Amanda Stevens ... over fifty nov els, includ ... The
... rd Queen. Her books have been described as
... d atmospheric, 'a new take on the classic ghost
... orn and raised in the rural South, she now resides
... ton, Texas, where she enjoys binge-watching,
... ng and the occasional margarita.

... assidy is an award-winning, *New York Times*
... g author who has written more than one hundred
... Mills & Boon. In 1995, she won Best Silhouette
... from *RT Book Reviews* for *Anything for*
... 1998, she won a Career Achievement Award
... nnovative Series from *RT Book Reviews*. Carla
... he only thing better than curling up with a good
... read is sitting down at the computer with a
... y to write.

Also by Amanda Stevens

Criminal Behavior
Pine Lake
Whispering Springs
Bishop's Rock (ebook novella)
The Restorer
The Kingdom
The Prophet
The Visitor
The Sinner
The Awakening

Also by Carla Cassidy

Desperate Strangers
Desperate Intentions
Scene of the Crime: Bridgewater, Texas
Scene of the Crime: Bachelor Moon
Scene of the Crime: Widow Creek
Scene of the Crime: Mystic Lake
Scene of the Crime: Black Creek
Scene of the Crime: Return to Bachelor Moon

Discover more at millsandboon.co.uk

INCRIMINATING EVIDENCE

AMANDA STEVENS

DESPERATE MEASURES

CARLA CASSIDY

MILLS & BOON

First Published in Great Britain 2019
by Mills & Boon, an imprint of HarperCollins*Publishers*
1 London Bridge Street, London, SE1 9GF

Incriminating Evidence © 2019 Marilyn Medlock Amann
Desperate Measures © 2019 Carla Bracale

ISBN: 978-0-263-27420-2

0619

INCRIMINATING EVIDENCE

AMANDA STEVENS

Chapter One

The hammer of rain on her umbrella obscured the sound of any footfalls behind her. Still, Catherine March cast an uneasy glance over her shoulder. Nothing seemed amiss. No darting shadows. No lurking silhouettes. But she knew she was being followed. The certainty tingled down her backbone as she hurried along the rain-slick sidewalk.

She gripped her umbrella and willed away the icy sensation. She was letting the gloomy day get to her. Grief clouded her common sense. Why would she be under surveillance? She lived a quiet and unassuming lifestyle. Most of her time was spent in a university lab or classroom. She consulted with various law enforcement agencies in and around Charleston, South Carolina, but a sleuthing, gun-toting forensic anthropologist was a figment of Hollywood's imagination. Catherine didn't investigate crimes or chase down criminals. Her job was to examine, analyze and inform. The cases on which she consulted were mostly cold, the skeletal remains of the victims picked clean by time, weather and predation.

Take her current assignment. She'd been tasked with creating biological profiles for fourteen separate sets of human remains recovered from an abandoned house on the outskirts of Charleston's famed historical district. The former owner of the residence, a paraplegic named Delmar

Gainey, had spent the last five years of his life in a nursing home and the previous two decades confined to a wheelchair. Before the accident that claimed his mobility, however, he'd murdered those fourteen women and sequestered their bodies in the walls of his home and in his backyard.

The remains of his victims might have stayed hidden forever if not for an ambitious house flipper, who had acquired the property at auction following Gainey's death. The first gruesome discovery brought the police. The coroner had brought in Catherine.

Butterfly fractures in the long bones told the story of the women's brutal captivity while striae patterns on the sternums and rib cages painted a vivid image of their deaths. The victims had been stabbed repeatedly with a serrated blade. All except one. Jane Doe Thirteen.

She was the anomaly. An outlier. An inconsistency that needled at Catherine even now as she thought about the single bullet hole in the back of the skull. In all likelihood, the entry wound had been made by a full metal jacket fired at close range from a 9 mm semiautomatic. An execution.

No bone trauma like the other victims. No nicks or fractures. Not even an exit wound.

Jane Doe Thirteen had definitely captured Catherine's imagination, but for now she had more pressing business.

Clutching the plastic bag to her chest, she plunged on through the puddles.

What were the chances? she wondered as she cast another glance over her shoulder. What were the odds that not one but two old serial-killer cases with seemingly no relation to the other had entered her quiet, ordinary world to wreak havoc on her peace of mind? Delmar Gainey had died in his bed at the Cloverdale Rest Home, no doubt savoring his monstrous deeds to the bitter end. Orson Lee Finch—the so-called Twilight Killer—was still very much alive but destined to spend the rest of his days in the Kirkland Correctional Institution, housed in a specialized unit for the state's most violent inmates.

Catherine had been little more than a baby when Gainey and Finch had stalked the streets of her city, each possessing a very different set of stressors, signatures and criteria. Then the remains had been found on Delmar Gainey's property and, soon after, headlines had exploded with startling new developments in the Orson Lee Finch case.

Catherine had experienced little more than professional curiosity until her mother's death unearthed a more personal revelation. Since early childhood, Catherine had known she was adopted. Her mother, Laura, had spoken openly about the circumstances of Catherine's birth. *You'll have questions as you grow older. At some point, you may even feel your loyalties are divided. That's only natural. But I want you to know that you can always come to me, Cath. There should be no secrets between us.*

No secrets? Then why hadn't Catherine known about the loose floorboard in her mother's closet or the box of newspaper clippings stashed inside the secret compartment? Why hadn't she been told about the photograph?

Why had Laura March, so pale and weak on her deathbed, pulled her daughter close and whispered a distressing message in her ear?

It's all a lie.

A car horn sounded in the distance, drawing Catherine's attention back to the present. She stood shivering on the curb as she waited for the light to change. It was a hot summer day, but the rain and her dark thoughts chilled her.

She took another quick check of her surroundings. She was alone on the street. No one else was about. No one that she could see. The rain had chased everyone inside. She was tempted to scurry across the intersection against the light, but she could almost hear her mother chastising her from the grave. *Careful, Cath. Always look before you leap.*

Grief settled heavily on her shoulders and tightened her chest. She couldn't remember ever feeling more alone than she did at the moment, huddled beneath her umbrella and missing Laura March more than she would have ever dreamed possible.

Wiping a hand across her damp cheeks, she drew a sharp breath. The feeling was there again. That frigid whisper up her backbone. She turned, almost expecting to find her mother's ghost floating toward her through the gloom. Instead, she saw a man watching her from a recessed doorway.

Their gazes collided before he glanced away, but in that fleeting moment of contact, Catherine experienced a flicker of recognition. She searched her mind for a time when their paths might have crossed. The man was memorable, not so much for his crudely tattooed arms but for the aura of danger that shrouded him. There was something sinister in his closely set eyes, something threatening in his body language. He looked to be middle-aged, his hair longish and slicked back, his cheekbones as sharp as razor blades. As if aware of Catherine's scrutiny, he tipped back his head and blew a long stream of smoke out into the rain.

Her heart raced as she considered her options. Run away or confront him. Before she had time to think, she found herself walking toward him.

"Excuse me!" she called out. "Do I know you?"

Even as she continued to advance, she admonished herself for provoking a stranger on a deserted street, but she couldn't seem to help herself. Grief did strange things to people. Maybe her emotions had been pent up for too long. Maybe her anguish had been suppressed to the point of explosion.

"Sir? Are you following me?"

He showed no visible reaction to the question, refused to acknowledge her presence with so much as a glance. He took another drag and then carefully flicked the cigarette butt into a puddle before he turned and walked away.

Catherine didn't follow him. She watched until he was out of sight before she went back to wait for the light, positioning herself so that she could keep an eye on the sidewalk behind her. She tried to tell herself again that she was imagining things. The man had been minding his own business. If anything, she'd likely scared him away. What had she been thinking, harassing a total stranger?

No one was following her. *Get over yourself.* The only other person who knew of her discovery was her mother's sister, and she couldn't fathom a scenario where Louise Jennings would have her watched. Catherine still had a hard time believing her mother had kept secrets from her all these years, but the proof was in the plastic bag she hugged to her chest. The confirmation had been in her mother's whispered confession.

It's all a lie.

THE HEADLINE IN the local paper had called her the bone doctor, a champion of the forgotten dead. Strange that Catherine March would be in the market for a private detective when Nick LaSalle had been reading about her in the paper. The article had highlighted her profession as a forensic anthropologist in general and, more specifically, her efforts to help identify human remains that had recently been recovered from an abandoned house.

Nick knew the woman slightly from his brief time as a homicide detective. He remembered her as dedicated and meticulous in her work. Quiet and thoughtful in her demeanor. He had forgotten how attractive she was. That part had taken him by surprise when she walked into his office.

He let his gaze drift over her features as he wondered why he'd never gotten around to calling her once he'd closed the case. The spark had been undeniable. He felt it now as he took in the long, dark hair, still glistening with raindrops, and the wide brown eyes that observed him with a hint of suspicion.

She wore a fitted gray top with slim black pants and sneakers soaked from the downpour. The only hint of color in the whole of her presentation was an emerald ring that glowed in the too-bright lighting of his office. He'd turned up the glare in order to chase away the dreariness of a rainy day, but a cozier ambience invited candor. He started to get up and adjust the dimmer, but he didn't want to interrupt her train of thought. Or his, for that matter.

"When did your mother pass away?" he asked as he pretended to jot notes on a yellow legal pad.

"Just over a week ago."

"I'm very sorry for your loss," he said, noting the shadow that flitted across her expression and the telltale sheen in her eyes, which she quickly blinked away.

"Thank you."

"You're here because you found some old newspaper clippings among your mother's possessions?"

"I'm here because I found them hidden beneath the floorboards of my mother's closet. I hadn't been by her house since she died. I wanted to gather up a few of her things to take home with me and to try and figure out what to do with the rest. Mostly, I wanted to feel close to her." She cleared her throat and drew a deep breath as she smoothed her hands down the tops of her thighs. She was nervous. That much was obvious. Uneasy, too. Her eyes kept darting to the doorway and to the corridor beyond as if she expected to find someone listening in on their conversation.

They had the second floor to themselves and the receptionist wouldn't be able to hear from her post in the lobby, but Nick got up and closed the door anyway. Then he surreptitiously dimmed the lights a notch. Catherine didn't seem to notice. She picked up the plastic bag at her feet and extracted a shoebox.

"You brought the clippings?" Nick walked back over to his desk and sat down.

She nodded. "I noted a loose floorboard when I went into my mother's closet. I pried it up and found this box inside."

"When we spoke on the phone, you said the articles are about a serial killer."

"Not just any serial killer." Her gaze lifted. "Orson Lee Finch. The most infamous monster in this city's history."

"But not the most prolific," Nick felt compelled to point out. "Delmar Gainey now holds that distinction."

"Yes, I know. I'm working on the remains that were recovered from his property."

"I've been keeping up with the case. I saw the article about you in the paper. How's it going?" he asked with genuine curiosity.

She tucked back damp tendrils and seemed to relax. "We're lucky in that most of the skeletons were found intact, with only a few missing bones. We also have all the skulls. I don't have to tell you how helpful that is. It allows us to check dental records and, if necessary, reconstruct facial features." She paused thoughtfully as if something had suddenly occurred to her.

He leaned in. "What is it?"

She said in surprise, "I'm sorry?"

"You look as if something just came to you."

"I was thinking about one of the victims. There's a rather puzzling inconsistency."

She had a way of making everything sound dreamy and mysterious. A conversation about human remains and serial killers should have evoked gruesome imagery, but instead her melodic voice mingling with the sound of raindrops against the windows mesmerized Nick. If he wasn't careful, he might find himself drowning in the unfathomable darkness of her eyes. "What kind of inconsistency?"

She seemed to catch herself then, shaking her head slightly as she clutched the box with both hands. "That's a discussion for the police. It has nothing to do with why I'm here."

Nick leaned back in his chair feeling oddly thwarted. "Back to Orson Lee Finch, then. The Twilight Killer." He took a moment to pretend to read his notes. He felt a little rattled and he didn't know why. For all his shortcomings—and he had more than a few—a lack of confidence in his cognitive abilities had never been one of them. Yet he couldn't seem to get a read on Catherine March. Beneath that ethereal demeanor, something dark and unsettling simmered. "When you called this morning, you mentioned a photograph."

She glanced down at the box. "It ran in the local paper at the time of Finch's arrest. The image is grainy, but it appears to be Finch. He's holding the hand of a little girl who looks to be about two. According to the accompanying article, the photo was sent to the paper anonymously and is the only known shot of that child. It was speculated at the time that she was Finch's daughter, but no one could ever locate her. Finch would never confirm or deny the rumor. Detective LaSalle... I mean... Sorry..." She faltered uncomfortably, realizing she'd addressed him by his former title. He wondered if she knew the circumstances of his departure from the police department. If so, he could only assume she'd reconciled the rumors to her satisfaction or she wouldn't be here.

"Call me Nick," he said.

She looked relieved. "There's no easy way to say this. I've reason to believe that I'm the child in that photograph. If true, then there is a very good chance that Orson Lee Finch is my biological father."

She'd shocked him, but he tried not to show it. "That's quite a leap from one old photograph. Do you have more substantial evidence?"

"No," she admitted. "Only that my mother saved every newspaper article written about Finch and she told me before she died that it had all been a lie."

"Meaning?"

"She didn't elaborate. *Couldn't* elaborate. It was near the end and she was in and out of consciousness, but she seemed lucid in that moment. Still, I might have chalked it up to delirium if not for the clippings and the fact that she took such pains to hide them from me."

"So, to be clear, you think Orson Lee Finch and your mother—"

"No!" Her voice rose. She took a moment to collect herself. "I was adopted when I was two. Laura March was the only mother I ever knew. The woman who gave birth to me had a relationship with Finch." She glanced away with a shudder. "At least, that's the assumption."

"How long have you known you were adopted?"

"For as long as I can remember. My mother and I spoke openly about it since I was a small child. She told me that my biological parents were very young. My father joined the military right out of high school. He died in a helicopter crash before they could marry, leaving my mother—my biological mother—alone and destitute. She tried to make a go of it, but she was too young and poor with no formal education and no job prospects. She gave me up so that I could have a better life."

"But you don't believe that."

She hesitated. "I did for a long time, but now I think Laura March invented the story because the truth was too painful...too stigmatizing. And perhaps she wanted to ward off my curiosity."

"What about your adoptive father?"

"Aidan March. He was a cop, killed in the line of duty when I was little. That much is true. Even though I was only five when it happened, I still have vague memories of him. His voice. His smile. The blue of his eyes." She glanced down at the ring on her finger. "This belonged to his mother. I'm told he wanted me to have it." She fell silent as she twisted the band.

Her phrasing wasn't lost on Nick. If Laura March had lied about Catherine's birth parents, might she also have fabricated a connection to her adoptive father?

"Go on," he prompted.

"I don't know how familiar you are with the specifics of the Twilight Killer case, but Orson Lee Finch was a gardener by trade. He went to college for a time majoring in horticulture, but his mother became ill and he had to drop out. Some say that fostered his resentment of the elite. They had what he so desperately wanted but could never acquire. His signature was a rare crimson magnolia petal, which he placed over his victims' lips."

"The kiss of death," Nick murmured.

She closed her eyes briefly. "Finch preyed on young, single mothers from affluent families. Despite their advantages—or maybe because of them—he deemed them unfit to raise children. The FBI profiler on the case called the kills mission-oriented. He speculated that the mother of Finch's child—possibly my biological mother—was his first victim. Her rejection may have triggered his spree. Finch denies it, of course. After all these years, he still maintains his innocence. At least to those who manage to get an interview with him."

"Have you talked to him?"

The question seemed to distress her. "I haven't gone to see him. Why would I?"

"You say you want answers. He would be the logical place to start."

She shook her head. "No. I won't see him. Let me be clear about that. I don't want Orson Lee Finch in my life. I don't want him to know who I am or anything about me. I only want the truth. I *need* to know the truth."

"Why?" Nick asked bluntly.

She regarded him for the longest moment. "If the answer to that question isn't obvious, then perhaps I've come to the wrong person for help."

Nick returned her stare. "Please don't take this the wrong way, but I have to ask—is it possible you're latching onto an implausible scenario as a way to distract from your grief? Stories about the Twilight Killer have dominated the news lately. The media has even managed to resurrect the mystique surrounding Twilight's Children," he said, referring to the moniker assigned to the offspring of Orson Lee Finch's victims.

"I'm well aware of the stories. I've read all the articles and watched the documentaries. If what I suspect is true, then I'm the ultimate child of Twilight." Her voice dropped to a near whisper. "Not just Finch's daughter but the offspring of his first victim."

Nick let that soak in for a moment. Catherine March didn't seem the type to court publicity—the opposite, in fact—but he'd been fooled before. If her story got out, he had no doubt the details would be sensationalized. She might even be offered a book or movie deal. Her profession would only feed into the public's fascination. The daughter of a serial killer devoting her life to forgotten victims.

He searched her face once again, staring deep into her eyes, waiting for a twitch or a blink that would give her away. Her gaze remained unwavering.

"Is something wrong?" she asked.

"No," Nick said. "I was just thinking about everything you've told me. At any other time, without the recent media circus, do you think you would have given those clippings a second thought?"

Annoyance flashed in her eyes. "A box of newspaper clippings hidden beneath a floorboard in my dead mother's closet? Yes, I think I would have given them a second thought."

"I'm not trying to offend you."

"I'm not offended. But if you knew me at all, you would know that I'm not the type to embellish or dramatize. I'm nothing if not practical. I'm not jumping to conclusions nor am I trying to distract from my grief. This isn't a bid for attention or some misguided need to feel special or important. For any number of reasons, I want to know who my biological parents are. Is that so hard to understand?"

"No," he said. "But you've heard the old saying, sometimes it's best to let sleeping dogs lie."

She removed a newspaper clipping from the cigar box and slid it across the desk. "That's a picture of Orson Lee Finch, is it not?"

He picked up the yellowed clipping and studied the subjects. "Hard to tell. As you said, the shot is grainy and there's a shadow across his profile. It could be Finch."

She nodded in satisfaction. "The child with him...the little girl...do you see a resemblance to me?"

Nick took his time studying her features before glancing back down at the clipping. Truthfully, there was a similarity but so vague as to be insignificant. "She has dark hair and dark eyes. Beyond that..."

She placed a photograph on his desk. "This is a shot of me taken in our backyard when I was three."

He compared the photo to the clipping. "There's a definite likeness, I'll give you that. But I'm still not willing to draw any conclusions."

"I'm not asking you to. All I need from you is a thorough investigation. Do you want the job or don't you?"

He waited a beat before he answered. "Why me? Why this agency?" He wondered if she would remind him that she had once consulted on one of his cases, but instead she withdrew a creased business card from the shoebox and handed it to him.

"Do you recognize this?" she asked.

He gazed down at the familiar logo. "It's one of our old business cards. The design was changed years ago."

"I found that card in the same box with the clippings. There's a number scribbled on the back."

Nick flipped the card and a shock wave went through him. This time he was unable to hide his astonishment.

"I take it from your expression that you recognize the number," she said.

"It's my father's home number," he conceded reluctantly. "It's been unlisted for years."

"Which means he must have spoken with my mother at some point. I think she came to him hoping that he could help her find out the truth about my biological parents. She must have had suspicions for a long time. Why else would she have saved those clippings? Why else would she have kept them from me? Ask your father if he remembers her. Or, better yet, check to see if there's a case file." Her gaze intensified. "It could be that the work has already been done for us."

Nick picked up the card and flicked it idly between his fingers. "I can tell this means a lot to you."

"Of course, it means a lot to me. Put yourself in my place."

"I've been sitting here trying to do just that and here's my conclusion… What if you are Orson Lee Finch's biological daughter? It won't change who you are. It won't diminish your accomplishments."

She sighed. "Nurture over nature. I get it. I may even believe it. Laura March was a wonderful person. Everything I am, I owe to her. I couldn't have asked for a more loving parent. But she kept things from me and I need to know why." Catherine's voice quivered and for the first time, she looked vulnerable. Lost. "A person needs to know where she comes from, Nick. A person needs to know the truth about her past."

He couldn't argue with that. "Okay," he said. "I'd like you to leave the clippings with me for now. The photograph, too, if you don't mind."

"Does that mean you'll take my case?"

"I'll look into it. If Orson Lee Finch will agree to see me, I'll press for a DNA test. That is what you want, isn't it?"

"Yes. That's what I want," she insisted, even as she looked anything but certain.

"If Finch cooperates—which I doubt he will—you'll have your answer in a matter of days. If not, we'll figure out where to go from there."

"You have no idea what this means to me." She stood.

"I realize how deluded I must sound. Thank you for hearing me out. You could have just sent me away."

"Don't thank me yet. Depending on the outcome, you may not want to thank me at all." He rose and walked her to the door. Their shoulders brushed as he reached for the knob. She moved away quickly and muttered an apology. But in that fleeting moment of contact, awareness sizzled. Nick found himself breathing in her scent. She smelled of raindrops and vanilla. A clean fragrance with more than a hint of mystery.

He cleared his head as he pulled open the door. "It was good seeing you again, Dr. March."

"You, as well. It's been a long time. And please call me Catherine." She smiled for the first time since entering his office. "I was surprised to hear you'd left the police department."

"Were you?" His smile felt brittle. "No one else was."

"Charleston PD's loss is my gain."

"We'll see, I guess." He handed her a fresh business card. "My cell number is on the back. Call me if you need anything or if you have questions."

She pocketed the card. "We haven't talked about financial arrangements."

"Jackie at the front desk will explain our terms."

"Thank you again."

Nick waited until he heard her footsteps on the stairs before moving into the hallway. He stood at the railing overlooking the lobby as she paused at the reception desk to speak with Jackie Morris.

Then fetching her umbrella and raincoat, Catherine March went out into the rainy afternoon, leaving Nick feeling oddly troubled as he stared after her.

Chapter Two

Nick turned away from the railing, anxious to have a look through the newspaper clippings, but the sight of his uncle Emmett lurking in the hallway stopped him cold. He hadn't expected to see anyone on the second floor. Since his father and uncle retired, Nick mostly had that area of the building to himself, although Emmett still retained his office and he almost always attended the weekly briefings.

He'd made a point of telling Nick not to expect him until the end of the week, but there he stood looking pleased with himself that he'd caught his nephew off guard. Emmett LaSalle was nothing if not competitive. He took great pride in one-upping the younger detectives in the agency.

"You're awfully jumpy," he observed.

"I tend to get that way when someone sneaks up behind me," Nick countered. "What are you doing here anyway? I didn't expect to see you until Friday."

"Change of plans." Emmett nodded toward the long row of windows in the lobby where rain still pelted the glass. "Can't take the boat down the coast in this weather."

"Fish bite best in the rain," Nick said. "Or so I hear."

"Rain is one thing, but a monsoon is something else. I may be crazy but I'm not stupid."

Like Nick's dad, Emmett LaSalle was a handsome man, tall and lanky with an easy grin. They were fraternal twins with physical similarities, but their personalities were like night and day. Emmett had always been a little on the slippery side whereas Raymond LaSalle was about as straight an arrow as one could hope to find. To Nick, his uncle looked as if he'd stepped from the pages of a noir detective novel. No matter the season or trend, he favored pleated slacks and fitted knit shirts topped with a weathered fedora. He claimed he'd given up gambling years ago, but Nick had his doubts. The detective agency had been a lucrative investment for the LaSalle brothers, and both Emmett and Raymond enjoyed fully funded retirements. But Nick couldn't help questioning some of his uncle's recent purchases, like the forty-foot fishing boat he slyly called *The Shamus*.

Emmett leaned both forearms against the railing and called down a greeting to Jackie, who had glanced up when she heard their voices. As always, her gaze lingered on Emmett before she turned back to her work. She'd had a thing for him for as long as Nick could remember. Everyone at the agency knew it but pretended not to. Nick sometimes wondered if they'd had a romantic relationship in their younger days. Maybe that explained why she'd stubbornly carried a torch through both of Emmett's marriages. Maybe she was waiting for him to wake up one day and realize the love of his life had been right in front of him all along.

Emmett gave him a sidelong glance. "The woman that just left. New client?"

"She could be. I'm looking into something for her. We'll see how it goes."

"Quite a looker, from what I could see. Way out of your league, though."

Nick was used to his uncle's ribbing. He gave a careless shrug. "Then I guess it's a good thing she's a client and not a date."

Emmett grinned, displaying a slight overbite that gave him a boyish air despite the silver at his temples. "My first wife was a client."

"And look how that turned out."

"Everything was fine until she got nosy."

"Yes, how dare she take offense to all those clandestine trips to Vegas," Nick said dryly.

Emmett's expression sobered. "What did you say her name was?" He stared down at Jackie until she glanced back up at him. Something flared between them. Not attraction or even affection, but the silent communication of an old and complicated liaison.

Nick paused at the abrupt change of subject. "You mean the client? Her name is Dr. Catherine March."

"Doctor, huh?"

"She's a forensic anthropologist."

Emmett repeated her name with a frown. "Has she been in before? I swear I know her from someplace."

"Maybe you recognize her from her work with the police department. An article ran in the paper yesterday about her efforts to help the county coroner's office identify the victims in the Delmar Gainey case."

Something flashed across his uncle's face, an emotion gone so quickly Nick wondered if he'd seen it all.

When Emmett didn't respond, Nick said, "Surely you've heard about the Gainey case. Human remains found in an abandoned house? You'd have to be living under a rock not to have heard all the breathless reporting."

Emmett frowned down into the lobby where Jackie had returned to her work. "Has she been able to identify any of the victims?"

"She's working up profiles for the coroner." Nick

thought about the enigmatic glint he'd caught in her eyes and the hesitant revelation about a puzzling discrepancy. He shrugged. "But to answer your question, I gather the work is ongoing. She didn't talk much about it."

Emmett glanced at him. "That's not why she came here, then. Good. I'd hate to see you get dragged into that mess. I hear heads are still rolling at police headquarters."

"I hear the same, but why would you even think that a possibility? Why would she come to me about a police investigation?"

"It was just a thought," Emmett said. "Wouldn't be the first time an overzealous consultant tried to go behind a detective's back. The last thing we need is to step on any CPD toes, especially in a high-profile case like this. If they thought you were trying to undermine an investigation, they could get your license yanked."

"You don't need to remind me to proceed with caution when dealing with the Charleston Police Department." Nick didn't have to elaborate. His uncle would get his meaning.

Emmett gave a grim nod. "All the more reason to keep your nose clean."

"My nose has always been clean." Nick turned to his uncle. "What's really going on here? You don't have reason to worry about the Delmar Gainey case, do you?"

"Why would I worry about a dead serial killer?"

Nick searched his uncle's profile. "Gainey was active while you were still a cop. Didn't you work some missing-person cases back then? You must have had a theory about all those disappearances. Fourteen women don't just vanish off the street without someone noticing."

"Happens all the time. Hookers, addicts, runaways. People live in the shadows for a reason," Emmett said. "They don't want to be noticed."

"You're saying not a single missing-person report was filed on any of the victims?"

"I'm saying if a report was filed, it would have been investigated like any other complaint."

"What about Gainey? No red flags?"

"Lived alone and kept to himself. Familiar story, right? From what I understand, he didn't have so much as an outstanding parking ticket. No one deliberately looked the other way, if that's what you're implying, but I'll be the first to admit, most of our resources were allocated elsewhere at that time."

"You mean to the Twilight Killer case," Nick said.

"Orson Lee Finch's victims were all young women from well-to-do families. They didn't just disappear from the street. He put their bodies on display. That generated a lot of attention. A lot of heat from the powers-that-be."

"I've heard Dad talk about that case. He was on the task force."

"Yeah, before the feds took over. Then Raymond and I left the department to open this agency. But you already know that story and, anyway, this is all ancient history. Personally, I'm a little sick of hearing about those old cases. I look forward to the time when Delmar Gainey and Orson Lee Finch fade back into the dustbin of history where they belong."

"I doubt that's going to happen anytime soon. Serial killers fascinate people. The fact that two were active in the city at the same time adds a new level of enthrallment."

"People are nuts," Emmett muttered.

"No argument there."

"So, this March woman."

Another abrupt transition. Nick gave his uncle a wary glance. "What about her?" He felt uneasy but he wasn't sure why. Maybe because his uncle was acting strangely.

Showing too much interest in Catherine March while dismissive of the two old cases that had taken the city by storm. If Nick didn't know better, he would almost believe something had struck a little too close to home for his uncle.

He cast another glance down into the lobby where Jackie pretended to type away on her keyboard. She didn't look up again, but Nick had no doubt she was listening to their every word. She was good at her job, efficient and loyal to a fault, but at times, she seemed to have eyes and ears everywhere.

"Let's go into my office," he said.

Emmett followed him down the hallway, but instead of taking the seat across from Nick's desk, he walked over to the window to stare down at the street. He folded his arms and leaned a shoulder against the frame, seemingly absorbed in the patter of rain against the glass.

"You wanted to know about Catherine March," Nick prompted.

Emmett turned. "I like to keep apprised of all our open investigations. Just because Raymond has distanced himself from the business doesn't mean I will. I still have a vested interest in the reputation and financial well-being of this agency."

"I know you do. That's why we have our weekly briefings. But since you asked, she came to see me about her adoption. Her mother died last week and she has reason to believe her birth father is Orson Lee Finch."

Emmett visibly started. *"What?"*

Nick nodded. "I had the same reaction."

His uncle just stared at him for a moment. "That's why she was here? Damn, Nick. What exactly is she asking you to do?"

"She insists she wants to know the truth about her birth,

so my recommendation is that we contact the attorney that handled Finch's last appeal and try to set up a meeting. If Finch will see us, I'll press for a DNA test since I no longer have access to any databases."

"Let me get this straight. You're asking a man who murdered all those women and is now serving consecutive life sentences for a sample of his DNA? Good luck with that, bud."

"It's a long shot," Nick agreed. "But what's he got to lose?"

"Are you going to tell him why you want the test?"

"I'll tell him as much as I have to. Catherine doesn't want to see him, though. She doesn't want him to know who she is."

"Smart woman. And if he insists?"

"I'll walk away. No deals. Protecting the client's privacy and safety is paramount."

Emmett gave him a reproving look. "I think you're being dangerously naïve. Psychopaths are by nature cunning, and as you just said, Finch has nothing to lose. He'll do whatever he has to in order to gain the advantage. If he does agree to see you, then you can bet he'll already have worked out an angle. You won't even see it coming until it's too late."

"I'll be careful. I'm not exactly a novice at this, you know."

Emmett turned back to the window. He looked glum as he watched the rain. "If Finch says no to a DNA test, what then?"

"Where we go from there will be up to Catherine. We'll see how far she wants to push this thing. Money could be a factor. If it was a closed adoption, then it'll take a lot of digging. A lot of billable hours."

Emmett hardly seemed to hear him. "What if Finch

does turn out to be her biological father? Have you or she given any thought to the consequences? You won't be able to keep something like that quiet. It'll get out. It always does. A bombshell like that could be a life changer."

Nick fiddled with a pen on his desk. He wished he didn't have such a bad feeling about all this. It wasn't too late to walk away, but he knew that he wouldn't. He was hooked already and he told himself Catherine March's deep brown eyes had nothing whatever to do with his interest.

"I don't know how well she's thought this through," he said. "To be honest, I'm not sure there's anything to investigate. She found some newspaper clippings hidden in her mother's closet, along with an old business card from this agency. That and her mother's mysterious last words are about all we have to go on."

"Sounds to me like she's holding out on you. She has to have more evidence or another angle. People save newspaper clippings for any number of reasons, and as to the business card, we used to hand those things out like candy. It's an understatement to say you don't have much to go on."

"The card is significant because Dad's home number is scribbled on the back," Nick said. "That's why she came here. She thinks her mother may once have been a client. Her name was Laura March. Does that ring a bell?"

"Not for me, but you can ask Raymond. Or, better yet, check with Jackie. She never forgets a name or a face."

Nick nodded. "I'll do that. Maybe I'll take a look through the archives, too. Anyway, that's it. That's the extent of our conversation. Do you want to hear about our other cases or should we wait until Friday?"

"Save it. I just remembered an errand I need to run." Emmett moved toward the door. "Don't forget your grandmother's birthday party later in the week."

"I won't forget."

"Buy her something nice. You can afford it now that we made you partner."

"Already taken care of."

"Nick?" Emmett paused on the threshold and glanced back. "I meant what I said earlier. You need to watch yourself with Finch. With Catherine March, too. Her story doesn't sit well with me. Might be best to take a pass on this one."

"Since when do we take a pass on interesting investigations? You and Dad built this agency by taking cases no one else would touch."

"This one is different," Emmett said with a frown. "Call it a premonition or a gut feeling, but I think that woman is going to be trouble."

Nick had had the same presentiment, but he shrugged. "I can look after myself."

"Yeah. That's what we all say until we're in too deep and there's no turning back."

"Voice of experience?"

Emmett shrugged. "Voice of wisdom. Take it with a grain of salt."

As he had earlier, Nick waited until he heard footsteps on the stairs and then he got up and went into the hallway. Instead of moving up to the railing, though, he lingered in the shadows at the top of the stairs as Jackie's voice rose.

"You said that was all taken care of—"

Emmett's gaze flicked to the second floor. "So I forgot to order the cake. It's not the end of the world. Your sister is a baker, right? I know you don't make all those Christmas cookies yourself. Give her a call. Convince her to help us out."

Jackie followed his gaze up the stairs as Nick pressed himself deeper into the shadows. Then she said a little too loudly, "I don't know why I'm surprised. Not the first time I've had to pull your bacon out of the fire." She gave an exaggerated sigh. "Don't worry. I'll take care of it. I always do."

They spoke for a few more minutes, and then Emmett left by way of the rear exit and Jackie returned to her work. She didn't glance Nick's way again, but she knew he was up there. He could tell by the rigid way she held her shoulders and by the overenthusiastic pounding of her fingers on the keyboard.

Whatever Emmett had said to her obviously upset her and Nick was certain it had nothing to do with his grandmother's birthday cake.

CATHERINE HAD A hard time falling asleep that night. She lay in the dark listening to the rumble of thunder as she went over the day's events in her head. She couldn't blame Nick LaSalle for questioning her frame of mind. The evidence she'd presented of her parentage was sketchy at best, but she could think of no other reason why her mother would have kept those clippings all these years. People often saved newspaper articles about events that were historical or even interesting, but why hide them in a secret compartment if she hadn't at least suspected the truth?

Rolling to her side, Catherine fixated on the flicker of distant lightning out her window. The wind was picking up and she could hear the patter of rain on the roof. Her landlady was away visiting family and Catherine suddenly felt very alone and isolated, set back from the street as she was. Her apartment was on the second floor, nestled in a thick canopy of oak leaves. Most of the time, she enjoyed the illusion of living in the trees and the peace and quiet of being located off an alleyway rather than a busy street, but tonight the solitude seemed oppressive, the shadowy yard and side street menacing. Who knew what danger prowled the dark?

She shifted to her other side, deliberately turning her back on the window, and fluffed her pillow. Insomnia had been a problem since childhood. Night terrors, too. Catherine had never understood her fear of the dark, but now she had to wonder if long-buried memories lurked somewhere in her subconscious. If she truly was Orson Lee Finch's daughter, what horrors might she have witnessed as a child?

The notion haunted her, so much so that when she finally drifted off, her sleep was filled with terrible visions of Finch's deeds. She dreamed of his victims' screams and of crimson magnolia petals raining down upon her. She awakened in a cold sweat, clinging to the covers as her gaze darted about her bedroom. Once her heart settled, she got up for a glass of water and then stood at her bedroom window peering out into the rainy night. Another image came to her—that of the man who had watched her from a recessed doorway. He had walked off when she called out to him, but Catherine couldn't suppress the worry that he had been following her, that he might even now be out there with his eyes trained on her bedroom window.

The dark and her nerves played tricks on her vision. She saw him everywhere—inside the back gate, hiding behind the azaleas, perched on her landlady's back steps. The intermittent lighting revealed the truth. The shadows dissolved into nothingness. No one was out there. She was perfectly safe ensconced as she was behind locked doors and a latched gate.

She went into the bathroom and took a melatonin tablet, determined to salvage what was left of the night. Then, shivering, she crawled back into bed and pulled the covers up to her chin. Turning her mind away from Orson Lee

Finch and his victims, she let her thoughts drift back to her meeting with Nick LaSalle.

She remembered him well from their previous encounter. Skeletal remains had been discovered in a wooded park after a heavy rain and Nick had been the detective assigned to the investigation. He'd come to Catherine for help in establishing a biological profile of the victim. Their consultation had been brief, but he'd made an impression. Tall and lean with dark hair and gray eyes the color of a rain cloud.

He'd struck her as professional and methodical with flashes of intuition that had surprised her. She'd been unexpectedly drawn to him and had been disappointed when he hadn't made further contact. Perhaps the attraction had been one-sided. Or perhaps other things had occupied his time. She vaguely recalled something unpleasant about his departure from the police department. She searched her mind for the details, but drowsiness clouded her memory and anyway, she'd never put much stock in rumors.

She drifted in and out of sleep, aware of her surroundings on some level even as she started to dream. She was in her bedroom, safely tucked beneath the covers. If she opened her eyes, she knew that she would see all her familiar possessions. The refinished dresser that had belonged to her mother, the vase of blue hydrangeas on her nightstand that she'd picked from her landlady's garden.

And yet the room that flitted at the edge of her consciousness was very different. Tiny and dim with pictures cut from a storybook taped to a drab wall. She could hear a man's voice, distant and angry, and a woman softly pleading. The sound frightened Catherine. She tried to rouse herself, but sleep tugged her deeper. The tinkle of a music box muted the voices and lulled her senses. She floated on those melancholy notes until her eyes fluttered open and she waited for the music to stop.

Fully awake, she bolted upright in bed. She could still hear a distant tinkle. She tried to convince herself that her landlady had returned. The older woman suffered hearing loss so perhaps she'd turned up the volume on her TV or radio. But the house was too far away and noise had never been a factor in the two years Catherine had lived in the apartment.

She clutched the covers to her chest, paralyzed with fear, though she couldn't say why exactly. The sound of a music box was hardly threatening, and yet dread clawed at her spine as she swung her legs over the side of the bed.

Barefoot and trembling, she crossed the bedroom and peered down the narrow hallway toward the living area. Nothing moved. She reached for the light switch but checked herself. She knew her way around the apartment with her eyes closed. If someone had broken in, the dark would give her an advantage.

Retreating back into the bedroom, she grabbed a baseball bat from the closet and then returned to the hallway, easing her way to the front of the apartment where she stood in the dark as the haunting melody washed over her.

The music box wasn't in her apartment, she realized. The notes drifted through her front door. Inching her way along the wall, she peeled back the curtain to peer out into the wet night. A set of wooden stairs led from the garden up to a tiny covered porch dimly lit by sconces on either side of her front door. An old-fashioned swing hung from a tree limb at the bottom of the steps. The chains squeaked ominously in the breeze, and for a moment, Catherine imagined someone sitting there staring up at her.

No one was there. But someone had just been there. The music box was only now winding down.

Gripping the handle of the bat, Catherine unlocked the dead bolt and pulled back the door.

She didn't see anything at first, but then her gaze dropped. The music box had been shoved up against the wall, protected from the rain by the porch roof. As the notes faded, the tiny ballerina froze in a suspended pirouette.

Catherine knelt to examine the box even as her gaze scanned the night. Someone had been on her porch moments earlier. They'd wound the spring and left the music box for her to find. But why?

Rising, she walked to the edge of the steps and stared down into the soggy garden.

"I know you're out there," she whispered. "Who are you? What do you want?"

The breeze blew through her hair and the rain dampened her nightgown. It almost seemed to Catherine that she could feel the cool caress of her mother's hand against her cheek. But Laura March hadn't left the music box on Catherine's porch nor had she followed her to LaSalle Investigations that afternoon.

Someone very much alive knew who she was. And they were trying to make contact.

Chapter Three

The oak trees were still dripping the next morning as Nick let himself in the gate and made his way along the flagstone pathway to Catherine's apartment. The rain had slackened sometime before dawn but the weather forecast called for more thunderstorms in the afternoon.

The gloom wore on Nick's mood, but the unexpected phone call from Catherine had given him a lift. He hadn't planned on contacting her until he heard back from Finch's attorney. If that source didn't pan out, he'd have to figure another way to get a visitor's permit for the Twilight Killer. He could always find a work-around, but first things first.

Pausing at the bottom of the outdoor staircase, he scoped out his surroundings. The garden was lush and redolent with the scent of flowers stirred by the heavy rains. The main house was historic, with gleaming columns and wide verandas, but the garage apartment was rustic and weathered. As his gaze moved over the facade, he saw a curtain flutter at a front window.

Catherine was up there watching him. He felt a prickle of awareness at the base of his spine, one that seemed equal parts attraction and trepidation. She hadn't elaborated on her need to see him, but there'd been a hushed quality to her voice and an underlying excitement in her tone that heightened his curiosity even as it deepened his unease.

He tried to shake off the foreboding as he climbed the steps. The door opened before he had a chance to knock and their gazes collided. Her hair was pinned up loosely and worry lines creased her brow. She looked as if she hadn't slept much the night before, but despite the shadows of fatigue beneath her eyes, she was far too appealing in her faded jeans and sneakers.

In that drawn-out moment of awkward silence, she gave him a return scrutiny before she motioned him inside. "Thank you for coming on such short notice. I could have met you at your office. You didn't have to make a special trip over here."

He shrugged as he entered her apartment, trying not to stare but curious about her living arrangements. The place was small, but the layout was efficient and the furniture had been arranged to accommodate an easy flow from one area to the next. Watercolors accented the white walls and area rugs warmed the tile floor. It was nice. Homey with a touch of eccentricity.

He turned. "It's no trouble. I pass right by here on my way to the office."

"Oh, well, that's good. Still, I don't want to take up too much of your time so we should probably get right to it." She walked into the small kitchen. "I made coffee. How do you take yours?"

"Black is fine."

She carried a tray into the living room and placed it on the coffee table. Perching on the edge of the sofa, she filled the cups while Nick took a chair across from her. He accepted the steaming brew gratefully. He'd gotten up early and he had a long day ahead of him. A jolt of caffeine was just what he needed.

"I suppose I should start at the beginning." Catherine lifted her cup and then set it back down without tasting the coffee. She adjusted her position and cleared her throat. "I neglected to tell you something yesterday. I didn't think it important, but in light of what happened last night…"

He leaned forward. "What did happen last night?"

"I'll get to that. Let me come clean first."

"By all means."

She absently rubbed the tops of her thighs. What was she trying to scrub away? Nick wondered.

"I think I'm being followed," she said.

"What makes you think that?" Reluctantly, he set his cup aside. The coffee was excellent. Strong and aromatic with a hint of chicory.

"On my way to your office yesterday, I had the strangest feeling of being watched. When I stopped for a light, I saw a man lounging in a doorway behind me. He was just standing there smoking, seemingly minding his own business, but he looked familiar somehow even though I couldn't place him." She paused with a frown as if trying to conjure a previous meeting. Then she shrugged. "I called out to him. I even asked if he was following me, but he just turned and walked away."

"It's rarely a good idea to confront a stranger, even if you think he's following you. Especially if you think he's following you."

"I know. I'm not usually impulsive, believe me, and I hate confrontations, but something came over me. Lately, I've been doing a lot of things that are out of character for me."

"Such as?"

"Hiring a private detective, for one thing." She clasped her hands in her lap as if she could somehow restrain her impulses. "I've read that grief can make a person behave oddly. That's why it's ill-advised to make important decisions for at least a year after the death of someone close."

She sat quietly for a moment. "Before my mother passed away, I would never have dreamed in a million years that I would require your services."

"You never considered searching for your birth parents before?"

"I had always been told that my biological father was dead. As to the woman who gave birth to me…yes, of course, I considered finding her, but I never pursued it seriously. It would have felt like a betrayal of the woman who raised me. Not that she would have seen it that way. She would have encouraged me had she known. I think I've been afraid to find my birth mother."

"Because you think she'll reject you?"

"No, it isn't that. There are things about myself that I've never understood. Certain anxieties. I've always had a fear of the dark and I don't know where that comes from. I was raised in a safe and loving environment. It makes no sense and yet…" She trailed off. "I don't sleep well because of that fear. Ever since I was little, I've had sporadic bouts of insomnia and night terrors."

"What are the night terrors about?"

"Nothing concrete. Vague images. A feeling of being lost and not being able to find my way home. A feeling of being pursued through the dark." She paused. "Typical childhood fears that I never outgrew."

"You think these night terrors are caused by something that happened before you were adopted?"

"I don't know. But maybe it's time I find out."

"Have you ever talked to a professional? Sorry," Nick muttered. "Maybe that's getting too personal."

"Not at all. I don't mind talking about it. My mother took me to see a therapist when I was young. After a few visits, he suggested the night terrors were a manifestation of deeper abandonment issues. Maybe he was right.

It makes sense, I guess. But ever since I found those clippings in my mother's closet, I haven't been able to shake the notion that I've suppressed memories from my early childhood."

"You said you were adopted at the age of two. Few people have memories that go back that far," Nick said.

"Few people *remember* back that far. Who's to say the memories aren't still stored somewhere in the subconscious? We know so little about memory and how it works. What if I saw something as a very small child? Something so terrible that I can only let those memories come out when I dream?"

"You think this is all tied to Orson Lee Finch?"

"That's my worry." She rose and went over to the window to glance out. "I know I shouldn't dump this on you. You're not my therapist."

"I'm here to help," he said. "In whatever form that takes."

She turned with a brief smile. On the surface, her gaze seemed guileless, even grateful, but her eyes looked troubled and Nick couldn't help wondering again what lay hidden in those endless depths.

Was she the offspring of Orson Lee Finch? He let his mind wander to that dark place and tried to imagine what the ultimate child of Twilight might have locked away in her subconscious.

She came back over to the sofa and sat down. "I'm sorry for going so far down the rabbit hole, but you're a very good listener. Patient. Nonjudgmental. I can talk to you more candidly than I ever could to my therapist."

Nick tried to shake off the disturbing images that had formed in his head. "There's a shrink in every good detective. You listen, you learn." He observed her for a moment.

"Why didn't you tell me any of this yesterday? Particularly your worry about being followed?"

"Because I already sounded delusional and I didn't want you to also think me paranoid. And now I've managed to sound completely unhinged. I can only imagine what you must be thinking."

"I'm thinking you've been through a life-changing event," he said. "You've suffered a devastating loss and you're still reeling. A week isn't a very long time. Cut yourself some slack."

"I'm trying. It's just all so confusing. So many things have happened since my mother died. Maybe I *am* still reeling."

"Then slow down. Take a breath. Drink your coffee before it gets cold." He picked up his cup.

She did the same, sipping slowly with eyes closed as if to savor the aroma while she collected her thoughts. "After I left your office yesterday, I felt better about things. Taking action gave me purpose. Something concrete to focus on. I even managed to convince myself that the man I'd seen in the doorway was nothing more than a stranger. He hadn't been following me at all. I'd let my imagination get away from me. But last night after I went to bed, I kept picturing him out there in the dark watching my apartment. The feeling was so strong that I even got up to look for him.

"I finally managed to doze off, but I wasn't completely asleep. I drifted in that gauzy, half-aware state where real-world sounds and scents are incorporated into a dream. Like falling asleep with the TV on. I saw myself in a strange room, tiny and dim with storybook pictures taped to the wall. I could hear voices and they frightened me. Then a music box started playing and when I awakened, I could still hear the melody. At first, I thought it was just a figment of my imagination or a lingering fragment of the dream. But the music was real."

Nick found himself enthralled by her story and once again mesmerized by the darkness of her eyes. Her skin was smooth and tanned, and when she turned her head, light glistened in her hair. For one split second, she seemed so ethereal she might have been a figment of *his* imagination. He could smell vanilla again and something more exotic like sandalwood or myrrh. The fragrances mingled into an intriguing dichotomy that disquieted Nick even as it aroused him.

He glanced around, taking in the candles on the kitchen bar and a small incense burner on one of the end tables. At the farthest end of the coffee table, she'd placed a small jewelry box, the kind that might adorn a little girl's dresser. The keepsake looked old. The hinges were tarnished and some of the decorative paper had peeled away from the cardboard.

His gaze went back to Catherine. She reached over and picked up the small box, running her finger along the top before opening the lid to display a tiny plastic ballerina. "While I lay sleeping in my bedroom, someone left this outside my front door. They wound the key and then shoved the music box up against the wall so that it would stay dry until I found it."

"You didn't see anyone? You didn't hear anything besides the music box? No footsteps, no car door...?"

"Nothing. But I didn't venture past the top of the stairs." Her voice lowered. "It was very dark out last night."

He wondered if she realized just how much she had revealed to him in that moment. "That was smart. Did you consider calling the police?"

"The thought crossed my mind, but what could I say? What could they do? No law was broken except trespassing, I suppose. I wasn't threatened. By the time the police got here, whoever left the music box would have been long gone."

"We can try lifting prints," Nick suggested.

"I'm afraid I haven't been careful with it," she said with regret. "I wasn't thinking straight."

"That's okay. We can eliminate yours. I still have a friend or two at CPD. If we're able to get a viable print, we can run it through the databases. I'm assuming you believe the music box is also connected to Finch and to those newspaper clippings."

She gave a helpless shrug. "How could it not be?"

He thought about that for a moment. "Did you talk to anyone else about those clippings?"

"My aunt. I wanted to know if she had any idea why my mother had saved them."

"Did she?"

"She said Mother had always been fascinated by true-crime stories, but I'm not sure I believe that. She never even watched the news when she could avoid it."

"Do you think your aunt deliberately tried to mislead you?"

"I think she was trying to protect me. I don't know how much she knows about my adoption, but if Mother suspected that Orson Lee Finch was my father, it stands to reason she would have confided in my aunt. Louise is an attorney. Mother may have even gone to her for advice."

"Is there anyone else your mother would have talked to?"

"I don't think so. She didn't have many close friends."

"And you didn't tell anyone else? Even a casual mention?"

"Only you."

He held out his hand. "May I?"

She reluctantly gave up the music box. Nick was careful to handle only the corners as he turned the box over to examine the bottom. Then he placed it on the coffee table and opened the lid with his finger. The ballerina turned jerkily then stopped. "It looks old," he said.

"Yes, though not an antique. It's cheaply made. Just cardboard and paper." Catherine paused. "Someone must have loved it, though. A child may even have cherished it."

Nick glanced up. "You've never seen it before?"

"Not that I remember. I've never been particularly drawn to music boxes until I heard the sound of one in my sleep last night."

"Did you recognize the song?"

"'Clair de Lune,' I think."

"Does that tune mean anything to you?"

"No, but someone left this on my doorstep for a reason. Someone is trying to tell me something. But why now? Why after all these years would my birth mother try to make contact?"

"Assuming it was her, maybe she heard about your mother passing away."

"That would mean she's kept tabs on me all these years. The notion that she's watched me from afar since I was two years old is disconcerting to say the least. But it makes sense in a way. I've always had these odd moments in my life. Something comes over me. A chill that I can't explain. A sensation of being watched." She shivered. "There I go, sounding unhinged again."

"Not at all," Nick said, but the hair at his nape had unaccountably lifted as she spoke. He didn't know what to make of this new turn of events. A trip to the prison to request a DNA sample from Orson Lee Finch had suddenly morphed into something darker and much more complex. He thought about his uncle's warning not to get involved and Nick's answering assurance that he could handle himself. *That's what we all say until we're in too deep and there's no turning back.*

Was he already in too deep? He was attracted to Catherine March, no question, but he had always prided himself on his level-headedness. On his ability to steer clear of dangerous distractions. He didn't know if he could do that with Catherine. He didn't know if he wanted to.

Beyond her physical allure, she had presented him with an intriguing case, the kind he hadn't come across since he'd left the police department. He hadn't realized until that moment how restless he was, how hungry he'd become, in more ways than just one.

"Do you mind if I take the music box back to the office? I don't have a print kit with me."

"No, I…no." She stood abruptly. "I'll get something to put it in, although I suppose we've handled it too much already."

She brought him a bag from the kitchen and he carefully placed the music box inside. "I'll take good care of it." He stood and she walked him to the door.

"Thank you again for coming."

"Anytime. I mean that, Catherine. If you see anything out of the ordinary or if you just feel uneasy, I'm only a phone call away."

She followed him out to the porch and stood at the top of the steps as he descended. When he got to the bottom, he turned with a wave, but she was no longer watching him. Her attention was fixed on something in the garden, and he turned with a frown, almost expecting to find the stranger from the doorway lurking beneath one of the dripping trees.

He saw nothing, heard nothing, but a chill swept across his nerve endings as his gaze returned to Catherine March.

THE WEATHER WAS still clear by the time Catherine set out for work and she decided to take a chance that the promised thunderstorms would hold off until she returned home that evening. She didn't much like to drive and the walk from her apartment to the university was so beautiful. Many of the homes in her adopted neighborhood were historic with walled gardens and secret courtyards that could be glimpsed through wrought-iron gates. The scent of jasmine clung to the humid air, tugging loose memories from her childhood. She missed her mother. Missed her soothing voice and gentle hand, her quiet smile and the too-rare glint of mischief in her blue eyes. *Everything will be okay, Cath. You'll see. Just keep breathing. One day at a time.*

What if another mother was still out there somewhere? Watching from afar? Trying to assuage Catherine's loneliness in the only way she knew how?

Catherine wasn't sure how she felt about that. She wasn't ready to move on. She wasn't ready to let Laura March slip away from her. She needed to clutch those memories tight.

Maybe it had been a mistake to hire a private investigator. She had no doubt Nick LaSalle would be good at his job. Maybe too good. Did she really want to know about her past? Was she ready to make peace with her DNA?

"Miss, you okay?"

She started out of her reverie. A man had approached her on the street. She'd been so deep in thought, she hadn't even noticed him. Now her hackles rose as she nodded. "I'm fine."

"You look a little lost," he said. "Need directions?"

She mustered a smile even as she backed away. "Kind of you to ask, but I know where I'm going."

She just had no idea where she'd come from.

Chapter Four

Catherine's grad-student assistants were already engrossed in their work when she arrived. The lab was located on the bottom floor of one of the university's oldest buildings, in what once would have been considered an aboveground basement. The overhead illumination was sufficient for their work, but even with every bulb burning, shadows seemed to linger in the corners.

A musty odor greeted Catherine as she walked through the rows of metal tables. Skulls grinned up at her. Here among nameless, faceless victims, she was in her element. Drawing in the scent of old death and mystery, she squared her shoulders. Time to start a new day.

"Morning, Dr. March." Emily Wooten looked up with a smile from the osteometric board she had been using to measure a femur. A hard worker in the lab and studious in the classroom, Emily was a pretty, petite brunette with a flawless complexion and an ingratiating disposition. Always cheerful, always eager to please.

Her male counterpart, Nolan Reynolds, was just as industrious, but he tended toward moody and intense. His curly brown hair was long and unwieldy, and he impatiently tucked it back as he leaned over his worktable. He was thin to the point of emaciation and the thick-rimmed glasses he wore gave him an air of scholarly absentmindedness. He was always alone on campus and in the class-room. He didn't seem to have any friends nor did he appear to want them. He was one of those people obsessed with his studies and content with his own company.

Catherine had once been a little like that herself. She'd entered college at seventeen, earned her bachelor's degree at twenty and, from that point forward, had kept her head down in pursuit of a PhD. She hadn't let anything or anyone interfere with her goals and ambition. No clubs. No sports. No social life to speak of. But that was before she'd known real loss. That was before she'd had an understanding of loneliness, the kind that ate away at you slowly. Solitude had little appeal for her now.

She returned Emily's greeting and said hello to Nolan. He spared a glance in her direction before adjusting his microscope.

"I was beginning to get a little concerned about you," Emily said.

"Why? I'm not that late, am I?" Catherine glanced at the large wall clock above the scrub sink.

"No, but you're usually so early," Emily explained. "And traffic is a real mess with all the rain. Glad you're here safe and sound."

"The weather has cleared for the time being, but you're right about the traffic. Luckily, I walked." Catherine slipped off her backpack. "What are you working on this morning?"

"Jane Doe Number Eight."

Catherine nodded as she glanced toward the skeleton one row over. She would return to Thirteen at some point during the day, but for now she and her assistants needed to complete biological profiles on the other Jane Does so that the measurements and calculations could be entered into missing-person databases.

She went over a checklist in her head as she walked through the maze of tables to her tiny office, stowing her lunch and backpack before checking her email. Then, donning a lab coat over her jeans and T-shirt, she went out to join the others. The lab was cramped with all the extra tables. Fourteen victims lay in the anatomical position awaiting further investigation and analysis. No time to waste. Catherine slid onto a stool and arranged her tools on the work surface.

The morning flew by. As always, she became so absorbed in her work that she lost all track of time. The sound of raindrops pounding against the high windows in the lab brought her out of her trance.

"It's really coming down again." Emily left her worktable and went over to stand on a stepstool to glance out one of the windows. "Wouldn't you know the sky would open up right at lunchtime?"

"Are you going out?" Catherine asked.

"Yes, I'm meeting someone off campus." Emily stepped down from the ladder and rubbed her arm. She didn't look at all eager to brave the weather and Catherine didn't blame her. Street flooding could make driving even a few blocks perilous.

"Can't you just reschedule?" Nolan asked.

"No, it's not that simple."

"What can be so complicated about a lunch date?" he wanted to know.

Emily hesitated. "I didn't say it was a date."

"What is it, then? A job interview?" Nolan's query surprised Catherine. He rarely showed interest in the people around him, but he was staring across the room at Emily with an enigmatic expression on his face.

Emily scowled back at him. "Since when do you care what I do?"

"I don't." Nolan went back to his work.

"Well, be careful out there," Catherine advised.

"I will." Emily gathered her belongings and headed for the door. "If I'm not back in an hour, send the coast guard."

The door clicked shut behind her and Catherine got up to stretch. "How about you?" she said to Nolan. "Are you going out?"

"In this weather? Not a chance. I'm not hungry anyway. Besides, I need to leave early today so I'd rather just work straight through. Don't let me stop you, though."

"Oh, I'm not going out. I brought my lunch." Catherine studied him for a moment. "You do realize that you've been hunched over that table for hours. Whether you eat or not, you need to at least take a break. It's not healthy to sit for so long in one place. Tell you what. Go wash up and then meet me in my office. I'll share my sandwich with you."

"Thanks, but that's not necessary, Dr. March. I'm really not hungry."

"Then keep me company while I eat. We don't even have to talk about work if you don't want to."

He looked perplexed. "What else would we talk about?"

"I don't know. The movies, the weather. Whatever you want. A change of scenery will do us both good."

"Your office is a change of scenery?"

"We could always walk over to the cafeteria," she said.

"Your office it is, then."

She peeled off her gloves and lab coat, washed her hands and then went back to her office to lay everything out. Her desk was uncharacteristically cluttered, so she spent a few moments rearranging files before placing half a turkey sandwich and an apple on a paper plate. She wouldn't have been surprised if Nolan had blown her off, but he sauntered in a few minutes later and took the chair across from her desk.

"I hope you like turkey on wheat," she said.

He shrugged and picked up the sandwich. "Dr. March, have you noticed anything peculiar about Emily's behavior lately?"

Catherine glanced up from her lunch. "Peculiar in what way?"

"It's hard to put my finger on it," he said with a pensive frown. "But something's been off with her for at least a couple of days. She stares at her phone when she should be working and she jumps when it rings. Then she goes out into the hallway to answer."

"I take calls here in my office because I don't want to disturb anyone else," Catherine said. "Maybe she's just being considerate."

He chewed thoughtfully. "If the phone calls were the only thing out of the ordinary, I would tend to agree. As I said, it's hard to put my finger on it, but something is definitely going on with her."

"Well, if something is going on, it's her business and we probably shouldn't speculate. How's your sandwich?"

Nolan took the hint and dropped the subject, but conversation fizzled after that so Catherine left him to his thoughts. She'd known Nolan ever since he'd wandered into one of her freshman anthropology classes, but he remained something of a mystery. He never talked about himself or his family, but his manner of speaking gave her the impression of old money. His clothing was generic in style and color, but the cut and fabric always looked expensive. Beyond her superficial observations and his work ethic in the classroom and lab, however, she knew next to nothing about him.

As soon as he finished eating, he disposed of his paper plate and napkin and went back out to the lab. Catherine sighed as she watched him exit her office. She wanted to remind him that there was more to life than work and studies. She'd learned that lesson the hard way. How many times had she begged off dinner or a movie with her mother because she'd been too caught up in her current project? How she wished she could go back now and have just one more evening together. But there was no going back. No point in wallowing in regret and self-pity, either.

She returned to work and tried to shake off a lingering melancholy, but she couldn't seem to settle or focus. It was an odd feeling for someone normally given to deep concentration. She felt restless and jittery and blamed it on a second cup of coffee. Or on the power of suggestion. Maybe Nolan's uneasiness had rubbed off on her.

Sighing, she let her thoughts stray to Nick LaSalle and she wondered if he'd made any progress on her case. Only a few hours had passed since she'd last seen him, so it was too soon to call. It was unreasonable to think that he would have already arranged a visit with Orson Lee Finch, much less had time to lift prints from an old music box and run them through a Law Enforcement database. Still, Catherine found herself glancing up with an accelerated pulse when the lab door opened.

Emily came in on a draft of damp air from the basement hallway. Her dark hair glistened with raindrops and, as Catherine's gaze swept over her, she couldn't help searching for the telltale signs that Nolan had mentioned earlier. Was something going on in Emily's life?

None of your business. Get back to work.

"Glad you made it back in one piece," she said lightly as she examined skull sutures.

"Barely." Emily shivered. "I almost got T-boned at a traffic light. Drivers go crazy when it rains. I just hope it lets up before it's time to head home. Especially for you,

Dr. March, since you walked. Although I'd be more than happy to give you a ride."

"Thanks, but I have an umbrella and I'm not going that far."

"An umbrella won't do you much good in this downpour. You'd be soaked before you ever left the campus."

"We'll see what the weather is like in a few hours."

"Okay, but the offer stands. It's the least I can do after everything you've done for me."

"I don't know what you mean," Catherine said. "Your work speaks for itself."

"Yes, but you have a lot of exceptional students. I'm grateful you chose me for this project. The experience has been invaluable. I just want you to know that." She seemed on the verge of saying something else, then changed her mind and abruptly turned to put away her things. Instead of settling down to work, she walked across the room to stare down at Jane Doe Thirteen. "I wonder who she is."

"That's what we're trying to find out," Catherine said.

Emily glanced up. "She's different from the others."

"Yes, but no more or less important." Catherine got up to join her and, for the longest moment, they observed the remains in silence. Jane Doe Thirteen didn't yet have a name or a face, but they already knew quite a lot about her. She'd been small in stature, likely in her early twenties at the time of death, Caucasian, right-handed and possibly a runner. She'd had her whole life ahead of her, but then she'd come into contact with a vicious serial killer named Delmar Gainey. He'd been an efficient and cunning hunter. He would have stalked her for days, watching from afar, biding his time until the moment arrived when he could take her.

Had he thrown her in the abandoned well where he'd kept his other victims?

If Catherine closed her eyes, she could almost hear their terrified screams. The moans and groans. The pleas for mercy and then for death.

Her scalp prickled a warning. She glanced over her shoulder to find Nolan staring at them intently.

Emily broke the silence. "You'll think I'm crazy, Dr. March, but I dreamed about her last night."

Catherine turned back to the remains. "You dreamed about Thirteen?"

"She looked just like my second-grade teacher. She said that I should check her teeth."

"Wait," Noland said from across the room. "Are you actually suggesting that the ghost of Jane Doe Thirteen came to you in your sleep?"

"I don't believe in ghosts," Emily insisted. "But I do believe my subconscious was telling me to go back over the remains in case we missed something." She ran a hand along the edge of the metal table. There was a strange note in her voice and an inexplicable glint in her eyes when she caught Catherine's gaze. For a moment, Catherine had the improbable notion that Emily had taken something before returning to the lab. Was that the purpose of her lunch meeting? The reason why she couldn't call and cancel at the last minute?

Catherine wondered if she would have entertained such thoughts if Nolan hadn't planted a seed of doubt in her head. She glanced at him. He still watched her and Emily with a bemused expression on his face.

"Dr. March?"

She cut her gaze back to Emily. "Yes?"

"Do you ever dream about our work?"

"I'm sure I have, but I don't often remember my dreams." Not altogether true. She remembered dreaming about the music box.

Emily's eyes glittered before she dropped her gaze to the table. "I keep asking myself what made this Jane Doe different. Why did Gainey shoot her in the back of the head, likely killing her instantly, when he obviously took his time with the others? They all suffered perimortem fractures. All except her. He must have broken their arms and legs so they couldn't escape and then he used a long serrated blade to end them. He started off slowly, barely nicking the rib cage, and then worked himself into a frenzy as he went deeper into the flesh, cracking the sternum."

"It's called piquerism." Nolan got up from his work and came over to stand at the end of the table. "The sexual and sadistic pleasure derived from penetrating the skin with sharp objects, sometimes to the point of death."

Emily grimaced. "The things you know."

"That's the textbook definition, but every case is different," he explained. "Jack the Ripper is probably the most famous example, but I've always thought Albert Fish the more fascinating subject. He was said to have engaged in piquerism not just with his victims but also with himself, flagellating his body repeatedly with a nail-studded board."

"As if this place wasn't gloomy enough," Emily muttered. "Now I can't get that image out of my head."

"And yet you're not the least bit fazed by decomposed bodies infested with maggots," Nolan observed. "Interesting."

"Decomposed bodies and maggots are just biology. The torture porn you described is psychological." Emily turned back to Catherine. "I have a theory about Thirteen."

"I'd like to hear it."

"Her bones and teeth were healthy at the time of death, unlike the others, whose teeth were worn down, chipped or missing altogether. We've also seen antemortem fractures in some of the others. Not uncommon in people who have sustained years of abuse. Prostitutes, junkies, runaways. But it appears that Thirteen led a safer lifestyle. She wasn't vulnerable like the others. She fought back. She got away from Gainey and made a run for it. He hunted her down, but the only way he could subdue her was by shooting her as she fled. Then he took her body back to the house and buried her in the backyard with the other victims."

"Not a bad theory," Nolan said.

"You have a different one?" Catherine asked.

"For all the reasons Emily just mentioned, I don't believe Thirteen was ever a target, much less a captive. Gainey hunted a specific quarry. Street people that could disappear without being missed. He would have viewed this Jane Doe as too much of a risk. I think he killed her because she was a threat to him somehow. Maybe she saw something. Or maybe she got between him and his target."

"Wrong place, wrong time?" Catherine asked.

"Think about it." Nolan impatiently shoved back his curls. "Gainey managed to kill fourteen women and secrete their bodies in the walls of his home and in his backyard without anyone ever suspecting a thing. That takes a certain amount of skill and intelligence. He wasn't the type to get careless. No one ever got away from him. No one ever lived to tell the tale. He worked efficiently, with purpose and without ego. Unlike, say, Orson Lee Finch, who taunted the police by putting the bodies of his victims on display. Arguably, Finch wanted to get caught."

The mere mention of Finch's name jolted Catherine. Something occurred to her as she studied the remains of Jane Doe Thirteen. What if her birth mother really had been the Twilight Killer's first victim? What if Finch was the one who had arranged for someone to leave that music box on Catherine's front porch? What if he was the one who had kept tabs on her all these years? Watching from afar, perhaps even silently celebrating the milestones in her life. That would mean he had always known who she was. Where she was. And he had always known how to get to her.

She shivered and rubbed the gooseflesh at her nape.

"Dr. March? You okay?" Nolan asked.

"Yes, I'm fine. Just lost in thought."

"What do you think about my theory?" His gaze seemed more intense than usual.

"I'll tell you what I think," Emily said. "You sound as if you actually admire Delmar Gainey."

Nolan answered with a shrug. "I can admire his resourcefulness without condoning his actions."

"Let's assume we're both right about Thirteen's lifestyle," Emily mused. "If she didn't live on the street, then why didn't anyone come forward to report her missing?"

"Maybe they did," Nolan said. "Everyone assumes Gainey's victims lived in or near Charleston, but this city alone is a small hunting ground for a killer as prolific as Gainey. Atlanta, on the other hand, offers a wider net and a greater probability of anonymity. And it's only a five-hour drive from here. Savannah is just over two hours. Charlotte, three and a half hours. A prostitute goes missing here, a runaway there. No one notices."

"You've given this a lot of thought," Emily said.

"Yes, but I haven't started dreaming about the remains yet."

She made a face at him.

"You've both presented interesting theories," Catherine interjected. "And speculation is fine up to a point, but we're getting away from our purpose and into the purview of the police. Let's just focus on our work right now."

She set an example by returning to her worktable. The

other two soon followed. In the aftermath of their discussion, the lab seemed unnaturally quiet, the drumming of rain against the windows the only disturbance. Catherine found herself glancing up now and then, surreptitiously studying her assistants. She noticed things that had never come to her attention before. Like the way Emily's gaze strayed back to Jane Doe Thirteen when she thought no one was looking. Like the way Nolan covertly studied Emily as Catherine observed him. She couldn't help thinking that something had changed and now the dynamics of the lab were discordant.

Maybe it was nothing more than her imagination.

Or maybe, instead of assuming the friction came from her assistants, she would be better served by looking in a mirror.

Chapter Five

Nick was out of the office for most of the day. By the time he returned late that afternoon, everyone but Jackie had gone home in anticipation of the storm. She was just clearing her desk when he came into the lobby brushing raindrops from his hair.

"Getting nasty out there."

She cut her gaze to the windows. "Understatement of the year, I'd say. I almost expected to see you float up in a boat."

Nick grinned. "Maybe Emmett had the right idea after all."

"That old fool? Throwing good money after bad is what he does best," she scoffed. "At the rate he's burning through his retirement, he'll be out on the street before his next birthday. Then what'll he do? Better not come whining to me is all I can say."

"You wouldn't take him in?" Nick teased.

"I would not. What does he know about operating a boat that size anyway? I give his love affair with the sea all of six months if he doesn't drown himself first." She checked her phone before dropping it in her purse, then removed a gold lipstick and compact.

In her fifties, Jackie Morris was still an attractive woman, meticulously groomed and determinedly blonde with a take-no-prisoners attitude. She glanced up with a stern glare and shook the lipstick tube in Nick's direction. "As for you, Mr. Slick, I've got your number. I know why you're hanging around here being all chummy and attentive. Don't even think about dumping work on my clean desk. It's after six and I've been here since seven. I'm done for the day. If you have an emergency, I suggest you handle it yourself."

Nick was used to her prickly disposition. He merely shrugged good-naturedly. "I was just going to say be careful out there. Weather is getting worse by the minute."

"Yes, well, some of us didn't have the luxury of leaving the office before the storm hit," she grumbled.

"You could always wait it out here," Nick said.

"Nice try." She opened the compact to powder her nose. "I'll see you in the morning."

"Are you sure you don't want me to drive you home?"

"I've been driving since before you were born. I think I can handle a little rain."

No doubt she could. She was one of those people whose competence and value far exceeded her job title, and she made sure everyone knew it.

"I won't keep you then," Nick said. "Just one quick question before you go. Do you remember the client who came in yesterday afternoon?"

Maybe it was his imagination, but Nick thought he detected a sudden tension in her posture.

She gave a little shrug as if to disguise a momentary anxiety. "Your two o'clock? Dark hair, big brown eyes?"

"Yes, that's the one. Dr. Catherine March."

"She's a doctor?"

"Why does everyone focus on her title?" Nick asked with a puzzled frown.

"Maybe because she didn't have the look of your usual clientele," Jackie offered.

"For the record, she's a PhD. A forensic anthropologist, to be exact."

"Okay. What's your interest in Miss PhD besides the obvious?"

"She thinks her mother may have been a client of ours some years back."

"How far back?"

"Twenty-five years or so. Her name was Laura March. Her late husband was a murdered cop named Aidan March. Do either of those names ring a bell?"

Jackie had been in the process of reapplying her lipstick, but her hand froze as she stared at her reflection in the compact mirror. Then her gaze lifted to Nick's. "I can't say that they do. Why does she think her mother was our client?"

"Laura March died last week. Catherine discovered a box of newspaper clippings hidden in a secret compartment in her mother's house. She also found one of our old business cards with Dad's unlisted number scribbled on the back."

"Your dad's number, you say?" Jackie busied herself with the lipstick and compact before returning both to her purse. She seemed to take an inordinate amount of time in completing the task. "Have you asked him if he remembers a client by that name?"

"Not yet, but we all know you have a memory like a steel trap. I've never known you to forget a name or a face."

"True, but I'm not infallible. And as much as I hate to admit it, I'm not the spring chicken I once was." She sighed heavily. "Anyway, I don't remember a client named Laura March, but it's possible your dad knew her away from the office."

"I'll ask him at my grandmother's party if I don't see him before then," Nick said. "In the meantime, maybe I'll stop by the warehouse and take a look through the archives."

"Best you wait until morning. After dark, the neighborhood becomes a war zone. I've been after Emmett for years to get rid of that place. I won't go over there by myself even in daylight. All those carjackings and home invasions. Makes you wonder what the world is coming to."

She picked up her purse and headed toward the back exit. Nick lingered to sort through a stack of mail on her desk. Then something propelled him down the hallway. He wasn't sure why he felt the need to follow Jackie, but something about her attitude and the overheard conversation with his uncle from the day before prodded Nick's curiosity. He had a feeling they'd both recognized Laura March's name. What he couldn't figure out was why they'd lied to him.

Jackie had popped open an umbrella and was hurrying across the small back parking area to her car. Before she could climb in, however, another car came around the corner of the building and the driver flashed the headlights. Jackie didn't appear alarmed or even wary, but Nick reached for the door. Before he had time to call out a warning, let alone intercede, she went around to the passenger side of the car and climbed in.

Nick couldn't see the driver's face even when the dome light flashed and he could only make out the first two digits of the license plate. He stood just outside the door under the shelter of the overhang as he watched the strange vehicle.

After about five minutes, Jackie got out and hurried back over to her car. The remote chirped and the lights flashed. The first car circled the parking lot and then sat with engine idling while Jackie backed out of her space. Nick automatically stepped deeper into the shelter of the overhang as both cars pulled out of the lot.

He told himself whatever relationship Jackie had with the driver of that car was none of his concern. For all he knew, he'd witnessed a romantic assignation, but he still couldn't shake the notion that both Jackie and Uncle Emmett had lied to him about Laura March.

He went back inside and climbed the steps to his second-floor office, but the noise of the storm and the rage of his own thoughts distracted him. He removed the clippings and the music box from a locked drawer and placed them on his desk. He'd only been able to lift one clear set of prints from the box and he'd matched those to Catherine's. Whoever had left the music box on her porch had wiped it clean. He wound the key and watched the little ballerina for a moment before turning his attention to the grainy photo of Finch and the child. He compared the image to the snapshot of Catherine at the age of three. Was there a resemblance to the child and to Finch, or had the power of suggestion planted the similarities in Nick's head?

What if Catherine's worst nightmare turned out to be true? Would Nick be drawn to her still, or would the sins of her birth father create a chasm of doubt and wariness no matter his intentions?

He sorted through the articles a second time and then locked everything back in the drawer. There were a number of avenues he needed to explore, including a follow-up call to Finch's attorney, but tonight he couldn't seem to settle down to work.

Rising, he walked over to the window to take stock of the weather before turning off the lights and locking up. He went out the back door, hunching his shoulders against the rain as he hurried to his car. He had the strongest urge to see Catherine even though he had nothing new to report and she might not appreciate him showing up on her doorstep unannounced.

Starting the engine, he backed out of his space and pulled around the building to the street, but instead of heading to Catherine's apartment or to his own place, he drove to the warehouse where the agency's old files were stored. He used a remote to open the gate and then pulled up to the front entrance. A clap of thunder and a keen bolt of lightning kept him pinned inside his car for a moment. Then, chancing the weather, he sprinted up the concrete steps, unlocking the garage-style door as he shook off the rain. The panel rolled up with a loud rumble. Stepping inside, Nick felt for the switch, and as the rows of old-fashioned pendant lights sputtered on, he hit the button to lower the door.

The warehouse was a cavernous place full of discarded furniture and equipment. Nick stood dripping on the concrete floor as he got his bearings. Metal shelving crammed with file boxes extended back into the shadows. Years after the agency had become fully digitized, the LaSalle brothers had remained stubbornly old school, insisting on paper copies of everything. No one bothered with the warehouse much these days. Boxes of files were periodically unloaded, but Nick doubted even his father and uncle knew everything that was stored there.

The place reeked of mildew. Water dripped somewhere toward the back of the warehouse and Nick made a mental note to have the roof checked. Wouldn't hurt to call an exterminator, either. He could hear rats in the walls and with the incessant splatter of rain against the skylights, the place was about as welcoming as a tomb.

He moved slowly down the cramped aisles, checking labels on boxes and glancing through the file folders inside.

Another clap of thunder rattled the windows and flickered the lights. He heard the unmistakable *womp* of a blown transformer and then the power went out.

He stood in the pitch black, listening to the rain against the glass and the crack of thunder overhead. Something heavy hit the roof and he reflexively covered his head as he moved away from the skylights. Using the illumination from his phone, he continued to scan the labels. He was just reaching for another box when a sound inside the warehouse stilled him. Not the scurry of rodents or the drip from a leak, but the stealthy rustle of someone moving toward the front of the warehouse.

Nick angled the beam through the shelving, catching a glimpse of a dark silhouette. "Hey! Stop!"

He was armed, but he didn't draw his weapon. The thought occurred to him that someone homeless might have sought shelter from the storm or some kid may have climbed in through a window on a dare. "Hey, you!"

The intruder dashed down the aisle, trying to beat Nick to the door. He heard a bump and a loud *clang*, and then the shelving units toppled like dominoes. He pressed back, stumbling in his haste to avoid the avalanche of metal braces and bulging cardboard boxes. He heard the rattle of the garage door as he scrambled to his feet and leaped over boxes. The intruder hit the floor and rolled through the partial opening before disappearing into the rainy darkness.

Ducking under the still-rising door, Nick paused at the top of the steps as an engine revved. The vehicle swung out of the alley between buildings and headed for the gate.

Nick vaulted over the handrail and climbed into his car. Wheeling away from the building, he floored the accelerator. The tires spun on the wet pavement as he careened through the gate and onto the street. Up ahead, he could see taillights through the rain.

He shot forward and then hit the brakes hard as a truck came out of nowhere. The driver swerved and laid down on the horn. Nick waited for the vehicle to clear the intersection, but the driver deliberately took his time. When the truck finally lumbered out of the way, the taillights in front of him had disappeared.

Nick drove on, peering down side streets and alleyways before he returned to the warehouse. Grabbing a flashlight from the glove box, he went back inside and walked each aisle, searching for evidence.

Toward the rear of the building, a box had been abandoned on the floor. As he knelt to scour the contents, his phone rang. He glanced at the no-caller-ID message on the screen before lifting the phone to his ear.

"Nick LaSalle."

"Are you the private investigator?" a male voice inquired.

"I am. Who is this?"

The caller paused. "I understand you were a police detective until certain accusations were made and you had to resign."

Nick frowned. "Accusations are not the same thing as the truth."

"How well I know."

Nick lost his patience. "I'll ask you for the last time. Who the hell are you and what do you want?"

"My name is Orson Lee Finch. You may know me as the Twilight Killer."

The moniker whispered down Nick's neck like the coldest of breaths. Suddenly, he became overly aware of his surroundings. He was alone in a pitch-black warehouse, talking on his cell to a notorious serial killer. He ran the flashlight beam up the tall racks and all along the walls. The place was eerily silent. Even the rats had gone still.

"Are you there, Mr. LaSalle?"

"I'm here. You took me by surprise. Your call came in as unknown. I take it you aren't calling from a prison payphone." The surreal aspect of the conversation strained Nick's voice.

"There are any number of ways of communicating with the outside world," Finch said. "We aren't as isolated as people like to think."

Was that merely an observation or a veiled threat? Nick remembered his uncle's warning about Finch. *Psychopaths are by nature cunning.*

"You certainly seem to know a lot about me," Nick said.

"I do my homework. People have all sorts of reasons for wanting to strike up a relationship with someone like me."

"I can imagine."

"Mr. LaSalle—may I call you Nick?"

"I'd rather you just tell me why you're calling." Nick walked over to the open door and stared out into the night. He wanted to hang up. The conversation gave him the creeps.

"What's that sound?" Finch asked.

"It's raining here. Has been for days."

"Rain." The word was almost a whisper. Nick could imagine Finch closing his eyes as he lifted his face to the sky.

"I remember reading that you were a gardener."

"I'm still a gardener, though I do my work these days in dreams and small containers." Finch sighed. "I understand you want to see me."

"Yes, the sooner the better."

"I don't agree to many meetings these days, but for you I'll make an exception. The administrative office usually slow-walks visitor applications. However, after all these years, I've earned a certain amount of consideration. I'll see what I can do about speeding the process along. Will Catherine come with you?"

The name shocked Nick. Finch's voice and his own exhaustion had almost lulled him into a dangerous lethargy. The very thing his uncle had warned him against. "How do you know about Catherine?"

"You should both take care. There is more going on than either of you realize."

NOLAN LEFT THE lab a bit early and Emily shortly after five. The rain was still coming down, but Catherine declined an offer of a lift. She wanted to get caught up on paperwork before she called it a day.

"Promise you won't work too late," Emily said as she headed for the door. "This place gets spooky after dark."

"I'll only be here for an hour or so," Catherine assured her. "If it's still pouring when I get ready to leave, I'll call a cab." She walked Emily out into the hallway. "See you tomorrow."

"Take care, Dr. March."

Catherine waited until Emily had disappeared into the elevator before taking a brisk walk up and down the corridor to loosen cramped muscles. Then, stopping by the restroom to freshen up, she went back to the lab, punching the key code to let herself in. The artificial glare from the overhead lights should have chased away all those lurking shadows, but Catherine found herself inexplicably unnerved as she wove her way through the tables. The lab was as familiar as her apartment, the skeletal remains no more off-putting to her than a next-door neighbor, yet Catherine couldn't seem to shake the unease that had gripped her since she'd found those clippings in her mother's closet.

The intense quiet seemed to mock her. *You are the*

daughter of the Twilight Killer. The blood of a monster runs through your veins.

"Stop it," she said aloud. "You're being very silly right now. How many times have you been alone in this lab? Have you ever once been frightened? Just get to work and stop talking to yourself."

Settling in at her desk, she opened her laptop and began the painstaking task of filing quarterly budget reports. She'd made her way through the first section and had barely started on the second when the lights flickered and went out.

She closed her laptop to preserve the battery and then dug a flashlight out of a desk drawer. Moving to the window, she stood on tiptoe to stare out. The blackout seemed widespread. She couldn't see lights in any of the nearby buildings. The campus looked dreary and deserted.

The dark made her feel claustrophobic, but she took a few deep breaths and forced herself to relax. She would just have to wait out the storm. Rain was one thing but she would be crazy to venture out in all that lightning. Her battery had plenty of juice so the sensible thing to do was go back to work to pass the time. But the notion held little appeal. Maybe it was the rain or lack of sleep, but she suddenly felt bone-deep weary. Grief bore down heavily in the dark. She curled up on the small sofa in her office and thought about her mother. About their last days together and Laura's cryptic message.

Catherine's eyes grew heavy as she lay there. The play of lightning across the ceiling mesmerized her and she felt worn down from recent events. *Close your eyes, Cath. Rest. Things will look better in the morning.*

Catherine had no idea how long she'd been out when a light outside her window awakened her. She stirred and wondered if the power had come back on. Then the light went out as thunder boomed and she thought the glow must have been lightning. She settled back down, dozing off once more only to startle awake a second time.

She stared wide-eyed at the ceiling, disoriented and frightened and not knowing why. Her office lay in complete darkness except for the intermittent lightning.

Rising, she reached for the flashlight on her desk, then froze. A sound came to her from the lab. The faintest of tinkles. She had the wild notion that someone had left another music box for her to find. Then reality hit her with a sickening shock. Someone had punched in the security code on the panel outside the lab door.

It's nothing. Don't panic.

Emily had probably come back to check on her or maybe Nolan had forgotten something. He'd left in a hurry earlier. He may even have decided to put in a few more hours of work before realizing the power was off in the lab.

Fighting panic, Catherine turned on the flashlight and moved toward the lab, but something stopped her again. The hair at the back of her neck bristled in warning. She flicked off the light and slipped to the office doorway, letting her gaze travel through the maze of tables to the exit. Someone was coming through the door. She could make out little more than a silhouette in the darkness. Tall, thin. It had to be Nolan.

But Catherine didn't call out to him. Instead, she stood listening as the door closed and the lock reengaged. She strained to hear the familiar *squeak* of Nolan's sneakers or the *thud* of his backpack as he dropped it to the floor.

Nothing came to her. No sound, no scent.

A flashlight came on, and in the back glow, Catherine caught the briefest glimpse of a black-clad figure lurking just inside the door. The beam swept across the lab, arcing over the tables, highlighting the skeletal remains, before coming to rest on the doorway of Catherine's office. She pressed back into the darkness, holding her breath, waiting, waiting until the beam moved away from her.

Even then, she told herself that, if not Nolan, the interloper must be a security guard making his rounds. Maybe he'd heard her in the office and had come to check out the noise. Still, she didn't call out. Her instincts warned her again to be silent.

She glanced around for her phone. She'd put it in her backpack earlier. But where was her backpack? She didn't dare look for the bag, didn't dare move from her current position for fear of making a noise. For fear of turning her back on that advancing silhouette.

Slowly—ever so slowly—he made his way through the lab, angling the beam over the gaping skulls and then pausing as if to check the numbers affixed to the stainless-steel tables. Catherine heard the *clang* of a bumped table and the clatter of a rolling stool. Unlike her, the prowler seemed unconcerned about noise. At that hour, he undoubtedly assumed everyone was long gone.

Her mind raced as her heart thudded. Why would someone break into the lab? The equipment was valuable but specific. It would be difficult to unload without drawing attention. But he hadn't broken in. He'd used the key code. He'd let himself in. All Catherine had to do was turn on her flashlight and catch him in the beam, but she didn't. She watched and waited in darkness.

All was still in the lab. Uncannily quiet. And into that heavy silence came the muffled *ping* of a text message on her phone.

Chapter Six

As the intruder whipped around, the flashlight beam shot like a laser across the lab, clipping Catherine before she could melt even deeper into the shadows. Light seeped through the glass panel in her office and she ducked, pressing against the side of the desk.

When the light finally shifted away, she let out a breath. She hunkered in blackness, desperately wanting to believe that she was overreacting, but what if she wasn't? Everything inside her warned that she needed to get to the exit. She was trapped in her small office, and the longer she stayed crouched by the desk, the greater her chance of discovery. Her best bet was to take advantage of the blackout.

Slipping to all fours, she crawled through the office doorway and out into the lab, taking shelter behind one of the tables. She had no idea who had invaded her domain or why, but she had to assume a devious motive. She positioned herself so that she had a clear path to the door. If she could make it to the hallway, she stood a greater chance of escape. She knew the building. Knew all the corners and crevices. Hopefully, the dark and the intruder's unfamiliarity with his surroundings would disorient him. So long as Catherine kept her head, she might be able to outsmart him.

Reaching a hand up to the table, she felt along the metal

surface until her fingers closed around a Boley gauge. Then she glanced around the table leg until she spotted the intruder outlined against the glass panel of her office. He held the light up to the window, peering in as if searching for her.

Catherine drew a breath and willed a steady hand. She flung the caliper through the office doorway and the metal tool landed with a loud *clang* against the tile floor. The flashlight beam shot wildly across the room as the silhouette lunged toward the office doorway. Catherine waited until his back was turned and then she rushed through the tables toward the exit.

She was halfway across the room when the flashlight beam caught her. She could hear him behind her, advancing quickly as he plowed through the metal tables. She grabbed a rolling stool, turned quickly and sent it flying down the narrow aisle toward him. He tripped, cursing, and Catherine rolled another stool in his path before she turned back to the door. Flinging it open, she burst into the hallway.

The elevator was to her left but useless without power. The stairwell was at the far end of the corridor. She plunged through the dark hallway, hoping to distance herself from the prowler, but she could imagine his footsteps behind her, could almost feel the tug of his fingers on her lab coat.

She needed to make it to the first-floor exit or find a hiding place. Most of the doors along the corridor would be locked at this hour and she only had the code for the lab. *Think, think.* There was a supply closet on her left, more rooms on her right, all of them undoubtedly locked and deserted. Hardly anyone besides the custodial crew and her students came down to this level. Catherine had always enjoyed the isolation, but now she saw the maze of hallways and closed-off rooms as another trap.

Keep going. Don't look back.

A sharp left turn took her down another short corridor to the stairwell.

The closed space was even darker. No windows, no flickers of distant lightning. The black closed in on her. For a moment, her throat closed and her chest tightened. It was like being lost in her worst nightmare, pursued through total darkness by some nameless, faceless entity who meant her harm. She tried to shake off the grasping fear as she put out a hand to feel her way along the wall. Her foot bumped against the bottom step and she stumbled. Using the handrail for guidance, she propelled herself up the stairs, making it to the landing before she heard real footsteps behind her.

He seemed to fly up the stairs. Before Catherine could move through the door, he grabbed her. She lost her footing and fell with a jarring *thud*, lashing out viciously as her survival instinct kicked in. Whether she caught him by surprise or the darkness disoriented him, Catherine didn't know. He stumbled back and went crashing down the stairs.

She grabbed the banister and pulled herself up. The assailant was already scrambling to his feet. Catherine lunged toward the exit. Flinging open the door, she rushed out into another narrow hallway that would take her to the lobby. If she could make it outside, she could find help. Someone would be working late. A security guard would be on patrol. Students would be leaving for a party. *Someone* would come to her rescue.

Fumbling with the lock, she shoved open the glass door and ran down the steps into the rain, not daring to look over her shoulder, not daring to stop for another breath. Headlights came toward her. She left the sidewalk and darted into the street, putting up her hands in desperation as the glare trapped her.

The vehicle slid to a stop and the door slammed. Only then did Catherine glance over her shoulder. No one was behind her. No one that she could see.

"Catherine?"

The familiar voice sounded incredulous. Hands gripped her shoulders. She found herself staring up into Nick La-Salle's rain-soaked face.

"Are you all right? What's wrong?"

She wiped raindrops from her lashes. "Someone was in the lab just now. He chased me down the hallway and attacked me in the stairwell."

Nick's grip tightened as he glanced behind her toward the building. "Are you hurt? Did you call the police?"

"I'm not hurt and I couldn't call anyone. I left my phone in the office." She paused to catch her breath. "No one should have been in the lab this late. I was only there because I fell asleep in my office."

Nick's grasp tightened. "Did you recognize the attacker?"

"I never got a look at his face. The power is out in the lab."

"It's out all over the city. Here, get in the car." He guided her around to the passenger's side and opened the door. Then he went back to the driver's side and slid behind the wheel.

"Where are we going?" Her teeth started to chatter as shock set in. She hugged her arms around her middle for warmth. She hated Nick seeing her like this—afraid and vulnerable. She hated anyone seeing her like this. *Pull it together. You're fine.*

"I need to get the car off the street before someone hits

us." He steered the vehicle to the curb and parked, then reached over the seat for a jacket. "Put this on."

Catherine gratefully complied, draping the jacket around her shoulders and sinking down into the fabric. It was a little like having Nick's arms around her.

"You sure you're okay?"

"Yes, I think so."

"Then stay right here." He handed her his cell phone. "Call 911. They'll alert campus patrol. Keep the doors locked until they get here."

Catherine glanced at him in alarm. "Where are you going?"

"I'll go have a look around. If the suspect is still in the building, maybe I can corner him."

"You can't get inside. The entrance door automatically locked behind me."

"Don't you have a key?"

"Yes, but I left it in the office along with my phone. I didn't take time to grab my backpack. I just ran."

"Then I'll have a look around outside. He'll have to exit the building somewhere. You just stay put. I'll be back before you know it."

The door slammed and he was gone. Catherine glanced around. The headlights and windshield wipers were still on. She reached over and turned both off. Silence and darkness enveloped her.

She made the call to 911, giving the operator her name, location and a brief rundown of the situation. The dispatcher promised to send an officer right away. All Catherine had to do was sit tight. But Nick was out there somewhere. What if the police mistook him for the prowler?

She reached for the door handle. Maybe she should go find him, warn him…

But someone was still out there…someone with evil intent. She shivered, imagining his eyes on her even now.

Nick's ringtone pierced the silence, causing her to jump. She answered his cell without glancing at the screen. "Yes, hello." When no one responded, she said in an urgent tone, "Is this the police?"

"I'm not the police."

Catherine tensed as a warning chill prickled her spine. The voice was unfamiliar and yet something about his tone inexplicably unnerved her. She told herself she was just upset and already frightened. A voice on the phone couldn't hurt her. *Sever the call and keep the phone free in case the police call back.*

Instead, she pressed the cell to her ear. "Who is this?"

"Who I am is irrelevant. Who you are matters a great deal."

"How do you know who I am?" And more importantly, how had he known to call her on Nick's phone? Was she being watched? Her heart pounded as she turned to scour the night. Blackened windows stared back at her.

"Listen carefully to what I say. The truth is not what you think. There's more at stake than you realize."

She squeezed the phone. "What are you talking about? *Who is this?*"

"Be careful who you trust. Aidan March found out the hard way that people with dark secrets never go down without a fight."

A PATROL OFFICER arrived a few minutes after Catherine's call. He arranged for a security guard to let them inside the building and then Catherine led everyone down to the lab. The intruder, of course, was long gone. They saw no sign of forced entry and nothing appeared to be missing from the lab, though a more thorough assessment would need to be undertaken once power was restored.

They regrouped outside under the covered main entrance, sheltered from the rain. Catherine had said nothing of the call she'd received on Nick's phone. She was still too shaken by that voice, too unsettled by his warning. Too frightened by the revelation that the only father she'd ever known had somehow died because of the secrets she was trying to uncover.

She twisted her emerald ring as she gave her statement to the officer. He was thorough, but he seemed to have doubts about her story. Maybe he could sense she was holding something back. She cast a surreptitious glance at Nick. Maybe he could, too.

"It's easy to let your imagination get the better of you during a power outage," the officer said. "You wouldn't believe all the crazy stories I've heard tonight. Must get pretty spooky in the lab when the lights go out. All those skulls would freak anyone out."

"This wasn't my imagination," Catherine said.

"I'm not saying it was. I'm just asking if there's a possibility you misjudged the circumstances. You said the suspect used the key code to unlock the lab door."

"That's right."

"Are you sure he wasn't a member of the faculty or staff, someone who had business in the lab? Maybe he even went down there to check on you."

"Then why didn't he call out my name? Why would someone who works for the university chase me out of the lab and attack me in the stairwell?" Catherine held out her arm even though it was too dark to see the discoloration. "I fought him off and I have the bruises to prove it."

"Yet you never got a good look at him?"

"The power was off. You saw for yourself. It's pitch black in the stairwell."

"Isn't it possible he chased you because he thought you were the prowler? He wasn't expecting to find anyone in the lab and you startled him. He reacted on instinct. Maybe he tried to subdue you in the stairwell rather than attack you." He canted his head as he studied her. "I'm just trying to consider every possibility so we can figure out what happened."

"She just told you what happened." The sharp edge in Nick's voice made Catherine shudder even as she shot him a grateful glance. "If this person thought Catherine was an intruder, why didn't he call the cops? Where is he now?"

The officer turned to Nick. "What did you say your name was again?"

"Nick LaSalle."

"And your business here?"

"He's a friend," Catherine put in. She didn't want to explain that she'd hired a private detective to prove Orson Lee Finch was her biological father. The officer had already questioned her state of mind. She could only imagine his incredulity at such a revelation.

"Your name sounds familiar. Do I know you?"

"I don't think so," Nick said coolly. "Why don't we just focus on what happened to Dr. March?"

The officer shrugged. "Without physical evidence or a description, there's not much more I can do except keep an eye out. If you hear or see anything else, you can call me directly at this number." He handed her a card.

By this time, Catherine was just glad to have the incident behind her. She nodded and thanked him, then waited until he was out of earshot before turning to Nick. "I don't think he believed me."

"I wouldn't read too much into his attitude. He's probably just anxious to get on to the next call. Nights like this are hell for patrol officers. He's right about one thing, though. Not much more we can do here tonight."

Catherine gave him an anxious glance. "You don't think I made all this up, do you? That I panicked in the dark? Let my imagination get the better of me? I could hardly blame you if you did after what I told you this morning about night terrors and my fear of being pursued in the dark."

"I don't think you made anything up," Nick said.

"Thank you for that."

"You don't have to keep thanking me. I haven't done anything yet."

"You came to my rescue tonight," she said.

"I happened to be at the right place at the right time."

"Yes, about that." She gave him a long scrutiny in the dark as the voice on the phone echoed in her ears. *Be careful who you trust.* "Why are you here?"

He hesitated for a fraction too long. "I wanted to talk to you about something, but it'll keep. Let me drive you home."

She caught his arm. "No, tell me now. You came all the way over here to see me so it must be important. How did you even know I'd still be here?"

He glanced at her hand on his arm, then at her. "Do you want to stand here in the rain all night, or do you want to go home and get some dry clothes on?"

"Why do I have the feeling you're trying to avoid telling me something unpleasant?"

"I'm not. We can talk on the way."

She nodded and they made a dash for his car. Catherine clicked on the seatbelt, and then settled back, hugging Nick's jacket around her as he started the engine. She studied his profile in the dash lights. The strong lines of his chin and jaw suggested resolve and resilience, along with what she imagined to be a stubborn streak. Let loose on a case, he would be relentless until he found answers, but was that really what she wanted? Was she ready to accept whatever secrets he uncovered?

And what secrets did *he* harbor? Catherine wondered. She racked her brain, trying to remember the rumors that had surrounded his departure from the police department. She hadn't paid much attention at the time. She'd been too preoccupied by her mother's illness. Other than the occasional twinge of regret that he hadn't called once their case concluded, Catherine hadn't thought much about Nick La-Salle at all. Now in the space of one short day, she couldn't stop thinking about him. Or looking at him, for that matter.

You're still in shock.

Right.

He caught her gaze as he turned onto the main thoroughfare. The impact was an electric thrill across her nerve endings. The drum of rain on the roof and the close confines of the car made it seem as if they were cocooned and isolated from the rest of the world.

As their gazes clung, she had the panicky sensation of falling. Butterflies quivered inside. Her pulse accelerated. She told herself to break eye contact and look away. *Take a breath.* This wasn't the time or place. She had a business relationship with Nick LaSalle, nothing more. Why muddy the waters? Her life was complicated enough as it was. Besides, what if she really was Orson Lee Finch's offspring? The ultimate child of Twilight? How would Nick feel about her then?

He turned back to the road. "You're awfully quiet for someone who wanted to talk. Are you sure you're okay? The ER is just a few blocks away. We could swing by and get you checked out."

"That's really not necessary. I'm just a little bruised. And a little frightened, if I'm honest."

"I'd be worried if you weren't. You've been through a lot tonight. But you're safe now."

She nodded and told herself to relax even as that strange voice on Nick's phone continued to goad her. *Be careful who you trust.* "Why did you come looking for me tonight?"

"We'll get to that, I promise. Right now, I think we need to go back over what happened at the lab while it's still fresh in your mind."

"What's there to talk about? You know as much as I do. You were there when I gave my statement to the officer."

"You recounted the facts, but we need to dig deeper. Think means, motive and opportunity. Someone came into the lab tonight when they had reason to believe everyone else would be gone. We need to figure out why. Who else has the code to the lab?"

"Any number of people," she said with a shrug. "It's hardly a state secret. My two assistants, the custodial staff, most anyone who works in the anthropology department. We take precautions, but people tend to get lax. I'm guilty of that myself. As far as I know, we've never had anything like this happen before. I've always felt perfectly safe in that building even when I work alone at night."

"Can you get me a list of people authorized to have that code?"

She tucked back her damp hair. "I'm not even sure there is such a list. Why? What do you want with it?"

"It could be one way of narrowing down suspects. Don't worry. I'll be discreet. No knocking down your colleagues' doors or anything like that."

"That's a relief, I guess, but tracking down suspects really isn't your job, is it? The incident at the lab is a police matter. Unless you think it's somehow connected to our investigation."

"I'm not willing to dismiss anything at this point. There may be more going on than either of us realize."

Catherine whipped around in surprise. "Why did you say that? Someone else told me the same thing earlier. Almost word for word."

He scowled at the road. "What are you talking about? Who told you that?"

"After I placed the call to 911, another call came in on your cell. I answered because I thought it might be the police. The man on the other end said the truth is not what we think. There's more going on than we realize."

Nick shot her a glance. "What else did he say?"

"He was very cryptic. He talked about my father. He called him by name. He said Aidan March found out the hard way that people with dark secrets seldom go down without a fight."

"Did this man give you his name?"

"He refused. But there was something about his voice… his tone…" She trailed off on a shudder.

Nick was quiet for a moment. "I know what you mean about his voice. I think the same man called me earlier. That's actually why I came looking for you. I wanted to tell you about that conversation in person. You weren't home so I decided to try the lab." Nick stopped at an intersection and turned to Catherine. "I think the person on the other end of that call tonight was Orson Lee Finch. The Twilight Killer."

Chapter Seven

Catherine's heart thudded as she stared out the rain-streaked window. The power was still out and the streets looked ominous. The alleyways and walled gardens that charmed by day became hiding places for the predators that hunted by night. Predators like Orson Lee Finch.

"How did he know to call you?" she asked in a hushed voice. "How did he even get your number?"

"I called his attorney to request a visit. I had to leave my name and number so that he could get back to me. I didn't mention you at all, but Finch somehow knew about you. He asked if you intended to come with me to visit him in prison."

Her mouth went dry. "How could he know that we're working together unless he's talking to someone on the outside? Maybe he even has someone watching us."

"That's possible." Nick studied the road. Catherine couldn't help wondering what was going through his head.

She tore her gaze away. "I wondered earlier if he was somehow responsible for the music box that was left on my porch this morning. What if he's been keeping track of me all these years? That would explain how he knows about our investigation. He knows everything about me. Where I live, where I work. Every move I make."

"Let's not get ahead of ourselves," Nick said. "Try to stay calm. We'll figure it out."

Too late to remain calm, Catherine thought. Panic pounded with every heartbeat. "Do you think the man I saw on the street yesterday works for Finch? He walked away when I called out to him, but he could have doubled back and followed me to your office."

"Can you describe him?"

"Middle-aged white male, tall, lanky, with longish brown hair slicked back from his face. His arms were tattooed. Crudely done from what I could see."

"Like prison ink?"

"I never even thought of that," Catherine said. "I suppose it's possible. I didn't get that good of a look and I'm certainly no expert." She glanced at Nick's profile. "Finch's phone calls change everything. It was one thing to search for answers when I thought I could remain anonymous, but he knows who I am. Who we both are. What should we do?"

"That's up to you." The play of shadows across Nick's face cast a sinister air and Catherine found herself wondering about him again. About his past, his character, his motives. What did she even know about Nick LaSalle?

Why had *her* mother kept a business card with *his* father's phone number scribbled on the back?

Why had Orson Lee Finch warned her to be careful who she trusted?

Doubts needled. Then she shook herself with a reminder that she was the one who had sought out Nick. She was the one who had gone to his office and invited him onto her quest.

As if sensing her agitation, his tone softened. "You have every right to be frightened. Finch's call shook me up, too. It's not too late to change your mind. We can shut down the investigation tonight if that's what you want. Just walk away and forget you ever found those clippings. Or..."

"Or what?" Catherine asked nervously.

"We keep digging until we uncover the answers you're looking for. You seemed convinced this morning that the truth is the only thing that will bring you peace."

"What would you do?"

"It doesn't matter what I'd do. This is your call. How far do you want to take it?"

She traced a raindrop down the window with her fingertip. Her hand was surprisingly steady now. "I don't want to drop the investigation. I don't think I can, especially after learning that my father may have been killed for asking the same questions I am. This isn't just about my adoption anymore."

"We don't know that. Psychopaths excel at mind games. Don't let Finch manipulate you. He could have a reason for wanting to misdirect us."

"I know. He's obviously a step ahead of us already. The notion that he has someone working for him on the outside, someone who may be following us even now..." She cast a glance over her shoulder. The road behind them was clear, but that didn't mean they were alone or safe. "Maybe this investigation is too dangerous. We're asking for the cooperation of a brutal murderer. Prison won't have changed his true nature." She bit her lip. "Are you sure *you* don't want to bail? There wouldn't be any hard feelings."

He gave her a careless smile. "Don't worry about me. I always have a card or two up my sleeve. I'll keep going until you tell me to stop."

"So what do we do next?"

"Finch said he'd let me know when to come to the prison for an interview. Maybe that was why he called my phone a second time tonight. If I don't hear from him again, I'll call the attorney tomorrow. With a little luck, I may be able to see Finch before the end of the week. If we're even luckier, he'll cooperate. I'm not holding my breath, but we'll see what happens. In the meantime, any records you can dig up concerning your adoption would be a big help. If you can't find the paperwork, then try to remember any conversations with your mother that might give us a clue. Of course, if Finch's DNA is a match, then you'll have all the proof you need."

Proof that her biological father was the Twilight Killer. "You didn't mention the number on the back of the business card."

"I haven't forgotten about it. My parents are throwing a birthday party for my grandmother tomorrow night. I'll ask my father when I see him what he remembers about your mother's case. If there was a case." Nick lifted a hand from the wheel and rubbed the back of his neck. "Speaking of that business card, there's one last thing I need to tell you."

She braced herself at the sudden tension in his voice. "What is it?"

"I went to the agency's warehouse earlier tonight to see if I could find a case file for your mother. For Laura March. Someone was already inside the building when I got there. I gave chase but whoever it was got away."

Her voice sharpened. "Why didn't you tell me about this earlier?"

"We had a few other things to discuss. Besides, I'm not sure it means anything. The building is in a bad location. We've had break-ins before. I don't want to worry you needlessly, but I don't want to keep anything from you, either."

"I appreciate that." Catherine sank back against the seat. "Your warehouse and my lab on the same night. What are the odds of that happening?"

"Pretty small, I'd say." Nick paused. "Besides the tattooed guy on the street yesterday, have you noticed anyone hanging out by the lab lately? Any strangers on campus? Anything at all out of the ordinary?"

"Lots of things have happened that are out of the ordinary," Catherine said. "But none that I haven't already told you about."

"You mentioned yesterday that you'd discovered an inconsistency with the remains."

"I don't see how that's relevant."

"Maybe it's not. But we've both been warned there's more going on than we realize. Just tell me what you can about your work."

"It's confidential. I shouldn't have brought it up at all."

"But you did. You found something that's obviously intrigued you. Maybe it's relevant to our case and maybe it isn't, but at this point, I don't think we can afford to overlook the possibility."

He had a point, but still she hesitated. She took her job seriously and she really didn't know Nick all that well. Didn't know yet if she could trust him. "The last thing I'd ever want to do is compromise an investigation," she said.

"I understand. And I admire your discretion. But I work for you. You're my priority. The more information I have, the better I'm able to protect you. If you're worried about my discretion, don't be. Whatever you tell me is privileged information."

She gave a reluctant nod. "I'll tell you what I can, but none of this has been made public yet. We both have to be careful not to let anything slip."

"You have my word."

"One of the victims died of a gunshot wound to the back of the head."

Nick glanced at her in surprise. "I thought Gainey's thing was a knife."

"He stabbed all the other victims, repeatedly and brutally. They also sustained bone fractures likely caused by days or even weeks of torture. And all but Jane Doe Thirteen have old injuries that are consistent with abuse or neglect. The kind that you would expect to see in people who've lived for years on the street. Jane Doe Thirteen is different. Her bones and teeth were healthy at the time of death."

"What's your conclusion?"

"I don't like to speculate, but my assistants each have a theory. Emily thinks that because of Thirteen's strength, she got away. Gainey tracked her down and shot her. Nolan believes she was never a captive or a target. She was someone who got in Gainey's way. Both theories are viable, but we may never know what really happened."

"How long have you known your assistants?" Nick asked.

"Since they were freshmen. The anthropology department is small. You tend to see the same faces year in and year out."

"Do you trust them?"

What an odd question, Catherine thought. "I don't know much about their personal lives, but in the classroom and lab, they're both smart and driven. You'd have to be in our field to understand their commitment. Competition is fierce. In any given year, there are more graduates than jobs. But do I trust them?" A day ago her response would have been an unequivocal yes, but now she remembered Nolan's subtle inferences about Emily and the enigmatic expression on his face as he'd watched her covertly. "I don't know if I trust them. I've never really thought about it before. Why?"

"Your attacker got that key code from someone."

"You think from Emily or Nolan?"

"Grad students are notoriously poor," Nick said. "Desperate people have a tendency to do desperate things."

"And people with dark secrets rarely go down without a fight," Catherine murmured.

NICK PARKED IN the alley at the back of Catherine's apartment and they got out of the car together. Glancing around warily, he unlatched the gate and stood back for her to enter. He probed the shadows and corners, all the places where someone might lurk, before following her into the dripping garden. The power was still off in the neighborhood so Nick used the flashlight app on his cell phone to guide them along the brick pathway. Climbing the steps to the apartment, they paused on the porch to look out over the nightscape.

Nick raked the beam over the entrance and then all along the floorboards. Satisfied they were alone and nothing had been left at her front door, he tapped off the app and put away his phone.

"It's so quiet and still," Catherine said in an awed voice. "Like the world stopped turning when the power went off. No car horns. No racing engines. No sound at all except for the wind in the trees."

"If you listen closely, you can hear traffic noises a few blocks over," Nick said.

Catherine shivered. "I find that oddly comforting."

He leaned a shoulder against a post as he gazed down at her. In the aftermath of the storm, a light mist settled over the garden and the clouds thinned, allowing the barest hint of moonlight to filter through. Even so, he could see little more than her silhouette as she stood staring out into the darkness. The exotic scents that drifted up from the flowers stirred his senses and he had no trouble conjuring her features. The curve of her lips. The slope of her nose. The shimmer of those dark, dark eyes.

She was average height, just topping his shoulder, but there was nothing else average about her. She was an enigma to him still. Smart, focused, dedicated. Those qualities were easy to read and he admired them. But the hidden facets, her mysteries and secrets, enthralled him.

As if drawn by his thoughts, she turned to him. "Can I ask you something? If I'm prying, just say so."

"You can ask me anything."

"Why did you leave the police department?"

He had been waiting for that question. Her curiosity was only natural and he didn't want to lie to her. What would be the point? An internet search would tell her everything she needed to know except for the whole truth. "Long story short, I was accused of taking a bribe."

"But you didn't."

It was a statement not a question. He appreciated that. "No, I didn't, but a witness swore otherwise. My word against his. I could have stayed and fought, but once you're labeled a dirty cop, no one wants to work with you. No one trusts you to have their back and you can't trust them to have yours. It became a dangerous situation so I left."

"That's too bad. You were a good detective."

"Water under the bridge. I was lucky that I had someplace to go. My dad wanted to retire so I was able to step in and take over his cases. I enjoy private security work. And for the record, I'm still a good detective."

He sensed her smile. "I admire your confidence."

"You wouldn't want to pay my daily rate plus expenses otherwise."

"No, I wouldn't." Their gazes clung in the dark before she turned away. She placed her hands on the porch rail and drew a deep breath. "I love the way the city smells after a rain. All green notes and jasmine."

"Have you always lived here?"

"Since I was adopted. I don't know about before. What about you?"

"Born and bred. The LaSalles go way back in this city."

She canted her face to the breeze. "Must be nice knowing your family's history. Where you come from. Who you are. Do you have brothers and sisters?"

"One sister. She moved to Atlanta after she divorced. She's raising three boys on her own, all under the age of seven. Hellions." He grimaced. "I don't know how she does it."

"I always wondered what it would be like to have siblings."

The wistful quality in her voice tugged at him. He had a rule about keeping emotional distance. Getting involved with a client rarely worked out well. It messed with your head and clouded your judgment. He told himself to end the conversation and call it a night. Regroup in the morning after a few hours rest. Instead he found himself asking, "Were you lonely as a child?"

"Sometimes. But I had my mother and my aunt, and we were close. Still, the grass is always greener. I think a big family would be nice, especially during the holidays."

"It has its moments. Both my parents come from big families so I have a bunch of cousins. Some of them are cops. Never a dull moment when we all get together. But families can also be a pain, especially if you're the go-to guy. Someone gets in trouble, you're the one they call. It gets old. And God forbid you should ever forget a birthday."

"But you wouldn't change anything," Catherine said.

"No, I guess I wouldn't."

She looked as if she wanted to say something else, but instead she shrugged. "It's been a long day. I should let you go."

"I don't mind staying," he said a little too quickly and then tried to convince himself he was just doing his job. Watching out for her. Protecting her from the night terrors. "I could keep you company until the lights come back on."

"That might be hours."

"I don't have anywhere else I need to be. I'd like to stay."

He heard the soft intake of her breath and he straightened as something flared between them. He told himself to ignore the tension. Keep things professional. No crossing lines, no regrets, no looking back.

Was it his imagination or had she moved in closer?

He kept his gaze fastened on her lips and waited.

"Do you remember the first time you came to the lab?" she asked.

"I do. I'd never consulted with a forensic anthropologist before. I had no idea what to expect. You were very impressive. The things you could tell from those bones." He shook his head in wonder.

"It was an interesting consultation. We got on well. At least it seemed so." She paused as if she didn't know how to proceed. "I thought you might call. You never did."

Was that regret he heard in her voice? He waited a beat before answering. "I wanted to, but you know how it is. You get busy. You think you misread the signals. Days go by. Weeks. Before you know it, the moment has passed."

"Do you think those moments ever come around again?"

The question caught him off guard. *She* caught him off guard. "Rarely, in my experience."

She fixed her gaze on the garden. "I've been standing here reminding myself that I barely know you. I don't even know what it is I'm feeling right now. Maybe it's the aftershock of everything that's happened. Just lingering nerves or something. Or maybe it's being alone with you in the dark. Whatever it is, I feel very drawn to you right now."

She was full of surprises. "Are you always this direct?"

"No. Sometimes people don't want direct. Maybe you don't, either."

"I appreciate your candor, but it does go against my assumptions."

"Assumptions about me?"

He resisted the urge to reach out for her, to run his knuckles along her jawline and tangle his fingers in her hair. She had been attractive to him before tonight. Now she was quickly becoming irresistible. "You're different than I remembered," he said.

She nodded. "I'm often misjudged on first impressions. It's the job, I suppose. I spend so much time in the lab people assume I'm an introvert. Or, worse, antisocial."

"But you're not."

"No, I like being with people. I'm quiet and I can be intense at times, but I'm not shy."

"You're also a puzzle," he said. "You have this way about you. You're mysterious and deep, and I think you have darkness in you."

He sensed her withdrawal. "I don't care for that description."

"Not darkness that harms, but the kind that makes you see the world in a very different way from the rest of us." He hesitated, choosing his words carefully. "It's one of the reasons I'm drawn to you."

He could almost hear the pounding of her heart in the dark. Or was that his?

She drew another breath as if to compose herself. "So it's not just me. This is a moment."

"This is a moment." He lifted his hand to touch her hair.

It was still damp and wavy from the rain. He almost expected her to pull away, but instead she peered up at him, daring him to move in closer. "You know this isn't a good idea," he murmured.

She tilted her face to his, rising on tiptoe so that she could meet his lips halfway.

Maybe it was the dark or maybe it was the woman. Maybe it was the sudden spike of adrenaline, but Nick felt the impact of that kiss all the way to his soul.

He hadn't expected this. Not the intensity. Not the explosion. He backed her against the wall, shielding her from the night as he deepened the kiss. He cupped her face and then dropped his hands to her waist, pulling her to him and holding her hard against him.

She broke away, staring intently into his eyes before letting her head fall back against the wall. "I've been wondering what it would be like to kiss you. Maybe I've wondered about it a little too much," she confessed.

He kissed her again, more measured this time as the urgency gave way to the reality of their situation. This was still a bad idea and he had time to do the right thing. *Call it a night and let things settle.* Whether he would have done so of his own accord remained a question. He heard the creak of a gate a split second before a flashlight beam caught them in the glare.

Then a female voice called out from the garden, "Cath, is that you up there?"

Catherine pulled away, rubbing a hand up and down her arm as she moved around Nick and walked over to the porch railing. "Louise? What are you doing here?"

The woman hesitated as if taking in the situation. "I was worried about you. The power is out all over the city and I know how you hate the dark."

"You didn't need to drive all the way over here to check

up on me. I'm fine." Catherine's voice had a breathless quality that might only have been Nick's imagination.

The flashlight beam captured him and lingered. "I didn't know you had company. I should have called first."

Catherine glanced over her shoulder where he hovered in the background. "No, it's okay. Come on up."

The beam bounced as the woman climbed the steps quickly. Nick remained near the wall as he observed her interaction with Catherine. He couldn't see her clearly, but in the back glow of the flashlight he had the impression she was in her mid to late fifties, a slim, attractive redhead.

"I texted you earlier," she said to Catherine. "I'd hoped we could have dinner, but obviously you had other plans." Her gaze moved to Nick. "Louise Jennings. Catherine's aunt."

"Nick LaSalle." He came out of the shadows to shake her hand.

"LaSalle." She gripped his fingers a moment longer than was necessary. "As in LaSalle Investigations?" Disapproval crept into her voice. She relinquished her hold and turned to Catherine. "You called the number on that business card. I thought we agreed not to rush into anything."

"I told you I would give the matter some thought and I did. I know you don't approve, but this isn't about you. It's about me needing to know my history. It's about finding out the truth. You don't have to be involved at all if you don't want to be. Just accept that I know what I'm doing."

The woman's eyes glinted in the dark. "All this trouble and expense, not to mention the emotional investment, because you found a bunch of old newspaper clippings in Laura's closet?" She shook her head. "I'm sorry, Cath, but that still doesn't make a lick of sense to me."

"What doesn't make sense is why Mother kept those clippings hidden from me," Catherine said. "But we've already been through this and I don't want to argue tonight. It's been a long day and I'm tired."

Nick said, "I should go and let you get some rest. Unless you want me to stay until the power comes on."

Louise broke in before Catherine could answer. "No need to trouble yourself. I'm happy to stay with my niece."

"No need for anyone to stay," Catherine insisted. "I'm perfectly fine. We should all call it a night."

"I'll be in touch as soon as I have news." Nick turned to her aunt. "It was nice meeting you."

She gave a curt nod in return.

Catherine walked him to the top of the stairs, their fingers touching briefly in the dark.

"Nick?"

He glanced over his shoulder as he started down the steps.

"Thanks. For everything," she said.

"I still haven't done anything."

"I would argue to the contrary."

Was that a seductive note in her voice or was he hearing what he wanted to hear?

He hesitated, overly aware of his feelings for Catherine and even more aware of her aunt lurking in the shadows, silent and reproving.

"Good night, Catherine."

"Good night, Nick."

He went out through the back gate, stopping by his car to grab a more powerful flashlight from the trunk. Then he walked down the alley to the main street, on the lookout for suspicious activity in the neighborhood. Earlier, he'd tried not to let on to Catherine how concerned he was about those ominous phone calls from Orson Lee Finch, but the investigation had taken a troublesome turn.

Finch had made it clear that he knew all about their investigation, which suggested he could get to them at any time. Nick wanted to believe the calls were benign, little more than malicious mocking, but even an imprisoned psychopath wasn't to be taken lightly. Finch was up to something. How the prowler in the warehouse and the intruder in Catherine's lab were connected to the Twilight Killer, Nick didn't yet know, but he didn't believe in coincidences.

The streets were still dark and by this time deserted, but he could see a faint glow to the east where power had been restored to the lower part of the peninsula. Bars and restaurants would be open, people talking, laughing, having a good time. Here in Catherine's enclave, nothing stirred. He glanced behind him, unnerved by the night's events and the memory of Orson Lee Finch's warning. *There's more going on than either of you realize.*

He circled the block, pausing at the front of the main house to play the flashlight beam up the driveway toward the garage. Candlelight flickered in the second-story windows, and he could almost conjure the scent of vanilla and the more exotic notes he'd noticed in Catherine's apartment that morning.

I'm quiet and I can be intense at times, but I'm not shy.

She was still a mystery, though. A dark-haired enigma that had already gotten under his skin.

And she was quite possibly the daughter of a serial killer, but Nick wouldn't let his mind go there. Not that it would make any difference to him. He would find her no less attractive or appealing, but the knowledge would change her. She would have doubts about herself. She would always wonder how Finch's DNA had shaped her.

His gaze lit on a parked car in the driveway. The driver had pulled to the back of the house so that only the rear of the vehicle was visible. He wondered at first if Catherine's landlady had returned from her trip, but then he realized that the car must belong to Louise Jennings. She would still be inside with Catherine, no doubt berating her niece for hiring a private detective. Her protectiveness was understandable. He felt it, too, even though he had little doubt that Catherine could take care of herself. She might have a thing about the dark, but when push came to shove, she'd taken on an attacker in a pitch-black stairwell and come out of the skirmish with only a few bruises.

Okay, this was getting ridiculous, Nick decided. He was far too preoccupied with Catherine March. He was letting himself get emotionally invested when he needed to keep a clear head, especially when his visit with Orson Lee Finch loomed. Catherine was right. Finch was already a step ahead of them. If he had an accomplice on the outside, then the last thing either of them needed was to underestimate his reach.

Nick headed up the driveway to check out the car. The late-model sedan was sleek but not ostentatious. The appropriate ride of a successful attorney who wanted to remain inconspicuous.

Something niggled as he played the light over the gleaming fenders. Why was he so fixated on Louise Jennings's car?

An image wavered at the back of his mind, that of a rain-drenched parking lot. Then the flash of headlights...

He went to the rear of the car and focused the flashlight beam on the license plate. The numbers and letters jumped out at him. The first two matched the digits he'd noted earlier on the car in the agency's parking lot. The vehicle that had approached Jackie Morris.

Steps sounded on the walkway. Nick tensed but he didn't melt back into the shadows. Instead, he straightened and flicked his light along the fence, catching Louise Jennings as she came through the gate.

Her hand went to her bag. "Who's there? I'm armed," she warned.

He moved the flashlight beam away from her face. "It's Nick LaSalle."

"LaSalle?" She dropped her arm to her side as she moved toward the vehicle. "What are you doing to my car?"

"Nothing. I saw it parked in the drive and decided to check it out."

"Why?"

"You can't be too careful. Blackouts tend to attract a bad element."

"That's a bit melodramatic." But she glanced around anyway.

"No place is completely safe," Nick warned.

"Nor any person." Her gaze came back to size him up. "What's going on between you and my niece?" Before he could confirm or deny a relationship, she said coolly, "Don't try to play coy. I saw the two of you together when I first walked up."

He merely shrugged. "You should talk to her, not me."

"I tried. She's defensive when it comes to you."

"Maybe she likes her privacy."

Louise canted her head, still taking his measure. "You seem very protective of her. Or is that just an act?"

"I try to look out for all my clients."

"I'll bet you do." Sarcasm thinned her voice. "It's actually a good thing you're still here. Saves me the trouble of tracking you down. As you undoubtedly gathered, I'm not a fan of this so-called investigation even though I understand the impetus. Catherine has experienced a life-changing tragedy and she's searching for answers." She used her remote to unlock the car doors, but she didn't get in. She remained at the front of the vehicle, allowing the flash of the headlights to briefly illuminate her. She wasn't a large woman in stature, but there was something imposing about her. Something unsettling. The impact of her harsh gaze pricked Nick's nerve endings.

"Again, you should talk to Catherine about this. I won't discuss my client."

"Then just listen. You're aware that her mother passed away little more than a week ago? They were very close. I don't think the impact of my sister's death has fully hit her yet."

Nick kept his voice neutral as he switched off his flashlight. "I'm sorry for your loss."

She barely acknowledged his condolences. "You seem like an intelligent man. Street-smart, I would guess. You must realize that Catherine's coming to you is her way of coping. She's grasping at straws in order to delay the worst of her grief. I would hate to see anyone take advantage of her pain. I wouldn't allow it, in fact."

"I understand your concern," Nick said. "But she knows what she's doing."

"Normally, I would agree, but these are extraordinary circumstances." Louise placed her bag on the car hood, within easy reach. "Let me explain something to you about Catherine. She doesn't have a lot of money. She's a brilliant, educated woman, but she will never get rich from her chosen profession. My sister was a schoolteacher so there's no inheritance to speak of. Since I doubt you're working pro bono, the expenses will quickly add up. If you think you can string my niece along with hints and vague clues until you divest her of thousands, you're sadly mistaken. All you will succeed in doing is prolonging her pain and squandering her meager life savings."

Nick wasn't quick to temper. He'd learned a long time ago the value of patience and resolve, but he felt his hackles rise, not just in defense of his honor but in response to Louise Jennings's cavalier dismissal of her niece's wishes and judgment. "You don't like me. That's fine. You're entitled. But I work for Catherine. Her opinion is the only one that matters."

"It's not personal," Louise Jennings assured him. "I don't know you. But in the nearly thirty years I've practiced family law in this city, I've witnessed the worst in your field. Ethics isn't a requirement to obtain a PI license and hang a shingle."

"I could say the same about your profession," Nick countered.

"True, but not one of those shady attorneys is a threat to my niece at the moment. I've tried talking sense into her, but she digs in her heels the moment the subject is broached. You saw that for yourself. She's setting herself up for a very hard fall if you don't convince her to drop this ridiculous search."

"She doesn't think it's ridiculous."

"A few old newspaper clippings and she's convinced Orson Lee Finch is her father. That doesn't sound ridiculous to you? That doesn't seem irrational?"

"If I drop the case, what's to stop her from hiring another investigator? You have no reason to trust me. I get that. But whether you believe me or not, I am looking out for Catherine's best interests. Another agency may not. And for the record, I was skeptical at first, too. Now I think she's on to something."

"On to something? On to what?" The woman's voice grew cold and cynical. "You've just proven my point. You can't possibly think Orson Lee Finch is her biological father. You'll say or do anything to keep the investigation alive."

"What do you know about Catherine's adoption?" Nick asked.

"Nothing. That's the point of a closed adoption. It protects both sides."

"Was an attorney involved?"

"That would have been a question for my sister," she said.

"Were you the attorney?"

The tension between them sizzled. "Handling an adoption that involved a close family member would have been a serious conflict of interest. I wouldn't have done anything then or now to risk my reputation, let alone jeopardize my sister's chance of becoming a mother when that's all she ever wanted."

In the ensuing quiet, Nick sensed her anger and another emotion that was even more compelling.

"There's something you need to know about me, Mr. LaSalle. I'm not a high-profile attorney. You will never see my name in the paper or my face on TV. I don't even have a website. But make no mistake. I'm very good at what I do. People respect me. I've made a lot of powerful friends in this city. Trust me when I tell you that you don't want me for an enemy. Walk away. Leave my niece to grieve in peace, or I'll see to it that your license is revoked before the end of the week. Then I'll bury your agency with so many lawsuits, you'll be years digging your way out of the legal system."

"Are you really that desperate to keep Catherine from the truth?" Nick asked.

"I'm not desperate, but I am determined to protect her. You have no idea who you're dealing with."

He stood aside as she climbed in the car and started the

engine, and then watched as she backed out of the drive and wheeled onto the street. He moved down the drive-way, tracking her taillights as she accelerated through the intersection.

Obviously, he'd touched a nerve. Louise Jennings seemed in a very big hurry to get away from his questions. Or to warn someone.

"What are you up to?" he muttered.

How did she know Jackie Morris and what the hell were the two of them hiding?

Chapter Eight

The next morning, Nick stared out one of the lobby windows, so lost in thought he barely took notice of the rush-hour traffic. He had awakened near dawn with Catherine on his mind, and he hadn't been able to get her out of his head even after a four-mile run, a shower and two cups of black coffee.

He'd driven into the office early so that he could jump-start his day before everyone else arrived, but there he stood, frowning at the rising sun and wondering how he'd managed to get himself in so deep in such a short amount of time. Wondering how the discovery of a bunch of old newspaper clippings had morphed into a complicated investigation that might well involve someone he had known for years.

He told himself he was jumping to conclusions. A partial license-plate number was hardly concrete proof that Jackie Morris and Louise Jennings were acquaintances, much less coconspirators. He hadn't gotten so much as a glimpse of the vehicle's driver in the parking lot, and the rain had been coming down too hard to determine make and model. Still, Jackie had known Nick intended to search the warehouse for Laura March's file. Maybe she'd tipped off someone. Maybe the intruder had gone there ahead of him to locate and destroy any connection that Catherine's mother had had to LaSalle Investigations. But why?

And then there was Louise Jennings's open hostility and threat of a lawsuit, Orson Lee Finch's enigmatic phone calls and Catherine's assault. Not to mention the music box that had been left at her front door. The incidents kept piling up, too many to write off as coincidental. Something was definitely going on. If ever Nick had need of a clear head, now was that time.

He reminded himself yet again that getting involved with a client almost never worked out. He had only to look to his uncle for confirmation. Too many times, Emmett's exploits and ill-advised liaisons had tainted his investigations and jeopardized the reputation of the firm. Nick admired a lot of things about his uncle, but Emmett LaSalle had never been a role model. Nick aspired to his father's professionalism, but when it came to Catherine March, objectivity was proving hard to come by.

He drew a breath and released it slowly. After the case ended and the dust settled, maybe then he and Catherine could explore their moment. But for now, at *this* moment, he needed perspective. Which shouldn't be that hard. They barely knew each other. He'd given her the highlights of his departure from the police department, but there was so much more she didn't know. So much more he didn't want her to know. He'd done nothing wrong, but his actions had hardly been noble. A man of character and conviction would have stayed and fought for his good name, but Nick had taken the easy way out. He'd convinced himself that his resignation was best for the morale of the department, but, deep down, he'd been worried what might surface in a protracted fight. The LaSalles had a long history in law enforcement, not all of it principled. Sometimes it really was best to let sleeping dogs lie.

Maybe he was more like his uncle Emmett than he cared to admit.

Footsteps sounded in the hallway behind him. Nick glanced over his shoulder as Jackie appeared in the doorway. She stopped short when she saw him and a myriad of emotions flashed across her face. As usual, she was dressed in a smart pantsuit, her blond hair styled and sprayed, her makeup heavy-handed but tasteful. "You're here early. And you've already made coffee. What's the occasion?"

"No occasion." Nick leaned a shoulder against the window frame. "We have a lot of open cases so I thought I'd get a head start."

"I can see you're hard at it."

Nick gave her a sidelong glance. "Just watching the street. Speaking of which, I saw a strange vehicle in the parking lot last evening. The rain was really coming down and I wanted to make sure you got to your car all right. A dark-colored sedan pulled around the building and the driver flashed the headlights. You got in for a few minutes and then after you went back to your own vehicle, the car pulled out behind you."

Instead of giving him the sassy comeback he would have expected, she turned and walked back over to her desk, calmly putting away her purse before opening a drawer to take out supplies. Finally, she looked up in exasperation. "What? I'm expected to explain myself now? What I do outside this office is my business."

Nick nodded. "I know that. I'm not trying to pry. I was worried about you. As long as you're okay, that's good enough for me." It wasn't, of course, but he didn't want to pressure her.

She scowled at him. "I'm allowed to have friends, you

know. Some of them even stop by occasionally to see how I'm doing."

"In the middle of a storm?"

She pumped lotion into her palm and rubbed her hands vigorously. "Maybe you weren't the only one concerned about me last night. I know you LaSalles think I have no life away from this agency, but I actually do have people who care about me."

"I've never thought otherwise," Nick said in a placating tone. "If I'm out of line, I apologize, but certain things have happened lately to make me cautious. We all need to keep an eye out."

She blotted the excess lotion with a tissue. "An eye out for what?"

"Suspicious vehicles. Strangers in the area. Anything out of the ordinary."

That got her attention. Her expression sobered. "What's going on, Nick?"

"I drove over to the warehouse after I left here last night. Someone was in the building. I gave chase, but the perpetrator got away."

"Did you see who it was?"

"The power was off. I barely got a glimpse."

"Man, woman…?"

"I couldn't tell. It was that dark."

She took a moment to digest his revelation. If Nick didn't know better, he would almost think she looked relieved. "Did you call the cops?"

"I figured the police had their hands full with the storm and power outage. Besides, I couldn't even tell if anything was missing. I'll go by later and check things out."

Jackie fiddled with a pen, her gaze thoughtful. "We were just talking about the warehouse before I left last night. You mentioned looking for a file, but I thought you said you were going over there this morning."

"No, you advised me to wait until morning," Nick said. "I never committed either way."

"You're like Emmett. No patience or common sense. Did you at least find the file?"

"Unfortunately, the transformer blew right after I got there."

"And then you chased off the perp."

"Correct."

Jackie glanced away. "Not the first time that place has been broken into. We've had problems with vandalism for years."

"It's the timing that concerns me. Someone also broke into Catherine March's lab last night and assaulted her."

Jackie's gaze darted back to him. "Your new client? You were looking for her mother's file, right? Something about an adoption. Do you think the break-ins are related?"

"How do you know about the adoption?" Nick asked.

For the first time that morning, her sly smile seemed pure Jackie. "I know everything that goes on in this office."

"But you still don't remember Laura March?"

"No." The smile vanished. "Is Catherine okay?"

"Yes, I think so. She's a lot tougher than she realizes."

"I imagine she's had to be."

The hint of tenderness took Nick aback. "What do you mean by that?"

"You said her father died when she was little. Losing a parent so young leaves a scar. And who knows what she went through before the adoption? Now the only mother she ever knew is gone. That's a hard row to hoe no matter your age."

Had he mentioned Aidan March's death to Jackie? Nick tried to recall their previous conversation. "She still has her aunt. They seem close, but the aunt is pretty hostile about the investigation." He watched Jackie's reaction. "She thinks I'm taking advantage of Catherine's mental state."

A brow lifted slightly. "Oh, *does* she?"

"She even threatened to sue the agency if I don't back off."

Jackie's lips thinned. "She said that?"

"In just those words. I didn't recognize her when we met, but her name sounds familiar to me. Have we ever worked with an attorney named Louise Jennings?"

Jackie opened her mouth to reply, but Emmett's voice from the doorway silenced her. "What's this about a lawsuit? Damn it, Nick, what kind of trouble have you gotten us into this time?"

"*This* time?" Nick's tone cooled. "The last lawsuit was before I joined the agency. That trouble was all on you."

Emmett didn't like having his past transgressions thrown back at him. "Water under the bridge," he muttered. "Have you notified our attorney?"

"Don't need to. Louise Jennings is blowing smoke. She has no grounds to sue. I work for Catherine, not her. I am curious why she's so worried about our investigation, though. It's almost as if she has something to hide."

"Like what?" Jackie asked anxiously.

"I don't know, but why else would she be so desperate to shut me down? Before last night, I wondered if Catherine might be chasing a dead end. I even brought the possibility up during our initial meeting. Now I'm convinced something is going on. Something that may involve more than her adoption. Until my client pulls me off the case, I intend to keep looking."

"Even if it causes trouble for the rest of us?" Emmett growled.

"It won't."

"You sound mighty sure of yourself."

"Since when do you get spooked so easily?" Nick challenged. "We've always taken on the hard cases. We thrive on the investigations no one else has the guts to pursue. Isn't that what you always say? Isn't that how you and Dad built LaSalle Investigations so successfully? We attract a messy clientele. People who lead perfect lives aren't the ones who seek us out."

"Yes, but sometimes you need to listen to your gut," Emmett said. "Sometimes you have to do what's best for the agency instead of the client."

"What is best for the agency in this case?" Nick countered. "There's no conflict of interest that I'm aware of. No grounds for a lawsuit. What is it about Catherine March that worries you?"

Emmett exchanged a glance with Jackie. "You don't hire an outfit like ours because of a bunch of old newspaper clippings. I told you on day one that she's holding out on you."

"Why would she do that?"

His uncle hesitated. "Maybe she thought you'd turn her down if you knew the whole story. Or maybe she's setting you up to be a patsy."

Nick almost laughed. "A patsy for what?"

Emmett scowled at him in displeasure. "Go ahead and yock it up, but it wouldn't be the first time one of our kind got suckered by a good-looking client."

"And who would know that better than you?" Jackie murmured.

"What was that?" Emmett demanded.

"I said, two LaSalles this early in the morning is almost more than a body can stand. I need another cup of coffee."

"Stay right where you are," Emmett barked as Jackie

pushed back her chair. "No one goes anywhere until I get some answers."

"What's the question?" Nick asked.

"You said someone broke into her lab last night. Do you have any leads?"

Now it was Nick who hesitated, his gaze jumping from Emmett to Jackie. "You heard that, too? How long were you listening at the door?"

"Long enough to hear things I didn't like."

"You might have alerted us you were there," Nick said.

"Old habits die hard. Do you have any leads?" Emmett repeated.

Nick ran a hand through his hair. "No, unfortunately. The incident occurred during the blackout. Catherine didn't get a look at her assailant. She called the police, but there's not much they can do without physical evidence or a description."

"Tell him about the warehouse," Jackie prompted.

"Oh, I'm sure he already knows," Nick said with a barbed edge as he turned to his uncle. "But I'll go over it again in case you missed something. I went to the warehouse last night to look for Laura March's file and ended up chasing off an intruder."

Emmett looked troubled. "When was this?"

"Sevenish. I got there just before a transformer blew. I didn't see much more than a shadow and I couldn't tell if anything was missing with just a flashlight. I was just telling Jackie that I'll go over there later and check things out. At the very least, we should have the locks changed."

"We should just get rid of that place," Jackie said. "Haven't I been saying that for years? If someone is injured on the property, the agency will be responsible. Or what if someone has the bright idea to steal files to try and blackmail our former clients? We need to get someone in there to shred everything. Anything worth keeping is already stored electronically."

"Not the really old stuff," Emmett said. "You never know when a need might arise for those files. Just like Nick here, trying to track down a former client. Besides, I don't trust computers."

"You don't trust anything or anyone," Jackie said.

"Not true. I've always trusted you." Another look, another silent communication. Nick felt as if he were on the outside peering in at something he wasn't meant to see. His uncle's pointed tone seemed more of a reminder—or worse, a threat—than an affirmation of support. Nick wondered again about their relationship. They went back a long way. No telling the secrets the two of them shared.

Jackie lifted her chin in defiance. "I'll remind you of that next time you question my judgment. Right now, though, I have work to do so I would advise you both to skedaddle and let me get to it."

"I'll be in my office if you need me." Nick moved away from the window and started for the stairs. The other agents were arriving by this time. He could hear muffled voices and the clatter of coffee cups coming from the kitchen. He didn't go down the hallway to greet them as he normally would have done. He needed a few moments of peace and quiet to ponder his conversation with Jackie and Emmett.

But his uncle wasn't through with him. He came up the stairs behind Nick. "Do I need to know anything else about this case? You've had, what, thirty-six hours? You must have made some progress."

Nick considered telling him about the music box and the ominous phone calls from Orson Lee Finch, but something held him back. He didn't like having doubts about his uncle and Jackie, but their behavior since his meeting with Catherine seemed curious to say the least. If either or both were somehow involved, he didn't want to tip his hand too soon. Or maybe he was still taking the easy way out. Maybe he wasn't ready to explore the implications and consequences of such an involvement.

"I've put in a call to Finch's attorney," Nick said. "I'm waiting to hear back."

"If you're lucky, that call won't come," Emmett said.

Nick shrugged. "You've made no bones about how you feel. First you warn me about taking the case and then Louise Jennings threatens to sue me. I'm starting to wonder why everyone is so insistent that I back off this investigation. The pressure just makes me want to dig that much deeper."

"Cases come and go, Nick. Best not to get too attached."

They paused on the landing. "Is there something you want to tell me about this case?" Nick asked.

"Like what?"

"Was LaSalle Investigations somehow involved in Catherine's adoption? Is that why her mother had a business card with Dad's private number on the back?"

"You need to ask Raymond about that."

"I intend to. But now I'm asking you."

Emmett glanced over the railing into the lobby. "I don't know anything about an adoption. Isn't my word good enough for you?"

Nick didn't answer. "What about Louise Jennings? We have arrangements with a number of law firms. Have we ever worked with her?"

"I never even heard of the woman until you mentioned her name this morning. And, personally, I'd like to keep it that way. Last thing we need is a vindictive attorney dogging our investigations. You make sure she isn't a problem or I will."

Nick frowned. "What's that supposed to mean?"

Something flickered at the back of his uncle's eyes. Something dark and shady and unpleasant. "If I've learned anything in the three decades I've been an investigator it's that no one's hands are completely clean. Everyone has a weakness, including Louise Jennings."

"I don't think I like where this is headed."

"Then take care of the problem," Emmett said. "Now talk to me about Orson Lee Finch."

"What about him?"

"If you insist on visiting him in prison, why don't I keep you company when you make that drive to Columbia? We could interview Finch together."

"I appreciate the offer, but I'd rather see him alone. He's more likely to talk if he doesn't feel cornered or threatened."

"He's more likely to talk if he thinks he can get something in return," Emmett said. "Be careful what you promise him."

"I'm not in any position to make promises." Nick tried to remain nonchalant, but Finch's warning niggled. *There is more going on than either of you realize.*

Emmett faced him. In the harsh light streaming in from the upstairs windows, his face took on a sinister edge. "I wish you would have let this one go, bud."

"I know you do." Nick studied Emmett's features, noting the odd glitter in his eyes and the almost cruel set of his mouth. He'd always thought of his uncle as slippery but also charming and mostly harmless. Now Nick felt an inexplicable chill up his spine as their gazes held. "It's an interesting case," he said. "Becoming more so every day."

"Careful you don't get in over your head," Emmett warned.

They parted on the landing. Nick went inside his office and closed the door. He paused for a moment, listening to the quiet as he contemplated his uncle's caginess. So much was going on that he didn't understand. So many buried secrets. Shaking off his uneasiness, he seated himself behind the desk and opened his laptop to check the day's schedule. Then he removed the box of newspaper clippings from his desk and sorted through the articles yet again as he went back over the previous evening's events.

No matter Finch's motivation, his phone calls had opened up a new dimension to the investigation. The Twilight Killer might well have an accomplice on the outside, someone keeping tabs on the case. But to what end? Nothing Nick uncovered would change the outcome of Finch's situation. No matter the killer's relationship to Catherine or to anyone else, he would remain incarcerated for the rest of his life. So why insinuate himself into this investigation? Why warn them about trusting the wrong person?

He heard his uncle's office door open and close and then, a moment later, his footsteps sounded on the stairs. Nick crossed the room and glanced out before easing onto the landing. Emmett paused at Jackie's desk and the two spoke briefly before he turned to leave.

Jackie stared after him for a moment and then she got up and went out the front door. Nick could see her standing in the shade of the building as she got out her phone and made a call. Obviously, she didn't want to be overheard and that made Nick wonder again about her connection to Louise Jennings. As his uncle's car rounded the corner of the building, Jackie pressed back into the shadows, as if she didn't want Emmett to see her. The behavior was odd to say the least.

Keeping an eye on Jackie, Nick went down the hallway and tried his uncle's office door. It was locked but the pin-and-tumbler apparatus wouldn't be that hard to pick. Or he could just go downstairs and look for a spare key in Jackie's desk. That might be pushing his luck, though. She could return at any time.

Checking to make sure no one lurked in the lobby, he took out a small tension wrench from his pocket set and inserted it into the bottom of the keyhole. Then he slid a rake pick into the top of the keyhole, scrubbing it back and forth while applying the slightest pressure on the wrench. The door opened with a soft click. Nick shot another glance over his shoulder before he slipped inside.

He'd been in his uncle's office countless times, but breaking in gave him a strange sense of displacement. He stood inside the door, getting his bearings as he wondered if a hidden camera had been installed somewhere in the room. Too late to worry about discovery. Too late to turn back now.

He strode across the room and sat down behind Emmett's desk, picking locks until he'd searched through every drawer. Then he rifled through the credenza and filing cabinets, saving his uncle's computer for last. The laptop was password protected. He tried a few birthday combinations before giving up.

Rising, he berated himself for invading his uncle's space for nothing. He'd crossed a line on the vague suspicion that Emmett and Jackie were hiding something. So what if Emmett had reservations about Catherine's case? Her connection to Orson Lee Finch was enough to give anyone pause. Nick was just being obsessive.

Moving away from the desk, he took one final glance around. His gaze lit on the paper shredder that had been placed between the wall and the credenza. He told himself to let it go. He needed to get out of the office before Emmett returned or before Jackie came looking for him. He raised the lid and glanced inside. The bin was clean. Not so much as a single paper strip remained.

But as Nick gave the machine a closer scrutiny, he noticed something gummed up on one of the blades. Upending the device, he used his penknife to remove the screws and snap off the guard. Mindful of the sharp edges, he scraped with the penknife until he managed to peel away the stuck file-folder label. Carefully he pieced together the mangled bits until he could make out a name: Aidan March.

He sat back on his heels, rocked by the discovery. Why would LaSalle Investigations have information about a cop who had been killed in the line of duty more than twenty years ago? And why had his uncle recently destroyed the file?

Nick's mind reeled as he quickly put the machine back together. Then, letting himself out of the office, he glanced over the railing. Jackie was still away from her desk, but he could no longer see her outside. He hurried back to his own office and sat down heavily behind the desk. What was going on here? How deeply involved was this agency in Catherine's adoption? Just how dark were the LaSalle family secrets?

He placed the tattered label on the surface of his desk as he contemplated the implications of that name. Aidan March.

Seconds clicked by before Nick realized that something was wrong. He glanced around, unnerved by a sense of violation. Nothing seemed amiss or out of place, yet the very air seemed agitated.

His desk drawers were locked just as he'd left them. He took out his key and opened the bottom compartment where he kept the articles. Lifting the shoebox lid, he checked the contents. He had to rummage through the clippings twice before the revelation hit him. The photograph of Orson Lee Finch and the child was missing.

He looked under his desk and all around the office. The clipping was gone. While Nick had searched his uncle's office, someone had gone through his desk.

Chapter Nine

Catherine hurried to answer the knock at her door, thinking that Nick might have news for her. She ran a hand through her still-mussed hair as her smile faded. "What are you doing here so early?"

"I wanted to catch you before you left for work." Louise Jennings held up a pink, striped bag from Catherine's favorite bakery on Rutledge. "Truce?"

"A truce? Are we fighting?"

"No, but things got a little tense last night. I couldn't go into the office until I knew everything was okay between us." She dangled the bag. "Fresh cinnamon rolls, peach muffins, blueberry scones. Take your pick."

Catherine stepped back so that her aunt could enter. "Great timing. I just made coffee."

Louise sniffed the air appreciatively as she followed Catherine into the kitchen. "Smells wonderful."

She got down plates while Catherine poured the coffee. As usual, Louise was stylishly put together but comfortable in slim black slacks and flats. Her red hair was pulled back from her face, highlighting the freckles across her nose and cheekbones. She would be fifty-five her next birthday, but looked a decade younger. Good genes and a disciplined diet kept her trim. She artfully arranged the assortment of pastries on a plate and then sampled the maple icing on a cinnamon roll. "Oh, my God."

"See what you've been missing?"

Louise broke off a piece of the roll. "This will go straight to my hips, but maybe it's worth it."

"Trust me, it is."

They sat down at the small table by the window. Outside, the sun hovered over the treetops. The raindrops clinging to the leaves shimmered in the early morning light, turning the garden into a fairyland. Last night's terrors were already starting to fade, but Orson Lee Finch's warning still echoed. Catherine tried to shut out his ominous words as she helped herself to a muffin.

Louise smoothed a napkin across her lap. "When did your power come back on? The trucks were just leaving my neighborhood when I got home. Must have been around ten."

"That sounds about right. I took a shower, went to bed and slept until my alarm went off this morning."

Louise gave her a critical appraisal. "You do look more rested than I've seen you in days. I've been worried about you, Cath."

"You shouldn't be. I'm fine. I've been on my own for a long time now. I can take care of myself." She picked at her muffin. "Let's just leave it at that, okay? I don't want to get into anything unpleasant this morning."

Louise was still watching her. "The last thing I want to do is upset you, especially now. You've been through so much. We both have. Losing Laura was a devastating blow. I keep thinking it's all just a bad dream. She'll walk through that door at any minute. She was such a good person and she loved you so much, Cath. She'd want me to look after you. You know she would. I can't sit back and do nothing while someone takes advantage of you.

It pains me to see you exhaust yourself on this nonsensical investigation."

"It's not nonsense to me."

"Because you're not thinking clearly. You haven't given yourself time to process your mother's death, let alone grieve."

Catherine frowned down at the garden. "People grieve in their own way. This investigation is important to me. It gives me something to focus on besides my loss. You of all people should understand that. I'm not walking away from this. I can't. Not when we've already made progress."

Louise looked skeptical. "What progress?"

Catherine hesitated. "It's too early in the investigation to talk about it. I'd rather wait until we have something definitive."

Louise reached across the table and placed her hand briefly on Catherine's. "Do you trust me?"

"Of course, I do."

"Then please listen to me. Whatever comfort you get from this investigation is temporary. You're only prolonging the inevitable. You're rushing to fill a void that can't be filled. Wait six months or, even better, a year, and if you still feel the same, then I'll do everything I can to help you track down your birth parents. *I* will help you. You won't have to rely on some sleazy PI. But for now, can you please just give yourself time to mourn?"

Catherine's hackles rose in defense. "He's not sleazy."

"What?"

"Nick LaSalle. He isn't sleazy. He's a good guy."

"And you know this…how?"

"I just know." Catherine sat quietly for a moment. "Why does this matter so much to you?"

"Why wouldn't it matter to me? You're the only family I have left and I want to protect you. Apart from the emotional issue, you have to be sensible about your finances. Private detectives don't come cheap. You say Nick LaSalle is a good guy, but how do you know? Did you do any research? Did you ask for references? How do you know he won't try to take advantage of you?"

Catherine lost her patience. "Oh, for crying out loud, give me some credit. Of course, I did my research. His agency has an excellent reputation, but I didn't hire him because of his Google reviews. I sought him out because of the business card I found with Mother's newspaper clippings."

"What did he have to say about that?"

"He's looking into it."

"I'm sure he is." Louise picked up her cup. "At the risk of offending you further, I also did some checking. Did you know he used to be a cop?"

"Yes. He and I once worked on a case together."

Louise looked surprised. "Then you must also know that bribery and shakedown rumors were rampant at the time he left the department. Nothing was ever proven, but the fact that he didn't stay to clear his name speaks volumes."

"Not necessarily. He could have had other reasons for leaving."

"Did he happen to mention that his father and uncle resigned years ago also under a cloud of suspicion? No, I don't imagine he did." Louise set aside her cup with deliberate composure. "I have friends who go way back with CPD. Ex-cops with long memories and old grudges. From what I've been told, Emmett LaSalle was always bad news. On the take for years while his twin brother, Raymond, turned a blind eye. When Emmett was forced to resign, Raymond left, too, and they opened LaSalle Investigations, an outfit that prides itself on taking problematic cases. Think about that for a minute, Cath. You've hired a private-detective firm run by a family of unethical, possibly criminal, former cops. Do you really think you can trust this man?"

"Until he gives me a reason not to." Catherine eyed her aunt coolly. "You have been busy, haven't you?"

"Yes, but you don't need to take my word for any of this. You know people in the police department. Ask anyone in law enforcement about the LaSalle family. You'll likely get an earful."

"So this is why you came over." Catherine had to work to keep her temper under control. She was by nature guarded and reserved, but she could be pushed too far. She was slow to anger and even slower to forgive, which was why she chose her words carefully. Whatever was said at that table couldn't be taken back. No matter their differences, Louise was her only family. "You didn't want to have breakfast with me and you certainly didn't want to make amends. You just wanted to drive a wedge between Nick and me."

Louise looked alarmed. "*Is* there a Nick and you?"

Catherine stood and began gathering the dishes. "We have a productive working relationship."

"You were certainly working hard last night," Louise murmured.

"Last night is none of your business."

Her aunt looked hurt. "What would your mother say if she heard you speak to me in that tone?"

"I'm sorry, but you're prying into matters that don't concern you."

"And you're being infuriatingly naïve."

"No," Catherine said calmly. "I'm sticking to my guns and you're not used to that. You can't bully me into getting your way this time." She carried the dishes to the sink, almost expecting her aunt to follow, but when she turned, Louise was still seated at the table staring at her thoughtfully.

"That's what you think of me? That I'm a bully?"

"You're very strong willed and you know how to intimidate." Catherine came back to the table. "But I told you already I don't want to talk about this today."

Louise shook her head regretfully. "I had no idea that's what you thought of me. I can be aggressive at times, perhaps even abrasive, but you must know I only have your best interests at heart."

"And you need to understand that I'm not going to change my mind no matter what you do or say. Mother saved those clippings for a reason. She had a purpose for keeping them hidden from me. I think you know why. She always confided in you. You were her rock. If you really want me to end the investigation, then tell me what you know about my adoption."

Louise turned to stare out the window, frowning down at the garden as she gathered her thoughts. Catherine observed her carefully, taking note of the deep creases in her forehead and the pulse that vibrated at her temple. She was clearly upset. And she was holding something back.

Catherine sat back down. "Whatever it is you can tell me."

Louise closed her eyes on a breath. "I hoped it wouldn't come to this. Laura never wanted you to know."

Catherine flattened her hands against the tabletop. She sat very still, but her heart flailed inside her chest. She asked herself again if she really wanted the truth. If she was prepared to face her past. "Just say it. If it's anything to do with my birth or adoption, I have a right to know."

Louise said nothing for the longest moment. Her gaze remained fixed on the window.

"Louise?"

She roused with a sigh. "You're right, Cath. We have been keeping secrets from you but not for the reason you think. Orson Lee Finch isn't your biological father. You aren't blood related to him at all." She turned to face Catherine. "But I am. Your mother was."

Catherine opened her mouth and then closed it again. She sat staring at her aunt, telling herself she couldn't have heard what she thought she had. *I must still be in shock from everything that's happened.*

Louise nodded. "It's true. He's a distant cousin. Laura and I knew him slightly when we were all children. He and his mother didn't come around much. They never really fit in so they kept to themselves. I remember that he was odd even then. A thin, pale child. Very quiet and intense but sweet in his own way."

"Sweet?" The Twilight Killer? Catherine had an image of his victims covered in blood and crimson magnolia petals. She shook her head to dispel the disturbing visions.

"Serial killers aren't born monsters," Louise said. "Something turns them. As I said, he was always a strange child and utterly devoted to his mother. Unnaturally so perhaps."

"Is this true?" Catherine demanded.

Louise frowned. "Of course, it's true. Why would make up such a disturbing story?"

"I can't believe you're telling me this now. I can't believe I never knew. Why would Mother keep it from me?"

"Why *wouldn't* she keep it from you? It's not exactly information either of us wanted to get out—that we're blood related to Charleston's most infamous killer. Can you imagine the reaction? It would be difficult enough now, but twenty-five years ago when all of this happened we would have been hounded."

"Why? No one could blame you for what he did."

"You have no idea what it was like back then. The horror and terror that came from the mere mention of his name. It would have been tantamount to saying I'm related to Jack the Ripper. My cousin is Orson Lee Finch, the Twilight Killer." She closed her eyes on a shiver.

"Was it really that bad?"

"After his arrest, the media went nuts. They tracked down former employers, camped out on sidewalks, made life a living hell for anyone whose path had ever crossed with Orson Lee Finch's. Even the slightest acquaintances were ruthlessly harassed, so Laura and I made a pact to keep silent. I was just out of law school and looking to be recruited by the kind of old-money firms that are adverse to even a whiff of scandal. Laura and Aidan were trying to adopt. They certainly didn't need that kind of public scrutiny. We hadn't seen Orson since we were children. Nothing we said would have changed the investigation or the outcome of his trial, but the revelation could have damaged our lives irreparably. That's the reason your mother saved those newspaper clippings, Cath. That's why she kept them hidden from you. She was both fascinated and repelled by Orson. I suppose I was, too."

Catherine felt numb. "I don't even know what to say."

Louise glanced across the table. "I know it's a lot to take in. I should have found a better way to tell you."

"I don't understand why you didn't say something when I first found the clippings. You could have saved me a lot of time and trouble. Instead you tried to make me feel as if I were acting irrationally. But I wasn't. Mother really did have a secret."

"I should have told you, but a part of me still feels as if that secret needs to remain hidden. I don't want people knowing that I'm connected to a monster. I don't want the looks and the stares and the questions. For so many years, the Twilight Killer was just a bad memory, an old nightmare, but now with the twenty-five-year anniversary of his arrest, there's an army of frenzied reporters running around the city looking for a new angle to an old story. I didn't tell you because I wanted you to drop the matter. But you're stubborn. Your father was, too. You aren't Aidan March's biological child, but you remind me of him in so many ways. He never knew when to give up, either."

Catherine's gaze darted to the framed photograph of Laura and Aidan March she kept on display in her bookcase. She remembered so little about him and yet there were times when she felt as if he were still watching over her. Still trying to keep her safe. She twisted the emerald ring on her finger. Melancholy tugged even as the Twilight Killer's voice insinuated itself in her head. *Aidan March found out the hard way that people with dark secrets never go down without a fight.*

What had he found out before he died?

Catherine had always been told that he'd been killed in the line of duty, but now she had to wonder.

"This may explain why Mother kept the articles hidden, but what about the business card I found among the clippings? Why would she want to hire a private detective?"

Louise shrugged. "I don't know why she kept that card. Maybe she wanted to find out who your birth parents were. She always worried about genetics. Always afraid that you might get sick someday and she wouldn't know anything about your background."

"She never talked to you about my biological parents?"

"No, not really. But I can assure you Orson Lee Finch is not your biological father."

Catherine sat with the revelation for a moment, wondering why she didn't feel more relieved. Wondering why doubt had already started to niggle. She wanted to trust her aunt. They'd always been close. But Louise's story seemed a little too convenient. "Did my father know about Finch?"

"I don't think Laura ever told Aidan. Not that he would have cared. He was crazy about her. I've never seen a couple more in love. When he died, a part of Laura died, too. That's why she never remarried. No one could ever measure up."

"What happened to him?" Catherine asked.

"You know the story. He was killed in the line of duty."

"Mother would never give me any specifics."

"The details were always a bit hazy. He worked undercover. Vice for a while and then Narcotics. He made a lot of enemies on the street. When his cover was blown, one of those enemies came after him." Louise paused. "Aidan was a good man. Heroic, even. He would have been very proud of you, Cath."

She glanced down at the emerald ring on her finger. "I wish I could remember him."

"All you need know is that he was a devoted husband and father. You and my sister were everything to him." Louise smiled. "I'll let you in on a little secret. He wasn't keen on the adoption at first. Working undercover was a hard life and having a family made him more vulnerable. Laura was the one who desperately wanted a child. But from the moment Aidan set eyes on you, he was hopelessly smitten. Never doubt for a moment that you were wanted and loved."

For some reason, Catherine thought of the photograph of Orson Lee Finch and the unknown little girl that had run in the paper. Somewhere in the back of her mind she could hear that child whispering to her: *Don't listen to her. She's telling you what you want to hear.*

"Do you know anything about my adoption?" Catherine asked.

"Nothing more than what you've already heard from your mother."

"She told me that my biological father died in the military, leaving my birth mother destitute and desperate. She was a teenager who gave me up for adoption so that I could have a better life. But Mother couldn't have known any of that if it was a closed adoption. She must have made up the story so I wouldn't question where I came from. Why would she do that unless there was something she wanted to keep hidden?"

"Why does any of this matter now?" Louise asked in exasperation.

"Because it does."

"*Why?* Nothing you find out will change anything. Why can't you just leave well enough alone?" Beneath her aunt's veneer of exasperation, Catherine glimpsed a cold, hard anger. "The kindest, gentlest woman I've ever known took you in and loved you as her own. She devoted her whole life to making you happy and this is how you want to honor her memory?"

Catherine felt a pang of guilt despite her resolve. "You said I'm stubborn like my father, but my mother is the one who encouraged me to go after what I want. She's the one who taught me to never quit."

Louise rose abruptly. "You have no idea what you're doing. What this investigation may cost you."

"Then tell me," Catherine demanded.

But Louise refused to respond. She walked away from the table and out the front door without another word.

Chapter Ten

"You think your aunt lied to you?" Nick asked a few hours later. He'd dropped by the university unexpectedly and after a quick tour, Catherine had brought him back to the lab. They were alone. Emily hadn't come into work that morning and Nolan had left for a late lunch.

Catherine wandered among the skeletal remains as she pondered his question. "Lying is a strong word. Louise is the only family I have left and I don't want to rush to judgment."

"Neither of them ever said a word to you about being related to Finch?"

"I'm pretty sure I would have remembered if they had." She stopped beside Jane Doe Thirteen, absently running her hand along the smooth surface of the table. "I suppose being related to a serial murderer would be reason enough to keep those clippings hidden. Sharing DNA with the Twilight Killer isn't something you'd want to broadcast. Still, I can't help wondering if Louise came up with that story just to dissuade me from the investigation."

"Are you dissuaded?"

"Hardly. I'm more determined than ever to get to the bottom of my mother's secrets." Catherine glanced around the room at all the unidentified remains. Compared to what those women had gone through at the hands of Delmar Gainey, her problems seemed insignificant.

"What is it?" Nick asked.

Catherine paused. "Am I just being stubborn? Maybe I'm making too much of all this. I grew up in a loving home. My mother was the best person I've ever known. Until her death, my life was close to perfect. I loved my job. I loved my family. Shouldn't that be enough? Why am I looking for trouble now?"

"You said you wanted the truth. You needed the truth."

"And you suggested I might be using the investigation to allay my grief. Do you still think that?"

"No. That may be part of it, but you seem clearheaded to me. For what it's worth, I want the truth, too. We're in this together."

Awareness flared as she met Nick's gaze. She tried to dismiss the butterflies in her stomach. Tried to tell herself this wasn't the time or place. Best not to think about last night's kiss. Best not to remember the velvety glide of his tongue in her mouth or the hardness of his body pressing against hers. Suddenly, though, that was all she could think about. His hands, his mouth, the warmth of his breath against her neck. She glanced down, focusing on Jane Doe Thirteen as she tried to calm her racing pulse.

"Catherine?"

His voice rippled along her nerve endings. "Yes?"

He was quiet for a moment. "In the interest of full disclosure, I need to tell you something."

She glanced up in alarm. "What is it?"

"Do you remember the receptionist at our agency? Jackie Morris?"

"Yes, of course. I met her when I came to your office the other day. She was very kind to me."

He looked surprised. "That's not an adjective I would

normally ascribe to Jackie. Professional, efficient, diligent, yes. Kind?" He shrugged.

"She was, though. She seemed very sincere."

"Maybe you brought out the best in her. Anyway, it may be nothing, but I saw her get into a dark sedan last night in our parking lot. The first two digits of the license-plate number match your aunt's car."

"You think they know each other?" Catherine frowned across the table. "That isn't much evidence."

"It's not just the car," Nick said. "I've been getting a strange vibe from Jackie ever since you came to the office. I can't put my finger on it. Maybe I'm looking for something that isn't really there. But I'm starting to wonder if Finch could be right. Maybe there is more going on than either of us realize."

"Did you ask her about the car?"

"She implied a friend had stopped by to check on her during the storm."

"But you don't buy it."

He thought about it for a moment. "As you said, it all seems a little too convenient. And weirdly connected. Intruders in your lab and my warehouse. Phone calls from Orson Lee Finch and now a possible link between my receptionist and your aunt. Things are getting complicated."

"And scary," Catherine said.

"I don't want to frighten you. If I thought you were in real danger, I'd say so. But it never hurts to take precautions. Keep your doors and windows locked and be aware of your surroundings." He glanced around. "You really are isolated down here, aren't you?"

"Yes, but I'm hardly ever alone. Emily and Nolan are almost always here during work hours. And I've already had the code changed on the key pad."

"Good. Things may start to break soon. I'm still waiting to hear back from Finch's attorney, but the sooner we can arrange a meeting the sooner we'll have some answers. Have you had a chance to look through your mother's records?"

Catherine's earlier words about moving on suddenly rang hollow. Her mother's spirit was still so strong in her home. The memories still cut too deep. "I've put it off, but I think I should go over there this afternoon after work."

"I have a few things scheduled that I can't postpone. Maybe you should wait until tomorrow when I can go with you."

She was tempted, but ever since the conversation with her aunt that morning, Catherine had felt a strange sense of urgency. "I appreciate the offer, but considering everything that's happened, I think I should get to those files before someone else does."

"Like your aunt, you mean."

"I want to trust her, but Jackie Morris isn't the only one acting suspect lately. I've never seen Louise this way. Maybe it's the grief. Everyone reacts to loss in different ways. I really want to believe she's being overprotective but…" Catherine's words trailed away. "The sooner I go through my mother's papers the better. But don't worry. It's a safe neighborhood and I'll be careful."

"Text me when you go and when you leave. And be on the lookout while you're there. You know the house and the neighborhood. If anything seems off, get out."

"I will."

"Keep your phone handy. Not just this afternoon but always."

She gave him a look. "Now you're being overprotective."

"Just cautious. It's the nature of my business." He searched her face and then, seemingly satisfied with what he saw, dropped his focus to the numbered label on the table. "So this is Jane Doe Thirteen."

Catherine was happy enough to change the subject. Her anxiety had only deepened since Nick's arrival. In part, the angst was personal, stemming from an attraction that grew stronger every time she saw him. But there was a darker reason for her disquiet. Delving into the adoption was one thing; uncovering disturbing secrets quite another. What if she found out something that tarnished her mother's memory? That was the real fear, she realized. That she would lose her mother all over again.

So call off the investigation. Send Nick away.

His gaze swept the room, taking in the magnitude of Delmar Gainey's atrocities. "Fourteen were recovered in all, I read."

"Seven inside the house and seven on the property. It's horrifying, isn't it? What one human being can do to another?"

"I've kept up with the case," he said grimly. "Like everyone else in this city, I was shocked by the discovery of so many bodies, but I'm not sure I fully grasped the depth of Gainey's depravity until now. Seeing them together laid out on these tables…sisters, mothers, daughters. Nothing left but teeth and bones." His attention lingered on each skeleton. "This is what greets you every morning when you come to work. No wonder you have night terrors."

"The night terrors have nothing to do with my work," Catherine said. "I love what I do."

"You're good at it, too. Passionate and dedicated." His gaze deepened. "I remember that about you."

"You were good at your job, too, but you gave it up. Why didn't you stay and fight the accusations? Why did you let them drive you out?"

If he was offended by the question, he didn't let on. "It

seemed best for everyone at the time. Morale was already low. The department had gone through one scandal after another. I didn't want people having to take sides. That wouldn't have been good for anyone, least of all those we swore to protect."

"But you left the impression you were guilty," Catherine said.

"Not to the people who knew me best." He eyed her sagely. "What is this really about? Has someone said something to you?"

She thought back to her aunt's harsh words about his family, about her reliance on a firm run by unethical and possibly criminal ex-cops. *Do you really think you can trust this man?* She shrugged off the warning. "It doesn't matter. I just wanted to hear it from you."

"If you're having second thoughts about the investigation—"

"I'm not. Not because of you anyway. A part of me has always been afraid of what we might find."

"It's not too late to pull the plug. Just say the word."

"And walk away with all these questions? I can't do that. I would always wonder about those clippings and about my connection to Finch. Besides, we've come too far. We have to see it through."

"Whatever you want. This is your show." Nick's voice softened, but Catherine refused to meet his gaze. She wasn't that great at hiding her feelings. What if he saw too much on her face and in her eyes? What if she scared him away?

She took her time snapping on gloves and adjusting her lab coat.

"Hey." He canted his head. "Is something wrong? Was it something I said?"

"What? No. You're fine. I was just lost in thought. Sorry

I got sidetracked. We were talking about Thirteen." Catherine slipped back into her professional persona with a brisk nod. "As you know, the first thing we do with any set of remains is determine whether the bones are human. The answer here is obvious because the skeletons are mostly intact. But that's not always the case. We determine sex by measuring the width of the pelvis and various points on the skull. We can tell Thirteen was a young adult, probably early twenties by the presence of wisdom teeth and by the fusion of cranial sutures. There are other measurements we take, too, but for the sake of brevity, let's just assume I did a thorough examination."

Nick glanced up. "You said she was shot in the back of the head."

"Correct." Catherine carefully rotated the disarticulated skull until he had a clear view of the entry point. "As you can see, the wound is fairly clean with minimal shattering. The result of a full metal jacket most likely. A hollow point would have caused a lot more damage to the surrounding area."

"No exit wound," he mused. "Which probably means the bullet was still lodged in her skull at burial. Was it recovered?"

"I was out of town when the graves were discovered. Unfortunately, the excavations took place without me and assumptions were made at the scene. Delmar Gainey was already dead, his victims deceased for much longer. There wasn't a case to be built, just human remains to be honored. I think the intent was to remove his victims from that house of horrors as quickly as possible."

"So the bullet could still be in the grave," Nick said. "Unless Thirteen's remains were moved at some point in the past."

"I don't think they were, though. It doesn't make sense

that Gainey would bury her someplace else when he already had a graveyard right outside his back door. Besides, we can tell when remains have been moved or disturbed by matching soil samples and measuring the rate of deterioration and the consistency of insect predation."

"So the bullet *could* still be in the grave."

"Yes, but given how much time has passed since her death and the rushed excavation, finding it would be like searching for the proverbial needle in the haystack." Catherine hesitated. "Why are you so interested in that bullet?"

"Once a cop, always a cop." He studied the wound pattern. "It occurs to me that whoever came into the lab last night was looking for something."

Catherine's breath quickened. "You think he was looking for the bullet? Wouldn't that suggest the break-in had nothing to do with our case or with me personally? The timing was just coincidental."

"I wouldn't go that far. Don't forget there was also an intruder in the warehouse. But as you said, it's an interesting inconsistency."

Catherine's phone rang just then. She slid it out of her pocket and held up a finger to Nick as she turned away from the table. "Nolan? Slow down. Where are you?" She had trouble hearing him. He was talking too fast and the connection kept dropping. She moved over to a window to see if she could get a stronger signal. "Are you there?"

His voice came through loud and clear. "I'm at Emily's apartment."

"Why? How did you even know where she lives?"

"I've given her a ride home a few times. I was worried when she didn't come in this morning. It's not like her. She would have called if she could. Her car is in the parking lot, but she's not answering her door or her phone."

"Maybe she's under the weather and turned it off."

"She'd have to be really sick to miss work," Nolan said. "Trust me, I know how important this project is to her. To both of us. Maybe I'm overreacting. I hope I am. But she hasn't been herself lately."

Catherine kept her voice calm, but alarm prickled along her spine. "Yes, you mentioned that yesterday. Have you checked with the neighbors to see if anyone has seen her?"

"No one else is around. This place is like a dead zone. I went over to the office to ask about a key, but they won't let me in because I'm not a relative and I'm not listed as an emergency contact on her application. The building manager seemed to think I'm a stalker or something. Dr. March, can you come over here? I think they'll be more inclined to listen to you."

Catherine paused. "You're really worried about her, aren't you?"

"I know it sounds strange coming from me, but I have a really bad feeling about this."

Catherine glanced at Nick. He was still at the table, watching her curiously. "Give me the address," she said.

Nolan complied and then severed the call. Catherine walked back over to Nick.

"What's going on?" he asked.

"Nolan says Emily's car is at the apartment complex but she's not answering her door or phone, and the building manager won't let him in. He's convinced something is wrong and now he's got me worried. It's not like Emily to miss work without calling. This is an important project. The experience of a lifetime. I told you before our field is extremely competitive. She wouldn't blow her chance when she knows there is a waiting list of graduate students eager to take her place."

"What do you want to do?" Nick asked.

"I think I should go over there before Nolan decides to break down her door."

Nick nodded. "I'll drive you. Do you have an address?"

"Yes, it's on Lockwood Drive, but I thought you had appointments this afternoon."

"I'll make a few calls on the way over," he said. "If nothing else, you may find my lock-picking skills an asset."

She gave him a wry look. "Let's hope it doesn't come to that. We could all end up in jail." She shrugged out of her lab coat and grabbed her backpack. They rode up the elevator in silence. Catherine tried to convince herself that Nolan really was overreacting, but she'd never known him to be dramatic or impulsive. He was normally pragmatic and thoughtful. But she'd heard a tremor of emotion in his voice. A jagged edge of fear in his tone.

The day was hot and muggy, but Catherine shivered as she climbed into Nick's car. "I don't want to tell you how to drive, but can we please hurry?"

He shot her a glance as he peeled out of the parking lot. "What did Nolan say exactly?"

She repeated as much of their conversation as she could remember. "He asked me yesterday if I'd noticed anything peculiar about Emily's behavior. I think that's why he went to her apartment today. He was already concerned about her."

"Had you noticed anything different about her?"

"She went out for lunch yesterday in the pouring rain. When she got back, she seemed a little wired. I even wondered if she might have taken something while she was out. But I figured I was overanalyzing the situation. Succumbing to the power of suggestion."

"But now you don't?"

Catherine turned to stare out the window. "I don't know what to think. You asked last night how well I knew my lab assistants. You speculated that one of them might have given the code to the intruder. Maybe I'm reacting again to the power of suggestion, but I can't help wondering if this is somehow related. If Emily had something to do with the break-in, maybe that would explain why she's gone missing."

"We don't even know if she is missing," Nick said. "We don't know anything at this point. Just try to relax, okay? We're almost there."

He took the next corner without slowing and Catherine gripped the seat. She tried to do as he suggested. *Take a deep breath and relax.* But all she could think about was Nolan's phone call. All she could hear was the echo of Finch's warning in her head: *The truth is not what you think.*

EMILY'S APARTMENT WAS in an older complex inhabited almost exclusively by college kids and grad students. The buildings had seen better days, but the pool looked relatively clean and the grounds were maintained. Nick located her building and found a place to park. Nolan waited for them on the front steps. He rose as Catherine climbed out of the car and met her on the walkway. He was dressed in his usual attire of khakis and a button-down. He tucked his curls behind his ears as he stared down at her anxiously.

"Thank you for coming, Dr. March."

"Of course. Nolan, this is Nick LaSalle. He and I are working on another project together. I didn't think you'd mind if I brought him along. He has experience in dealing with…complicated matters."

He didn't look too pleased by Nick's presence, but he offered his hand. After they shook, he said awkwardly, "Did Dr. March fill you in?"

"As much as she could," Nick said. "When was the last time either of you saw Emily?"

Nolan answered without hesitation. "Yesterday at work. I left a little early. Four thirty or thereabouts. I guess that means you were the last one to see her, Dr. March."

Catherine nodded. "She left around five. She offered to drive me home, but I stayed to do some paperwork."

"How did she seem to you?" Nick asked.

"She was concerned about me walking home in the storm, but I told her I'd wait it out or call a cab."

"Did she mention where she was going? Or if she was meeting anyone?"

Catherine thought back. "No. I assumed she was going straight home."

Nick turned toward the building, trailing his gaze over the weathered facade, as if noting the layout and exits. Catherine marveled at his focus. *Once a cop, always a cop.*

"I just phoned her again," Nolan offered. "The call went straight to voice mail."

"You said her car is in the parking lot?" Nick asked.

Nolan hesitated, his gaze going to Catherine before he nodded. "It's that little beat-up red compact at the end." He pointed to the area reserved for residents. "I'm not good with cars. I don't know the make or model."

"Good enough," Nick said. "Have you checked it out?"

Nolan frowned. "No. I mean…checked it out for what?"

"Are the doors locked? Any sign that she left in a hurry? Did she leave her purse or phone behind?"

Nolan looked stricken. "I never even thought to look."

"Probably a good thing," Nick said. "Best not to leave fingerprints in case of foul play."

"Foul play?" Catherine and Nolan exclaimed together.

Nick glanced from one to the other. "Forget I said that. We shouldn't get ahead of ourselves."

Nolan visibly paled. "I thought she was just sick or something, but you're suggesting that someone—"

"Nolan." Catherine placed her hand on his arm. "We shouldn't get ahead of ourselves."

"Too late," Nolan muttered. He wiped a hand across his clammy brow as he drew in several deep breaths.

"I'll have a quick look at the vehicle," Nick said. "You two stay here." His gaze seemed to mean, "Keep an eye on him." Catherine nodded.

Nolan watched him with a scowl. "Dr. March, who is that guy? Should he even be here? This isn't his business."

"He can help," Catherine said. "He used to be a cop."

Nolan's expression darkened. "You think something terrible has happened to Emily, too, don't you?"

"No, I don't. I think she's under the weather and is having a good rest. She probably turned off her phone so she could sleep. As for Nick, he was in the lab when you called. He offered to drive me over here. Let's just try to relax and let him do his thing. Maybe you should sit down. You look as if you're ready to fall apart."

She wasn't used to seeing Nolan so upset. He was usually unflappable. His agitation was rubbing off on her and she found herself tracking Nick anxiously as he examined Emily's car. He glanced inside and then circled the vehicle slowly, even going so far as to check the tires.

"Did you find anything?" Catherine asked when he came back to the sidewalk.

"There's mud in the tread."

"Meaning?"

He shrugged. "Probably nothing considering all the rain we've had lately. Which apartment is hers?"

Nolan pointed to a third-story balcony. "Second one from the end."

Nick glanced back across the parking lot to the office. "I'll go talk to the manager. You two go up and try the door again." Turning to Catherine he said, "Maybe she'll answer if you call out to her."

"Shouldn't I come with you to the office? I have a university ID. My credentials might help."

"I'll call if I need you." His voice lowered so that only she could hear. "Be careful. You can knock on the door, but don't touch anything else."

Dread iced her blood. "Did you see something in the car?"

"No, just being cautious."

She watched him stride across the parking lot before turning to Nolan. "Let's go up."

They climbed the stoop steps and he opened the outside door for her. Inside, the foyer was cramped and dark. A narrow hallway led straight back to the ground-floor apartments and a staircase rose to the next level. Catherine could hear music playing in one of the units and a baby cried in another. The building was overly warm and a musty smell permeated the stained carpet. The bleak space made her all the more appreciative of her secluded garage apartment.

"This way." Nolan took the lead up the stairs. They climbed the two flights in silence and then paused on the third-story landing. It was quieter on the upper floor. No music, no babies. The worn carpet muted their footsteps as they made their way down the narrow corridor, pausing once again at the door marked 312.

"This is it," Nolan said as he lifted his hand to knock.

"Wait." Catherine took out her cell. "Let me try her phone first."

"I just did."

"I know, but she could be awake by now. If she sees my number, she might pick up." The phone rang several times before switching to voice mail. Catherine left a brief message and then hung up.

"What do we do now?" Nolan asked.

Catherine stepped up beside him and knocked on the door. "Emily? It's Dr. March. Are you in there? Nolan is with me. We're both very worried about you." She put her ear close to the door, listening intently. "I don't hear anything inside. She may not even be home."

"Then where is she?" He ran a hand through his tangled curls. "I know you think something is wrong, too, Dr. March. It's not just me."

"Let's wait for Nick. In the meantime, we should move away from the door. It's probably best we don't touch anything."

"Fingerprints," he said with a grim nod.

Another few minutes went by before footsteps sounded in the stairwell. They watched anxiously as Nick appeared in the corridor along with a man Catherine assumed was the property manager.

Nick quickly introduced him as Dennis Oakley. "He's agreed to let us in."

"I said I would let one of you go in," he corrected. "I'm not about to let a bunch of strange men traipse through her apartment." His gaze lit on Catherine. "You're her boss?"

"Yes, she works for me at the university. I'm also her professor."

"Okay, you can go in just long enough to make sure everything is okay. Then you come right back out. I don't like violating a tenant's privacy. We have laws about that sort of thing."

Catherine nodded. She didn't relish the idea of going in

alone, but she understood the manager's reluctance. "I'll be quick."

He used his master key to turn the dead bolt and then stepped back for Catherine to enter. The three men watched her from the hallway.

"I don't like this," Nick said as she stepped across the threshold. "I don't think you should go in there alone."

"That's the deal," the manager said. "Take it or leave it. We can call the cops instead if you want."

"No, let her go," Nolan said. "Time could be of the essence."

"I'll be fine," Catherine said as she glanced around.

The lights were off in the apartment and the drapes were pulled at the windows. She paused just inside the door to get her bearings. The kitchen was to her right, the living area to her left. A tiny hallway led back to the bedroom and bathroom.

"What's wrong?" Nick asked from the doorway.

"It's dark in here. I'm letting my eyes adjust." She moved into the apartment and called out to Emily. "Are you home? It's Dr. March."

No answer. No sound at all except for the low hum of the air conditioner. The temperature had been warm in the hallway, but the apartment was freezing. The chill seeped into Catherine's bones, along with an ever-growing sense of unease.

You're being ridiculous. Check the bedroom and bathroom and get out.

Nick said from the doorway, "What do you see?"

"Everything seems fine in here. Nothing out of place that I can tell. I'll go check the bedroom and bathroom."

"Wait!" This from Nolan.

She whirled in surprise. "What is it?"

"I don't know. I just…" He turned to the manager. "Let me go in there with her."

"You heard what she said. Everything seems fine," the man said impatiently. "Let her finish up so we can all get out of here."

Nolan appealed to Nick. "Mr. LaSalle, was it? You said yourself she shouldn't go in there alone."

"And you correctly pointed out that time could be a factor. Catherine? You okay?"

"Almost finished."

"Hurry," Nolan urged.

His jitters did nothing to alleviate Catherine's nerves. She tried to shake off the disquiet as she crossed the room and started down the hallway. She called out Emily's name again and then glanced in the bathroom. The shower curtain was open, the counter littered with cosmetics and brushes.

"Bathroom is clear," she called over her shoulder. She moved back into the hallway. The bedroom door was open. A sour smell emanated. Like cheap wine. Like vomit and urine.

Catherine faltered, her hand going to her nose as her stomach churned. No. *No.* Emily was fine. She had to be. Maybe she really was sick. A stomach bug or even a hangover. Maybe that explained the smell…

She stepped up to the door, preparing to knock or call out again, but the odor grew stronger and she stopped to draw her shirt up over her nose and mouth.

She pushed open the door with her toe. It was dark inside. The drawn drapes blocked the light from the narrow window directly opposite the bed. Catherine could just make out a silhouette on top of the covers.

"Emily? Is that you? Can you hear me? It's Dr. March. Emily?"

The silhouette didn't move or utter a sound.

Catherine was trembling by this time. She felt for the light switch, disregarding Nick's caution not to touch anything.

The illumination blinded her. Or maybe a protective instinct had kicked in, temporarily shielding her from the horror.

Chapter Eleven

Emily lay on her back staring blindly up at the ceiling. She was fully dressed, her hair splayed out against the pillow. She might have been lying there in deep contemplation except for the glazed eyes and the blood that had soaked through the sheets and dripped down into the carpet. A kitchen knife lay on the pillow beside her head. A dark film stained the blade.

Catherine gaped. For a moment, she couldn't seem to take it all in. Her brain refused to accept reality. Then with a gasp, she stumbled back through the door into the hallway. Bending double, she fought back the nausea in her throat as she drew in deep breaths.

Nick called to her from the entry. "You okay?"

She drew in another breath. "Call 911," she said weakly.

"What is it? What's happened?"

She could hear chatter from the hallway, but she couldn't respond. She clapped a hand over her mouth as she tried not to heave.

"Catherine?" Nick's voice was close. Right in front of her. She glanced up to find him headed down the hallway toward her. "What happened?"

She pointed to the bedroom as she gulped in more air. He touched her shoulder as he brushed by her. She heard the sharp intake of his breath and a muttered oath before he got out his phone. He supplied the address and a brief description of the scene to the 911 operator before he returned to Catherine.

He put his arm around her. "Come on. Let's get you out of here."

"Did you see?"

"Yes."

"Emily's dead."

"I know."

"I feel sick."

"You'll be okay. We'll get you some air while we wait for the police."

"Nick…"

"Don't say anything. Don't touch anything. We need to keep the others out of here."

She welcomed the warm, stale air of the hallway. Leaning a shoulder against the wall, she listened as Nick spoke in low tones to the others. Nolan reacted viscerally to the news. Surprising for him. He was usually contemplative. He knocked Nick's hand from his arm and backed away, eyes wide with shock. Then he turned toward the apartment, calling out Emily's name. He would have gone inside if Nick hadn't stopped him. Nolan struggled for a moment before collapsing to the floor, drawing his knees up to his chest as he rocked back and forth.

The manager quickly closed and locked the door. "You sure she's dead?" he asked Nick.

"Yes."

"We don't need to call an ambulance or anything?"

"I called 911. The police will be here soon."

"This is bad. Really bad. I've worked in property management for nearly twenty years. Never had anything like this happen in any of my units. Someone shot up the parking lot once. Plugged a few cars, but no one was hurt." He glanced back at the closed door. "Dead, huh?"

"Yes."

Catherine vaguely followed the conversation. The dizziness had passed, but her brain still lagged. After a few minutes, she went over and sat down on the floor beside Nolan. She didn't try to touch him.

He lifted his head from his knees and stared blankly at the wall in front of them. Then he turned bleary eyes on Catherine. "I knew something was wrong. Didn't I tell you? I could feel it."

"Yes. You were right, unfortunately."

"She was acting strangely for the past couple of days. I said that, too."

Catherine nodded. "You don't have any idea what was bothering her?"

"She wouldn't have confided in me. We were friendly competitors but we weren't friends. Not really. The only time we interacted outside work was when we gave each other rides." He scrubbed a hand down his face. "I should have made more of an effort. I should have told her..."

"Told her what?" Catherine asked when he trailed away.

"It doesn't matter now." He hugged his knees as he glanced around. "Shouldn't the police be here by now?"

"It's only been a few minutes."

"I feel sick."

"I know. Me, too."

Nick squatted beside them. "You two okay?"

Nolan looked affronted. "No, we're not okay. What kind of question is that?"

"Take it easy," Catherine murmured. She glanced at Nick. "Do you think it would be all right if Nolan and I go downstairs for some air? It's warm in here."

"Yes, go on. I'll wait here with the manager. He looks a

little shaky. Are you sure you're okay?" This to Catherine. He took her arm as she struggled to her feet.

"I'll be fine." She put a hand down to Nolan. "Come on. Let's go outside."

He rose, leaning a shoulder against the wall for support. "Shouldn't we wait for the police?"

"We'll be right downstairs. We'll see them as soon as they arrive."

He glanced back at Emily's door before he nodded and allowed Catherine to lead him to the stairs. They went down side by side, arms linked, and remained that way until Catherine broke away to open the front door. The day was hot and humid, but the fresh air felt good. She sat down on the top step and turned her face to the sun. After a moment, Nolan joined her.

"Dr. March, you never said how it happened, but it was bad, wasn't it?"

"Yes, but Nick said it was best if I wait and talk to the police about what I saw."

Nolan closed his eyes briefly. "You don't have to say anything. I saw your face when you came out of the apartment. She...someone hurt her, didn't they?"

"Try not to think about it," Catherine said.

"Who would do such a thing? To Emily, of all people."

"I don't know. We'll have to leave those answers to the police. Do you know anything about her friends or family? Is there anyone we should call?"

"Her family doesn't live here. She came to the university on a full-ride scholarship. That's about all I know."

Catherine nodded, her gaze on the parking lot. On Emily's little red car. "What did you mean earlier when you said you should have told her?"

"Nothing." Nolan stared straight ahead, hands on knees, his curls stirring in the breeze.

"You cared for her, didn't you?"

"Of course, I cared for her. We went through college and grad school together. I saw her every day in the lab."

"Did you have deeper feelings for her?"

He turned with a probing gaze. "You mean like the kind of feelings you have for Nick LaSalle?"

The question startled her. "Why would you think I have feelings for Nick?"

"I saw the way you looked at him earlier. The way he touched you in the hallway. You should tell him how you feel."

"This isn't the appropriate time for such a conversation," Catherine said uneasily.

Nolan's gaze intensified. "You should tell him how you feel before it's too late."

His long stare made her uncomfortable. "You've misinterpreted our relationship."

"Have I?" He seemed on the verge of pressing his point, but then changed his mind. "You asked if I knew what had been bothering Emily before she…before this happened. I don't, but I think she may have been involved in something dangerous. Her murder wasn't a random attack."

"What do you mean?"

"Look at this place. Look at her car. She was out of money and couldn't get another loan. She was afraid she'd have to drop out of the program."

"She told you that?"

"Not directly, but I overheard her on the phone talking to a loan officer. She was very upset. That's when her behavior changed and she became so secretive. I tried to talk to her about it once, but it was a sensitive issue and she was embarrassed. She told me she'd worked things out. I took that to mean she'd gotten the loan after all. Now I wonder if she came into money a different way. Maybe that's why she's dead."

Catherine said quietly, "I thought you said the two of you didn't talk."

"It wasn't much of a conversation. I offered to help and she blew me off. Should I tell the police about it?"

"You should tell the police everything. They can decide if it's worth pursuing."

"Dr. March?"

"Yes?"

"Thank you."

"For what?"

"For coming over when I called. For sitting here with me now. You could have blown me off, too."

"I'm glad I didn't. Your instincts were right. But it's been a shock for both of us. After we talk to the police, you should go home. The lab can wait."

"Thank you." He lifted his head. "I hear sirens."

Catherine rose as the sound grew louder. "Let's go back inside and join the others."

"Dr. March?"

She glanced down at him.

"You really should tell him."

A PAIR OF uniformed officers arrived first, followed by a homicide detective, the coroner and a crime-scene investigator. Statements were taken from Catherine and the others and then they were all told they could go. The building manager went back to his office, Nolan disappeared and Nick hung around in the hallway to see what he could glean from his former colleagues.

Catherine went back outside to wait for him. She sat down on the steps as her thoughts ran rampant. She was still in shock. Even with the sun beating down on her shoulders, she couldn't stop trembling. Images bombarded her. Emily on the bed, the knife on her pillow. Blood everywhere.

She closed her eyes and hugged her arms around her middle until the trembling subsided.

Where was Nolan? He'd been there one moment, gone the next. His disappearance worried Catherine. Emily's death had affected him deeply. His image as a moody loner had fallen apart before her very eyes.

She thought back over their conversation and his advice that she should tell Nick how she felt. But what did she really feel for him? A spark of attraction that would soon be extinguished? Or something deeper and longer lasting? It was too soon to tell. Adrenaline was running too high. Now was not the time to trust her emotions.

Her gaze returned to Emily's car and she realized she was once again masking her grief by dwelling on her feelings for Nick. But she couldn't hide from the dark reality of her assistant's death. A young, brilliant woman had been viciously murdered in her apartment, in her own bed, the murder weapon left beside her pillow out of panic or in mockery. She had been stabbed repeatedly, the detectives told Catherine. Overkill, one of them said.

It's called piquerism. The sexual and sadistic pleasure derived from penetrating the skin with sharp objects, sometimes to the point of death.

The memory flitted away as a chill swept through her. Across the parking lot, a man stood watching her from the corner of a building. Nothing unusual in that, she told herself. People had come out of their apartments to monitor the police activity. Small groups gathered on walkways. Neighbors spoke in hushed tones. It was to be expected. Residents of the complex were naturally curious and concerned.

But there was something disturbing about the man across the way. Something…familiar. As Catherine sat watching, he leaned a shoulder against the building and blew a thin plume of smoke toward the parking lot, toward her.

Catherine's heart jumped. She *knew* him. She recognized his lanky form, the long hair brushed back from his face and the crude tattoos up and down his arms. She had seen him on her way to Nick's office that first afternoon. She had been certain he had followed her.

And now here he was at the scene of a grisly murder.

She half rose—to do what, she wasn't quite sure—when a voice said behind her, "Dr. March?"

She jumped, her hand flying to her thudding heart.

"I'm sorry," Nolan said. "I didn't mean to startle you."

She took a moment to calm her nerves. "I wasn't expecting to see you. You disappeared earlier. I thought you'd gone home."

"I couldn't stay up there while they…you know. I've just been wandering the hallways." He paused with a frown. "What are you doing out here alone? Where's Mr. LaSalle?"

"He's still inside. Nolan—" she placed a hand lightly on his arm "—there's a man standing at the corner of that building directly across the parking lot. Do you see him?"

Nolan glanced past her. "I see a lot of men standing around. They're all staring at us." His frowned deepened. "They should go back inside and mind their own business."

"They live here. They have every right to be concerned." Catherine lifted a hand to shade her eyes as she turned back to the building. "He's gone."

"Who was he? Did he do something to upset you?"

"I thought I recognized him, but maybe I'm imagining things."

Nolan looked uneasy. "Should we tell the police?"

"Tell the police what?" Nick asked as he came through the door.

"Dr. March saw a man watching her just now."

Nick's gaze roamed the area. "You always get gawkers at times like this."

"She thought she recognized him," Nolan said.

Nick's gaze came back to fix on her. "Is that right?"

"I don't know for sure. The sun was in my eyes. I had the impression he was tall and lanky with longish hair and tattooed arms."

Recognition flared in Nick's eyes. "That's pretty specific."

"It could have been my imagination," she said.

"Wait here." He hurried down the steps and strode across the parking lot.

Nolan watched for a moment before glancing back at Catherine. "What's going on? You look frightened. Do you think that man had something to do with Emily's death?" He clutched her arms. "Tell me!"

The action took Catherine aback. She shrugged out of his hold and stepped away from him. "Calm down. I don't know any more than you do."

He looked instantly mortified. "I'm so sorry, Dr. March. I shouldn't have grabbed you like that. I don't know what came over me."

"We've both had a terrible shock. We're not ourselves." Catherine paused, her pulse still racing. "The police said we're free to leave. Why don't you go home? Are you okay to drive? Do you need a lift or should I call someone for you?"

"I'm fine now. I'm really sorry I did that to you." His eyes were earnest and remorseful. "I hope my actions today don't leave a lasting impression."

"Today is an exception. We both get a pass."

He nodded gratefully. "What about you? Are you going back to the lab?"

"I don't think so. I wouldn't be able to concentrate." She saw Nick coming across the parking lot out of the corner of her eye. "I'll get an early start in the morning, but you take as much time as you need."

"Dr. March?" He swallowed. "Do you think they'll find who did it?"

"I hope so."

His expression hardened as he glanced away. "Nothing will bring her back, but it would at least be a comfort to know that her killer got what he deserved."

Chapter Twelve

It was late afternoon by the time Nick drove Catherine home. The sun was still hot and bright as it shimmered down through the oak leaves, but her upstairs porch was cool and shady.

"Do you want to come in?" she asked.

He propped a shoulder against a post as he regarded her. "You look beat. You should try and get some rest. You'll need your energy in the coming days."

His comment alarmed her. "Why do you say that?"

"The police will be all over campus interviewing Emily's friends and acquaintances. You can expect them to visit the lab. They may even want to talk to you and Nolan a few times before all is said and done. That can be stressful." He paused, as if trying to gauge how much more he wanted to pile on her. "Our case is heating up, too. I heard back from Finch's attorney a little while ago."

Her head came up. "Why didn't you tell me?"

"You had other things on your mind. Besides, I wanted to wait until we were alone. Finch was good as his word. He somehow accelerated the paperwork. We can go see him as soon as we hammer out the details with his attorney."

"'We'? No," Catherine said fervently. "I already told you, I don't want to see him. I hate that he knows anything about me at all. I just want you to go to that prison and get him to agree to a DNA test."

"And if his DNA contradicts your aunt's story?"

Catherine sighed. "I'll deal with that when the time comes. I want the truth, no matter what, but I also want a speedy resolution. I didn't realize what I would be getting us both into when I came to your office that day."

"It does seem like we've kicked a hornet's nest," he agreed. "For now we'll stick to the original plan. I'll go see Finch alone."

"When?"

"I'm stopping by his attorney's office as soon as I leave here so we can establish ground rules and schedule a time."

"Ground rules?" Catherine frowned. "I don't like the sound of that."

"It's not unusual for an attorney to set parameters on a meeting like this. If all goes smoothly, I may be driving to Columbia as soon as tomorrow. Once I see Finch, we'll know where we need to go from there." He gave her a warning look. "Things could get even crazier. You should rest while you can."

"I know you're right, but I don't even want to close my eyes after what I saw today. I should just go back to the lab. At least there I can be useful."

"It's getting late. You don't want to do that."

Catherine gripped the porch railing as she gazed down into the dappled garden. "I can't just sit here and brood. Maybe I should go over to my mother's house and search through her files. I was planning to do that anyway."

"You should hold off on that, too," Nick said.

She turned with a frown. "You don't want me to leave my apartment, do you? Why? You said you'd tell me if you thought I was in any real danger."

"I also said it never hurts to be cautious." He straightened as he scanned their surroundings. "The truth is, I don't know if you're in danger. You've already been attacked once. Maybe that incident was the result of catching the intruder by surprise, but now someone you worked with has been murdered. We can't discount any possibility."

Catherine moved back from the rail, as if suddenly afraid of what she might see in the shadows. "It still seems so surreal. All that blood. The knife on her pillow." She shivered.

Nick's voice softened. "I'm sorry you had to be the one to find her."

"You couldn't have known. None of us could. I thought she was probably sick in bed. At worst, she might have fallen and hit her head. Who would ever have dreamed of a scene like that? She was so young and smart and ambitious. She had her whole life ahead of her and now, just like that, she's gone." Catherine's eyes burned with emotion. "Do you think she knew her killer? Do you think she invited him into her apartment?"

"There was no sign of forced entry at the front door. No sign of a struggle inside the apartment. By all indications, she wasn't alarmed by his presence. He caught her unaware. He may even have drugged her."

"My God."

"The police will know more after the autopsy and toxicology screens. I still have friends at the lab. I'll see what I can find out. In the meantime, try not to dwell."

"Easier said than done, but don't worry about me. I'll be fine." She moved to the front door. "You go do what you have to do."

"Are you sure you're all right?"

"I'm safe enough here. I have a strong dead bolt and there's no outside access to any of the windows. I'm up in the trees. No one can come in unless I let them in." *Which was exactly what Emily had done.* Catherine suppressed another shiver as she unlocked the door and stepped inside. The apartment was cool and airy, but already the walls seemed to close in on her. She retreated and turned to Nick. "Maybe you could come in for just a minute."

"I've got some time." He followed her inside and closed the door.

She glanced around. "Why does everything seem so different now? Like everything has been turned upside down? Even my own apartment."

"You've suffered a shock," he said. "It'll take time before you feel normal again."

She ran a hand up and down her arm. "I can only imagine what poor Nolan must be feeling. He was so distraught earlier."

"Were he and Emily close?"

"I never thought so before today. They were competitive with one another. The best students usually are."

"Did they ever have any problems? Arguments? Anything like that?"

She looked at him, startled. "You can't think Nolan had anything to do with her death."

"I'm just trying to get a feel for the people in Emily's life. Her everyday relationships."

"I can't tell you much," Catherine said. "Only what I observed in the classroom and lab. Nolan could be abrasive and superior at times and he knew how to get under Emily's skin. I always thought that was just his personality. But after we talked to today, I wonder if he was trying to disguise his true feelings for her. I think he was in love with her."

"Do you think she knew?"

"He wouldn't have said anything, but she may have sensed something. That could explain the change in her behavior. Maybe she tried to put some distance between them so that he wouldn't get the wrong idea."

"Rejection is a powerful motivation," Nick said.

She frowned. "And you think, what? That his distress today was just an act?"

"It's been known to happen."

"Come on. Nolan has his quirks, but he isn't a killer." Catherine dropped down on the couch and motioned Nick to a chair, but instead he went over to the window to glance out.

"People can sometimes fool you," he said.

"Yes, and sometimes what you see is what you get." She studied his profile, wondering again about *his* secrets. Wondering if she had seen the real Nick LaSalle. He was in the business of subterfuge. Maybe he'd kept a part of himself hidden even from her. Especially from her. "Nolan told me earlier that Emily had been having financial problems. He overheard her on the phone with a loan officer. She was very upset. When he offered to help, she said she'd taken care of the problem. He took that to mean she'd come up with the money another way. Perhaps a dangerous way."

"Like selling access to the lab?"

That jolted Catherine out of the numbness she'd been trying to sink into. "Nothing was taken from the lab. I doubt the police have even followed up on the complaint. Even if Emily gave that code to the intruder, why would he kill her? And in such a brutal fashion?"

"Because she could recognize him," Nick said. "The overkill could have been calculated misdirection."

Catherine thought about that for a moment. "But there's nothing incriminating in the lab. Certainly nothing worth murdering someone over."

Nick turned. "How about the remains of fourteen homicide victims?"

"Delmar Gainey is dead. Who else would have any concern about those remains? Unless you think he had a partner."

"No. But one of the victims is not like the others."

That stopped her again. "You think someone broke into the lab because of Jane Doe Thirteen? Why?"

He hesitated, glancing back out the window before he came to take a seat opposite her. His expression was dark, intense, a little excited. "Maybe her killer is still alive."

Catherine's breath caught and she found herself clutching the edges of the sofa. "What?"

"Don't tell me the thought hasn't crossed your mind."

She stared at him in disbelief. "Why would it cross my mind? It's too farfetched. What are you even suggesting? That someone shot Thirteen in the back of the head and conveniently buried her body on the property of a serial killer?"

"It's not that farfetched if her killer knew about Gainey," Nick said. "In fact, it would be the perfect way to cover his tracks. If the bodies were ever recovered, she would be lumped in with Gainey's other victims. Which is exactly happened."

Catherine's mind reeled. "I admit, it's an interesting theory, but it still doesn't explain why someone would break into my lab. The bullet was never recovered and any other incriminating evidence would have been placed in police custody, either at the police lab or in the evidence locker."

"He couldn't have known whether the bullet was recovered or not. And anyway, maybe Thirteen's killer wasn't looking for evidence. Not yet. Maybe he just wanted to know if his victim had been recovered."

Catherine thought back to the day before, when Emily had returned from lunch. She'd immediately gravitated to Thirteen's remains. Had she just come from a meeting with her killer? "Assuming Emily was somehow involved, why not just tell this person about the bullet hole in Thirteen's skull? She could have sold that information as easily as the access code and it would have saved them both a lot of trouble."

"Because he wouldn't have told her *why* he wanted in the lab. Buying access is one thing. Admitting to homicide is another."

Catherine said pensively, "Do you think that's why he killed her? Because she figured it out on her own? Maybe she tried to blackmail him."

"It's possible."

She fell silent, her thoughts still raging. "We keep saying *he*. The brutality of the attack would suggest a male assailant, but we can't know that for certain. As you said, the overkill could be misdirection. I can't even swear that the intruder in the lab was a man. I never got a look at him. Even when I was grabbed on the stairs, my back was turned." Catherine froze as the implication hit her. "My God, Nick. What if the person who attacked me is Emily's killer? I was that close to him. If I could have stopped him that night, she might still be alive."

"You can't think like that. You did everything right. You reported the incident. You cooperated with the police. There was nothing else you could do."

"It just makes me feel so helpless." She glanced toward the window, searching the sky through the trees before turning back to Nick. "What do we do now?"

"About Emily?"

"About everything we just discussed. Maybe the police need to know about your theory."

"Right now it's nothing but idle speculation. Until something breaks, we should concentrate on our own case.

Speaking of which…" He got out his phone to check the time. "I should probably go."

Catherine rose to walk him to the door. "It's just so odd, isn't it? I'm professionally tied to Delmar Gainey and there is every possibility that I'm personally connected to Orson Lee Finch. Ever since my mother died, my life has revolved around those two serial killers. And now another killer has taken the life of someone close to me."

"It's been a strange couple of days," Nick agreed. He turned at the door to search her features. "Are you sure you're okay? I still don't like leaving you alone."

"I'll be fine. I'll lock up and my phone is charged and ready." She held up her cell.

They moved onto the porch. "My grandmother's birthday party is tonight, but I'll check in with you later and you call if you need me." He paused at the railing, his gaze sweeping over the garden before returning to her. In the late afternoon sunlight, his eyes had deepened to charcoal. "I'll come no matter the time."

They stood very close, his body mere inches from hers. Catherine wished that he would put his arms around her. She wanted nothing so much as to feel the solidness of his chest beneath her cheek, to feel the rhythm of his heartbeat against her hand. She didn't know him well, but she somehow trusted that he would protect her with his own life and that certainty both stunned and humbled her.

It was a powerful moment. A turning point. Yet she was cautious enough not to act on her feelings. Emotions were still running high and grief still weighed too heavily on her heart.

"You're trembling," he said.

"I think I'm still in shock."

He slipped his fingers through her hair, lifting her face so that he could stare into her eyes. "Maybe I should stay."

Yes, please stay. The sun will be setting soon and I don't want to be alone in the dark.

"I'm fine. Go to your grandmother's birthday party. You shouldn't disappoint her."

"She'll understand."

"I don't want her to understand. I don't want you to think that I'm some frightened little bunny who can't take care of herself. I'm *fine*." She paused on a sharpened breath. "I really wish you wouldn't look at me that way."

"What way?"

"You know what I mean. You should go before we make a very big mistake."

He leaned in ever so slightly. "Would it be a mistake, though?"

"Yes," she said, without much conviction. "Under these circumstances, it would be. I'm not thinking clearly. And I need to think clearly when I'm with you."

He murmured her name and she sighed.

"You're going to kiss me anyway, aren't you?"

He teased her for a moment, leaning in and pulling back before he brushed his lips against hers. She wished that he would deepen the kiss, but he didn't. He respected her hesitancy, whether she really wanted him to or not.

His fingers were still tangled in her hair as he gazed down at her. "You're right. We'll wait. I've never thought it wise to mix business with pleasure even under ordinary circumstances. And this case is far from ordinary."

"How will it end, do you think?"

His eyes glinted. "I have some idea."

Her pulse thudded. "No, I mean the case. How will it end?"

"Not well for someone. Too many people have been keeping secrets."

"Like my aunt Louise? Like Jackie Morris?"

His dark gaze drew her in. "Yes, among others. But we'll figure it out. I won't give up until we find the answers you need."

The hard certainty in his tone unnerved her. She dreaded the coming days. Dreaded what would be revealed when all those secrets were uncovered. She wanted to turn back the clock to a moment ago, to the intimacy of their kiss. She wanted his lips on hers again, his tongue in her mouth and his hands all over her body. She wanted to tempt him back into her apartment and into her bed, but now was not the time and she didn't feel quite that bold.

"I'll call you later," he said, smoothing a hand down her hair. "I'll come back sooner if you need me."

Before she could say another word, he turned and bolted down the steps.

Catherine watched him go. The gate clanged shut, his car started up and then the sound of the engine faded into silence. She watched the sky. The sun still hovered over the treetops. Darkness was hours away and yet already the claustrophobia of night crept over her. Somewhere out there, a killer had crawled back into the hidey-hole of his everyday persona. He had scrubbed the blood from his hands while smiling pleasantly to himself in the mirror. He had killed one woman, possibly two. Had he already set his sights on another?

Catherine lingered on the porch until the shadows in the garden lengthened and the oak leaves began to whisper of nightfall.

Chapter Thirteen

Nick checked his watch and then his phone. It wasn't even ten o'clock, but the night felt endless. His grandmother had already gone to bed so the party should start to wind down soon. He wanted to make a beeline for the door, break away from the crowd before the goodbyes started, but if he left too early, he'd catch hell from his mother.

Besides, he hadn't yet had a word alone with his father. Every time he started toward the study where his father had retreated, well-meaning friends and relatives waylaid him. His head pounded from the aimless chitchat. He wondered if Catherine was still up or if she'd succumbed early to exhaustion.

The peace and quiet of her little apartment in the trees beckoned like a cool glass of water on a steamy day. He pictured her there now, curled up on the couch, dark hair tucked behind her ears as she scowled at her laptop screen.

Or was she huddling under the covers, trying to ward off her night terrors?

He chided himself for his fixation. Catherine wasn't the only attractive woman who had ever come to him for help. She wasn't even the most beautiful, but she had a quality about her that was hard to define and even harder to forget. He wondered again why the dark brought monsters to her doorstep, why the secrets of her past still triggered her nightmares.

There was so much about her he didn't know. Who would have ever thought on that rainy day when she'd first come to his office that a box of old newspaper clippings would open such a Pandora's box of intrigue? That he would be standing in the middle of a raucous family gathering, worried about night terrors and bloodlines and the unexpected twists in an already-tortuous investigation?

He scanned all those familiar LaSalle faces, thinking about his father's private number scrawled across the back of a business card found among Laura March's secret clippings. Wondering again about the label he'd discovered in his uncle's paper shredder and the clandestine meeting he'd witnessed between Jackie Morris and the driver of a dark sedan. He thought about his confrontation with Louise Jennings and the warning call he'd received from Orson Lee Finch. His mind went round and round with possibilities, but he still had no real answers for Catherine. He was as much in the dark as the day he'd opened the investigation. What did that say about his skills?

Extricating himself from a good-natured dispute, Nick moved through the crowd, nodding and smiling before slipping down the hallway to his dad's study. He knocked on the door and then stuck his head inside. Raymond stood at one of the long windows, staring out at the woods. The drapes were open and Nick could see moonlight glimmering on the pond in the distance.

"Dad?"

He turned with a welcoming smile. He was tall like Emmett but a few pounds heavier, and his hair had gone almost completely gray while his brother's had only silvered at the temples. Raymond was the eldest by only a few minutes, but the responsibilities of raising a family and running a business hadn't worn as gently as Emmett's freewheeling lifestyle.

His smile broadened as he motioned Nick inside. "Managed to give your mother the slip, did you? Well, come in and close the door. I was just about to break open the good stuff."

"Nice." Nick closed the door, shutting out the sounds of music and laughter that drifted down the hallway from the front of the house. "It's getting a little wild out there. Emmett is teaching the younger cousins some of his dance moves."

Raymond winced as he poured the whiskey. "That won't end well. The man has no sense of rhythm, but you'll never convince him of that."

"You should see him out there," Nick said. "The cousins are egging him on and he's eating it up with a spoon."

"That's Emmett. Whatever his shortcomings, he's always had more than his fair share of confidence."

"Confidence or bravado?" Nick asked.

"A little of both maybe." His dad handed him a glass and they both took seats. "He's not alone in that. The LaSalles have never been known for humility and self-reflection."

"I guess that's why Grandma thinks I'm the only one around here who has a good head on his shoulders," Nick teased.

"She said that? Seems she's conveniently forgotten some of your earlier stunts." Raymond's eyes glinted as he lifted his glass. "Like skateboarding down the roof and breaking your leg in three places. Or plowing over the neighbor's mailbox with your three-wheeler. Wrapping your first car around a light pole. I could go on and on. You and speed were a dangerous combination." Raymond ran a hand through his hair. "See this? Gray-headed by the time you were in high school."

"I guess it took me a while to learn my lesson," Nick said.

"At least you did learn it, which is more than I can say for most of your cousins out there."

Nick sipped thoughtfully. "I've always wondered about something. When all that trouble started up in the department…all the rumors and accusations…you never once asked me if any of it was true."

"I didn't need to. I already knew the answer."

Nick studied his father's careworn face. "The thought never crossed your mind that I could be a dirty cop?"

"Not once. I know you better than that. I also know when something's on your mind." Raymond paused. "What's troubling you tonight, son?"

"A lot of things," Nick admitted. "But that question is something I've wanted to ask for a long time. Now seemed as good a time as any to bring it up."

His dad met his gaze. "Did you really have any doubt about my answer?"

Nick shrugged. "Maybe not, but it was good to hear just the same. There aren't too many people who have that kind of faith in me these days." He hoped Catherine was one of them, though.

Raymond gave him a hard look. "Don't sell yourself short. You're a better man than I ever was."

The response surprised Nick. "That's not true. I've always looked up to you. Always respected the way you've conducted yourself personally and professionally. I couldn't have asked for a better role model."

Raymond glanced away. "Don't put me on a pedestal. I've made plenty of mistakes. Some of them still come back to haunt me now and then."

"We all make mistakes," Nick said. "As a matter of fact, Emmett thinks I'm making a big one right now."

"How so?"

Nick swirled his drink. "He doesn't approve of one of the cases I took on. I've been meaning to speak to you about it."

"I'm listening."

Nick was silent for a moment. "I hardly know where to start. A woman came to me two days ago with a bunch of old newspaper clippings she'd found hidden beneath the floorboards in her deceased mother's closet. Based on the content of those articles, she wanted me to open an investigation into her adoption because she thought Orson Lee Finch might be her biological father."

Raymond's hand froze in midair. Then he set down his glass without drinking. "That must have taken you by surprise."

"To say the least," Nick muttered.

"Besides the clippings, what other proof did she offer?"

"Nothing beyond circumstantial. I agreed to look into it because it seemed important to her. But opening that investigation has turned out to be a real can of worms."

"So you're saying Emmett was right to be concerned?"

"Yeah, I guess that is what I'm saying. He was at the office the day Catherine first came in. He said then he had a bad feeling about the case. About her."

"Catherine is the client?"

"Catherine March."

His dad toyed with his glass. "And how do you feel about the case? About her?"

"She's been through a lot. I trust she's being straight with me, but the investigation has turned out to be a lot more complicated than either of us ever dreamed. I've wanted to talk to you about it because I think it may tie back to one of your old cases."

"How old?"

"At least twenty-five years ago. Does the name Laura March mean anything to you?"

Maybe it was Nick's imagination, but he detected a slight hesitation. He watched his dad's expression, thinking, *No, not you. Don't you keep things from me, too.*

"I don't recall the name," Raymond said. "But I've conducted hundreds of investigations since we opened the agency. I can't remember them all."

"She may have approached you about finding her daughter's biological parents. When Catherine first came to see me, she brought along one of our old business cards that she'd found with the clippings." Nick fished the card out of his pocket and slid it across the desk to his father.

"That is an old one," Raymond said as he picked up the card. "We haven't used this design or logo in years."

"Check the back."

Raymond flipped over the card and raised a brow.

"You still don't remember Laura March?" Nick pressed.

His dad looked up. "No reason why I should. I didn't write that number."

"You're sure about that?"

Raymond held up the card. "It's not my writing. See how the sevens are crossed? I've never done that. Maybe this woman, this Laura March, got hold of one of my cards and jotted my number on the back. Maybe she meant to contact me but never did."

"How would she have gotten your private number?"

"Someone must have given it to her. All I know is that I didn't write that number."

Nick sat back in his chair. "Laura March's husband was an undercover cop named Aidan March. From what little I've been able to dig up, he was killed in the line of duty when his cover was blown. That would have been a few years after you left the department. Do you remember anything about that case?"

Raymond hesitated again as he glanced back down at the card. "Emmett and I didn't have much to do with CPD once we left. Hard feelings lingered. It seemed best we sever ties."

"Hard feelings about what?"

"Built-up resentments. Bruised egos." Raymond shrugged. "I got along with most of the officers, but Emmett liked to throw his weight around as a detective. He was never much of a team player. Never much of a cop, to be honest. He didn't like playing by the book and that made him a loose cannon. But he was a damned good investigator. Still is. Tenacious as a bulldog. He would keep digging when everyone else had given up. You're like him in that respect."

"He said the same thing about you."

Raymond's smile tightened. "That's about the only thing he and I have in common."

Nick thought about the label he'd peeled from the blades of Emmett's paper shredder and the intruder in the warehouse. Had his uncle beat him to those files that night? Had he destroyed evidence that could have linked their agency to Catherine's adoption?

Maybe they'd had this all wrong. Instead of Laura March having a connection to the LaSalle agency, maybe Aidan was the one who had come looking for help. But how did that make sense? He'd been a police detective with a lot of resources available to him. Why would he need to hire a private investigator unless he intended to go outside the law?

So many things about this case still didn't make sense. So many leads didn't seem to relate. Nick had never felt so lost in an investigation.

He glanced across the desk at his dad. Raymond was still gazing down at the card, apparently lost in thought. "Did you ever meet Orson Lee Finch?"

Raymond's head snapped up. "Finch? No, why?"

"You worked that case for a while, right? I thought your paths might have crossed."

"They kept him locked down pretty tight once he was in custody. The only time I ever saw him was on TV, just like everyone else."

"What did you make about the rumor of him having a child?" Nick asked.

"That's all it was as far as I knew—a rumor. But if I were Finch and I did have a kid? I'd have made damn certain she was hidden from the public."

"Like making arrangements for her to be taken in by another family? What better way to protect her than by giving her a new name and a new identity?"

Raymond nodded. "But if the adoption wasn't official, you'll have a hard time proving it."

"That's why I intend to ask Finch for a DNA sample."

Raymond's brow lifted again. "Do you have any reason to believe he'll give you one?"

"He's already reached out. I think he'll cooperate."

His dad's gaze flicked away. "Then it's only a matter of time before you and your client have an answer."

"As to whether or not Finch is her biological father, yes. But there's another issue that may or may not be connected." Nick explained about Catherine's role in the Delmar Gainey case. "Last night someone entered her lab and assaulted her. Earlier today, we found her assistant murdered in her apartment."

Raymond sat forward. "You think it's the same suspect?"

"It seems too much of a coincidence to believe they're

unrelated, and all this happening the day after she came to see me." He glanced back at the door to make sure he'd closed it when he came in. "What I'm about to tell you can't leave this room. It involves Catherine's work and the coroner hasn't made any of this public."

Raymond looked uneasy. "Go on."

"If you've kept up with the Gainey case, you know that fourteen sets of remains were found on his property. The news reports would lead you to believe that all the victims were brutally tortured while in captivity and then stabbed repeatedly before they died. That was Gainey's MO. But one of the victims was shot."

"And you think that's significant?"

"It breaks a pattern," Nick said. "No stab wounds, no sign of torture. By all indication, this Jane Doe was a healthy young woman until someone shot her in the back of the head. Either she was trying to run away or someone executed her."

Raymond said quietly, "Someone?"

"I don't think she was killed by Delmar Gainey. I think whoever murdered her knew about Gainey. She was buried on his property so that if the remains were ever recovered, the police would assume that she was another of his victims."

"That's a pretty big leap," Raymond said. "You're suggesting someone let a serial killer go free just to cover his own tracks."

"People get desperate. You have to admit, it would be the perfect cover. According to Emmett, Gainey was never on the police's radar."

"You've talked to Emmett about this?"

"A little. He seemed to know something about the Gainey case. He said Gainey had never been stopped for so much as a traffic violation. But someone knew about him. I think the person who broke into Catherine's lab was looking to verify that his victim had been recovered with the other Jane Does."

Raymond pondered the possibility. "Why would he take such a risk after all this time? He had to know that someone might see him."

"Maybe he was afflicted by the same compulsion that drives a murderer back to the scene of his crime," Nick said. "He probably thought the lab would be empty, but Catherine stayed late that night. She never got a look at his face because it happened during the blackout."

"Then why go after the assistant?"

"That's what I'm still trying to work out," Nick said. "It's possible she was the one who gave him access to the lab. If that's the case, then he's tying up loose ends. Getting rid of anything or anyone that can link him to the Jane Doe. Which means he'll try to get his hands on any evidence that was recovered from the gravesite."

"Was evidence recovered?"

Nick hesitated. "That I don't know."

Raymond got up and paced to the window. He stared out for a moment, in deep thought, before turning back to Nick with a pensive frown. "You weren't kidding when you said you'd opened a can of worms."

"No, but maybe I'm overreaching. Overthinking. Maybe I'm crazy to try and link up all these threads. But I know in my gut that something more is going on than Catherine's adoption. I'm hoping my visit with Finch will shed some light."

"Be careful, Nick."

"Don't worry about me. Emmett has already warned me about allowing myself to be manipulated by a psychopath."

"I'm not talking about Finch. I'm talking about you. Some cases aren't worth what they cost you. The things you uncover…the things you have to do." Raymond turned back to the window. "Some of them you don't come back from."

CATHERINE STOOD AT the window watching the night sky. A halo encircled the moon. The refracted light heralded another storm. She hoped the bad weather held off until morning. She didn't relish another blackout. The dark hid too many bad people. Too many evil deeds. She understood now the panic that had consumed the city during Orson Lee Finch's bloody reign, when even the smallest sound or movement must have struck terror into every young woman's heart.

She glanced over her shoulder; she couldn't help herself. Her gaze moved across the living area into the kitchen and then down the short hallway to the bedroom. The door was open and a lamp glowed inside. She'd left a light on in the bathroom, too. The whole apartment was well lit, the front door locked tight and the windows closed against the night air. She was up in the trees. Safe and sound from any intruders. She could keep watch all night, if need be. No one could approach the steps without her seeing them.

Even as she braced herself for a long, sleepless night, she had to stifle a yawn. Exhaustion had set in hours ago. Weariness tugged. She told herself she should go to bed. Nothing was going to happen. But as tired as she was, she still fought sleep. The night terrors were only an arm's length away tonight. If she closed her eyes, they would come. Already she could feel an icy tingle at the base of her spine and a strange prickling across her scalp.

She'd been battling the sensation ever since Nick left, although she told herself she was just unnerved by the day's events. Who wouldn't be? She'd tried to comfort herself with a normal routine—an early dinner, a long shower and then a bit of reading before bedtime. But the disquiet had been insidious. It had crept along her nerve endings, raising chill bumps on her arms and undermining the calming effect of the wine she'd had with leftover pasta. Closing her laptop, she'd risen from the couch and paced to the window where she had remained nearly motionless for the last ten minutes.

Her gaze dropped to the garden. The streetlights filtered over the wall so that she could see all the way across the backyard into her landlady's screened porch. Palmettos stirred in a mild breeze. Gardenias gleamed in the moonlight. If she opened the door, the scent would invade her senses, but she did not move.

Even so, the dreamy fragrance seeped in through the glass, evoking strong emotions and conjuring vague images. She turned away from the window, away from the shivery nudge of something she didn't want to face. She had no recollection of the time before her adoption. She'd been far too young. She wanted to believe the nebulous images meant nothing. Her imagination had taken those old newspaper clippings and pieced them together with her lifelong fear of the dark to create a sinister past—the ultimate child of Twilight.

But if her connection to Orson Lee Finch was nothing more than a flight of fantasy, then why had he made contact? Why had he taken it upon himself to warn her about whom she should trust?

She toyed with her ring as Finch's warning came back to prod her. *Aidan March found out the hard way that people with dark secrets never go down without a fight.*

Plucking the photograph of her parents from the bookshelf, Catherine placed it on the coffee table so that Aidan and Laura March's smiling faces were turned toward her. Then she lay down on the couch and pulled a light throw over her legs. She told herself she would just close her eyes for a moment while her guardians watched over her. After she rested for a bit, she would go back to her vigil at the window. She wouldn't sleep. Nick might call. The night terrors might come. She wouldn't sleep.

But exhaustion weighted her lids. All too soon she sank down into a dreamy haze, searching through her memories and probing along the edges of her subconscious until those vague images took on sharper form and substance.

She pulled the blanket to her chin and settled more deeply into sleep. She was no longer in her apartment but somewhere dark and scary. There was a little girl in her dream. Was she that child?

She could hear the familiar creaks and pops of an old building, but the traffic noises that sometimes kept her awake were muted. Her breath came in terrified gasps.

Mama?

Hush, baby. Mama's right here. I need you to be quiet, okay? Stay in the closet until I tell you to come out.

Dark.

I know it's dark, but we're going to play a game. Crawl way back into the corner and don't make a sound. Hurry now! We don't have much time!

Mama!

It's okay, it's okay. Take your dolly with you and hold her tight. I have to leave you now. It'll be even darker when I close the door, but don't be afraid.

Mama! Mama!

Shush. You have to be quiet. No matter what you hear, don't come out. Do you understand me? Don't come out!

The door closed and the child was alone in the dark.

A part of Catherine's brain was cognizant enough to realize that she was lost in a dream. She knew that dark, scary place wasn't real. Maybe the child wasn't real, either.

Yet she could feel the hard floorboards beneath her huddled form. She could hear the rasp of her shallow breaths.
A loud crash sounded somewhere in the apartment and
her pulse jumped. Then all was silent.

It was warm in the closet. So hot that sweat trickled
down her back and dampened her pajamas. She lay very
still, clutching her dolly until the heat became unbearable.
Until the noises subsided and her fear gradually turned
into curiosity.

Then she crept from her hiding place and pressed her
ear against the door. All was quiet on the outside.

She opened the door a crack and peered out.

The lamp was off in her tiny bedroom, but enough light
filtered in from the street that she could see the familiar
lines of her furniture. She could even make out the storybook pictures on the wall and her music box on the dresser.
Every night at bedtime, Mama wound the key. The melody
would fill the room while the tiny ballerina spun and spun.
The music brought sweet dreams, Mama said.

The child wished that she could wind the music box
now. The apartment was so quiet and she was so scared.
Where was Mama?

She slipped across the room and listened at the bedroom
door. No sound came to her from the other room. Mama
wasn't watching TV or listening to music. She wasn't crying, either, like she sometimes did. There was no sound at
all. Nothing but that terrifying hush.

Standing on tiptoes, she turned the knob. The door
clicked open. She didn't call out for Mama now. An instinct
warned her to silence. She clapped a hand to her mouth.

Mama lay on the floor facing the bedroom. She was
very still, her eyes open, her skin as pale as Dolly's. The
carpet beneath her was dark with something wet. Something red.

Someone stood over her. A stranger...

The child let go of the knob and eased back into the bedroom. Her chest hurt and tears burned her eyes. She couldn't remember ever being so frightened. She wanted to run into Mama's arms more than anything at that moment, but she couldn't. The stranger would hurt her if she made a sound. She had to be quiet. She had to stay hidden.

She climbed upon a chair and grabbed the music box from the dresser. Then she eased herself down and dashed into the closet, dropping to her knees to crawl back into those dark, closed depths.

She hugged Dolly tight as she opened the music box, but she didn't dare turn the key. She could hear the music inside her head, though, and she pretended to hum along to drown out the quiet.

Footsteps sounded on the wooden floorboards. They moved slowly around the room before pausing outside the closet door.

She hummed silently, louder and louder.

The door creaked open and the light came on.

She didn't stop humming until someone stood over her. She slowly lifted her head.

Her mother's killer stared down at her.

Chapter Fourteen

Catherine awoke with a start. Panic bloomed in her chest and a scream clawed at her throat. For a moment, she thought she was still hiding at the back of that closet and she put up her hands as if to ward off something—someone—frightening. Then realization slowly dawned. She was in her own apartment. Safe and sound and all grown up. She'd fallen asleep on the couch.

It was just a dream.

"It *was* just a dream," she whispered aloud, as if to bolster her conviction.

Not a memory, but a nightmare.

She rolled onto her back and stared up at the ceiling. Already the images were fading. The harder she tried to recall the disturbing vision the hazier it became, like writing in sand. Only a vague imprint remained.

Picking up the beloved photograph, she pressed it to her heart as she imagined Laura March's soothing voice in the quiet. *There's nothing to be afraid of, Cath. See? No monsters hiding in the closet. No creatures lurking under the bed. Would you like for me to read to you until you fall asleep? Here, snuggle up close. Poor baby, you're trembling. What happened to you, I wonder. Never mind that. You're safe now. That's all that matters.*

How long had she been out? Catherine wondered. It seemed as if she'd just closed her eyes, but when she checked the time on her phone, she realized nearly two hours had passed. How could she have fallen so deeply asleep after everything that had happened? What if someone had tried to get in the apartment? Did that explain the loud crash she'd heard in her dream? What if someone was out there right now, lurking in the garden and staring up at her windows?

She threw off the blanket and rose, taking a quick glance around the apartment before returning to her vigil at the window. A few clouds had moved in, drifting across the lower edge of the moon and partially obscuring the halo. But it was still bright outside. She skimmed the garden, peering into all the dark corners as she poked and prodded the shadows. Even as she searched the night, she told herself she was overreacting. Caution was one thing, but paranoia could be dangerous. It was time she got over her fear of the dark.

She glanced at her phone again, checking for texts and recent calls. Nothing from Nick. Nothing from anyone. She told herself that was a good thing. No reason to call if all was well. No reason for her to call him, either. *Let him enjoy his grandmother's party.*

She started to turn away from the window when something down in the garden caught her eye. She stared for a very long time, thinking that she'd only imagined movement. Or else the wind had stirred a tree branch. *No one is out there. Come away from the window.*

But she remained motionless, her gaze locked on the garden. Just inside the gate, a silhouette took shape. Catherine stared and stared, telling herself again that it was just a bush or a tree. A figment of her imagination. But the form was unmistakably human—hunched in the shadows. Head tilted toward her window.

Catherine jerked back from the glass. She'd turned off the overhead light in the living room earlier, but a lamp glowed from a nearby table. She reached over and pressed the switch, allowing the darkness to hide her.

For all she knew, she could be in grave danger. No one without dire purpose would trespass on private property, let alone take such care not to be seen. The intruder's dark clothing had melded so seamlessly with the night that even now Catherine couldn't help but question whether or not she'd actually seen anyone. She hadn't made out facial features. Had only a vague impression of stealth.

She eased up to the window, fingering back the curtain so that she could peer out without being seen. *Where are you? Who are you?*

Her mind conjured Emily's bedroom. She imagined a knife in the intruder's hand, blood lust in his eyes...

She clutched her phone. *Call Nick. Call 911.*

She did neither, not because she was frozen in fear but because the presence strangely intrigued her. Catherine had no idea why, but she no longer felt frightened. Visions of blood and gore vanished as an imagined voice whispered in the dark, *Hush, baby. Mama's right here.*

NICK SAID GOOD-NIGHT to his mother and then made the rounds before he left. He called Catherine as he walked back to his car. She answered on the first ring.

"Everything okay?" Nick asked anxiously.

She waited a beat before answering. "I'm fine."

"You hesitated. Are you sure you're okay?"

"I thought I saw someone down in the garden. It could

have been my imagination. Things have been so crazy lately. But what if someone really was watching my apartment?"

Nick's grip tightened on the phone. "Did you call the police?"

"I didn't want to bring them out on a false alarm. I've been standing guard at the window. I haven't seen anything else."

"I'm leaving the party now," Nick said. "I'm coming straight to your place."

"You don't have to do that."

"Yes, I do. This isn't about your fear of the dark or your ability to take care of yourself. I know you're more than capable. This is about me, okay? My peace of mind."

She sighed. "I don't really believe you, but I'm grateful for your concern. I'll be waiting."

"Catherine?" Now Nick was the one who hesitated. "We need to talk."

"About the case?"

"Yes. I haven't been completely honest with you. There are things going on that you should know about. They may not mean anything. I hope they don't. But you need to know just the same."

He heard a slight catch in her voice. "That scares me a little."

"It'll be okay. We'll figure things out. I'll be there in a few minutes."

He slipped the phone in his pocket as he left the driveway. Another vehicle was parked up the road. He gave the gleaming silhouette a cursory glance as he unlocked his door. Then he paused and turned back. The car looked familiar, but he didn't think the luxury sedan belonged to any of his relatives. Maybe to a friend or a neighbor. He hadn't known everyone at the party.

Nick scanned his surroundings. The road was clear. Odd that the driver had parked so far away.

He kept watch from his periphery as he walked toward the vehicle. If anyone came out of the woods, he didn't want to be caught unaware. He wasn't the type to let his imagination get the better of him, but a brutal murder that might or might not be connected to his investigation tended to make him cautious.

The windows in the sedan were tinted. He couldn't tell if anyone was inside until he was upon the car. Then he walked to the rear of the vehicle and got his phone back out to illuminate the plate. The digits matched Louise Jennings's car.

He stood back in contemplation. Why would Catherine's aunt be at his grandmother's birthday party when both Emmett and Jackie Morris had claimed not to know her?

Angling the beam toward the ground, he noticed a set of footprints in the soft shoulder. He flicked the light into the trees. He'd grown up at the house in town so he wasn't that familiar with the country property, but he remembered a footpath that led back to the pond. He searched until he found the trail and then he put away his phone, using only the light of the moon to guide him.

He moved as quietly as he could, but the layer of dead leaves rustled beneath his boots. As the trees thinned, he could see the shimmer of moonlight on water. Near the pond two women stood talking. A third person came out of the woods from the direction of the house. When the man turned, he saw that it was his dad.

Stunned, Nick moved in as close as he dared. A twig snapped underfoot and he froze as all heads turned in his direction.

"What was that?" Louise Jennings asked nervously.

"Probably just a deer," Raymond said. "They come to the pond at night."

"Are you sure you weren't followed?"

"Followed from my own house? I doubt it." Raymond's tone held an edge that was unfamiliar to Nick. He barely recognized his dad's voice. "You're the one who needs to be careful. What were you thinking, coming out here in the middle of a family party? If someone spots you, your presence won't be so easy to explain."

"It wouldn't have been necessary if you'd taken my calls."

"I didn't take your calls because we all had an agreement, remember? You were never to come to my home or place of business. We were never to have contact of any kind."

"I tried to remind her of that," Jackie put in. "For all the good it did me."

"Things have changed," Louise insisted.

"Nothing has changed," Raymond said firmly. "We swore we would never talk about that night. We put it behind us. We all moved on. As far as any of us are concerned, it never happened."

"But it did happen," Louise said. "And now your son is poking around in our past. Sooner or later he'll start putting the pieces together."

Raymond turned to glance out over the pond. "I don't think so. We had a long talk earlier. He's making some connections, but he doesn't know anything yet."

Louise moved up beside him and placed her hand on his arm. "Then I suggest you shut him down before he does."

Nick could see his dad's profile in the moonlight. He might have been a stranger standing there, colluding with the others. "How do you propose I do that?"

"He works for you, doesn't he?"

"I know my son. If he's pressured to drop the case, he'll just dig harder."

Her tone turned coercive. "Then give him a reason not to. I don't mean anything specific, but a general suggestion that it would be in everyone's best interests to let sleeping dogs lie."

"You mean make him choose between his family and his conscience? I won't do that to him. I won't put that burden on his shoulders."

Louise dropped her hand. Anger and fear crept into her voice. "What's the alternative? That we stand by and let everything we've worked so hard for come tumbling down around us?"

"We keep our heads," Raymond said. "We don't do anything rash."

"Or we could just tell them the truth," Jackie suggested.

Louise whirled. "That's not an option and you know it. Tell her, Raymond."

He took a moment before he answered. "If we don't panic, this could all blow over. There's no proof. We didn't keep anything from that night." He turned to Jackie. "You got rid of everything, right?"

Now Jackie paused. "Don't I always follow orders?"

He ignored the tinge of bitterness in her voice. "Then there's nothing to worry about."

Nick didn't dare move in any closer for fear of giving himself away. But another twig snapped nearby and his pulse jumped. Someone else was in the woods.

His father left the women and moved to the edge of the trees. "Who's out there?"

No one answered. There was no sound at all except for the breeze rippling through the trees.

Nick remained motionless, his senses on full alert. He

could have sworn someone was watching him through the trees. *Who are you? Where are you?*

"Best you go now," Raymond said to Louise. "Make sure no one sees you drive away." He turned to Jackie. "You go back to the party and wait for me there."

"What are you going to do?" Louise asked anxiously.

"I'll take a look around and then I'll go back to the house, too." Raymond peered into the trees, his eyes steely in the moonlight.

For a moment, Nick could have sworn their gazes collided in the dark.

"ALL CLEAR," NICK said a little while later as he came back up the steps to Catherine's apartment. She'd watched from the porch as he made the rounds through the garden and the alleyway in the back. Now she moved inside and he followed.

"I told you on the phone it may have been my imagination," she said. "I fell asleep on the couch and I'd just woken up. Maybe that shadow in the garden was still part of my dream."

"I don't think it was a dream or your imagination," Nick said as he closed the door. "You still seem pretty shaken up."

She rubbed her arms against a lingering chill. "I had a nightmare. It was unlike any dream I've ever had before."

"Do you want to talk about it?"

The concern in his eyes touched her. "It was just a dream."

"Are you trying to convince me of that or yourself?"

"Honestly, I don't know. There was a child in the dream. A little girl. She was hiding in a closet. When she came out, she saw her mother bleeding on the floor and someone standing over her. The child ran back to the closet and crawled to the very back, but he found her anyway."

"He?"

"Her mother's killer."

He gazed down at her tenderly. "You think you were that child?"

His tone melted her. From the moment she'd walked into his office with a box of old clippings and the farfetched notion that she was the daughter of a serial killer, Nick had remained open-minded and nonjudgmental. He had always been willing to listen. "I know it was a dream and yet it seemed like a memory."

"Dreams can seem all too real," he said.

She sat down on the edge of the couch and picked up the photo of her parents. "It was disturbing. I'd rather believe it was just a dream."

Nick sat down across from her. "Tell me about the shadow you saw in the garden."

"There's nothing to tell. It's possible it was just a bush or a tree, but it seemed to have substance and form. I could have sworn I felt eyes on me in the dark."

"Why didn't you call me?"

"I didn't want to bother you at your grandmother's party and, as strange as it sounds, I wasn't really frightened. I told you once that I've had these odd moments in my life. A feeling that someone is watching over me."

"And you think this watcher is your biological mother?"

She shook her head sadly. "Not anymore. I think she's dead, too. But I keep going back to that music box. It was in my dream so it must have been important to me. Who else could have known about it?"

"Your biological father?"

"Finch." She said his name with a deep shudder. "I'd almost managed to put him out of my mind. Strange, since he's the reason I came to see you in the first place."

"A lot's happened since that first day."

"Yes. Poor Emily." Catherine rose and paced to the window.

"What do you see out there?" he asked.

"Nothing but darkness and shadows." She pressed her forehead against the cool glass. "You said on the phone you needed to talk to me about something."

Nick got up and came to stand beside her. "I searched my uncle's office this morning."

She turned in surprise. "Why?"

"I've had the feeling all along that he hasn't been truthful with me. I don't think any of them have been completely honest. Not Jackie, not your aunt, not even my dad."

"Your dad? You talked to him tonight? Did you ask him about the number on the business card?"

"He said the writing wasn't his."

"Do you believe him?"

"There was a time when I would never have thought him capable of lying to me." Nick stared out into the darkness. "I don't know what I believe anymore."

"Did you find anything in your uncle's office?"

"There was a label stuck to the paper shredder blades, like he'd put a file folder through. The name on the label was Aidan March."

Catherine jerked around. "Why would he have a file on my father?"

Nick switched up the question. "Why would he have a file on a murdered cop?"

She put her hand on his arm. "Nick, what's going on?"

He shook his head. "I don't know. But the reason you came to me in the first place was because of my dad's phone number on that business card. The connection was there from the very beginning and yet so much of what we've learned still doesn't make sense to me. Like why your aunt met with my dad and Jackie Morris in private tonight."

"They did?"

He looked grim. "I overheard enough of their conversation to know that they've been hiding something for years. They've been lying to both of us ever since you found those newspaper clippings."

Catherine stared at him in shock. "You saw them all together tonight?"

"Yes. I have no idea what's going on but I intend to find out."

"Even if it involves your father?"

Nick's gaze intensified. "Do you trust me?"

She answered without hesitation. "Yes."

He searched her eyes as if looking for the confirmation he needed. "I've suspected Emmett and Jackie were keeping something from me, but my dad... I've always looked up to him. Admired and respected him. But the man I saw tonight was like a stranger."

Catherine said softly, "That must be hard for you."

"It's not pleasant."

"You keep telling me that I can drop the investigation anytime I want. The same goes for you, you know. You can walk away from this."

"I did that once. Put family before justice. It wasn't that I turned a blind eye exactly. I just never bothered to look because I didn't want to know the truth. I didn't dig because I was afraid of what I might uncover. I lost my self-respect when I walked away from the police department. I won't do that again. Not to myself and not to you."

"Nick." She said his name on a breath.

"You shouldn't look at me that way."

"I can't seem to help myself tonight."

He muttered something under his breath. "We agreed this wasn't a good idea, remember?"

She nodded. "But you're going to kiss me anyway."

"I know."

There was no teasing this time. No playful back and forth. He was all business. The way he backed her against the wall. The way he captured her hands above her head.

He kissed her until her heart thudded and her knees grew weak.

He kissed her all the way down the hallway to her bedroom. Kissed her as he slid off her top and then pressed her back on the bed to tug off her jeans.

Then he dropped to his knees and pulled her to the edge of the mattress, kissing her so intimately she gasped in shock and threw back her head as she shuddered.

Rising, he whipped off his shirt, but when he reached for the button of his jeans, she pushed his fingers away and undid the waist slowly as she gazed up at him. Then came the zipper. Then *him*.

She kissed. She teased and tasted as he plunged his fingers in her hair.

She fell back against the bed and drew him into her. Her heart pounded like crazy. Her breath came in tiny gasps. She clenched the sheets, clutched his shoulders. She couldn't get close enough, couldn't get enough of him.

When it was over, they fell back against the pillows and laughed in that awkward, wondrous way of new partners.

"Wow," he murmured.

"I know."

They turned to face each other, still smiling.

There was no talk of Nick leaving. No discussion about what it all meant. Just a knowing intimacy that gradually faded into deep contentment.

After a while, Catherine rolled over and tucked his arm around her breasts. Her eyes grew heavy and she fell into a dreamless sleep.

Chapter Fifteen

Orson Lee Finch was a small, wiry man with an unassuming yet fastidious demeanor. He was clean-shaven, his prison uniform smoothed out and tucked, his hair freshly buzzed. Out on the street, his nondescript appearance would never be noticed, but through the Plexiglas partition, Nick detected the gleam of a sly intelligence in his eyes.

He gave the inmate a nod as he picked up his handset. "I'm Nick LaSalle."

"I know who you are, young man. You look just the way I pictured you."

Nick didn't know if that was a good thing or not. He'd seen photographs of Finch, but the images hadn't prepared him for a face-to-face meeting with the notorious serial killer. Nor had their previous conversation primed him for Finch's formal manner of speaking. He didn't look or sound like a monster capable of butchering young women, but a jury of his peers had found otherwise and Nick's guard went up.

"Thank you for agreeing to see me. And for making the arrangements so quickly."

"It was in both our interests to do so, Mr. LaSalle. Or may I now call you Nick?"

"So long as you remember we're not friends."

"I'm not likely to forget. I don't make friends easily, although there have been strong bonds over the years, even in here."

"Hard to survive on the inside without them, I'm told."

"That was once true, but I've been in here for a long time. No one bothers with me anymore."

"That's a good thing, I guess."

"Yes, although the isolation can get lonely at times. I don't have many visitors these days. Real visitors. Writers and reporters request interviews, as does the occasional FBI agent. I sometimes see them out of boredom. Your visit is different. There is a reason I was eager to meet with you. We have a lot to talk about."

Nick nodded. "Let's get to it then. You already know why I'm here."

"You want a DNA test to prove that I'm not Catherine March's biological father. We aren't related, but I doubt either of you will accept my word. So I'll submit to any kind of test you like, but I need something from you in return."

Nick braced himself. "What is it?"

"I don't know Catherine March personally. I've never met the young woman. But I was close to her mother, Laura, and I made her a promise before she died. I'm asking you to help me keep that promise."

Nick stared at the man through the partition. "How did you know Laura March?"

"We were family. Once my mother passed, Laura was the only blood relation who ever gave a care to my predicament. We were cousins several times removed, but we became quite close after my incarceration."

"What about your daughter?"

Finch's gaze flickered. "I don't have a daughter."

"A lot of people have thought differently over the years."

"If I could control what people think, I wouldn't be in this place."

"That's a fair point," Nick said. "Will you tell me more about your relationship with Laura March?"

"I saw her only a few times as a child. Our families barely knew each other so we lost touch over the years. I never expected to see her again, but she came to see me after the arrest. She told me that she had been following the case closely and that she was convinced of my innocence. Even after I was sent here, her faith in me never wavered. Can you imagine how much that meant to someone in my position?"

Nick thought about his conversation the evening before with his father. "I have some idea. What about her sister, Louise?"

"I've seen her only once since we were children. She came to tell me in person of Laura's passing. I was grateful for that, but the visit was hardly selfless. She also wanted an assurance that I wouldn't reach out to Catherine."

"Why?"

"She didn't want Catherine's career or personal life tainted by association with the Twilight Killer. At least that's what she said."

"But you don't believe her?"

Finch paused. "I will only say this about Louise Jennings. Even as a child, she had none of her sister's kindness or compassion. Laura was...angelic. That may sound overly sentimental, but she was truly someone special. She reminded me of my mother." He fell silent again as the eyes behind the wire-rimmed glasses glittered.

Nick told himself not to fall for the emotion in the killer's eyes. People like Orson Lee Finch were notoriously good actors. That was what made them so dangerous. "You said you made a promise to Laura before she died."

"I promised I would look out for her daughter. That I

would do everything in my power to keep Catherine safe. I see that surprises you."

"Given your circumstances, yes."

He smiled for the first time. "Guardian angels come in many different forms, Nick. Some of them even have prison tattoos."

"Be that as it may, I'm not sure I'm buying what you're trying to sell me," Nick said. "If Laura March thought her daughter needed protection, why didn't she go to the police?"

"Because her husband was a cop and he ended up dead when he started looking into Catherine's background."

Nick frowned. "You're saying he was murdered by someone connected to Catherine?"

"I'm saying you can't trust anyone."

Nick lowered the phone while he digested everything Finch had told him. Why the implication about Aidan March's death came as such a shock, he didn't know. He'd been toying with a similar theory for the past two days. If true, the repercussions were huge. Nick was on the right track, but where that trail led filled him with dread.

He lifted the phone. "How do I know you're telling me the truth?"

"Why would I lie? Laura March was my cousin and my dearest friend. Is it so hard to accept that she would confide in me? That she might actually value my unique perspective?"

"I guess not. You seem like a personable, intelligent guy." Sociopaths were often charming and persuasive. "I am surprised that Catherine never knew about your relationship, though. If you were as close as you claim, why did Laura never say anything?"

"She thought it too dangerous. She never even let on that she had doubts about her husband's death. She only told me because she knew she could trust me. She knew that I would have the resources to help her if and when the time ever came."

"Did she know anything specific about Aidan March's investigation?"

"Only that he had stumbled upon something while working undercover. He found out about a young woman and her child who had gone missing just days before Laura's sister had approached them about a private adoption."

Nick sat forward. "Are you telling me Louise Jennings was somehow involved in Catherine's adoption?"

"She wasn't just involved," Finch said. "She's the one who made all the arrangements."

Nick gripped the receiver. "That would explain why she's been dead set against my investigation."

"She has a lot to lose. They all do."

"They?"

"Louise didn't instigate the adoption on her own. She had help."

Nick thought again about the business card with his father's private number on the back, the meeting at the pond he had overheard the night before. "Who helped her?"

"That's for you to uncover. But think about this while you continue to dig—Laura had suspicions about the adoption from the very first, but she kept them to herself because she didn't want to lose her daughter. After her husband's death, she stayed silent because she feared for the child's safety. She didn't dare confide even in her sister." Finch leaned in, his eyes intense. "These people have kept their secret for over a quarter of a century. Now that you're closing in, they are undoubtedly desperate and dangerous. One of them is a killer. I told you from the first, there is far more going on than you realize."

IT WAS LATE afternoon by the time Catherine heard back from Nick. She'd been working in the lab all day with Nolan. Other than a few cursory exchanges that morning, they hadn't talked about Emily. Instead, they had both settled into work, keeping their heads down and their thoughts occupied.

Nick wouldn't say much about his meeting with Finch, only that he would fill her in once he got home. In the meantime, she should remain cautious.

"I have a few stops to make when I get back to town," he said. "But I'll see you back at your apartment tonight."

Tonight. At her apartment.

Catherine shivered as she slipped the phone in the pocket of her lab coat.

She'd gone into her office to take the call, and when she returned to the lab, she found herself gravitating to the remains of Jane Doe Thirteen. The skull gaped up at her. The bones called out to her.

"Dr. March?"

She glanced up to find Nolan's gaze on her.

"Are you okay?" He looked worried. "You had the strangest look on your face just now."

"I was just thinking about Thirteen. About all of them, really. Wondering if anyone is still out there looking for them."

"I don't think anyone ever looked for them," Nolan said. "Not even the police."

Catherine nodded. "You're probably right. We can't do anything about that, but we can at least honor them by finding out their names. Giving them back their identities. Making sure they aren't reburied in unmarked graves. We owe them that."

Nolan watched her intently. "You really love this job, don't you, Dr. March?"

"Yes. It's all I've ever wanted to do."

"Then you're lucky." He took off his glasses and scrubbed the lenses. His naked eyes looked watery and distant. "Most of us won't be so fortunate. We'll end up teaching and writing papers. Withering away from boredom in some dark, cramped office."

"I still teach," Catherine said. "And in case you haven't noticed, my office is pretty cramped."

"But you also have this." He waved a hand around the lab. "Positions like yours are few and far between. I've been thinking a lot about what you once told us. Our career path is fiercely competitive. In any given year, there are far more graduates than jobs so we have to be willing to work twice as hard as anyone else. We have to be insanely dedicated." He put back on his glasses and peered across the room at her.

"You're not having second thoughts about your career choice, are you?"

"Let's just say I'm contemplating my options." He pushed back his stool and stood. "No one ever leaves a job like this voluntarily."

The way he looked at her...the slight shift in his posture...

Alarm tingled at the base of Catherine's spine. She told herself she'd imagined the sinister note in his voice, the cunning gleam behind his glasses. She'd known Nolan for years. He was intense and driven and he definitely marched to the beat of his own drummer, but he wasn't dangerous. She would have seen signs before now.

Still, she found herself gripping the edge of the table. "I wouldn't worry. You'll have plenty of opportunities. Your classroom and lab work are impeccable. You're naturally gifted. One of the most talented students I've ever worked with."

He tucked back his curls. "More talented than Emily?"

"That hardly matters now, does it?" Catherine's gaze flitted to his hands. How was it she'd never noticed before how long his fingers were? How slender and strong they seemed? She imagined them curled around a knife handle and her heart started to pound even though she told herself again she was being silly.

"Still, I'd like to know," he said. "If a position had become available—let's say, if your job opened up for whatever reason—who would you have been inclined to recommend as your replacement?"

"The question is moot. Emily isn't here and I'm not going anywhere. Let's just get back to work. Or, better yet, call it a day. It's late and you've been here since early morning. Go home and get some rest."

"It's later than you think, Dr. March."

She tried to keep her tone even. "What do you mean?"

He lifted his gaze to the ceiling. "Everyone upstairs will have gone home by now and the security guard won't make his rounds for another few hours. We're all alone down here." Slowly, deliberately, he started toward her through the maze of tables.

Catherine straightened. "Nolan, what are you doing?" She put up a hand. "Stop right there. This isn't funny. You're making me nervous."

"I'm not playing games, Dr. March. I'm deadly serious."

"Nolan—"

"Don't beg. It won't do any good and it'll just make us both uncomfortable."

"I'm not begging."

Admiration sparked in his eyes. "You're brave. I didn't take that into account before. I underestimated your quickness, too, and your strength. I won't make that mistake again. You've done well, Dr. March. You should be proud. You've taught me a lot about preparation and the need for improvisation."

She slipped her hand in her pocket and felt for her phone. "What are you saying, Nolan? You're the one who attacked me?"

"I'm saying it's a dog-eat-dog world out there. Sometimes you have to make your own opportunities. I eliminated the competition. Now I have to create a job opening."

Catherine stared at him aghast. "You did that to Emily?"

"Don't worry. She didn't feel a thing. I'm not that much of a monster." He ran a slender finger along a skeletal arm. "Not yet anyway."

A wave of nausea rolled over Catherine. She willed away the dizziness as she focused in on Nolan. She knew this young man. Knew what made him tick. If she could keep her cool, she could outsmart him.

He shook his head as if he'd read her mind. "You underestimated me, too, Dr. March. I was always the better student. Smarter than anyone in any of your classes and I worked twice as hard in the lab. And yet Emily was always your favorite."

"That's not true. I gave you both the same opportunities." Catherine backed into another table. "Think about what you're doing. Emily is dead. If you kill me, who do you think the police will come looking for?"

"They may come looking, but they won't be able to prove anything. I'm very persuasive in case you haven't noticed." He kept advancing little by little. "I'll come out of all this a victim and the job will be mine for the asking."

"I wouldn't be too sure about that. You still have to kill me first."

"I'm not going to kill you, Dr. March."

"Then—"

"Oh, make no mistake, you are going to die tonight, but it won't be by my hand. You see, someone else wants you just as dead as I do and we have an agreement. All I have to do is leave the door open."

He moved quickly then, shoving tables into one another until they pressed up against Catherine, pinning her between the metal surfaces. In the split second it took for her to push back, he whipped out an aerosol can and sprayed something into her face. Fiery needles pricked her skin and eyes. In that first moment of intense pain and panic, she thought he had doused her with acid.

Eyes squeezed closed, she lashed out blindly, but he was on her in a flash, holding her against the floor and then pressing a cloth to her mouth and nose until the room spun and the world went black.

As soon as Nick got back in town, he drove straight to the office. He'd planned to go out to the country to confront his father, but when he called, Raymond had suggested they meet at the agency.

Nick came in the back way, expecting to find Jackie at her desk. The lobby was empty and he thought at first the building was deserted. Then he heard voices coming from the second floor. He climbed the stairs slowly and approached the open door of his office with apprehension.

Raymond was at the window staring out. Jackie stood behind Nick's desk. She jumped when he cleared his throat. "Nick! I didn't hear you on the stairs."

His gaze dropped to the music box on his desk. "What are you doing in here, Jackie?"

"We were just…" Her words trailed away helplessly.

"You have a key to my desk, I take it."

"I'm sorry, Nick. There is an explanation, but I'm not

the one you should hear it from." She glanced at Raymond. "I'll just leave you two alone."

"Dad?"

"Come in and take a seat, son."

"I'd rather stand until you tell me what's going on."

Raymond turned back to the window. "It's a long sordid story, I'm afraid."

"I'm listening."

"You were in the woods last night, weren't you? How much did you hear?"

"Enough to be concerned. Enough to know that you've been keeping secrets." Nick shoved his hands into his pockets. "I'm surprised you agreed to see me when I called. Last night you seemed to think this would all blow over. Whatever this is."

Raymond turned with a slight smile. "I know you too well, Nick. You would never let this go."

"Then maybe you should just tell me the truth."

Raymond leaned a shoulder against the window frame. With the late afternoon sun streaming in through the glass, he resembled his brother, more so than Nick had ever noticed before.

"You know your uncle," Raymond said. "I told you before that he wasn't well regarded in the police department. He was always pushing boundaries, always crossing lines. Those rumors about shakedowns and bribes…" He sighed. "Probably more truth in them than I wanted to believe, but he was my brother."

"You turned a blind eye," Nick said. "I know a little something about that."

"He came to me one night, desperate and panicked. He'd gotten into trouble with some very bad people. A waitress at some dive bar had witnessed something. He wasn't very specific. I figured it had been a payoff. He found out where she lived and went to warn her that she needed to get out of town, but he was too late. There was blood on the floor and the woman was missing. He found a child hiding in a bedroom closet. He was already panicked so he grabbed her. He was afraid she'd seen something, too, and the bad guys would come back and find her. He came to me that night, as he always did, to help clean up his mess."

"What did you do?"

"We took the child to Jackie. This was before she came to work for us, of course, but we were friends even back then. She and Emmett had dated for a while. The relationship didn't work out, but she'd remained close with the family. She agreed to keep the child until we could figure out if there was a father in the picture or some other relative that could take her in."

"It never crossed your mind to file a report?"

"A lot of things crossed my mind that night," his dad said. "But my primary concern was to keep that child safe."

"And your brother out of trouble."

Raymond closed his eyes. "I should never have protected Emmett. Not that time, not any of the other times, but I didn't want him to get blamed for something he didn't do. With his history, no one would have believed him. There wasn't a cop in the city who would have taken his side."

"So what did you do?"

"We went back to the apartment," Raymond said. "From everything we could glean from the landlord, the woman and child had lived alone. There wasn't anyone else in the picture. He assumed from our questions that the mother was in some kind of trouble with the law. He said she was behind on rent and had likely skipped town."

"And you let him believe it."

"It made things easy. We cleaned up and left. I've told

myself all these years that we did the right thing that night. We saved a child's life. If we'd turned her over to Child Protective Services, what chance would she have had? You've seen what happens to so many of those kids that come up through the system. We gave her a fighting chance."

"You believed what you wanted to believe," Nick said. "How did Louise Jennings get involved?"

"I knew her slightly through Jackie. They were friends and I'd heard about some of her work through the grapevine. She knew how to facilitate private adoptions."

"Private or illegal?"

"Both."

"You didn't think it a risk to place the child with Louise's sister?"

"At the time, we didn't know about the sister. We were told the child would be placed with a family out of state. We never had a clue until Aidan March came around asking questions."

"He was the one who wrote your number on the business card," Nick said. "How did he know about you?"

"Charleston is a small town in many ways. He would have heard about our agency through mutual acquaintances."

"How much did he know?"

"He had a hunch, but nothing concrete. He was just starting to put it together when he was shot."

"A timely execution," Nick said.

Raymond's expression hardened. "I had nothing to do with his death. Cleaning up my brother's messes was one thing, but I would never knowingly be a party to murder."

"Knowingly?"

Raymond let out a sharp breath. "All this time, I believed the story unfolded just as Emmett had said. I even managed to convince myself that Aidan March's death was a tragic coincidence. He was in a very dangerous business and he'd made a lot of powerful enemies. It was just a matter of time before one of them came looking for him. Then last night you said something to me that made this whole house of cards come tumbling down."

Nick watched his dad, watched the creases and worry lines deepen around his eyes.

"What did I say?" Nick asked quietly.

"You told me about the Jane Doe with a bullet hole in her skull. I remembered something Emmett said to me once. It was during the Twilight Killer case. He told me he thought two serial killers were active in the city. One of them preyed on street people. Victims that no one would ever miss. He said if he set his mind to it, he could find that killer. He already had a suspect in mind. I thought he was just bragging. He was always so full of himself and police work was just a game to him. A means to an end."

"You think he knew about Gainey?"

"I think he must have suspected. I think he shot that girl in the head and buried her body on Delmar Gainey's property."

Nick stood. "Where is Emmett now?"

"He said something earlier about taking the boat out." Jackie had reappeared in the doorway. Nick doubted she'd gone far. Now she caught his arm as he started out. "Everything Raymond and I did was to protect that child. Louise, too. We didn't just give her a fighting chance—we gave her a loving home. Ask yourself this, Nick. Would she be the same woman she is today if we'd done anything differently?"

Nick was angry and sick of the excuses, but she gave him pause. "I don't know. You may have a point, but nothing about this sits right with me." He glanced back at his desk. "You left that music box on her porch, didn't you? Why?"

She lifted a shoulder. "I don't know. I just remember how scared and helpless she was. How lost she seemed. Maybe I saw something of that lost little girl when she came to the office to see you. The music box was the only thing that could calm her."

"Do you have any idea where I can find Emmett?"

"Check the marina," she said. "He may not have left yet."

His dad turned from the window. "What are you going to do?"

Nick glanced over his shoulder. "Has it not occurred to either of you that Catherine saw him that night? She's the only one who can identify her mother's killer."

"It was over twenty-five years ago," Raymond said. "People change."

"Not Emmett."

Chapter Sixteen

Chapter Sixteen

Catherine awakened to a rocking motion. The floor beneath her rose and fell and she could hear water sloshing nearby. Could feel a cool breeze on her upturned face. She opened her eyes and saw the gleam of eyes above her.

The man moved in closer and she gasped as she tried to scramble away.

"Nowhere to go," he said.

She glanced around frantically. "Where am I?"

"You're on *The Shamus*," he said. "We're at sea."

The last thing she remembered was being in the lab with Nolan.

Her eyes widened as it all came back to her. "Where's Nolan Reynolds?"

"Your little psycho assistant is back at the lab getting his story straight. Just so you know, I didn't have anything to do with what happened to that girl. I only wanted access to the lab. To you. The rest was his idea. He said she'd seen us together, but I think he was just looking for an excuse. I know a thing or two about compulsions and that kid's got some real issues. You're lucky he left you to me."

"Who are you?" Catherine pushed herself up and gazed around. Twilight had fallen. She could see nothing in any direction but dark water.

"Oh, come on," he said. "You must have figured it out by now."

She peered at him through the dusk as her skin tingled with awareness. "I've seen you before. I've dreamed about you." In the back of her mind, an image wavered. A terrified child, a dark closet, her mother dead in the other room. She could hear the faint strains of a music box as a killer stared down at her.

And then another image formed. The skeletal remains of a young woman who had been shot in the back of her head. That victim was Catherine's mother. Had a part of her always known? Did that explain her uncanny fascination with Jane Doe Thirteen?

Catherine jerked herself back to the present. "Why did you bring me out here?"

"I think you know why," Emmett LaSalle said as he drew his weapon. "I knew when you came to see Nick that first day that it would eventually come to this. Once you started looking into your past, memories were bound to come back."

"I was just a baby," Catherine said desperately. "If you'd stayed away from me, I would never have known who you were."

"How was I going to stay away when you and Nick were getting so tight? I know my nephew. Once he started digging, he was never going to stop."

"You think he'll stop now?" Catherine moistened her dry mouth as she eased away from him.

"He won't want to, but I'm family. Raymond will see to it that he does the right thing. I'll disappear for a while and let things calm down. By the time I come back, it'll be like it never happened." He motioned with the gun. "Get up." When she resisted, he said, "I don't want to mess my deck up, but I'll shoot you right here if I have to."

She scrambled to her feet.

"Now go over and kneel at the side. Face the sea."

Catherine hung back. "Why? So you can shoot me in the back of the head like you did my mother?"

"It'll be quick and painless that way. I know what I'm doing."

Catherine's heart pounded as she stared at him. "You'll never get away with it."

"That's what they all say. Now get down on your knees."

She clung to the rail as she lowered herself to the deck, gazing around frantically for a weapon. Far out to sea, she saw a twinkling light. She thought it was a star at first, but it drew closer as she watched.

"Someone's coming," she said.

"Right."

"No, I'm serious." She pointed to the light.

In the split second he took his eyes off her, she slipped through the rail and dove into the water. Deeper and deeper she swam to escape the barrage of bullets.

She wasn't worried about air. She could hold her breath for a very long time. She'd practiced as a child, hiding underneath the covers to wait out the night terrors.

When she finally surfaced, she could barely make out the silhouette of *The Shamus*. The boat moved steadily away from her. He must have thought she'd drown out here, miles from anywhere.

She treaded water and tried to determine the direction of land. Not that it mattered. She was a strong swimmer, but already her muscles were tiring. She floated on her back to rest. A spotlight moved slowly over the water. She thought at first *The Shamus* had turned, but then she remembered the twinkling light she'd glimpsed earlier. She waved her arms when the spotlight passed over her again, but she didn't call out. Sound carried on open water.

A motor started up. She followed the sound to a small boat heading straight toward her. She waved again and then treaded water until the hull swung around beside her. A pair of tattooed arms reached overboard to grab her.

The twilight had deepened while she'd been in the water. She could just make out her rescuer's longish hair, his lanky form, the piercing eyes that gazed down at her.

"Don't worry. You're safe," he said as he hauled her into his boat. "Finch sent me."

CATHERINE'S GUARDIAN ANGEL dropped her downstream with a cell phone and his well wishes.

"I don't even know your name," she said as she scrambled onto the dock.

"No worries," he said as he reversed the throttle. "It's better that way."

And then he was gone.

Catherine tried reaching Nick, but the call went straight to voice mail. She signed into her Uber account and called for a car. The driver arrived a few minutes later and they were on their way out of the marina when she spotted a commotion up ahead. *The Shamus* had pulled into a slip and was now surrounded by police cars and the harbor patrol. She could see Emmett LaSalle on deck arguing with two uniformed cops and a man she believed to be Nick.

She asked the driver to stop and then got out of the car and made her way through the crowd. She could hear Emmett's voice now. He was surly and indignant.

"Last time I checked, there's no law that says I can't take my boat out any damn time I please."

"Where is she?" Nick demanded. "If you've done something to her, I swear to God I'll kill you."

The officer put out his hands to hold each of them back.

"Okay, both of you, just take it easy. Mind if we take a look around your boat?"

Emmett swept his hand out across the deck. "Be my guest. I've nothing to hide."

"We'll see about that," Nick said.

"I haven't done anything wrong. You'll have a hard time proving otherwise."

"I can prove it," Catherine called out as she shouldered her way through the crowd. Dripping and shivering, she stood at the edge of the dock and gazed up at Nick.

Her dramatic entrance caught him off guard for only a moment, but it was the advantage Emmett had been waiting for. He slipped underneath the railing and leaped to the dock, grabbing Catherine around the neck and thrusting a gun to her temple. Someone screamed as the crowd scattered. Nick jumped off the boat after his uncle. The police officers surrounded them with drawn weapons.

"Let her go," Nick said. "It's over and you know it."

"Give me your car keys," Emmett demanded. "Now!" Nick took out his keys.

"Hand them over slowly. Don't try anything cute."

Nick tossed them just out of Emmett's reach. They landed with a plop in the water.

"You son of a bi—"

Emmett's grip eased. Catherine caught Nick's gaze. He nodded imperceptibly and she dropped. Emmett grabbed for her, losing his balance, and Nick lunged. They toppled backward into the water. A shot went off. Another. Catherine scrambled to the edge of the dock in terror. She couldn't see anything in the murky water.

Finally, Nick's head broke the surface and he hauled up his uncle. The police took custody of Emmett as Nick hitched himself out of the water. Catherine went straight into his arms.

He held her close. "I thought you were—"

"It's okay. I'm okay. But, Nick… Nolan was in on it. He killed Emily."

"I know. He's in custody lying through his teeth, but another grand entrance from you should shut him up. I know what happened to your mother, too." He pulled away and cupped her face. "I know everything, Catherine. We've got a lot to talk about, but it'll have to wait."

"I'm not going anywhere, ever."

"Neither am I. When this is all over—"

She clung to him. "I know, but for now just kiss me."

He complied as the moon rose over the watery horizon and the first stars began to twinkle through the clouds.

"Now, *that's* a moment," she whispered.

* * * * *

DESPERATE MEASURES

CARLA CASSIDY

Chapter One

"And the winner of this year's most innovative design in the Kansas City area goes to Jake Lamont of Lamont and Star Architects Incorporated," the emcee for the night announced.

Jake rose as the people in the ballroom stood and clapped. He pasted on a fake smile, the same one he'd been wearing for the past couple of years, and made his way to the podium to retrieve the large shiny trophy.

He wove through the white-draped tables holding the remnants of a dinner that had consisted of a piece of dry chicken with a strange, mysterious green sauce over the top and potatoes and purple cauliflower on the side.

The meal had been horrible. The night already seemed endless, and he knew after the official itinerary was over there was still a cocktail party that would be filled with congratulations and glad-handing.

He should be thrilled with the recognition he'd just received, but it was an empty victory without

Suzanna standing by his side. Unfortunately, she couldn't stand beside him because she was dead. He shoved these painful thoughts away as he accepted his award with a short speech.

Twenty minutes later he stood in a circle of other architects talking about the huge renewal projects taking place in the Kansas City downtown district.

"I've got to admit it, your building at Tenth and Main is a real visual beauty," John Davis said. "And you're working on another one, aren't you?"

Jake nodded. "Third and Main is also mine."

"That's going to be some addition to the skyline," Richard Burke said. "What is it? Eighteen…twenty stories high?"

"Actually, it's twenty-two stories," Jake replied.

He stiffened slightly as Tim Lathrop joined the group. Jake and the dark-haired man with his cold blue eyes were often in competition for a job, and Tim had a reputation for not always playing nice.

"You know that award should have gone to me," he said.

"You can take it up with the members of the committee if you think a mistake was made," Jake replied.

Suddenly he was exhausted. He was tired of the fake smile he'd sported all night long. He wanted to rip off his gray-and-black tie and get out of his black suit and into something casual. The polite social chatter was wearing on him. He had so many other important things on his mind…things like murder.

It took another half an hour before he finally took

his leave. He stepped out of the building where the celebration had been held and into the oppressively hot late-August night air. He made his way to his car parked down the block and as he walked he yanked to loosen the tie around his neck.

He couldn't wait to get home in his own space. All he wanted at the moment was a drink and his recliner, where he didn't have to smile or interact with anyone.

This was the first real social event he'd attended in the past two years and he'd found it beyond exhausting. He wouldn't have attended at all if it hadn't been for him receiving an award.

He'd only gone a short distance when a female voice called out from behind him. He turned and saw a petite, dark-haired woman hurrying toward him.

He frowned. She looked vaguely familiar, but he couldn't quite place her and in any case had no idea what she wanted with him. She wasn't one of the attendees of the night's festivities, for instead of wearing a cocktail dress she was clad in tight blue jeans and a royal blue tank top.

Despite her casual dress, she was quite attractive, but when she drew closer to where he stood beneath a streetlamp, recognition slammed into his gut.

Monica Wright. Oh, hell no. What was she doing here? The last person he wanted anywhere in his life was the investigative reporter with her popular podcast. And why did she want to speak to him?

"Mr. Lamont, could I just have a moment of your time?" She finally reached where he stood.

Despite his initial impulse to turn and hurry away, he smiled at her and played dumb. "And you are…?" He looked at her quizzically.

"Monica Wright of *The Wright News* podcast." She offered him a bright smile.

He'd found her attractive when he occasionally tuned in to her podcast, but in person she was even prettier. She was petite and shapely. Her eyes appeared more blue, a startling and beautiful contrast to her long dark hair. She had a heart-shaped face and full lips that were more than a little bit appealing.

"I see you brought home the big prize," she said with a gesture to the large trophy he held.

He relaxed. Maybe that's why she wanted to speak to him. "Yes, I'm very honored."

"The building you won for is a real beauty."

"Thank you. It's always nice when people recognize your hard work."

"And how did you feel when Max Clinton was murdered two nights ago?"

He stiffened, gut-punched by the unexpected question. "No comment." He turned on his heel and once again headed in the direction of his car.

"Mr. Lamont, I'd really like you to come on my podcast. I'm sure you have an interesting story to share."

She followed him like an annoying, yappy Chihuahua. "You must have some thoughts and feelings about Max Clinton being murdered by the Vigilante Killer."

Thankfully by that time he'd reached his car. He

opened the door. He then turned back to face her. "I told you no comment and that's all I have to say on the matter." He got into the car and slammed the door.

He ignored her presence as he started his engine and then roared out of the parking lot. He headed north and tried to keep his mind empty.

But of course, that was impossible. With a single question, Monica Wright had stirred up a lot of thoughts...all of them bad. Why had she singled him out? Had she talked to some of the other men who had found their personal justice through a pact forged in hell? How had she possibly learned about them... about him? The last thing he wanted was to get tangled up in any discussion concerning the Vigilante Killer.

Home was a four-bedroom brick house on an acre of land. He'd had it built three years ago. At that time, he'd believed the bedrooms would eventually be filled with children. He didn't believe that anymore. He hadn't believed in anything like happiness or family since he'd lost his sister.

He pulled into his garage and then entered the kitchen, where he placed the trophy on the countertop. Eventually it would find its way into his downtown office, but not right now.

The first thing he did was head to his bedroom, where he changed out of the suit and into a pair of jogging pants and a T-shirt. He went into the family room and to the minibar in the back corner. He poured himself two fingers of Scotch over ice, and collapsed in his black leather recliner.

He took a sip of the drink, leaned his head back and closed his eyes. Instantly, a vision of Suzanna filled his head. Whenever he thought of her, it was with her head thrown back and her eyes twinkling with laughter.

She'd been so beautiful, with her short dark hair and sparkling green eyes. She'd had an exuberance, a love of life that had been intoxicating to the people around her. She'd been the star in Lamont and Star. She'd been Jake's inspiration, his partner and his twin sister. And since her murder two years ago, Jake had been utterly lost.

He took another drink as his thoughts shifted to Max Clinton, the man who had killed Suzanna. He'd been Suzanna's boyfriend. He should have been her champion, the man who had her back, and instead he had beaten and strangled her in a fit of jealous rage. Unfortunately, his lawyer had managed to put enough doubt in the minds of the jury that he'd walked away a free man.

How did he feel when he'd learned that Max was the latest victim of the person the news had labeled the Vigilante Killer? He'd felt so many emotions that it had been difficult to sort them all out.

There had been the intense relief that Max Clinton would never again be in a position to hurt another woman. There had also been a renewed grief as Max's murder had caused a rush of memories to torment him…memories of his beautiful sister's life and torturous memories of the brutality of her death.

Two nights ago, Max had been killed by the Vigilante Killer, who liked slitting his victim's throats and then carving a deep V into their foreheads. Some would call Max's death karma, but Jake knew better.

Max's murder had come out of a meeting of Jake and five other grieving, angry men who had entered an agreement that assured them each a place in hell.

Finally, Max's murder had evoked a chilling, confirming fear as Jake recognized that he and those men had unleashed a monster on the community.

MONICA CURSED BENEATH her breath as she slit the tip of her finger on a piece of paper. So far, she was having a horrible morning and it was only nine o'clock.

She'd been up far too late the night before, waiting for her police department source to return her call. She wanted anything new he might have on the Vigilante Killer. Unfortunately, he hadn't returned her call.

Then first thing this morning her single-serve coffee machine had gasped and sputtered and refused to give up a cup of coffee. Her shower had spurted out only a trickle and had reminded her she'd been meaning to buy a new shower head. And when she walked outside to retrieve her morning paper, she stepped squarely in a pile of fresh dog poo.

And now this…a tiny cut that hurt like hell and refused to stop bleeding. She grabbed a tissue from the box on her desk and wrapped it around her finger, then leaned back in her chair and released a sigh of frustration.

And the source of her frustration wasn't the events of the morning, but rather that she hadn't been able to get Jake Lamont to be on her podcast that evening.

He would have made a compelling guest. He was the only surviving member of his family after his twin sister had been brutally murdered. The alleged perpetrator had walked scot-free and then two years later was murdered by a killer who seemed to be on a bloody journey of justice denied in the Kansas City area.

So far the police had admitted this particular killer had murdered four men, each of whom had been suspects in heinous crimes and each of whom had walked free due to glitches in the judicial process. And the killer seemed to be on a fairly fast track—four kills in less than two months and with no end in sight. So far he'd left no clues behind for the authorities to follow.

Monica wanted to be the one to break the case wide open. It was a lofty aspiration for a woman who had a nightly news podcast with just over twenty thousand subscribers and news that focused on the Kansas City and surrounding areas.

She wanted to break the case not only in hopes of expanding her visibility, but also to quiet the self-doubt that had driven her for most of her life. She needed to prove to her father that...

She jumped as her landline rang. She never answered this phone. It was a tips line of sorts that she advertised each evening when she ended her show.

So far, she'd received eleven marriage proposals, countless invitations to be a baby mama and several phone calls that had offered her the chance to be involved in strange sexual situations.

Lately she'd also been getting calls from Larry Albright, a local contractor. Monica had done an exposé on him three days ago when it came to light that he was scamming people out of thousands of dollars.

In the past two days he'd left dozens of nasty and threatening messages for her. She now chewed on the nail of the index finger that didn't have the paper cut on it as she waited to see who was calling this time.

"Hi, Monica. My name is Janet McCall. You don't know me, but I'm a huge fan of yours. Uh…but that's not why I'm calling. I know you've been asking for any information anyone might have concerning the Vigilante Killer."

The woman paused and Monica leaned forward, the paper cut on her finger forgotten. "This might be nothing at all and I could be wasting your time. I run the Northland Survivor Group and I just thought it was an odd coincidence that the Vigilante Killer has killed four men who perpetrated crimes against four of the men who attended my group for a short period of time."

Monica picked up the phone. "Janet, it's Monica Wright."

"Oh… I didn't expect to speak to you in person." She released a nervous laugh. "I'm a huge fan of yours."

"Thank you, I appreciate it, but I want to make sure I understand what you're telling me."

"Okay…hmm…according to the reports, the Vigilante Killer's first victim was Brian McDowell, who beat Matt Harrison's mother to death. The second victim was Steven Winthrop, who raped and killed Nick Simon's wife. The third kill was of Dwight Weatherby, who killed Troy Anderson's daughter, and now this fourth victim was Max Clinton, who beat and strangled Jake Lamont's sister. Matt Harrison, Troy Anderson, Nick Simon and Jake Lamont all belonged to the Northland Survivor Group for several months and then they all stopped coming to the meetings about the same time."

There was a long pause as Monica slowly digested the information. Janet gave another small, nervous laugh. "That was clear as mud, right?"

"Not at all, I'm just trying to wrap my mind around it," Monica replied. "Have you spoken to the police or any of the authorities about this?"

"No. I didn't really know if the information meant anything or not."

"Right now I don't know, either, but I'd like a little time to check into it before you give it to the police," Monica said.

"Of course," Janet replied slightly breathlessly. "So you think this might mean something?"

"To be honest, I don't know, but I really appreciate you bringing this to me."

Minutes later, Monica reared back in her chair, her mind racing with the information she'd just been given. Was it just a coincidence that the Vigilante Killer had murdered the bad guys of four men who attended a small survivors' group?

There were dozens of survivors' groups around the Kansas City area, yet according to what Janet had just told her, the Vigilante Killer had focused in on this particular group. Why?

And now she had another reason to talk to Jake Lamont. Although she couldn't see how this information worked in the puzzle she was trying to piece together, it definitely warranted further exploration. And that's what she did for a living.

For the rest of the morning she worked on the material for her podcast that night, and then she left the house to shop for a few groceries and to buy a new coffee machine. There was no way she was going to go a full day without her coffee.

It was nearly three by the time she got back home. The whole time she'd been shopping, her brain had worked overtime on the information Janet had given her. She made herself a cup of coffee and once again sat in her office chair.

Rather than thinking about the killer, she found herself thinking about Jake Lamont. He was definitely one hot hunk of a man. His suit had fit perfectly over his broad shoulders. His dark hair had been slightly shaggy and his eyes had been the deep green of a primal forest.

She'd come home the night before and had done a

search on him. She'd learned that he was single and a successful architect. She'd reread articles about his sister's murder, and she'd also used a search engine that had provided both his work and home phone numbers and his home address.

At four she left her small ranch house and drove the fifteen miles to where Jake Lamont lived. She had no idea what time he got home from work. She didn't even know if he did work today, considering it was Saturday. But she intended to go to his house and try to talk to him again.

She especially wanted to speak to him now, armed with the new information she'd received from Janet. If he wasn't home when she arrived, then she intended to be there waiting for his return.

She still hoped to get him on her evening podcast and now she also wanted to ask him about the time he'd spent at the Northland Survivor Group and the other three men who had attended with him.

Jake's house was a large, beautiful brick with a huge bay window in the front. The lawn was neatly manicured, with trimmed bushes and flowers surrounding a beautiful fountain. Both the oversize plot and the expanse of the house whispered of money and success.

The first thing she did on arriving was knock on his front door. When there was no answer she assumed he wasn't home, and she pulled out of his circular driveway and parked down the street where she could see him when he arrived.

She'd taken him by surprise last night. She was

hoping tonight he'd be more willing to talk with her. She'd just settled in to wait when her cell phone rang. There were only a few people who had this number.

Looking at the caller identification, her stomach instantly clenched tight with a familiar stress. "Hi, Dad," she answered.

"What are you doing?" Neil Wright's deep voice boomed over the line.

"I'm working."

Her father's dry chuckle twisted the nerves in her stomach even tighter. "I was hoping by the time you hit thirty you'd put that podcast silliness aside and get a real job."

"Dad, this is a real job," she replied, knowing it would do no good. She'd been a disappointment to her father since the moment she'd been born a girl instead of a boy.

She was the youngest of three girls and according to her father, was the last chance for him to get the son he'd desperately wanted.

It hadn't been so bad when her mother had been alive to soothe the hurt her father sometimes caused, but her mother had died from breast cancer when Monica had been eight.

"So, what's up?" she now asked.

"I'm heading out early in the morning for a day of fishing with Harry and Frank, but those parts I ordered for my truck came in at the Liberty location so I was wondering if while you're out running around tomorrow, you could pick them up for me."

Monica stifled a deep sigh. "Sure, I can do that."

"Great, just drop them off in the garage. I'll be home late tomorrow night."

When the call ended, she released the sigh she had stifled moments before. Her father often asked her to run errands for him and to her it was just another indication of how little he respected her and her job.

She knew she could gain his respect if she went back to school and became a nurse or a lawyer, like her two sisters had become.

But news was her passion and she absolutely loved what she did. Always in the back of her mind was the notion that if she became big enough, if she reached a certain number of followers or one of her stories got picked up by a national news source, maybe then she'd be good enough for her father to love.

All insecurities and thoughts of her father flew out of her head as Jake Lamont's car passed hers and turned into his driveway.

She started her engine and followed behind him, her heart beating with the excitement of a potential story. He stopped outside his garage door and got out of his car.

She quickly parked behind him and did the same. Good lord, the man had been a hunk in his suit last night, but he was even hotter in his jeans and a navy T-shirt that showcased his muscled chest and flat abdomen.

"You're trespassing." His handsome, chiseled features were taut with obvious anger.

"I thought with a night to think about it, maybe

you changed your mind about being on my podcast." She offered him her most charming smile.

"My mind hasn't changed," he replied, and headed toward his front door.

She followed closely behind him. "Since the latest man murdered by the Vigilante Killer is tied to you and your sister's death, I'd really like to get how you feel about the murder on the record."

"What don't you understand about no comment?" he replied tersely. He unlocked his front door and then turned back to look at her. "And now it's time for you to get off my property."

"Just one more thing," she said hurriedly. "Can you confirm to me that you attended meetings at the Northland Survivor Group at the same time Nick Simon, Troy Anderson and Matt Harrison attended?"

He appeared to freeze. Once again he turned to face her. The anger that had ridden his features appeared to relax. "Okay, I'll give you five minutes. Come on in," he finally said, and to her surprise he opened his door wider.

Chapter Two

She'd shocked him. How in the hell had she managed to learn about the four men attending the Northland Survivor Group together? And what other information might she have?

His need to know what she knew was the only reason he invited her inside. Watching her podcast the few times he had, he'd recognized she was tenacious and ambitious…two dangerous traits when it came to her digging into the Vigilante Killer case.

He guessed the killer was one of two men, but he needed to know what Monica knew about the case, because if the truth came out he'd be charged as an accomplice.

Keep your friends close, but keep your enemies closer, he told himself as he ushered her into his family room. "Drink?" he asked as she eased down onto his sofa and he walked over to his minibar in the corner of the room. Maybe he could get her relaxed enough she would give up all the information she'd already gleaned about the case.

She gazed at him with a sudden wariness in the

depths of her amazing blue eyes. "I just want you to know that my producer and my cameraman are in a car just up the street. Warren and Wally always have my back and they know I'm here. And with that said, I'd love a cold glass of water."

What did she think? That he'd invited her inside to kill her? He had no idea if she really had a Warren and Wally just waiting to run to her rescue, but he certainly had no intention of harming her in any way.

He handed her a glass of ice water and then carried his Scotch and water to the recliner chair opposite her. "Let's get one thing straight right now—I'm not going to be on your podcast," he began. "But I'll tell you off the record how I felt when I learned that Max Clinton was murdered by the Vigilante Killer."

"Do you mind if I record this?" She pulled a cell phone out of her oversize bright red purse.

"Actually, I do mind," he replied. He didn't want anything about this on tape. "I told you this was off the record. Besides, I'm not sure you need a recording for what I'm going to tell you. When I heard that Max Clinton had been murdered I felt nothing except for a bit of relief that he would never harm another woman again."

"Yes, I'm so sorry for your loss," she replied.

He nodded and for just a moment his thoughts were filled with Suzanna. They had always seemed to know what the other was thinking or about to say. "It's a twin thing," they'd say to their friends. He'd felt gutted since her death, as if half his soul had been stolen and would never be returned.

"And where were you on the night that Max was murdered?" Her question made the here and now slam back into him.

But, God, she was attractive. Today she was clad in a pair of black jeans that hugged her legs and a red tank top that matched her red heels and hinted at a bit of cleavage.

How many men had lost themselves in the depths of her blue eyes or in the utter charm of her smile and spilled their guts? She smelled of something citrusy with mysterious spices that were incredibly evocative.

"Where were you when Max was murdered?" she asked again.

He mentally shook himself and focused on the question, not on how sexy he found her. "I was at Doug's Tavern in a meeting with the mayor, half a dozen city councilmen and some local architects. We were discussing the renovation and renewal project going on downtown. Then I came back here and slept."

"Alone?"

He gave a curt nod. "Yes, I was alone." He knew Max's time of death was sometime between midnight and two in the morning. And that meant he had no real alibi for the time of the murder. He'd been questioned briefly by the police the day after the murder, but he hadn't heard anything more from the authorities.

"And how did you learn about Max's murder?"

"I read it in the newspaper like most of the people in Kansas City."

"Would you like to tell me something about your sister?" Her features radiated a soft sympathy.

Oh, he'd love to talk about his sister…about the loving, wonderfully magical woman she had been. But it would cheapen Suzanna to talk about her to this stranger who was only looking for her next scoop.

"No," he answered simply. "Why are you here talking to me?"

"When Max Clinton was murdered, and a V was carved in his forehead, I knew he was a fourth victim of this particular killer. The police tried to keep the V out of the new reports from the very beginning, but somebody leaked it to the press."

He looked at her in surprise. "How do you know that?"

"I have a friend on the police force," she replied.

"You mean you have a snitch."

"Friend…snitch…whatever you want to call him, he occasionally gives me a little inside information that keeps me up to date with what's going on with the crime in Kansas City. I also heard there's going to be a news conference tomorrow and the police are going to ask the community for their help in catching this person."

Interesting. Jake would definitely like to know what was going on in the investigation into the Vigilante Killer, and Monica Wright just might make an interesting partner of sorts.

"You still haven't told me what, specifically, you want from me?" he said.

"Initially I thought you would make a good human interest story for my podcast, but then I got a tip about you and the three other men attending the Northland Survivor Group."

"Who was your source for that?" he asked.

She smiled and her eyes gleamed with both intelligence and wit. "I don't give up the name of my sources. So do you know Nick Simon, Troy Anderson and Matt Harrison?"

"I do. You're right, we all attended meetings there around the same time, but what does that have to do with anything?"

"So it's just an odd coincidence that the killer has gone after the men who ruined all your lives?" She shook her head and once again her eyes shone with keen intelligence. "I'm sorry, but I don't believe in those kinds of coincidences. The killer seems to have a connection to the survivor group, and that means you might know him." She leaned forward. "If you know something about the killer, then please tell me."

"Why should I tell you anything?" he countered. "I don't even know you. You're just somebody who showed up unannounced on my doorstep."

"So why did you invite me?" she countered.

"Because you caught my interest when you mentioned the survivor group and the other men."

"Have you ever seen my podcast?"

He took another sip of his drink before replying. "I've caught it a couple of times."

"Then you should know I'm good at what I do. I dig into investigations and there's nobody in this city who wants to identify this killer more than me. I want this… I need this to prove to everyone that I'm here to stay, that what I do with my podcast is a real job." Her cheeks flushed pink, as if she hadn't meant to say so much. She leaned back.

He studied her for a long moment. "Then we both want the same thing. I want this killer caught and I intend to bring him down. He's obviously unhinged and enjoys killing, and I don't see him stopping any-time soon."

She frowned, the gesture doing nothing to detract from her attractiveness. "He's smart and he's thor-ough. He hasn't left a single clue behind for the po-lice to work with. They are frustrated by their lack of leads. Right now he's killing what most of soci-ety would deem bad guys, but that still makes him a murderer."

"I totally agree."

She gazed at him for a long moment. "What's your story? You're a successful, award-winning architect. What would make you want to suddenly become a killer-hunter?"

He certainly wasn't ready to trust her with the details of the murder pact six men had made in the woods behind an abandoned baseball field.

To give the information he had to anyone pre-sented a huge risk, not only to himself but also to the four other innocent men in the group. He felt responsible for the birth of the Vigilante Killer and he had to somehow figure out how to point a finger for the police. But first, he had to see which one of the remaining two men was the guilty one. And the only way to do that was to do some investigating of his own.

"Let's just say I feel a moral obligation to go after him," he finally replied.

She narrowed her eyes. "So you do know something."

"I might," he admitted.

Her eyes lit with an obvious hunger, and he momentarily wondered what it would feel like if her eyes lit up like that when she looked at him as a man and not just as a source for a big story.

"If we both want the same thing then there's no reason why we couldn't partner up. I can share with you all the information I have and you could share with me."

The offer surprised him. He had to admit there was a part of him that had longed to talk about what he knew with somebody. But he'd never dreamed he'd share any of this with anyone, especially not with an ambitious reporter.

"I need some time to think about it," he finally said.

"How much time?"

"I don't know…give me twenty-four hours." He wanted to stop the Vigilante Killer, but he'd certainly never thought about having a partner who may have some resources to help him achieve that goal.

She checked her wristwatch and then stood. "Okay, twenty-four hours it is. I've got to get home now to do my podcast."

He rose as well. "I hope nothing we discussed here is in your podcast tonight," he said as they walked to his front door.

"Contrary to what you believe about me, I know how to keep secrets. How can I catch up with you tomorrow?"

"How about you have dinner with me at D'Angelo's. Do you know where it is?" Even as he asked the question he wondered what in the hell he was doing.

"I do. What time is good for you?"

"Shall we say around six?"

She nodded and then smiled. "I'm looking forward to it."

"Tell Wally and Warren I said hi."

Her smile turned slightly sheepish. "Will do. I'll see you tomorrow." With that she turned and hurried out to her car.

He watched until she pulled out of his driveway and then he closed and locked his front door. His brain spun wildly as he returned to his recliner and picked up what was left of his drink.

What in the hell was he doing even thinking about sharing what he knew with her? And he'd definitely lost his mind in inviting her out to dinner.

If he was going to work with her in any way, it would be a fine line he'd have to walk to make sure he didn't incriminate himself or the others. But she was a wild card in this whole mess and he knew she wasn't going to stop digging. At least if he worked with her he might be able to guide her investigation on a path he wanted to keep it on.

Still, he had to remember that she would throw him under the bus in a minute to get her story.

IT WAS JUST after five thirty when Monica angled her car into a parking place down the street from D'Angelo's Restaurant. It was a popular place to dine with great Italian food and reasonable prices, but on a Sunday evening there would be fewer diners.

She'd come away from Jake's house last night with the gut-burning certainty that he had some knowledge that would help move the investigation forward.

There had been shadows in his deep green eyes that had whispered of secrets, secrets she definitely wanted him to share with her.

Had she worn her royal blue cold-shoulder blouse tonight because she'd had several people tell her she looked sexy in it? Had she decided to wear her black skinny jeans because she knew they hugged her thin but shapely legs? Was it all in an effort to use her womanly wiles on him?

Maybe, but she had to admit part of it was for him to see Monica Wright not just as a sharp investigative reporter, but also as a desirable woman.

Which was completely ridiculous. The very last thing she wanted in her life was a relationship that would suck time and energy away from her work, but there were times she was lonely. It was really rather silly, but something about talking to Jake the evening before had made her think about her loneliness.

Maybe it was because from the moment she had met him, butterflies had danced in her stomach. And she hadn't felt butterflies about any man in a very long time.

She raised a finger to her mouth and then dropped her hand back to the steering wheel. She was desperately trying to stop chewing her nails. It was hard to have pretty nails when you gnawed them ragged. Instead she now clicked them against her steering wheel as her thoughts continued to cascade in her head.

It's about the story, stupid. This had been her mantra for the last five years, when she had really gotten serious about what she wanted to do. The advertising on her podcast paid her bills, but she wanted more than just financial security. She wanted respect. And identifying the Vigilante Killer and being responsible for his arrest would gain her that respect.

This was the first case where she didn't just want to report the facts; rather, she wanted to make the facts. She wanted to hunt the killer.

It was definitely interesting to her that Jake had wanted nothing more than to kick her off his property until she'd mentioned the three other men and the Northland Survivor Group. He had suddenly become quite amenable after that.

He'd started out just being a possible human-interest story. Janet McCall's phone call had changed all that. Talking to him last night had also changed that. He was so much more than a human-interest story. She had a feeling he might be the key to discovering the identity of the killer.

Her clicking fingernails stopped and she sat up straighter in her seat as Jake's car pulled into a parking space on the opposite side of the street.

The butterflies took flight again in her stomach as he got out of the car and headed inside the restaurant. His black slacks fit perfectly on his slim hips and long legs, and he also wore a dark green short-sleeved shirt she knew would perfectly match his eyes.

She waited five minutes and then, ignoring the dancing butterflies, she got out of her car and headed for the restaurant's front door.

It was cool and semi-dark inside. Scents of garlic and onion and rich Italian spices filled the air, and soft music played overhead. A pretty, young hostess greeted her. "Hi, is there just one this evening?"

"No, I'm meeting somebody here. Jake Lamont?"

The hostess smiled again. "Oh yes, if you'll follow me."

The hostess guided her through the main dining room and into a smaller private room with a table for two.

Jake stood as they entered, and for just a brief moment she wondered what it would be like if he had gotten the private room because he wanted to know her hopes and dreams…because he wanted to spend time gazing into her eyes and whispering sweet nothings in her ear.

Of course nothing could be further from the truth. He'd gotten the private dining room because they had things to discuss, things like murder and a serial killer working in her hometown.

"This is nice," she said once the hostess was gone and the two of them were seated at the table.

"I figured it would be good to meet in a neutral place to have this discussion," he replied. "But how about we eat first and then talk about the main issue."

"That works for me," she agreed.

He gestured toward the menu. "I've already decided what I want," he said.

She opened the menu but as she read the offerings, she was acutely aware of his gaze on her. She made her decision, closed the menu and met his gaze.

He looked away and for a moment an awkward silence ensued. Thankfully a waitress entered the room and broke the silence.

She served them water and a mini loaf of garlic bread and whipped butter. She took both their drink and meal orders, and then left the room once again.

"How was your day?" he asked when they were alone again.

She looked at him in surprise. She couldn't remember the last time anyone had inquired about her day. "Do you really want to know or are you just being polite?" she asked.

"I'd really like to know," he replied.

"My morning was rough. Most of them are rough.

I'm not a morning person and everything that can go wrong in a day usually happens then. Yesterday my coffee machine quit working. I bought a new one and this morning I went to make coffee and realized I was out of pods."

A corner of his mouth lifted. "Sounds disastrous."

"Oh, trust me. It was. I am not a happy camper without my morning coffee. Anyway, the rest of my day was good. I'm working on several stories right now and things are coming together nicely on them. How did your day go?"

"It was quiet. I watched a little television and then sketched for a while. I hate Sundays, when the job site is closed down and there's nothing much for me to do."

"Do you have family here in town?"

"I don't have family anywhere," he replied. "My parents are gone and it was just Suzanna and me. What about you? Do you have family here?"

"My mother died when I was eight, but I have my father and two older, overachieving sisters. Addie and Elizabeth are the apples of his eyes."

"Which implies that you aren't?" He raised a dark brow.

"I've been his disappointment for years," she replied, and fought against a hurtful hitch in her heart.

Their conversation was interrupted by the arrival of their meals. He'd ordered the spaghetti and meatballs while she had opted for cheese ravioli. "Oh my gosh, this looks yummy."

"Can I cut you off some bread?"

"Yes, please."

He cut her a piece. "Butter?"

"Definitely," she replied.

He slathered the bread with butter and then handed it to her. As their fingertips touched, the butterflies in her stomach flew once again. Good Lord, what was wrong with her?

"I think Italian food is my favorite type of food," he said as he cut himself a piece of the bread.

"Italian is good, but Mexican is my very favorite," she replied. "There's nothing better than chips and salsa and cheese enchiladas."

For a few minutes they were quiet as they focused on their meal. On the one hand, Monica wanted to hurry up and eat so they could get to the conversation she wanted to have with him. On the other hand, there was a small part of her that wanted the meal to go slow so she could somehow pretend this was a normal first date between a man and a woman who were interested in each other.

Jeez, once again she wondered what was wrong with her. All she wanted from Jake Lamont was any information he might have about the Vigilante Killer. She wanted her big story, and that was it.

She had to stay focused and not get caught up in his beautiful green eyes with their thick dark lashes and the sexy slide of his lips curving into a smile. Okay, she found him vastly attractive, but she needed to maintain her emotional distance from him. She had to remember that he was nothing more than a means to an end.

"So, why news?" he asked as they continued to eat.
She shrugged. "Why architecture?"

"I loved the way buildings looked. I always knew
I wanted to design amazing buildings."

"And I was always fascinated with the women
reporters on the news. I studied them and tried to
figure out what made them popular. I always knew
I wanted to be an investigative reporter and really
dig into the stories I thought impacted the Kansas
City area."

"Why not work for one of the big networks?" He
cut himself off another piece of the bread.

"It's a whole new world. More and more people
are getting their news from alternative sources and
I wanted to be one of those alternative sources." She
offered him a smile. "Besides, I like being my own
boss. I don't always play well with others."

He raised a dark brow once again. "Ah, good to
know, especially when you want to partner up with
me."

"I'll let you in on a little secret about me…if
you're working with me, then I'll be the most loyal
person in the whole world to you."

"Now all I have to do is believe you."

"Trust me, you can believe me," she said fervently.
Their gazes locked for a long moment. She couldn't
tell if he believed her or not, but what she'd told him
was the honest-to-goodness truth.

It was she who broke the gaze, finding it suddenly
too probing…too intimate. "I'd go to prison before
I'd ever give up the name of a source. Despite my

ambition, I like to think I have a big streak of integrity inside me."

"Integrity is a good thing to have," he replied.

They finished their meals and he pushed his empty plate aside. "How about some dessert with coffee? I never miss a chance to have something sweet to finish off a meal."

She flashed him a cheeky grin. "Nothing I like better than chocolate and murder. Let's get to it then."

HE HAD TAKEN the last twenty-four hours to think about what he was going to tell Monica. Could he trust her? Even though he had absolutely no reason to, his gut instinct was that he could. After all, they both wanted the same thing.

Or maybe it was because he desperately wanted to trust her. He needed somebody like her to know what had taken place in the woods that night...in case something happened to him. If she ran directly to the cops with what he told her and he was arrested, well, maybe that was okay as well. Maybe it was exactly what he deserved.

He ordered tiramisu and she opted for chocolate lava cake. They both ordered coffee, and once they'd been served and were alone again, he studied her closely.

Was he deciding to trust her because she looked amazing in the sexy blue blouse that bared her slender shoulders and matched her eyes? Was he weakened by the fact that when she smiled at him a crazy warmth filled him? No, he wasn't that stupid. This was far too important to make that kind of a mistake.

It was the directness of her gaze and the honesty, and yes, integrity he sensed in her that finally made up his mind to confide what he could to her. Besides, he needed an insurance policy so that if something did happen to him she could take the information he gave her to the police and hopefully get the killer behind bars.

"Let's just assume there were six angry men," he began. "They had all suffered the loss of a loved one by bad men. Not only that, but due to jury nullification and technical glitches and other problems in the judicial system, those bad men all got away with their crimes."

He stared down into his coffee as he remembered the killing rage and grief that had made him half-crazed after Suzanna's murder. His rage had been further fired by the fact that Max Clinton walked away a free man.

He gazed back at her. "Anyway, these six men all found themselves at the Northland Survivor Group. They were all looking for ways to deal with their emotions. They were hoping to learn some new coping skills or something to help them with their overwhelming pain."

"And did they find what they needed?" she asked softly.

"No, they didn't. They met several times for drinks after the meetings, talking about their grief and their rage at the system, but they found no relief until they decided to hatch a plan."

Once again he paused, this time to take a drink of his coffee and eat a bite of his dessert. It was tasteless and he knew it was because his mouth was filled with the taste of grief and shame and the enormous bitterness of deep guilt.

He still couldn't believe he'd actually been a part of the plot they had all come up with on that crazy night. It had definitely been a moment of temporary insanity.

"Anyway," he continued, "the more these men all got together, the greater their anger grew." A knot expanded and twisted tight in his chest. "And then one night they all met in the woods next to an old abandoned baseball field. It was on that night they came up with a stupid plan."

This was the part where he had to get a little inventive in order to protect not only himself but the other men who had come up with what now was a horrendous plot. He definitely believed that one of them was the killer, but that meant he and four others were innocent.

"A stupid plan?" She put her fork down and stared at him intently.

He was afraid to tell, but there was also a part of him that wanted to spill his guts to her about everything…a part of him that needed to get this burden off his chest.

"You have to remember that we were all crazy

with grief," he said, as if that somehow mitigated what they'd planned to get the justice they all wanted.

"This is a judgement-free zone," she replied.

He released a deep sigh. "To be honest, I don't know for sure who came up with the idea, but it was planned that we would each kill another man's killer. For instance, I'd kill the man who murdered Nick Simon's wife. Nick would kill the man who beat Matt Harrison's mother to death, and so on."

He paused and watched her features carefully, seeking a sign of shock and revulsion. But none was there. All he saw was open curiosity.

"Looking back at that meeting in the woods, it seems like a bad dream, not something that really happened. But it did." He paused and drew a deep breath. "And we all walked away from that meeting thinking we were going to act on that plan. But when it came right down to it, I would have never been able to kill a man, no matter what heinous crimes he'd committed, and I believe the others were just like me. Don't get me wrong, the idea of the murder pact was appealing, but I didn't believe any of it would really happen."

The waitress's entering the room with a coffeepot interrupted the conversation. She topped off their coffee, and he handed her his charge card and then once again she left the room.

"Anyway," he continued, "I didn't believe any of it was really going to happen until the first man was killed." His chest tightened with tension as he remembered reading about the murder in the paper.

"Brian McDowell," she said. "He's the man who beat Matt Harrison's mother to death."

"Right. Nick Simon was supposed to kill him, but Nick didn't kill him, and that's when I believe the Vigilante Killer was born."

"So, you believe the Vigilante Killer is one of four men?"

"I don't believe that any of the men who got their so-called justice through the Vigilante Killer is guilty. I think the killer is one of the last two men. He's either Clay Rogers or Adam Kincaid."

"What are you going to do about it?" Her eyes were lit with an eagerness that made him second-guess his crazy decision to trust her.

Still, he figured in for a penny, in for a pound. "I've been thinking about it since Max Clinton was murdered." An idea had been whirling around in his head since the morning he'd read about Max's death in the paper. "I know all the murders have happened between midnight and two in the morning, so I figure the only way to identify the killer is to watch these two men during those hours until one of them makes a move."

"And then what?"

"Once I know for sure who the killer is, then I'll take him down. Hopefully I can subdue him and then contact the police. I need to get him behind bars." He frowned. "I think this person likes to kill, Monica. And the carving in the foreheads of his victims speaks of a bloodlust that is absolutely disgusting."

"I completely agree. There's only one thing I ask.

Once we identify the killer, I want time to break the story before anyone else gets it," she replied. Her eyes gleamed brightly.

He didn't miss her use of "we" in her sentence. "I can give you that," he replied. "But this is something I need to do for myself and there's no reason for you to get involved in this at all. I'll let you know when I have confirmation on who the killer is and you'll have your story."

"But I am involving myself. I want to be a part of this. Jake, I want to do the surveillance with you," she protested.

There was one more interruption by the waitress to bring back his receipt and credit card.

"Monica, this could be dangerous," he said once they were alone again. "Whoever the killer is, the last thing he wants is to get caught. He's ruthless."

"I know that, but think about it—two people are better than one. We could do surveillance from your car one night and then from mine the next night to make sure nobody gets suspicious. We can wake each other up if we drift off to sleep."

He shook his head. "I just don't think it's a good idea. One of the reasons I told you all this is that I want somebody else to know in case something happens to me."

"Why would something happen to you?"

"I don't know, but if this man is as ruthless as I believe him to be, then all the rest of us in the pact are loose ends. If he catches wind that I'm hunting him, then there's no question he'll come after me."

"I still want to be a part of this. I have the two names of the men you think it might be. I'll just conduct my own surveillance if I'm not doing it with you." Her chin shot up a notch and her eyes held a definite challenge.

"Don't make me regret I told you all this," he said. Damn, he should have never given her the names of the two men he suspected. That had been careless of him.

"Then don't try to cut me out of the action," she replied. She reached out and covered his hand with hers, the unexpected pleasant touch sparking an electric jolt in him. "Please, Jake. Don't try to shut me out of this." She pulled her hand back. "Why don't I plan on being at your house tomorrow night at eleven thirty and we can get started."

"Okay," he finally relented. The last thing he wanted was for her to go off all half-cocked and either screw things up or get herself killed. He already had enough guilt in his heart to last a lifetime. "Are you ready to get out of here?"

"I am," she agreed.

He'd already taken care of the tab, so they left the private room, walked through the main dining area and then stepped out into the hot night air.

"Hey, bitch," a deep voice shouted from behind them.

They both turned and Jake got a quick look at a dark-haired scruffy-looking man standing on the sidewalk. The man raised his hand and threw something.

Jake grabbed her to his chest and whirled her

around to protect her as a beer bottle shattered on the sidewalk next to them.

"What the hell?" With Monica behind him he turned to confront the man. But he was gone, the sound of his running feet on the pavement letting Jake know the man was retreating. A few moments later a car door slammed in the distance and then a car roared by them.

"Bitch!" the man yelled out of the window as he drove by.

"What was that all about?" he turned and asked Monica.

"That was Larry Albright. He's a local contractor I did an exposé on a couple of days ago. He had ripped off dozens of homeowners, mostly elderly people, by telling them they needed new roofs. He then not only overcharged them but also used substandard materials. Needless to say, he's not happy with my reporting."

"What's he doing? Stalking you?" Jake asked in alarm.

"Apparently that's what he did tonight."

"Have you called the police?"

"No, I don't think he's a real threat to me. And in any case, he's been charged with half a dozen crimes and he was released on his own recognizance. He knows one phone call to the police from me and he'll wind up in jail to await his trial. He's just blowing off some steam. And now, thank you for dinner, and I'll see you tomorrow night."

He watched as she walked to her car. She looked

gorgeous with the last gasp of sunlight playing in her dark hair. She walked with a sexy confidence despite the height of her heels.

Still, no matter how attractive he found her, no matter how eager she was or how much he implicitly trusted her, he couldn't help but feel this whole situation just might have disaster written all over it.

Chapter Three

"Join me again tomorrow night for part two of 'Gang Violence in Kansas City.' And as always, make sure you're getting the right news with Monica Wright."

She clicked off her microphone and camera and scooted away from the desk. This spare room in her house was her "newsroom." She had her high-dollar microphone, camera and computer. There were three televisions tuned to news stations. She also had a red, white and blue backdrop that looked professional.

Tonight she'd started a six-part investigative report on the growing gang activities in the area. Each weekend there were more shootings and more deaths, mostly happening in the south of the downtown area.

She'd been thrilled to snag an interview with a self-proclaimed gangbanger who, surprisingly, was an intelligent young man who had chosen a life as a dope dealer because he he'd seen no other future for himself.

A life of poverty and a lack of opportunity had stolen his hopes and dreams of a different kind of future. It had ended up being a compelling piece that she was proud of, but it was her plans for later that night that had her pumped up and excited.

Tonight she and Jake would begin their quest to catch a killer. A shiver of excitement worked up her spine as she changed from her business attire to a short-sleeved black blouse and black jeans.

There was no question that she'd been shocked the night before when he'd told her about the plan the six men had come up with. She'd been shocked and yet oddly humbled that he had decided to trust her enough to give her that information.

If she was a different kind of woman, a different kind of reporter, she could have taken what he'd told her and run with a sensational story of six blood-thirsty men on a quest for murder.

She was far more interested in the end game of getting a killer off the streets and in jail. Besides, she found it hard to believe that anyone could find six men, no matter how angry or how much they were grieving, who would actually commit cold-blooded murder.

The really big story would be identifying that killer and getting him arrested. That's what she wanted: the final story of a killer's end.

She especially didn't think Jake Lamont was the kind of a man who could murder another human being. Call it women's intuition or her hope that she was a good judge of character, but she didn't believe Jake Lamont had it in him to kill anyone no matter how crazy he'd been with grief and rage. Otherwise why would he have told her his story? Of course, she could always be wrong about him. Time would tell.

At eleven she packed some snacks in her purse, grabbed a small cooler that held several cold drinks and then went out to her car. As she walked in the darkness toward where her car was parked in the driveway, she kept an eye out for anyone else in the area.

Larry Albright's attack the night before had shaken her up more than just a little bit. She'd never had anyone she'd reported on come after her. What she'd told Jake was true—she didn't see him as a real threat—but still he'd surprised her by stalking her to the restaurant and throwing that bottle. She hoped that was the end of him bothering her.

She reached her car and settled in, confident there was nobody watching her. Once she pulled out and got on the road, she kept her gaze on the rearview mirror for several miles, but didn't see anyone following her.

She'd spent much of her day researching what she could find out about the five other men Jake had named as belonging to the group.

There had been two engagement announcements. Both Nick Simon and Troy Anderson had gotten engaged in the last month. She couldn't find much information about any of the other men, but she assumed Jake would fill her in about them tonight.

When she was about five miles from his house a new kind of excitement filled her. There was no question she found Jake attractive. She'd met a lot of attractive men in the past, had even dated a couple, but she had never allowed herself to get too close or emotionally involved.

It's about the story, stupid, she reminded herself. And over the next couple of nights hopefully she could get the information she needed to break the biggest story of her career.

Light spilled out of Jake's bay window. She parked in his driveway and then grabbed her things and headed for his front door. He answered on her first knock. He wore a pair of black jeans, a black T-shirt and a deep frown.

"I was hoping you'd have changed your mind about coming with me," he said.

"No way," she replied firmly.

"I still think this is a bad idea." His frown deepened.

"I don't know why," she replied. "Starsky needed his Hutch, Batman needed his Robin. Heck, even Turner needed his Hooch."

The corner of his lower lip curled up. "Hooch? Really?"

"Hey, you never know when you might need a big, slobbering dog. Woof."

His lips completed a full smile and then he shook his head. "I have a feeling this might be a long night."

She laughed. "Well, let's get this party started."

Minutes later they were in his car and headed to Clay Rogers's house. "Tell me about Clay," she said as she tried to ignore the very pleasant spicy scent of Jake's cologne.

"He works the financials at a car dealership. His girlfriend went out for a run one night and never came back. Her body was found the next day in a field. She'd been raped and strangled."

"That's tragic," she replied, unable to even comprehend the kind of pain such an event would cause in a loved one.

"Yeah, what's even more tragic is they found the killer by checking out video in the area. His name is Charlie Cohen. He was seen following her in his car and then parking and getting out of his car and chasing after her."

"Let me guess, for some reason he walked free."

Jake nodded. In the dim lighting from the dashboard his handsome features appeared grim. "He had a high-dollar lawyer who argued Charlie had just wanted her to make a phone call for him because he had a flat tire. There was no actual footage of him actually grabbing her, and the jury hung. The prosecutor didn't feel like he had the evidence to retry."

She fought the impulse to touch him, to reach over and stroke the tension out of his shoulders. "So you all not only felt the pain of your own loss, but it sounds like you shared each other's pain as well."

"We did." He released a deep sigh and some of the tension left him. "Clay was the youngest of all of us, and I liked him, but if he is the Vigilante Killer, then he needs to be stopped."

"And that's why we're in a car in the middle of the night," she replied.

They fell silent as they continued to drive the dark

streets to Clay's house. They had no idea when the killer would strike again, but Monica had a feeling it wouldn't be too long.

She believed Jake was right. This person liked what he was doing. It took a sick mind-set to slit somebody's throat, but that's how this man was killing his victims. And what was he going to do when he'd taken care of all the men who had wronged the six of them? Would he then move on to murder other people?

She sat up straighter in the seat as Jake slowed the car. He turned onto a tree-lined street. The houses were modest and most of them were completely dark at this time of night.

Jake pulled up to the curb and stopped the car. He doused his headlights and cut the engine. "That's Clay's house," he said, and pointed to the house on the opposite side of the street from where they were parked.

It was a small ranch house with a neat and tidy yard. It, too, was dark, but if he was the killer, it was possible lights could come on at any minute and he would leave the house with murder in mind.

"Might as well get comfortable," he said. He unfastened his seat belt and moved his seat back to give himself more legroom.

She did the same and then opened her purse. "Want some licorice?"

"No, thanks."

"What about some corn chips or spice drops or dried apple slices?"

He turned in the seat to look at her, his features barely discernible in the faint illumination from a nearby streetlight. "Do you really have all those snacks in your purse?"

"Ah, this isn't an ordinary purse tonight. It's a surveillance survivor kit. Not only do I have snacks, but I've also got antibiotic cream and bandage strips, a bottle of pain reliever and ChapStick just to name a few things."

"So I can eat spice drops while you bandage up a wound and make sure my lips don't get chapped," he replied.

"Exactly. See, this is why you need me with you for surveillance."

"I've got a surveillance kit, too," he said.

"Really? What do you have?"

"A flashlight and a gun."

His words instantly sobered her. This wasn't just two people sitting in a car in the middle of the night laughing and eating junk food. This was a potentially dangerous situation. If the murderer saw them watching him, she had a feeling he wouldn't hesitate to kill them.

"You do realize this could take more than a night or two," he said, breaking into her frightening thoughts.

"I know that, but I don't think it's going to be too long before he strikes again," she replied.

"I agree." He stared past her and toward the house. "It's also possible we're sitting on the wrong man. I hope it isn't Clay."

"Tell me about the other man… Adam Kincaid."

"Adam's wife was murdered after she withdrew two hundred dollars from an ATM. A drug addict pulled her out of the car and beat her for the money. She might have survived, but he slammed her head into the pavement so hard it killed her. Before it went to trial, the perp was offered immunity in order to bring down a drug ring operating in the city."

"My God, I can't believe how badly the justice system let you all down," she replied.

"Thank God cases like ours don't happen every day and for the most part justice prevails."

"Still, it's horrible how the six of you saw no justice," she replied. "It must have been incredibly difficult for you to know Max was still walking around free after he murdered your sister."

"It was difficult," he admitted.

Once again she fought the impulse to reach out and touch him. She could understand the grief and rage that all these men felt.

He grabbed a flashlight from the console. "I need to get out and check to make sure his car is in the garage. Otherwise he could already be gone, and we wouldn't know we were sitting on an empty house."

"No," she exclaimed, reaching out and grabbing hold of his arm. "I don't want you to do that. It's too dangerous."

"How dangerous could it be for me to just take a peek into the garage?" he asked.

"Lights could flash on and an alarm could sound.

Guard dogs could suddenly appear...dogs with big sharp teeth and trained to kill."

He gently pulled his arm out of her grasp. "If that happens, we implement plan B."

"And what's plan B?" she asked.

"You duck down and I run like hell."

HE GOT OUT of the car as silently as possible and for a moment remained in place and stared at Clay's house. Around him the night was silent other than the insects that clicked and whirred their normal night songs. The three-quarter moon overhead helped him see clearly.

But that also meant the moonlight might help somebody else see him. He looked at all the other homes, assured by the darkness within each one. Hopefully the occupants were all soundly sleeping and would never know that he had been here.

He didn't need his flashlight as he raced across the street and toward the doors of the two-car garage, which each held a small window. His heart beat a steady rhythm and the scent of freshly mowed grass filled his nose.

He reached the garage doors. A bright light suddenly bathed the area in front of the garage. His heart stopped. Was an alarm now ringing someplace inside the house? He took a moment to peek into one of the windows and then he took off running.

His heart beat so hard it felt as if it was going to burst right out of his chest. He didn't look back. He just ran. When he was three doors down from Clay's place, he spied a large tree and ducked behind it.

He drew in several long, deep breaths in an attempt to slow his heartbeat. Was this whole plan an act of stupidity? Maybe, but it was the only way he knew to identify the killer. And he felt morally responsible to do so.

Several minutes passed and the light over Clay's garage went off. There was no indication that anyone on the inside of the house had been roused out of sleep, no sign of anyone rushing to check things out.

A simple motion detector light, that's what Jake bet it was. Not an alarm or anything like that, just a light that came on to warn people away. A meandering cat or a dog could have set it off.

He waited another couple of minutes and then, assured that nothing more was going to happen, he raced back across the street and headed to his car.

Monica was hunkered down half on the floor, her eyes huge as he slid back inside. "Are we safe?" she asked worriedly.

"We're safe. You can get up now."

She settled back in the seat and released a deep sigh. "That was a little bit scary."

"I warned you this could get a little scary. Are you ready to let me do this by myself? I could still keep you informed when I manage to identify the killer."

"No way," she replied. "We're partners in this until the very end."

He'd half hoped that she would insist he take her back to her car and that she'd allow him to do this by himself. She was a bit of a distraction with her citrusy-spicy scent eddying in the air. He was far too conscious of her, not as a partner, but as a woman... a very desirable woman.

For the past two years he'd kept himself isolated. He'd shunned any kind of a social life and had focused only on his work. He would remain alone forever, as penance for the events that had unfolded on the night his sister was murdered.

Monica was the first woman in the last couple of years to tempt him just a little bit. He couldn't help but notice her petite but perfectly proportioned body. Her skin looked soft and touchable, and he liked the way her eyes sparkled and the shape of her mouth.

But more than his physical attraction to her was the fact that he was somehow drawn to the energy that wafted from her. It was an energy that spoke of curiosity and intelligence and a real zest for living that reminded him of what life had been like for him before Suzanna's murder.

Thankfully, she obviously saw him only as a means to an end, so she wouldn't be too much of a temptation for him. He just wanted to get the Vigilante Killer before he struck again.

"Did you see if his car was in the garage?" she now asked.

"It was there."

"I've got to admit, I was terrified for you when those lights went on."

"I was a little bit scared for myself," he admitted. "Thank goodness it was just a motion detector and there were no guard dogs with big, scary teeth."

He settled back in his seat and stared down the road. They were betting that the killer would adhere to the timeline he'd set up with the four previous murders. It was close to midnight now, and they'd remain in place until just after two and then head back to his house.

"This is going to play hell with our daily schedules," he said.

"I really don't have much of a regular schedule," she replied. "As long as I take several hours to research and do my homework for the podcast each night, then I can sleep until noon if I want to."

"I don't have that luxury right now. We're in the middle of putting up a high-rise building and I like to be on-site every day to work with the builder."

"Whatever you do, don't go up in a high-rise and then get sleepy and fall off."

He smiled. "Trust me, I always wear a safety belt when I go up high. Generally, I don't do crazy things."

"Sitting in a car in the middle of the night to try to catch a serial killer...you don't consider this crazy?" Her tone was teasing.

"Oh, it's crazy all right, but I also feel like it's my duty. I don't believe anyone else is trying to stop him and we both know so far he hasn't made a mistake to help the police in their investigation."

She reached over and placed her hand on his forearm. Her fingers were warm and soft, and he fought the need to overreact to the touch and jerk his arm away.

"Jake, I find what you're doing right now to be quite admirable."

"I'm the last person anyone should admire," he scoffed, grateful when she removed her hand from him.

The car was suddenly too warm. He started the engine and turned the air conditioner on high. He felt her gaze lingering on him, but he didn't turn his head to look at her.

"Jake, I have a feeling this man would have eventually killed with or without anyone else's involvement. He's playing God and from all indications he likes it."

"That's why he needs to be stopped. I'm afraid that after he kills all the men who hurt us, he'll move on to killing other people. Not all people charged with a crime are guilty and there's no way of knowing who he might move on to next."

Strange, he was far more comfortable talking murder with her than talking about anything else. He didn't want to make small talk with her. He didn't want to get to know her better. They were partners with a common goal, and that was it.

With the interior of the car sufficiently cooled off, he cut the engine.

"You told me both of your parents were gone. What happened to them?" she asked.

Apparently, she intended to make small talk. He

sighed. He rarely thought of his parents, who had spent their lives making bad choices.

"They were both drug addicts from the time Suzanna and I were four or five. Our father overdosed and died when we were eleven. Mom tried to clean up and pull it together, but she never managed it. She wound up overdosing and dying when we had just turned eighteen."

"Oh, wow. I'm so sorry," she replied.

"Thanks, but it was a long time ago." His childhood had been more than difficult, but he'd always believed it had made him strong, and it had bonded him and his sister together in a way that even went beyond their twin connection. They'd always had only each other to depend on.

"Tell me about your sisters and your father." Even though he didn't want to know too much about her, it seemed the proper thing to ask. In any case, he was grateful to keep the conversation off him and his miserable life.

She shifted positions in the seat and leaned closer to him. "My sisters are five and six years older than me. Addie is the eldest. She's married and has two daughters. She's also a nurse. Elizabeth is also married and has a little girl. She and her husband have their own law firm. At birth I was a disappointment to my father. I was supposed to be the boy he'd wanted."

"I'm sure that didn't change how much he loved you," Jake replied.

"I don't know, I always felt as if I had to work

extra hard to please him. Of course, my two sisters being overachieving Goody Two-shoes didn't help, and I did go through a couple of years of a little rebellion in high school."

Somehow this didn't surprise him about her. "How much of a rebellion?"

She grinned. "Not that bad. It was the usual teenage stuff. I blew off curfews and partied a little. More recently, Dad isn't exactly thrilled at my choice of careers. He thinks I'm just wasting my time and playing at a job. He doesn't understand that this is my passion and my chosen path."

For the next hour and a half they talked about their jobs. She told him about past stories she had run, including her investigation into gang activity, and he told her about the buildings he'd envisioned and had the pleasure to see through to completion.

He broke down and ate a handful of corn chips and they opened sodas that she had brought. There followed a good-natured argument about what was the best snack food. He liked salty and nutty, and she was definitely into sweet candy. She was so easy to talk to and he found himself completely relaxing with her company. They talked briefly about politics and agreed to disagree on some issues.

When two o'clock rolled around he was surprised by how quickly the time had gone by. "I think we're safe to get out of here now," he said. "If Clay is our man he would have already made a move if he was going to do anything tonight."

"I agree." She pulled her seat belt back around her, and he did the same and then started the car.

"Are you positive we just have to worry about one of these two men being the killer?" she asked as he headed back to his house.

He frowned thoughtfully. "I know without a doubt that the killer isn't Nick Simon or Troy Anderson. Both of those men were shaken up and freaked out when the men they were supposed to kill in the plan were killed. I also know those two men have moved on from this whole mess. They've found new love and want nothing to do with this. I'm not as sure in Matt Harrison's complete innocence. But I think the odds are the killer is either Clay or Adam."

"Are we back on Clay again tomorrow night?" She stifled a yawn with the back of her hand.

"I think we stick on him until something happens." A knot formed in Jake's chest. That something would be another man's murder unless he could stop it from happening. He prayed that he would be able to prevent the killer before another man was murdered.

They were quiet on the rest of the drive. "Will you be okay to drive home?" he asked as he pulled into his driveway next to where her car was parked.

"I'll be fine," she assured him. "Same time tomorrow night?" she asked when they got out of the car.

"Unless you want to have dinner with me again. You mentioned that you like Mexican. How about I take you to El Chappo's?"

The moonlight bathed her face in a silvery light and her pleasure was obvious in the shine of her eyes and the curve of her lips. What in the hell was he thinking? What in the hell was he doing?

"I'd like that," she replied. "I've eaten there often and I love their food. Why don't I meet you there at around six?"

"Sounds good," he replied, even though he already wanted to take the invitation back.

Minutes later he watched as her car pulled away. He continued to watch until her lights disappeared and then he turned and went into his house.

Exhaustion filled him as he went into his bedroom and got ready for bed. It had been years since he'd had any kind of social interaction with anyone. He'd pushed away the friends he'd once had in his grief and rage.

They had been not only his friends, but Suzanna's as well. After her murder, seeing any of them had just been too painful.

Even though he and Monica had talked about nothing important, sharing conversation with her had felt good. It had stirred a hunger in him for more social talk, more time with her, making her even more of a temptation to him.

He shouldn't have asked her to eat with him again. He'd been foolish to invite her. He didn't want her to think that she was anything to him except part of his plan to catch a killer.

He'd liked being in her company and that wasn't good. She'd made him laugh, and there was no place in his life for laughter or fun. Max Clinton might have killed his sister, but Jake could never forgive himself for what he had done on that terrible night.

Chapter Four

Monica walked into El Chappo's and all her senses came alive. Rousing music played overhead and the walls were painted with colorful murals. The scents of tortillas and pork, of onions and enchilada sauce, rode the air.

Still, it was the sight of Jake sitting in a booth toward the back and waiting for her that really stirred her senses. He was such a hunk and she knew he'd smell wonderful. She liked the sound of his deep voice and especially enjoyed the rumble of his laughter.

She hated to admit it, but she'd been looking forward to having dinner with him all day long. She really hated to admit that she wanted to get to know him better.

She certainly hadn't expected to like him this much. She definitely needed him to break the biggest story of her career and of course that was her top priority. She just had to keep reminding herself of that. She wasn't ready for any kind of a relationship in her life. She needed all her energies and attention focused on her career.

"Good evening, Mr. Lamont," she said as she scooted into the booth seat across from his.

He smiled. "And good evening to you, Ms. Wright. I hope you brought your appetite."

"I'm starving." She reached for the basket of chips that sat in the center of the table. She grabbed one, dipped it in the bowl of hot sauce and popped it in her mouth. "Hmm, I love these things."

"They are addictive," he replied, and took one.

"You don't look too tired considering our overnight hours." In truth he looked amazing in a white short-sleeved shirt that complemented his glossy black hair and tanned skin.

"I managed to sneak in a nap this afternoon. What about you?"

"I slept in until almost eleven."

A waitress appeared at their table and took their drink orders. He got a soda and she opted for a strawberry daiquiri. Within minutes their drinks arrived and they placed their meal orders.

"Other than your nap, how was your day?" she asked once the waitress had left.

"It was good. Everything is going as scheduled on the new building and that's always a good thing. What about you?" He gazed at her with an intensity that threatened to steal her breath away. Under different circumstances it would be so easy to fall into the depths of his green eyes. Instead she grabbed another chip.

"It was okay. I ran some errands for my dad, because, you know, I don't have a real job." She couldn't help the touch of irritation that colored her voice. She crunched on the chip.

"Does that happen a lot?"

She nodded and swallowed. "More often than it should." She cast him a bright smile. "But all that will change once we complete our mission and I break the big story." She just knew then she'd get the respect from her father that she so longed for. That was her ultimate goal, to gain the love and re-spect from her father that she felt was missing in their relationship.

Despite the fact that a lot of the tables and booths were filled with diners, their meals arrived fairly quickly. He had ordered a pork-stuffed burrito and she had the cheese enchiladas. The servings were generous with sides of beans and rice.

"I could eat this kind of food every night for din-ner," she said.

"I like it, but I'm not sure I'd want it every sin-gle night."

"So, what's your very favorite go-to food?"

"A good steak," he answered immediately. "With a baked potato on the side. Now that I could eat al-most every night."

"Butter and sour cream?"

He grinned at her. "Absolutely."

"Do you cook?" she asked him curiously. He couldn't be as perfect as he appeared.

"I can cook enough to stay alive," he replied.

"But I certainly don't try anything too fancy. What about you?"

"Same, although I have to confess I prefer things that go from carton to microwave. It's always seemed like too big a hassle to cook for just one."

"I guess I should have asked you before, but you don't have a significant other?" Once again his eyes gazed at her intently, as if she were the most fascinating creature on the face of the earth.

"Yes, I have a significant other. It's my work. I can't remember the last time I went out on a date. That's why this is so nice. I mean, not that this is a real date or anything like that," she hurriedly added as a blush warmed her cheeks.

A small frown cut across his forehead. "No, this isn't a date. I don't date. I have no interest in having a relationship."

She wanted to ask him why he didn't want to have a relationship and why he'd invited her out to dinner. But his eyes suddenly appeared dark and shuttered, definitely not inviting any further questions on the topic.

"The one thing I do miss about having somebody in my life is that I have never really enjoyed eating alone," she finally said.

"I'm the same way and that's why I invited you out. I like a good meal, but it's even better if you have good company."

She smiled at him, grateful to see that the darkness that had been in his eyes momentarily was no longer there. "At least you consider me good company."

He returned her smile. "I can't imagine anyone considering you bad company."

A wave of warmth rushed through her. Jeez, what was wrong with her? Why did she want to get to know him better not as a story, but rather as a man? Why on earth did his smile, his intent gaze, make her heart skip a beat?

Loneliness. The word leaped into her head as she took another bite of her enchilada. Most of the time she kept busy enough she didn't have time to feel lonely.

But there were times, like when she saw a gorgeous sunset or thought of something funny or was just sitting alone in her living room, when a hollow wind of loneliness blew through her.

But she didn't intend to do anything about it. Work first; there would always be time for a meaningful relationship after she had firmly established herself as a real success.

"I've refilled my surveillance bag for tonight," she said. "It now has corn nuts, potato chips and peanuts in it just for you."

Once again, he smiled. "You didn't have to do that. Did you also add some sweet stuff for you?"

"Definitely. I've been trying to quit chewing on my fingernails so I always have a bag of candy or packs of gum around the house."

"Is that helping?"

"Not really," she replied with frustration. "Most of the time I'm not even aware that I'm chewing on them."

"Haven't I heard something about putting hot sauce on your nails?"

She smiled. "Yes, I've heard that, too. The problem is I really love hot sauce so it wouldn't be a deterrent to me." She then frowned. "Is it just my imagination or is it getting a little smoky in here?"

"Now that you mention it, it is. They must have burned something in the kitchen."

"At least we know it isn't our dinners burning back there," she replied. "How is your burrito?"

"Absolutely delicious. What about your enchiladas?"

"I don't think I've ever had a bad cheese enchilada," she replied. "These are wonderful."

"What other kind of Mexican food do you like?"

"Anything on the menu," she replied with a laugh.

The words had just left her mouth when shouts could be heard coming from the kitchen. The mood of the dining room changed, quieting as the shouts from the back got louder and more frantic.

Several men wearing white aprons ran from the kitchen and into the dining room. "Fire," one of them yelled.

"*El incendio*," another man shouted.

Panic ensued. Diners got out of their seats and pushed and shoved one another toward the entrance. There was an exit door two booths down from where she and Jake were seated. It was closer to the kitchen area, but easier than battling the rest of the people headed toward the main entrance.

They got up and Jake guided her toward that door.

They weren't alone. Several others also headed in that direction.

The smoke grew thicker and heat radiated from the kitchen. They reached the door and Jake pushed on it. Apparently, it was locked, because it didn't open. However, the people behind them didn't seem to realize it. They pushed and shoved, getting more frantic.

As people pressed against her, panic crawled up the back of her throat. If the smoke and fire didn't get them, then they were going to be crushed to death in the panic.

"Let us out, man," a male voice yelled from behind them.

"It's locked," Jake yelled back. "The door is locked. We can't get out this way."

The heat from the kitchen grew more intense and still people pushed and shoved. Finally, the group at the exit door realized it was no way out and turned to head toward the main entrance. Jake threw his arm around her and pulled her close to his side as they also made for the entrance.

When they finally got outside two fire trucks, three police cars and several news vans had arrived. Everyone who had been in the building stood around, as if unsure what they should do.

Light bulbs flashed as photos were taken, microphones were shoved in people's faces and two ambulances roared into the parking lot with sirens screaming.

Jake pulled her closer and leaned into her. "Must

be a slow news night," he murmured in her ear. "How about we get out of here."

"Sounds good to me," she replied.

They headed for their cars in the parking lot. The crowd began to break up as other people hurried toward their cars, too. She was grateful to see that none of the emergency vehicles had them blocked in.

"Well, that was exciting," she said as they reached her car.

"Definitely more excitement than I expected for a meal out," he agreed. He looked back at the restaurant and the emergency vehicles. "At least it looks like nobody got hurt."

"That's a good thing. For a minute there I thought I was going to be crushed by the crowd."

"I wouldn't have let that happen," he replied.

Warmth washed over her at his words. "Well, thank you, and I'll see you later tonight." She wanted to get home and write up a few notes on the fire to add to her podcast that night.

Besides, she needed just a little bit of distance from Jake. When he'd put his arm around her and pulled her close to his side, she'd wanted to stay there forever, and that was the last thing she needed from him.

"It's about the story, stupid," she muttered to herself as she drove away from the restaurant, where the fire was finally out.

JAKE AWAKENED THE next morning with a sense of dread. He'd tried not to think about this particular date for the past several days, but it slammed into him the moment he opened his eyes.

Two years ago today he had unlocked the door of Suzanna's house and had found her dead in her bedroom. The memory of that moment and the vision of his sister beaten and broken would remain with him forever. He would never forget the smell of death that had hung in the air.

At that moment he'd wanted nothing more than to run to the side of her bed. He'd wanted to gather her into his arms and weep...and scream. But he hadn't.

Even with wild grief clawing at his insides, someplace in the back of his mind, he'd known not to touch anything. He'd backed out of the bedroom and called the police. He'd then collapsed in the hallway and fallen apart.

It had been a kind policeman who had finally pulled him up and taken him out of the house. He'd sat in his patrol car with Jake while he screamed and sobbed.

When his tears had momentarily subsided, he'd managed to give a statement. The policeman had followed Jake in his car to ensure Jake got home safely.

He now finally roused himself out of the bed to shower and dress, and then he went out to retrieve his morning paper. He needed to keep busy today. He needed to keep the memories at bay and not dwell on this horrible anniversary.

He made coffee and then sat at his table to read the paper. He was vaguely surprised to see on page two a report on the restaurant fire the night before.

The brief article was accompanied by a photo of the restaurant and in the background, along with some of the other diners, Jake could be seen with his arm around Monica.

Once again last night they had spent several hours in front of Clay's place, where nothing had happened except he'd learned that Monica's favorite color was lavender, her favorite kind of music was old rock and roll and she made delicious throaty happy sounds when she ate gummy bears.

When he'd thrown his arm around her the night before to lead her out of the restaurant it hadn't been lost on him that she fit perfectly against him.

He was grateful to read the paper, drink his morning coffee, and then he needed to get to the job site where he didn't have to think about Monica's redolent scent. He didn't have to imagine her lavender bedroom or what it would be like to hear those throaty noises coming from her when his lips took hers.

The last thing he wanted to do was think about her and he certainly didn't want to dwell on memories of Suzanna and the last time he'd seen her.

It had been so terrible. He'd known she might be in trouble when noon rolled around and he hadn't heard from her. Not only had she not called him, but she hadn't answered any of his calls.

He'd driven to her house in a panic, knowing in his gut that something terrible had happened. And it had. Suzanna's death had been a defining moment that had changed his life forever.

He stuffed his memories deep inside and left the house at eight. He headed for the building site, hoping that talking to the men would keep his mind clear.

"Hey, Jake," Brett Cummings, the foreman on the job, greeted him as he got out of his car. "I was waiting for you to get here today."

"How's it going?" Jake asked. When the foreman came looking for him, generally there was a problem.

"I was wondering if you could go up with me and do a little review of the prints for the next two floors."

"Sure," Jake agreed.

The two men got in the cage that would carry them up to the sixteenth floor, where the foreman's tiny shack sat across a spiderweb of beams.

When they reached the floor, they each snapped onto the safety line that would keep them from falling to their deaths with a single misstep.

"At least the good weather is keeping us on deadline," Brett said as they maneuvered across the beams.

"Before deadline and under budget is always a good thing," Jake replied. "That will make Sam a happy man." Sam Watterson was the owner of the project. Sam was a well-known developer in Kansas City and was involved in dozens of projects.

For the next hour Jake clarified what he needed to with Brett and when he finished he walked around and greeted the workers. He'd always believed being on a first-name basis with the men who were doing the actual work of bringing his blueprints to life was important.

Today it was difficult to make pleasant small talk, but he forced himself to do just that. When he'd finally made the rounds, he returned to his car and sat and watched the work being done.

This building design had been one of several he and Suzanna had worked on together right before her murder. It had been ambitious and bold, and it had taken him the last two years to find the right people to invest in seeing their dream come to life.

It was bittersweet to see it actually being realized without her. There were many nights he and Suzanna would go up and sit on the high beams of one of their construction sites and gaze up at the stars overhead.

Suzanna had always loved the stars and she would point out the various constellations to him. That was why he'd named his business Lamont and Star.

God, he missed her so much. He missed her smiling face. He missed brainstorming with her about new visions of building. He missed talking to her. They had been such an integral part of each other's lives.

An overwhelming grief and a killing guilt pressed down on him. If he'd just made a different decision on that night, then Suzanna would probably be alive today. If he just hadn't been so damned selfish.

He didn't know how long he'd been sitting in the car and thinking of his sister when Monica's car pulled up next to his. He looked at it in surprise. What in the hell was she doing here?

He got out of his car and waited while she exited hers. "Hi." She greeted him with a bright smile. "Did you see the morning paper?"

"I did," he replied.

"We're now famous."

"Not that famous. Our names weren't even mentioned. Is that why you're here?" Clad in white shorts and a bright yellow blouse, she was like a ray of sunshine in what had been a very dark day for him.

"Actually, yes and no," she replied. "I was curious to know if you saw the paper, but I also brought you lunch."

"Lunch?" He stared at her blankly.

"Yeah, you know it's when people eat a meal around noon."

"Did we talk about having lunch together today?" Maybe in the wee hours of the morning while they'd been sitting on Clay's house last night he'd somehow missed something.

"No, we didn't talk about it, but I thought maybe today would be a good day for you to have lunch with your partner."

Her smile and her soft gaze made him realize she knew. She knew it was the anniversary of the day he had found Suzanna's dead body and she had come here to help him get through it.

There was a part of him that wanted to growl at her to go home, to leave him alone with his dark thoughts. She didn't need to be here because she pitied him. That was the last thing he wanted from her.

But then she turned and pulled a picnic basket

from her passenger seat and her eyes held a touch of apprehension, as if she knew she might not be welcome. "I hope you like ham and cheese."

And just that quickly he was oddly grateful she'd shown up. "I love ham and cheese," he replied.

She lit up like a Christmas tree, her eyes sparkling as she smiled widely. "Should we sit in one of the cars?"

"You brought lunch, so I'll provide a dining room." He took the picnic basket from her and then grabbed her hand in his.

He led her around the side of the building where there were several lawn chairs and a couple of sawhorses with sheets of plywood on top. He set the picnic basket in the center of the plywood and then pulled up two chairs.

"It isn't exactly the Ritz," he said.

"But it's perfect for a picnic," she replied, and then opened the picnic basket. The first thing she pulled out was a red-and-white-checkered tablecloth. He helped her put it down, still touched that she was here.

Not only did she have ham-and-cheese sandwiches, but there was also a container of potato salad, small bags of chips, a container of fruit salad and cookies.

"This isn't lunch, this is a feast," he said as she pulled out two cans of soda, then moved the picnic basket to the side.

"I wasn't sure what you normally did for lunch."

"Sometimes I just skip it and other times I grab a hamburger from a joint down the street," he replied.

The noise of the work site quieted as the men all knocked off for the lunch hour. As he and Monica ate, she asked him questions about the building.

"What's it going to be?" she asked.

"The first floor is going to be a grocery store. They're hoping to draw more people into living in the area and those people will need a place to buy their food."

"And the rest of it?" She looked past his shoulder to the skeletal building.

"The next fifteen floors are office space and the rest of it is going to be lofts for sale."

"I'm not sure I'd want to live in a loft that high up," she replied.

"Are you afraid of heights?" he asked.

"Maybe a little, why?"

"There is no place better to stargaze than on the beams near the top. Suzanna and I used to go up in the high beams and look at the stars. I was just thinking that one night when we aren't doing surveillance, you might be interested in doing a little stargazing with me."

Once again, she looked up at the top of the structure and then gazed back at him. "I imagine it's kind of an exhilarating experience."

"It is."

"There are safety belts or ropes or whatever involved?"

"Definitely."

She looked at him. "Then I'd be up for it."

"We'll do it some night soon." He hadn't been up on the beams at night since Suzanna had died. It was something he hadn't wanted to do by himself when he knew memories of her would assail him.

With Monica it was difficult to be depressed. Something about her filled him with an inexplicable optimism. She reminded him that there was still laughter, and moments of real contentment, real happiness left in the world.

However, none of that really mattered. He could fall madly and wildly in love with her, but he wouldn't act on his feelings.

In any case if she ever learned the role he had played in his sister's murder, she would look at him with revulsion. He'd made a decision that night that he would never forgive himself for and he had a self-loathing that would last for the rest of his life.

"What do you think about dogs?" Her question pulled him back from his dark thoughts.

"I like them better than cats."

"Have you ever thought about getting one?"

"I've thought about it from time to time, but with my work schedule the way it is, it wouldn't be fair to the dog. I'm gone most of the day. Why? Are you thinking about getting one?"

"Maybe. There are times I'd like a little fur baby to keep me company. You know, somebody who thinks I hung the moon and loves me unconditionally." For a moment she looked incredibly vulnerable. Her eyes appeared wistful and then she released a small, uncomfortable laugh and the vulnerability was gone.

"Have you ever had a dog before?" he asked.

"We had a dog when I was young. His name was Pooky and he was the sweetest little schnauzer you'd ever want to meet. He was my cuddle buddy at night and I adored him."

"What happened to him?"

She sighed. "He got heart failure and we had to put him down. I was devastated for a while."

"That's one reason why I don't want a dog. I don't want to bond with a dog that won't live as long as me," he replied.

"But then you miss out on years of laughing and doggy kisses and having a little fur friend that loves you unconditionally. Besides, a dog is a thing to have before babies. It's practice for taking care of something helpless."

He didn't respond to that. He couldn't, because there would never be any babies in his life.

They finished eating and cleaned up and then he walked her back to her car. He hadn't forgotten why she'd shown up and her thoughtfulness humbled him.

She had pushed away the darkness that had threatened to descend on him. When they reached the car she placed the picnic basket in the seat and then turned back and smiled at him.

"Thank you for taking time out to have lunch with me," she said.

"No, thank you," he replied. She looked so gorgeous, and for just a moment he wanted to pull her up close to him and kiss her smiling, lush lips.

"And now I have a favor to ask you."

"A favor?" He consciously shoved away any thoughts of kissing her.

"I have these two huge steaks and a barbecue grill I don't know how to use. You'd be doing me a big favor if you'd come over this evening and fix them for us."

He looked at her skeptically. "Do you really need me to grill the steaks or are you just being kind?"

"Oh, I definitely need you on the grill." She looked at him innocently. "My father insisted I get one when I bought my house, but the idea of gas and flame scares me a little bit so I've never used it. Besides, you told me you could eat a steak and a baked potato every night, and tonight I'm offering them to you. Besides, I'm really hungry for steak tonight and they just don't taste the same broiled in the oven."

He wanted to tell her no. Things were definitely getting a bit too cozy between them. But when he thought of being at home alone during the long hours of this particular evening with nothing to keep him company but his dark memories, he finally relented.

"Okay. How about six?" He was already going to hell for his role in Suzanna's murder and his part in a pact of death. He might as well add using Monica for company on a difficult night to his sins.

"Perfect," she replied. "I'll text you my address and I'll see you then."

Minutes later he frowned thoughtfully as he watched her drive away from the job site. His desire to have dinner with her tonight was at least partially selfish.

She was like a panacea to his grief, a magic potion that would keep dark memories away. But there was also a bigger part of him that just wanted to spend all his spare time with her, and that's what had him worried.

She was getting under his skin. He found himself thinking about her way too often. Each time he was with her a simmering desire filled his veins. Her spicy citrus scent enticed him and her easy laughter enchanted him.

He'd go to her house tonight and grill the steaks. He'd enjoy having dinner with her, but after tonight there would be no more meals with her.

They would continue their surveillance, but that would be the extent of the time they spent together.

HE STARED AT the picture in the paper and then slammed his fist onto the faces of Jake Lamont and Monica Wright. Oh yes, he knew who she was. She was a freaking reporter.

Why were the two of them together? Even as he asked himself that question he knew the answer. Jake had turned on them.

How long had the two of them been talking? Why hadn't a news story already appeared detailing the murder pact? Why hadn't any cops come knocking at his door?

He'd known none of the other men would really adhere to their plan of murder. They had all talked a good game that night in the woods, but he knew when push came to shove they wouldn't be able to kill anyone.

He'd taken it upon himself to ensure that four foul pieces of humanity got what they deserved. What he had discovered on that first night when he'd slit Brian McDowell's throat was that he liked it. He'd liked the feel of blood on his hands, the smell of it and the swell of power that filled him as he took the man's life.

He also liked that he had a name…the Vigilante Killer. Only really good killers got names. Hillside Strangler… Son of Sam… Zodiac… Someday the Vigilante Killer would be as well known as those other killers.

He was good at what he did. He'd left no clues, nothing for the police to find him. He had no intention of getting caught or stopping. There were lots of bad people walking around free as birds who needed to be killed.

This was his mission in life. It was his passion and it excited him and he wasn't about to let Jake Lamont run his mouth to a reporter and ruin it all.

He leaned back in his chair and sipped his now-cool coffee. He had no idea why a story hadn't broken yet, but he knew what he had to do. There was no question about it.

They needed to die...sooner rather than later.

Chapter Five

That evening as Jake drove to Monica's house, he couldn't help the way his heart lifted at the anticipation of spending more time with her. And he was still determined that this would be the last time they would spend any social time together. They would continue to do the surveillance together, but that was it.

He sensed that she might be a little bit romantically interested in him, and he wasn't and could never be the kind of man she wanted or deserved. He needed to make sure she understood that he wasn't in the market for any kind of a relationship with her except for a working one. The problem was it was just so damned hard to remember that when she was around him.

He turned down a tree-lined street with small, neat homes and eyed the addresses for hers. Halfway down the block he spied her house. He was interested to see her personal space. He imagined vibrant colors and comfortable furniture.

Her house was a ranch painted a soft gray with

darker gray shutters. It sported a maroon front door, and a large picture window in the front reflected the clouds that had moved in late this afternoon.

Pulling up in the driveway, he steeled himself, needing to stay strong and keep his growing feelings for her in check. Maybe she just acted as if she liked him in order to get the story.

He immediately dismissed this idea. She didn't strike him as a woman who would be that disingenuous. He'd already pegged her as a straight shooter and nothing so far had changed that initial assessment of her.

She answered the door on his first knock, and despite all his desires to the contrary, his heart skipped a beat at the sight of her.

Clad in a pair of white shorts and a pink T-shirt that clung to her small waist and emphasized the thrust of her breasts, she looked sexy as hell.

She gestured him into a small but pleasant living room that held a navy blue couch and matching chair and a large flat-screen television anchored on one wall. Bright yellow throw pillows and yellow-based lamps added the vibrant touches he'd imagined would be in her living space. She also had several candles burning and their scents filled the air along with her fragrance.

"The steaks are marinating, baked potatoes are in the oven and a salad is in the fridge," she said as she led him into the kitchen.

It was also a pleasant room, with yellow-and-white curtains hanging at the windows and a bouquet of artificial sunflowers in the center of the round wooden kitchen table.

"How about I check out that grill," he said. Already the scent of her now-familiar perfume eddied in the air as if to torment him.

"It's on the deck." She opened the back door and together they went out on the deck, where a table with a bright blue umbrella was already set with navy-and-yellow-ringed dinner plates.

"Since the clouds moved in and it's not as hot as it has been, I thought we'd eat out here if that's all right with you."

"Perfect," he replied. At least out here he wouldn't have her scent surrounding him.

The grill was a standard gas one and it took him only minutes to get it lit and warming up. "How does a cold beer sound?" she asked.

"It sounds great."

"I'll be right back." She disappeared into the kitchen.

He walked over to the deck railing and gazed out to her backyard. There were several pretty trees and a birdbath in a round flower bed. The grass was neatly cut and the whole thing was surrounded by a privacy fence.

He turned as she came back outside. "Thanks." He took the icy beer bottle from her. He twisted off the top and took a drink. "Ah, there's nothing better than a cold beer on a warm day."

"I completely agree." She took a sip of her beer

and then set it down on the table. "Just let me know when you're ready for the steaks."

"We'll let the grill warm up for a few more minutes. I was just admiring your backyard. With the fence it would be perfect for that little fur baby you mentioned."

She smiled. "I know. I'm trying to decide if I'm ready to make that kind of commitment."

"Do you know what kind of dog you'd like?"

"I've been thinking about it and I'm leaning toward a miniature schnauzer, since that's what I had growing up and a girlfriend of mine has one now and he's a little sweetheart."

"Sounds like a good choice," he replied. "You have a very nice home."

She laughed. "Thanks, but it's nothing but a mud hut compared to yours."

"That's not true," he said with a laugh of his own. "Besides, I had to build a house that reflected my profession. It's a big house for just one person to ramble around in and it's easy to be lonely there." Embarrassment filled him and he mentally kicked himself. Even though it was true, why had he said that out loud?

She looked at him for a long moment. "I get lonely, too. I guess it doesn't matter how big or small your house is. People can be lonely anywhere."

He broke eye contact with her. "Maybe we both need dogs." He walked over to the grill. "I think it's ready for the steaks."

She brought him two beautiful T-bones and as

they sizzled on the grill they talked about the weather and the clouds that had moved in. They argued about what made a perfect steak—he believed it should be medium-rare and she insisted well-done was better.

What they didn't talk about was loneliness or anything else personal. The easy conversation continued as they ate. They shared more about their work and then talked about sports. They both loved football and supported the local Chiefs team.

"There's nothing better than tailgating at a Kansas City Chiefs game."

"I know, all you can smell is good barbecue," he replied.

"When you're at home and watching a football game what kind of food do you eat?" she asked.

"Hot wings and french fries."

"Ah, a man after my own heart." Her eyes sparkled brightly. "I love hot wings dipped in blue cheese dressing."

"No way," he replied. "They're better if they're dipped in ranch dressing."

Then followed a discussion about the best foods to eat while watching a football game.

He pushed his empty plate away. "That was one delicious steak, and the potato was baked to perfection."

"I hope you have enough room for dessert," she said. "I bought a peach pie."

"For peach pie, I might have a little room left."

When she was finished eating night had fallen, and they cleared their dishes and moved inside where she made coffee and then cut them each a piece of the pie.

They settled on the sofa side by side to eat the dessert and once again her scent surrounded him. She placed her hand on his arm. He'd come to realize that she was naturally a toucher. He was sure she had no idea how her frequent touches warmed him.

"Tell me about your sister, Jake," she said. "Tell me what Suzanna was like."

He stared at her and for a moment his heart stopped beating. What was she doing? Why did she want to talk about his sister? He hadn't talked to anyone about Suzanna in the past two years. He wasn't even sure he could. He placed his empty pie dish on the coffee table and then looked at Monica once again.

Her gaze was soft, inviting him to share. "Why do you want to know about her?" He heard the thick emotion in his voice and coughed in an effort to clear it.

"I want to know all about her because she was so important to you."

He closed his eyes for a moment, wondering if he could do this. Could he reach beyond the darkness to find the light that had been his sister? "She had the most incredible laugh," he finally said, and opened his eyes.

Speaking that simple sentence seemed to loosen not only the lump in his throat, but also a dam inside him. "It was one of those kinds of laughs that invited everyone around her to share in it even if they didn't know what they were laughing about."

"That's a wonderful gift." She scooted closer to him on the sofa. "Tell me more, Jake. Isn't today a good day for celebrating her life instead of dwelling on her death?"

Celebrating her life? He'd never thought about it before, but that's exactly what he wanted to do right now with Monica. "I liked to tease her about being a pesky little sister. She was almost two minutes younger than me and I never let her forget that I was the older, wiser one."

He leaned back, suddenly immersed in good memories. "She was so full of life. She loved roller coasters and scary movies, but she also loved growing flowers and stargazing and listening to classical music."

He took a sip of his coffee and then continued, "She used to tell me I had the social graces of an ox. But she drew people to her. She had lots of friends and she was loyal and supportive of all of them. Have you ever seen a picture of her?"

Monica shook her head. "No, I haven't."

He pulled his wallet from his back pocket and with fingers that trembled slightly, he pulled out the picture he carried of the sister he'd lost. He handed the small photo to Monica.

She studied the picture for several moments and then handed it back to him. "She was beautiful."

"She wasn't just beautiful on the outside, she was also beautiful on the inside." He tucked the picture away and returned his wallet to his back pocket.

"I had to start scaring guys away from her when we were only about thirteen." He smiled. "I have to admit there were a couple of years where she hated me for playing the role of big bad father."

Monica laughed. "So you scared all the boys?"

"I did. I finally eased up a bit when she was about seventeen. She dated a lot but managed to keep up her grades. And she always seemed to date nice boys, which also helped me relax."

"You mentioned that your parents were both drug addicts and died when the two of you were young. How on earth did you two manage to survive?"

"Needless to say, we both had to grow up really fast. There were many nights we were the caretakers for them rather than the other way around. We hoarded any change or dollar bills we'd find and use that to buy food. We quickly learned what food went the furthest, but of course there were days when there was no food to be found. I'm not telling you this so you will feel sorry for me, but rather to show you that it was always Suzanna and me against the world."

"How did you manage to put yourselves through college?"

"We figured out early on that education was the only way we were going to get out of the life we were living and make something of ourselves. We both got scholarships and grants, and then when we turned twenty-one we were shocked to learn that our mother's father left us an inheritance that helped us. We both worked and then used the inheritance to pay off college debt. We used what was left over to open our business."

"Your mother's parents…they didn't step in to help you and Suzanna?"

"My mother's mother died when she was fairly young so it was just our grandfather, who we'd only met once. He died when we were young, and I don't think my parents even knew about an inheritance. A lawyer contacted us on our twenty-first birthday, which was the term set up in his will."

"And you and Suzanna worked well together?"

"We did. It was nice for me to have a partner who could finish my sentences and who saw the world like me. Yet her weaknesses were my strengths and vice versa. She was good at visualizing the amazing buildings, and my strength was the actual drawing up the blueprints of her vision."

"You hear horror stories about family going into business together," Monica replied.

He nodded. "We talked about that and both of us agreed our relationship came first and was far more important than the business. Everything worked beautifully until she started dating Max Clinton."

He frowned and his jaw clenched tight as he remembered the first time Suzanna had introduced him to Max Clinton. Even then there had been several little red flags that had waved in his head, but he'd kept his concerns to himself.

At that first meeting Max had shown hints of being a control freak and gave the impression that Suzanna was a piece of property he'd just newly acquired. Then he'd told himself he had misunderstood and was just imagining things.

"She was absolutely crazy about him. He was a good-looking guy and smooth as silk." He got up from the sofa and walked over to the picture window. He stared out even though he couldn't see anything except the darkness of the night.

"Within three months of them dating she'd moved him into her house. I started getting worried when I realized not only was he slowly isolating her from all her friends and me, but he also had a huge jealous streak."

"Definitely two big red flags."

He turned back around to face Monica. "Yeah, and it got worse from there. She started showing up at the office with cuts and bruises. She even had a couple of black eyes during that time. But she always had some kind of crazy explanation for the injuries."

He drew in a deep breath and released it slowly. "She finally confessed to me that he had a temper and she was tired of being his punching bag. She threw him out of her house, and I hoped and prayed that was the end of it."

"But it wasn't," Monica said softly.

"No, it wasn't." His chest tightened with a twist of turbulent emotions and once again he clenched his jaw at the memories that now raced to the forefront of his mind.

"She became a cliché for an abused woman. He'd send her flowers and sweet-talk her and she'd welcome him back. I now know that's called the honeymoon period in an abusive relationship. Then he'd beat her again and she'd throw him out. It was a vicious cycle that I couldn't break. I tried to talk to her, I yelled at her, but ultimately all I could do was just sit back and watch it all happen."

He was vaguely aware of Monica getting up from the sofa and joining him in front of the window. But he was deep now into memories that weren't a celebration of his sister's life, but rather the utter tragedy of her untimely death.

"He was in and out of her house a dozen times, and each time when she threw him out, he got more and more angry. The last time she seemed determined to make a final break with him. First, he pleaded and cajoled her to take him back, and when she refused, he stalked her and he left messages that he was going to kill her...the 'if I can't have you, nobody will' kinds of threats."

Jake's emotions threatened to spiral out of control. His chest was so tight he could hardly draw a breath. The back of his throat had closed up as pain and regret pummeled him.

Monica placed her hand on his shoulder and moved closer to him. He couldn't talk about this anymore. They both knew how it had ended. Only he knew his part in it all and he would never voice his own culpability aloud to anyone. That was a shame, a guilt that was too enormous for words.

He stared at Monica helplessly, unable to speak and caught in emotions too deep to share. She returned his gaze and moved closer to him. She raised her face. "Kiss me, Jake."

Her words shocked him, and that shock cast his memories aside. He gazed down at her and became aware of the heat of her body so tight against his and how soft and welcoming her slightly parted lips appeared.

Even though he knew it was wrong on so many levels, he lowered his head and captured her lips with his. All thoughts of Suzanna slipped out of his mind as Monica raised her arms to curl around his neck and opened her mouth to deepen their kiss.

He hadn't realized how cold he'd been until the fire in her kiss, the intimate press of her body against his, warmed him. And he welcomed the warmth by deepening the kiss and tangling his fingers in the long, silky strands of her hair.

She welcomed him. Her tongue swirled with his as her arms tightened around his neck. He was quickly lost in her; any other thoughts were impossible.

Suddenly, the picture window exploded as rapid gunshots filled the air.

MONICA SCREAMED AS Jake threw her down to the floor and then covered her body with his. Bullets whizzed into the wall opposite the window, shattering the glass on the pictures that had hung there. They slammed into the Sheetrock, chipping out chunks with their impact.

Terror shot through her, making it difficult for her

to draw a breath. And yet she had to be breathing because in some place in the back of her mind she knew she was screaming and sobbing.

The noise was deafening, and she clung to Jake, squeezing her fingers into his shoulders as she continued to sob. What was happening? Why was this happening? Her brain couldn't wrap around it. Who was shooting into her house?

It seemed to go on forever. Finally, it stopped. There was the squeal of tires on pavement. And then silence. Except for the deep sobs that Monica couldn't seem to control.

"It's okay. We're okay," Jake whispered in her ear. She knew he meant to comfort her, but his voice was deep with tension. "Monica, we're fine."

Fine? No, she wasn't fine. Somebody had just tried to kill her and terror still squeezed her throat half-closed, still iced her entire body.

"I'm going to get up and I want you to crawl down the hallway and into the bathroom," he said.

The bathroom? At the moment it felt like it was a million miles away from the living room. Still, it was an interior place in the house. He was sending her to an interior room.

"Do…do you think they'll be back?" Oh God, this was a nightmare, the worst nightmare she'd ever suffered. And she couldn't wake up.

"I don't think they'll be back, but just to be on the safe side, I want you in the bathroom until the police arrive. Now, are you ready?"

No, no, she wasn't ready. She didn't want him to

get up from her. She needed his body next to hers, making her feel safe despite the horrifying event that had just occurred.

"Monica?"

"Yes, okay," she replied. Her sobs had subsided for the moment, but her heart still beat so quickly she felt dizzy and breathless.

Jake rose from her but remained in a low crouch as she crawled toward the hallway. She tried to avoid moving through the broken glass that littered the floor, and by the time she reached the bathroom she was crying once again.

She closed the door and sat with her back against the tub. Her tears half-choked her and her ears still rang with the sound of the bullets flying.

Somebody had just tried to kill her...them. Who had done this? Who was responsible? Never had she felt such terror.

What was Jake doing out there? Surely he had called the police by now. And even if he hadn't she would imagine one of her neighbors had called. Gunshots in this neighborhood never happened.

There had been so many bullets. She didn't know much about guns, but if there had only been one person shooting then they had to have used some sort of a semiautomatic weapon.

Who had done this? The question pounded in her head like a bad headache. And would they come back again? Was it possible this had to do with the gang podcasts she'd been doing?

Nothing in her life had prepared her for something

like this happening. Even when she'd pressed to be Jake's partner in finding the Vigilante Killer, she hadn't believed she'd be in any real danger.

Tonight had been real and present danger.

She drew in several deep breaths in an effort to stanch her tears. Who did this? The question repeated again and again in her head.

The sound of sirens caused a shuddery relief to flood her. She swallowed the last of her sobs and then quickly swiped at her cheeks.

Surely the shooter wouldn't come back with the police here. She got to her feet and opened the bathroom door. The sound of Jake's voice along with several others assured her that it was okay to leave the bathroom.

She walked on unsteady legs into the living room, where Jake was speaking to three police officers. Jake gestured her to his side and, on legs that still shook, she joined them.

Jake introduced her to Officers Tim Moran, Brad McDonald and Stephanie Boen. "So, what do you think happened here tonight?" Officer Boen asked her.

"I don't know what happened," Monica replied. "We were just talking and all of a sudden the window exploded and bullets were flying." Her voice trembled, and she was grateful when Jake threw an arm around her shoulder and pulled her closer to his side. "We could have been killed. We should be dead right now." She stopped talking and drew in another deep breath as she heard her own hysterical voice.

"I've caught your podcast several times, Ms. Wright," Officer McDonald said. "Is it possible one of your stories is the cause of what happened here tonight?"

Monica told them about the gang series she was running, and then Jake reminded her about Larry Albright. She told the officers about the threatening messages he'd left her and about him following her to the restaurant and throwing a beer bottle at her.

"It's a big leap from throwing a bottle at me and what happened tonight," she said. Looking around the room her chill returned, and she began to shiver once again. "Whoever did this wanted to kill me." A new hollow wind of fear blew through her.

Jake tightened his arm around her. "We aren't going to let that happen."

For the next hour or so they were questioned over and over again while other officials dug bullets out of her walls. When that evidence had been collected, all them left except Officer McDonald.

"I'll be honest with you, this has all the markings of a typical gang-related drive-by shooting," he told them, and then looked at Monica. "Do you have some place you can stay for the rest of the night?"

"She does," Jake answered for her.

"In fact, I would recommend you stay away from here even longer than a night," the officer continued. "If you have ticked off somebody in the gang world, then you probably need to see if a little time will cool things off and maybe talk to the men who were on your podcast."

This couldn't be her life. It couldn't be true that somebody wanted her dead. And yet it was true, and she'd never been so frightened.

She listened absently as Officer McDonald said they would investigate the crime. But he also said that drive-by shootings were particularly difficult to solve. "I'll sit out at the curb until you two leave here." And then he was gone.

Monica became aware of the hot air wafting in where the front window used to be. Somewhere in the neighborhood several dogs barked. It was all so surreal. Her house now felt like an alien space and not the sanctuary she'd always believed it to be.

"Do you have anything we can use to cover the window until we can get it fixed?" Jake asked.

"Uh… I think there might be some plywood out in my shed," she replied. Her voice sounded weak and trembling even to her own ears. "There's also a hammer and nails in there."

"Why don't you come into the kitchen and sit while I see about finding material to board up the window."

"Okay." She was suddenly eager to get out of the living room, where despite the officer's car being parked, another round of bullets could come in un-impeded by a glass window. Would the shooter or shooters come back?

In the kitchen she handed him the shed key and then she sank down in a chair at the table. "Jake… be careful. They might come back." Sadly, even policemen could be killed in a hail of bullets. She bit back tears that threatened to fall again.

"I don't think they'll be back," he replied. "For all they know right now, we're both dead. Sit tight and I'll get this taken care of in no time." He disappeared out the back door.

For all they know right now, we're both dead. His words played and replayed in her mind. She chewed on her index fingernail as a million other thoughts flew through her head.

If the shooting was gang-related, then she didn't know why. Her interviews with the gang members had not focused on their criminal activities, but rather on what had drawn them to that lifestyle and what they believed needed to be done to solve the gang issues in the city. The men she had talked to had been more than cooperative. They had appeared pleased that somebody was actually listening to them. So why would they come after her now?

And if she needed to stay away from here for a few days, where would she go? Her father lived in a small house and he didn't even have a bed in either of the guest rooms. One held workout equipment and the other room he used as a storage area. She would die if she had to go to one of her sister's homes. She didn't want to hear them tsk-tsking her over her lifestyle or career.

She'd go to a motel even though the idea of being all alone was abhorrent right now. Tears once again pressed hot behind her eyes.

What was taking Jake so long? Had somebody

been hiding in her shed? Or in the darkness of her backyard? Had he been attacked? She stared at the back door, her heartbeat accelerating with a new fear.

What if Jake had been jumped? Maybe he was right now in the backyard unconscious or…

Just when she thought she might scream, he came back in. He carried a hammer and half a sheet of plywood. He leaned the plywood against the wall. "This should do it," he said. "But I'm going to need your help."

She jumped out of the chair. "Let's do it." Anything to take her mind off her horrible thoughts.

It took them only fifteen minutes to position the wood over the opening the missing glass had created and nail it solidly in place.

"Now pack some bags. You're going to stay with me," he said.

"Really? I'm supposed to stay away from here for more than a night." She stared at him, wanting nothing more than his arms around her.

He seemed to sense her need, for he pulled her into his arms. "You'll be safe at my place for as long as you need to be there," he whispered into her ear. "I have lights and alarms and mean guard dogs with sharp teeth who will go after anyone who gets close to my house."

A small laugh released from her. He held her only a moment longer and then let go of her. "Now go pack up what you'll need to be away from here for a week or so. While you're doing that, I'll do a little cleanup in the living room. Broom?"

"In the pantry," she replied.

As he began to sweep the hardwood floor, she went into her office. The first thing she packed was her work equipment. She'd wanted a story and now she had one, but she wished she didn't. Tonight real danger had come far too close. If it wasn't for Jake's quick action in pulling her to the floor, they both would have been dead, their bodies riddled with bullets.

With her equipment all packed up, she went from her office into her bedroom and pulled out a large suitcase from her closet. She had moved from paralyzing fear to a curious numbness.

The numbness kept its grip on her as she packed clothes and toiletries. She then went back into the living room, where Jake was sweeping up the last of the broken glass from the floor.

Even without the broken glass, the room looked like a war zone. The wall was riddled with holes and all the pictures she'd had hanging were ruined. Even though she knew it wasn't true and it was just her imagination, right now the room smelled evil.

Would she ever feel safe here again? She didn't know the answer. All she knew for sure was she was ready to go anyplace but here.

"Let's get your things loaded into my car and get out of here," Jake said, as if he'd read her thoughts.

She didn't breathe easier until they were in his car and driving down the street away from her house.

"Are you okay?" he asked softly.

"I'm not sure," she admitted. "Right now I just feel kind of numb."

"Maybe numb is good for right now."

"At least I'm not screaming or sobbing. I'm sorry you had to put up with that. There's nothing worse than having to deal with a hysterical woman."

He flashed her a quick glance. "Don't be silly. Trust me, I was definitely screaming on the inside."

She studied his profile, illuminated by the dashboard lights. "Are you sure you want me at your house?"

He smiled reassuringly at her. "Monica, I have a big house with two guest rooms. I want to make sure you're safe, so yes, I want you at my house. I just hope you're not an irritatingly cheerful morning person."

To her surprise she laughed. "Trust me, I'm not anything near a cheerful morning person. Truthfully, I'm pretty grouchy when I first wake up." She sobered and continued to gaze at him. His handsome features looked strong and she found comfort in the strength that emanated from him.

Suddenly she was thinking about what had happened just before the bullets had flown. The kiss. Oh, that amazing kiss. It had torched a wonderful heat that had sizzled through her from the top of her head to the very tips of her toes.

His mouth had been demanding and hungry against hers and she wondered what else might have happened between them if the window hadn't been shot out.

Now she was going to be staying in his house and despite everything that had happened, right now all she could think about was if and when he might kiss her again.

Chapter Six

Jake sat at his kitchen table with his hands wrapped around a cup of coffee. Dawn's light drifted in the window, bringing with it the promise of a new day.

He was exhausted. He'd barely slept the night before. He'd gotten Monica settled into one of his guest rooms and she had immediately gone to bed.

He'd been too pumped up with adrenaline to sleep and had sat in his recliner for hours with his brain working overtime. Many of those same thoughts still whirled around in his head right now.

Death had come far too close to them the night before. If they hadn't hit the floor quickly enough they both would have been killed.

His inclination was to believe it had been a result of Monica's podcast. It was the only answer that really made sense. Still, he'd considered that it was possible it was the Vigilante Killer who had somehow gotten word that he was talking to a reporter. He supposed it was possible the murderer had seen their picture in the paper. But the attack wasn't the style of that particular killer and so he'd dismissed that idea.

Even though the odds were against them, he hoped like hell the police could figure out who was behind the assault and get him, her or them behind bars.

He took a sip of his coffee and thought about the woman who was now asleep beneath navy sheets in his guest room. She had caught him by surprise last night. *Kiss me, Jake*. When she'd said that to him he hadn't been able to do anything else but comply.

Kissing her had been breathtaking. The softness of her lips…the warmth of her body against his, had dizzied his senses with desire. She had immediately banished the grief that had welled up inside him when he'd been talking about Suzanna.

If the bullets hadn't flown, what else might have happened between them? If she'd said, "Make love to me, Jake," would they have wound up in her bedroom? Or would he have come to his senses and stopped that from happening? He honestly didn't know the answer to that question.

His feelings for her were crazy and all wrong. The last thing he wanted was to lead her on, to make her believe he was interested in a long-term relationship with her.

Despite the fact that she was now under his roof, he had to keep his distance from her. There was no question she was a temptation, but kissing her had been wrong and he couldn't let anything like that happen between them again.

Once they identified the Vigilante Killer, the odds were good he'd never see her again. She'd have her

big story and he'd go back to the life he deserved…
forever alone and without love or laughter in his life.

He was still seated at the table sipping coffee and
thumbing through the morning paper at just after
nine o'clock when Monica appeared. Clad in a navy
blue robe and with her hair sleep-tousled, she looked
utterly charming…except for the frown that rode
her features.

"Coffee is in the pot," he said. "Cups are in the
cabinet above the coffeepot."

She nodded and beelined in that direction. He
watched as she grabbed a cup, filled it, and then
walked to the table and sat in a chair opposite him.

She didn't speak and neither did he. She also
didn't look at him. She took a drink of her coffee
and then stared into the cup as if it might hold the
answers to all the age-old questions.

He'd been warned that she was crabby when she
first woke up and she definitely looked crabby. There
was nothing about her that invited any conversation.
When she'd finished off one cup of coffee, she went
back to the countertop and refilled her cup. When
she returned to the table she took a couple of sips,
leaned back in her chair and released a deep sigh.

She looked at him with a sheepish grin. "Thank
you for respecting my morning crankiness by not
trying to talk to me."

"The frown on your face was enough to scare
anyone mute," he teased.

She winced. "Was it that bad?"

He nodded. "It was that bad."

"I don't know why I wake up in such a bad mood. I've been that way since I was a little girl and of course both my sisters and my dad are bright-eyed, cheerful morning people. I remember wanting to smash them all in their happy faces with a waffle."

He laughed and then sobered. "How did you sleep?"

"I was afraid I would have nightmares all night long, but I went out like a light and didn't suffer from any bad dreams."

"That's good."

"What about you?"

"I had a restless night," he admitted. "I didn't have any bad dreams but I just couldn't shut off my brain enough to fall asleep."

"I hate nights like that. I'm sorry, Jake. I'm sorry about all of this."

"Did you hire somebody to shoot up your house?" he asked gently.

Her eyes widened. "Of course not."

"Monica, you have nothing to apologize for."

She offered him a small smile. "Thanks, I guess I needed to hear that." She leaned forward and he caught a whiff of her scent. "I was wondering if there's someplace in your house I could set up my equipment so I can continue to do my podcasts in the evenings."

Of course her first thought would be about her work. She was ambitious. And he was an arrogant fool to think that her asking him to kiss her the night before had anything to do with her wanting a relationship with him.

He'd been emotional about Suzanna's death at the time she'd asked him to kiss her. It had probably been done in an effort to comfort him and had meant nothing to her.

"We can set you up in my office. I'm not doing any work in there right now. It has a big drafting table that can be folded down to give you plenty of space for all your equipment."

"That sounds awesome." She gave him a bright smile. Even with a bit of raccoon eyes and no other makeup, she looked beautiful.

He got up from the table. "Are you up for some breakfast?"

"Thanks, but I'm not really much of a breakfast eater." She lifted her cup. "I prefer to drink my breakfast."

"Yeah, I'm not much of a morning eater, either." He leaned his back against the counter. The smell of her had stirred him and he found himself wondering what she had on beneath the short blue robe.

Get a grip, Lamont, he told himself firmly. If he couldn't keep those kinds of thoughts out of his head then it was going to be one hell of a long week.

She finished her second cup of coffee and then rose. "I think I'll go jump in the shower and get dressed for the day. Then if you could show me your office, I'd appreciate it."

"I'm ready whenever you are," he replied.

He breathed a sigh of relief when she left the kitchen. He had a feeling having her here was going to be more difficult than he'd initially thought.

He had to keep a tight control of his emotions where she was concerned. She was just a houseguest who needed a place to stay, not a potential lover he was wooing.

He rinsed their cups and placed them in the dishwasher and then stepped outside on his back deck. The clouds from the night before had brought no rain and it looked to be another dry, hot day. No rain was fine with him; it kept the construction on the job site going.

Thank God there had been no report of another Vigilante murder in the morning paper. Going to sit on Clay's house had been the last thing on his mind the night before. All he'd wanted to do was get Monica out of her house and here where he could assure her safety.

When he'd driven her here from her house he'd made sure they weren't followed. If the shooting was gang-related, there was no way anyone from that world would think to look for her here.

He wouldn't be surprised if she wanted to put the whole Vigilante hunting on hold. If that was the case, then she could stay here, and he would continue to sit on Clay's place during the killing hours.

Although he had joked about having alarms and killer dogs to guard the house, what he did have was a state-of-the-art alarm system and strong locks on each of his doors and windows. He was confident she would be safe here.

Thirty minutes later she returned to the kitchen. Wearing a pair of denim shorts and a red-and-white-striped tank top, she looked fresh and ready to officially face the day.

"All ready for me to set you up in the office?" he asked.

"I just need to grab my equipment from my bedroom."

"I'll help you with that." He knew her bags were heavy from carrying them into the house the night before.

He followed her down the hallway to the room he'd given her to stay in. It was a nice room, big and airy and with its own bathroom.

She'd made the bed up with the navy-and-light-blue spread and matching throw pillows. The room smelled of her scent, that wonderful, slightly exotic fragrance that made his pulse race just a little bit faster.

It would have been so much easier if he hadn't kissed her. If he didn't have the memory of her soft lips beneath his, then he wouldn't be thinking about kissing her again right now.

Minutes later they were in his home office, where they unloaded her equipment and she set it up on the desk. Behind the desk was a historic picture of downtown Kansas City, which she proclaimed would make a wonderful backdrop for her podcast.

"This is great, thank you so much," she said when they were finished. "What are your plans for the rest of the day?"

"I'm leaving here pretty quick to check in at the

job site and I thought you might want to come take the ride with me."

"Oh, I was hoping I'd be here all alone so I could sneak a peek in your underwear drawer and then go through your closet." She paused a beat, as if waiting for his outraged response.

He smiled at her. "I'm afraid you'll be bored to death by both. I prefer boxers over briefs and there are no skeletons rattling around in my closet."

She laughed. "Ah, you're quick, Mr. Lamont. I'm happy to go with you as long as I have enough time later this afternoon to do some research and work on this evening's podcast." Any laughter that had been in her eyes disappeared. "I have to tell you, it's really hard for me to believe that last night's shooting was in any way tied to my podcasts about the gang issue."

He frowned. "Then what do you think it was about?"

Her eyes darkened. "I think it's possible it was the Vigilante Killer." Her voice was a whisper, as if she was afraid the killer might hear her talking about him.

Jake frowned. "I wondered about that earlier, but what happened last night really isn't his style."

"Forget his style. I'm wondering if he saw our picture in the paper and freaked out. He was watching my house and when he saw the two of us together in the window. We made perfect targets and he tried to kill us both."

She stared at him, as if willing him to protest that particular scenario. But he couldn't. He didn't know who had been behind the attack the night before and he didn't know what was worse: a gang that wanted Monica silenced or a killer who feared identification, knew where he lived and now wanted both Monica and him dead.

MONICA HAD TO ADMIT, she wasn't over last night's attack. She'd never considered that her choice of career would put her in any danger. Sure, she'd known on some intellectual level that when she partnered up with Jake to find the killer there was a possibility of danger. However, thinking about it intellectually and actually experiencing it were two very different things.

Jake told her she could stay at the house while he checked in at his job site. He'd even shown her the alarm system and how to set it, but the truth of the matter was she wasn't ready to be left alone.

Before they left the house he went into his bedroom and came out wearing his jeans and a lightweight navy blazer over a white T-shirt. "You're looking pretty spiffy to go to the job site," she observed.

"Get used to the blazer," he replied, and opened one side to reveal a shoulder holster with a gun. "I have a concealed carry license and I intend to carry anytime we leave the house."

It was a sobering moment and yet she had to admit she felt safer knowing he was armed.

As they drove to his job site she found herself looking over her shoulder to the cars behind them, needing to make sure they weren't being followed by anyone.

"Try to relax," Jake said. "Whoever might be after us, they're like cockroaches that only come out at night."

"Do you really believe that?" she asked anxiously.

"I do. If it's gang-related, those kinds of things usually happen after dark. If it was the Vigilante Killer, I know those men we suspect have day jobs, and it would be important for them to show up there every day so when an investigation happens nobody thinks there's anything odd going on with them."

She settled back in her seat and tried to relax, but her heartbeat remained slightly accelerated and her nerves were on edge.

"While you're out talking to the men on the site, I'm going to make some phone calls. I'm going to try to make contact with some of the gang members who are part of the podcast series. Maybe one of them can tell us what's going on."

"Sounds like a good plan," he replied.

It wasn't until they reached Jake's job site that she began to relax. She remained in the car as Jake checked in with the men who were working.

He was greeted with wide smiles and obvious respect from each of the men he spoke to. She wasn't surprised. Jake was a stand-up, regular kind of guy and Monica found those traits very appealing.

In fact she was finding everything about Jake appealing. His body was hot and his laughter was as infectious as he'd described his sister's. He was smart and he made her feel safe and he...

She consciously willed her thoughts away from the man who was supposed to be her business partner of sorts and instead focused on what she wanted to run on her podcast that night.

She definitely intended to report the shooting that had occurred at her house and she had another gang member interview to run. She also had to take some time to research what else was big, local news that her audience would be interested in.

She only had a phone number for two of the men who had agreed to be a part of the gang series. She dialed the first number and a robot voice declared that it was not a working number. The second call she made went to an answering machine. She left a message but she doubted she'd hear anything back.

As she thought of her podcast for the night, she realized she'd better call her father to let him know she was okay. If her family watched, they'd know she was all right, but she seriously doubted any of them had ever watched her show. If they heard about the shooting from any other source, they might freak out. Of course, nobody had called her so she doubted they even knew what was going on in her life.

Maybe she just needed to hear the sound of her father's deep voice. She dialed him and he answered on the second ring. "What's up?" he asked.

She explained to him about the shooting and before she was completely finished he was already cursing. "If you had a real damn job, crap like this wouldn't happen."

Instantly, hot tears burned at her eyes. "Dad, I just called to let you know I'm safe and staying with a friend."

"A friend? Last I heard you didn't have any friends because you always have your nose in the internet. So, who is this friend?"

"His name is Jake and I'm going to be staying in his house for the next week or so."

"Is this guy a boyfriend?" There was a touch of hope in his voice.

"No, we're just friends," she replied quickly.

"Hmm, too bad. It's past time for you to find a good man and get married. You know you aren't getting any younger. I don't want you to wake up one day and be one of those old ladies living with a bunch of cats."

She laughed. "Dad, you know I'm not fond of cats and I just turned thirty. I have plenty of time to get married and have babies."

"Maybe you could give me a grandson. All your sisters have managed to spit out are more girls."

"And you're crazy about those girls," she replied. Her father might be gruff and outspoken, but he was a marshmallow when he was around his grand-daughters.

"But if you don't get off this podcast nonsense you're never going to have a normal life."

She sighed. "I'll call you tomorrow, okay?" She was grateful to end the call. The conversation had been depressing. Most of her conversations with her father were depressing.

Why couldn't he be proud of her, of what she did and who she was as a person? Why did she always get the feeling that she was never quite enough for him?

Fifteen minutes later Jake returned to the car. "I thought we'd drive through and get some Chinese to take home and warm up for dinner tonight."

"Sounds good to me." *Is this guy a boyfriend?* Her father's question whispered through her head. As they pulled away from the job site, she shot surreptitious glances at the man behind the wheel.

She wouldn't mind if he was her boyfriend. She wouldn't mind at all if they ate Chinese for dinner and then they went into his master bedroom and got into bed together. As her boyfriend, he would hold her and make sweet love to her and then she'd fall asleep in his arms. That scenario sounded far too appealing at the moment.

Casting her gaze out the passenger window, she chided herself. She couldn't get all crazy about Jake. It wasn't time for her to find her one true love. She needed to prove herself a success in her work before she could even think about falling in love.

"You're awfully quiet," Jake said, breaking into her thoughts. "Are you okay?"

"I'm fine. I just had a conversation with my father and he usually manages to depress me a little," she confessed.

"I'm sorry," he replied. He reached over and placed his hand over hers on the console. The physical touch lasted only a moment and then he returned his hand to the steering wheel.

But the warmth of that simple touch remained with her.

She had to get her head on straight. Jake had to remain a means to an end and nothing more. "I hope you're planning on us sitting on Clay's house again tonight."

"Given what happened last night, I wasn't sure where your thoughts might be about resuming that," he replied.

"I'm still all in," she replied firmly. "The sooner something breaks in that case, the sooner I'll be out of your life."

He cast her a glance. "I'm in no real hurry for you to be out of my life." Butterflies flew in the pit of her stomach. "I want to make sure you're completely safe before that happens."

The butterflies halted their flight and disappeared. He wanted her safe. He didn't want her in his life any longer than necessary. He just wanted her...safe. Once again, she stared out the passenger window and wondered why his words somehow depressed her all over again.

HE'D MISSED. THEY hadn't died. Although he would have preferred to slit their throats like he had so many before them, his main goal had been to kill them as quickly and as efficiently as possible.

When he'd seen them standing in the window at Monica's house he'd made his move, firing as many bullets as possible before driving away.

He'd been so sure he'd killed them, but the morning news had only had a short report of the shooting, indicating that nobody had been hurt.

Damn. Damn! How had they survived that hail of bullets? Besides needing to take care of them as soon as possible, he was also hungering for the feel of blood on his hands again.

The morning news had also included a story about a man who was arrested for killing a dog and he had been released to await his trial. He hadn't been arrested for the death of the dog, but rather for carrying a handgun without a license.

The man, Greg Bellows, insisted the dog had attacked him and he'd had to kill the animal to save his own life. He'd been carrying a friend's gun that morning on his walk because the dog had attacked him before.

He didn't believe Greg's story and anyone who could hurt an innocent animal was scum of the earth.

And he was the self-anointed destroyer of scum. Greg would never make it before a judge. He had already judged him guilty, and his sentence was death.

His fingers tingled and his heart raced as he thought of the look of surprise Greg would have on his face right before his throat was slit.

Tonight the Vigilante Killer would take care of Greg. After that his next kills had to be Jake and Monica. They had to die before Jake talked too much and Monica broke a story that might lead the cops to him.

It was important that the Vigilante Killer survive and thrive. There were just so many people who needed to die.

Chapter Seven

Dammit. The killer had struck again. Jake read the article in the morning paper and a wave of anger and renewed guilt swept through him.

He didn't know the victim, but what scared him was Greg Bellows had been charged, but not yet tried for his offense. He should have been presumed innocent, but the Vigilante Killer had not only tried him and found him guilty, he'd also handed out the ultimate punishment…death.

This had been Jake's biggest fear. The killer was escalating, no longer murdering the last of the men's perpetrators connected to the pact, but apparently going after anyone he deemed guilty. The thought was absolutely horrifying.

Last night they had continued their surveillance on Clay's house and now Jake knew with certainty Clay wasn't the killer. That left Adam. Jake felt the pressing need to get him arrested, but he had no real evidence to offer the authorities.

He needed to catch Adam in the act. Unfortunately, it would probably be a week or so before the killer acted again. Just the thought of the man going after somebody created a knot of tension in the pit of his stomach. He hoped like hell the killer made a mistake with this latest murder. He hoped the police found something that would lead them to making an arrest.

He looked up from the paper as Monica stumbled into the kitchen. She got a cup of coffee, sat across from him and offered him a half smile.

He raised an eyebrow. "This can't be cranky Monica actually smiling before a couple of cups of coffee."

"I'm trying to change my ways." She took a sip of her drink and released a sigh of obvious satisfaction. "Ah, elixir of the gods." She gestured toward the paper. "Anything exciting in there?"

He hesitated a moment before replying. He hated to ruin her morning as his had been ruined. "I wish you wouldn't have asked me that."

"Why?" She took another sip from her cup and eyed him over the rim.

"There's a story in here that will take that smile right off your face," he finally said.

"What is it?" Her beautiful eyes darkened as she held his gaze.

"There was another killing last night." He told her what had happened overnight with Greg Bellows and sure enough, any smile that might have curved her lips disappeared.

"This is just what you feared," she said. "This Greg Bellows had nothing to do with the pact."

"Even worse than that is the fact that Greg Bellows hadn't been found guilty of anything. And he didn't murder a person. I mean, I don't believe in any kind of animal abuse, but if Greg Bellows was telling the truth he had no option but to kill the dog. And it was possible he'd just get a fine for the gun charge."

"So the killer is definitely escalating," she replied.

"Yeah." He sighed in frustration. "But with this latest murder happening last night, that means he might not act for another week or so."

"Or he could go back out tonight," she countered. "We just don't know. We're doing all that we can do right now, Jake."

"I know, but it's just not enough."

For the next half an hour they talked murder, and then she went to shower and get dressed for the day.

For the next three days they fell into an easy routine. They went to his job site for about two hours in the mornings and then returned home where he sketched at the kitchen table and she worked on her podcast for that night. At noon they ate lunch together and then at eight o'clock each evening she went back into his office and did her podcast for half an hour. She then returned to the family room where they watched television. Then at eleven thirty they left the house to go watch Adam's house.

The evenings were the most difficult for him, when they sat on his sofa to watch television and all he could think about was the kiss they had shared and how much he wanted to kiss her again.

She made him laugh and she made him feel more

alive than he had in years. She was so easy to talk to. They had spent one evening talking about their childhoods and he'd told her more than he'd ever told anyone about the struggles he and Suzanna had encountered as children of addicts.

He had told her about living in squalor and never having enough to eat. There had been endless seedy motels and even seedier men lurking around.

Child Protective Services had never gotten involved, probably because they were never in one place long enough.

He confessed to her that the times when their mother cleaned up were the scariest times of all, because he and Suzanna had known it wouldn't last. They both knew not to believe or trust that their home life might really get better because it never really did.

Monica made him forget every other woman he had ever dated in his life. Being around her was intoxicating and he was desperately trying to stay sober. The problem was that more and more, she seemed to be attempting to seduce him.

She sat too close to him on the sofa and she touched him often…light and simple touches that nevertheless kept a coil of tension twisted tight in his stomach.

He often felt her gaze lingering on him. He was afraid to return the gaze, feeling as if he'd fall into the depths of her blue eyes and do something really stupid.

This evening was no different, except the tension

inside him was at an all-time high. Once again they were seated on the sofa after having eaten a pizza he'd had delivered.

Monica sat close enough to him that he could feel her body heat as her scent filled his head. She'd been quiet all evening, which was unusual.

"Have you spoken with your father today?" he asked to break the silence that had become heavy between them.

"No, why?"

"You've just been really quiet, and I wondered if maybe you'd spoken with him and he depressed you."

"No, I didn't talk with him today," she replied. She looked back at the television, which was playing some inane comedy show that she hadn't been paying attention to.

She watched television for several minutes and then turned back to face him. "You know what's really bothering me tonight?"

"What?"

Her cheeks took on a pink hue. "Maybe I shouldn't say anything."

"What is it? You know you can say anything to me."

"Forget it," she said, and looked back at the television.

"Monica, what's wrong?"

"Nothing is wrong." She looked down at her hands in her lap and then gazed back at him. There was a bold look in her eyes. "It's just… I can't stop thinking about the kiss we shared."

He stared at her and his breath caught in the back of his throat. "Have you been thinking about it at all?" she asked.

He swallowed hard. "It's crossed my mind a time or two."

"Then why haven't you tried to kiss me again?"

God, she was killing him. He raked his hands through his hair and drew in several deep, steadying breaths. "Because it wouldn't be fair to you."

She leaned closer to him. "What do you mean? Why wouldn't it be fair?"

He felt as if he was being strangled with his desire for her and she was helping him tighten the noose. "Because I told you before that I don't want a relationship with anyone."

She frowned and didn't take her gaze off him. "But what if we were both on the same page about that? What if I don't want a relationship with anyone, either, and I just want you to kiss me again?"

He tried to look away from her. He desperately fought for self-control. One of them had to be the smarter one in this situation.

Her frown deepened. "Maybe the truth is I'm a bad kisser. Maybe the real problem is you just really don't want to kiss me again."

"Oh, woman, you have no idea how badly I've wanted to kiss you again," he half growled.

She moved so close to him on the sofa she was practically sitting in his lap. "Then kiss me, Jake. I desperately need you to kiss me again right now."

He had the single thought that he was an absolute

fool, that they were both complete fools, before his mouth captured hers. Instantly fire leaped into his veins as he tasted her soft, pillowy lips.

She moaned deep in the back of her throat as she allowed him to deepen the kiss. Her arms rose and her hands moved to the back of his head as she moved closer and closer still to him.

She was so warm and her breasts pressed against him as if to torment him further. Someplace in the back of his mind he knew he should stop this, that he should pull away from her and halt the sweet rush of adrenaline that filled his veins. However, that voice was just a whisper beneath the shout of his desire for her.

She certainly didn't seem inclined to stop the kiss. She moved her hands from the back of his head to his shoulders and actually continued to pull him closer.

He was lost to her, in her.

He couldn't think rationally when he was kissing her. When she was in his arms his brain froze and he was nothing more than his need and want of her.

Finally she pulled back from him. Her eyes appeared to blaze a blue he'd never seen before. He took a moment to breathe.

"Jake, I want you to make love to me."

Her words punched him square in the gut and all the air left his body. All he could think about was having her naked and in his arms. Right or wrong, foolish or not, he didn't want to think anymore.

"Please, Jake." She got up from the sofa and held

her hand out to him. "Take me to your bed and make love to me."

He stumbled to his feet and took her hand. "Are you sure?"

"I've never been more sure of anything in my life." Her certainty shone from her eyes and filled her voice.

There were a dozen steps or so where either one of them could have changed their mind about what was about to happen. But neither of them spoke a word as they headed down the hallway toward his master bedroom.

MONICA HAD FOUGHT her growing desire for Jake for what seemed like forever. Kissing him again had only made her want him more. Over the last couple of days the sexual tension between them had been off the charts. And tonight she decided to follow through on that desire.

They entered his large bedroom and the butterflies that danced in her chest had her half-breathless. The only light in the room was the soft illumination that shone from a lamp on his nightstand.

He immediately pulled her back in his arms and took her lips with his once again. His mouth was hot and demanding as his hands tangled in the length of her hair and he held her so close she could tell he was fully aroused.

His mouth left hers and he trailed kisses behind her ear and down the side of her throat. A shiver shot down her spine at the hot sensations he evoked in her. Then once again his lips returned to hers.

It had been a long time since she'd allowed herself to be this vulnerable with any man, and yet something about Jake made her feel safe…safe to explore an intimate moment with him.

She ended the kiss and stepped back from him. Holding his gaze, she unfastened her shorts and stepped out of them, leaving her in the wispy pink silk underpants she'd put on that morning.

She heard his breath catch as his gaze swept down the length of her bare legs. He yanked his shirt over his head and tossed it to the floor.

He had a beautiful chest with well-defined muscles and skin that looked so warm and touchable. His eyes burned with a wildness that only excited her more.

He walked over to her and began to unfasten the buttons on her blouse. She held her breath as he caressed and then kissed each inch of skin that was revealed. When he finished with the last button, he gently pushed the blouse off her shoulders. It fell to the floor behind her.

She watched breathlessly as he stepped back from her and took off his jeans. He had a beautiful body. His stomach was flat and his hips were lean and his long legs were perfectly shaped.

They got into the bed and instantly their legs entwined as they kissed once again. It was another hot kiss that stirred her desire for him to a new level.

He stroked up and down her back with hands that

felt fevered against her skin and she did the same, loving the play of his back muscles beneath her fingers.

His lips slid off hers and once again he trailed nipping, teasing kisses down the side of her neck. At the same time his fingers unfastened her bra. He plucked it from her and tossed it away.

"You are so beautiful," he whispered in her ear. "And I feel like I've wanted you since the moment you barged into my life."

"I feel the same way about you," she said breathlessly, and then gasped as his hands moved to caress her breasts. Then his mouth was there, licking and sucking first one taut nipple and then the other. Electric currents ran through her and her need for him grew.

Within minutes they were both naked and exploring each other's bodies with kisses and touches meant to bring the most pleasure.

It was beyond pleasurable. She was lost in a haze of sweet sensations. As his hand moved down her stomach to touch at the very core of her, she thought she might explode.

Gently at first, his fingers moved against her in a rhythm that had her gasping. She arched up, needing…demanding more from him. He increased the pressure of his touch and quickened and suddenly she was there, falling over a cliff as wave after wave of pleasure washed through her.

"Yes…oh yes," she cried breathlessly.

For a moment she was limp, boneless in his arms

as she attempted to catch her breath. He leaned down and kissed her, the kiss filled with his own hunger.

She reached down and took hold of him. He was fully aroused and he released a deep moan at her touch. Just that quickly she wanted more of him. She wanted all of him.

She stroked his velvety length slowly at first and then more quickly. He moaned again and grabbed her hand to stop her.

He disentangled from her and rolled over to the nightstand. He opened the top drawer and withdrew a condom. She took it from him, ripped the foil and then rolled the condom onto him. For a long moment their gazes locked. She lay back and silently invited him onto her, into her.

He eased into her with a deep sigh and she closed her eyes as new waves of pleasure shuddered through her. Slowly he began to stroke into her as she gripped his taut buttocks.

She thrust her hips up to meet him, half-wild and out of control. It didn't take long for him to start to stroke faster…deeper, and then she was there again, her climax making her cry out his name.

He stiffened against her and groaned as his own climax gripped him. Neither of them moved; the only sound in the room was their panting breaths slowing to a more normal rhythm.

Languidly she stroked a hand up and down his back. "That was wonderful," she said.

"It was better than wonderful." He kissed her gently on the forehead. "I'll be right back." He rolled off her and then disappeared into the master bathroom.

She stared up at the ceiling and released a deep sigh. She'd half hoped that he sucked in bed, that he would be a selfish or lazy lover. If that had been the case then she'd be over him and she would have easily gotten him out of her head.

But he hadn't been any of those things. He'd been tender and giving and more than wonderful as a lover. Right at this moment, with her body sated and the scent of him lingering on her skin, she knew it was going to be very hard to get him out of her head.

She'd like to stay in bed and cuddle with him, remain in his arms and talk about dreams and hopes and the kind of afterglow conversation most couples indulged in after making love. And that's why she got up.

She was half-dressed when he came out of the bathroom wearing a black robe. He sat on the edge of the bed and gazed at her thoughtfully. "Uh…maybe we should talk about things?" he said tentatively.

"There's really nothing to talk about." She pulled her blouse on and began to button it. "Neither one of us wants any kind of a romantic relationship and nothing about what just happened between us changes that."

She finger-combed her hair and smiled at him. "Let's not make this complicated, Jake. We desired each other, we acted on that desire, and there's nothing wrong with that. We're both single adults. Look at it this way, we're friends with benefits, right?"

He looked relieved. "Okay, then I'll just get dressed and we can go back to television watching until it's time to sit on Adam's house."

"Perfect," she replied, and left him alone in his bedroom. She returned to the family room and sank down on the sofa. She'd talked a good game with Jake just now, but the truth was her heart was starting to get involved with him.

They definitely needed to identify the killer soon so she could get back to her own life and try to forget about Jake Lamont. In the meantime, she definitely needed to hang on to her heart.

Minutes later he rejoined her in the family room but instead of sitting next to her on the sofa, he sank down in his recliner.

"I was just thinking I've been very lax," she said.

He raised an eyebrow. "I would definitely dispute that statement, especially given this evening's uh...activities."

Warmth leaped into her cheeks. "I wasn't talking about this evening. I'm talking about since I've been here. I haven't even called a glass company to get my front window fixed."

"There's no real hurry on that," he replied. "Surely you're not thinking about going back to your house anytime soon?"

"Jake, I need to go home eventually. I'm going to call first thing in the morning and set something up. Would you mind taking me there sometime tomorrow so I can get it done?"

"Just let me know what time and of course I'll take you there," he replied.

They made small talk and watched television until eleven and then drove to Adam's house and parked across the street. Despite the fact that he had just had her in his bed, she was acutely aware of him. His scent…the memory of his touches, just his very presence in the small confines of the car ignited a new flame of desire in the pit of her stomach.

The sex had been amazing, but her desire for him went beyond the actual physical act of lovemaking. She wanted his arms wrapped around her. She wanted to cuddle with him and press her face in the hollow of his neck where she knew she'd smell his scent. She wanted to gaze into his beautiful eyes and talk about their innermost hopes and fears.

What was wrong with her? The last thing she wanted was an emotional connection with him. Sex was fine, but anything deeper or more profound than that was out of the question.

Their surveillance that night passed uneventfully. He was unusually quiet and she filled the silence chattering about her desire to get a little black schnauzer when this was all over.

The next morning she called the glass company to set up an appointment. "He can't meet us until four thirty this afternoon," she told Jake as they sat at the table drinking coffee.

"We'll be there," he replied.

He'd been a bit distant all morning… quiet and

withdrawn. Was it because of their lovemaking? Or was he just tired of having her as a houseguest?

Maybe it was time she really thought about moving back home. While the gunfire that had nearly killed them was still fresh in her mind and the idea of being there all alone was daunting, perhaps she had worn out her welcome here.

They could still do their nightly surveillance, but during the days they'd have their distance from each other.

"I guess the police didn't figure anything out about who shot at us since nobody has called us with any follow-up information," she said, breaking the silence that had built up to be oppressive between them.

"I didn't expect them to have anything for us," he replied. "Drive-by shootings have got to be one of those crimes that are difficult to solve."

"Along with crazy serial killers," she added.

He frowned into his coffee cup and then looked back at her. "I keep thinking there's got to be a more efficient way to out the killer, but damned if I can come up with anything." His frustration was rife in his voice.

She reached out and covered his hand with hers. "We're doing the best we can, Jake."

"I can't go to the police with my gut instincts and without any kind of evidence." He pulled his hand from hers. "I need to stop him before he kills another person."

"So, if it's Adam, then you intend to call the police when he leaves his house in the middle of the night?"

"Monica, it isn't against the law to leave your house no matter what time it is. I intend to follow him to his victim's house and wait until he breaks in, then I'll take him down and call the police."

She stared at him. "Jake, that's way too dangerous," she said softly.

"I told you before I intended to do that," he replied.

"I guess it didn't compute in my brain before. I don't want you to put yourself in that kind of situation."

His eyes were dark. "It's the only way to take down a killer I helped create."

"Jake, you can't take credit for creating a monster. Whether this is Adam or somebody else, they had more than a little bit of monster already inside them before you six got together."

His gaze searched her face. "Do you really believe that?"

"I definitely believe it," she said firmly. "For God's sake, let yourself off that particular hook, Jake. This person is broken, and was probably broken long before you ever met him."

He leaned back in his chair and released a deep sigh. "I guess I'm just feeling discouraged this morning."

"I'm sorry you're discouraged. What else can we do? Do you want to call the police and tell them you believe Adam is the killer? You don't have to tell them about the pact. You can just say you know him and you believe he's the killer."

He shook his head. "No, I don't want to ruin an innocent man's life and I'm still not one hundred percent sure Adam is our man. It's possible the killer could be Matt Harrison."

"Why haven't you talked much about him before?"

He sighed once again. "Because of all the men, I really didn't want it to be Matt. Matt and I got particularly close when we were attending the meetings. He's my age, and separate from our grief and anger, we had a lot of other things in common. We'd stay at the bar after the others had left and just talk."

"So, what's his story?" she asked.

"His mother was beaten to death by Brian McDowell. Matt believed that McDowell didn't know she was home when he broke in. She surprised him and he used a baseball bat to kill her."

"Another tragedy," she replied softly. "Brian McDowell was the first victim of the Vigilante Killer.

He nodded. "That's right. Is that a clue? Did the Vigilante Killer murder the man who had wronged him and he then moved on to the others?"

It was a question that hung in the air with no answer. She fought the impulse to reach out and touch him again. She could feel the weight of discouragement wafting off him and she wished she knew how to take it away from him.

He remained quiet through the course of the day and at a little after four they were in his car and headed to her house to meet the glass guy. Jake wore a pair of jeans, a navy T-shirt and another lightweight blazer. She knew beneath the blazer he had on his shoulder holster, which he'd worn each time they'd left the house since the night of the shooting.

"At least with the window fixed the house will be ready for me to come home to," she said as they pulled up in her driveway.

"You're still going to have some work to do on the wall that got shot up," he said. "Don't be in too much of a rush to get back here." He shut off the engine and together they got out of the car.

"You've been so quiet today I thought maybe I'd worn out my welcome."

"That's definitely not the case," he replied. "I guess I have been quiet today, but it's just because I've spent the day trying to see how this all ends and right now I just don't see it.

She withdrew her key from her purse, unlocked her front door, and then turned and smiled at him. "I hope it ends with us being friends long after this is all over."

"I'd like that," he replied.

She shoved her door open but he pushed her behind him and drew his gun. "Let's just check things out before we get comfortable.

She followed him into the dark living room. With the board on the window, it felt like an alien space. His gun led them into the kitchen, where he opened the pantry door to make sure nobody was inside.

Her heart was once again thudding an unnatural

rhythm as they left the kitchen and he then led her down the hallway. Was there somebody hiding out in one of her bedrooms? Somebody just waiting for their return here?

He whirled into the first room…her guest room. He walked past the queen-size bed covered in a turquoise spread and right to the closet. He threw open the closet door and then relaxed, but a knot of tension still worked in his jaw.

They cleared the hall bathroom and the room she used as her office and then approached her bedroom. If anyone was in the house they were somewhere in this room.

Her heart beat more rapidly as they stepped into the room, where the bed was covered with her lavender floral spread and wispy lavender curtains hung at the window. This room had always brought her a sense of calm and peace, but not now.

He checked her master bathroom and then stared at her closet door. There was no sound in the air except for her slightly panicked breaths.

He jerked open her closet door and they both breathed a sigh of relief. "It looks like we're alone," he said, and holstered his gun.

"Thank God," she replied.

Together they returned to the living room, where she quickly turned on one of the lamps on the end table next to the sofa, but even that illumination seemed inadequate to chase away the darkness of evil the room held to her.

Would this ever feel like her home again? Not only

did she need to get the window replaced but she also needed to contact somebody about fixing the walls where the bullets had hit. Once all the damage was taken care of, would she be able to embrace this space as her own little haven once again?

"Are you okay?"

Jake's question pulled her from her thoughts. She forced a smile. "I'm fine. It's just that this doesn't really feel like my home right now."

"Once you get things taken care of here I'm sure you'll feel better. Did you contact your insurance company?"

"I gave them a call that first morning at your house. Unfortunately, I have a fairly high deductible so I think these repairs will be out of pocket for me."

"Do you have the money to take care if it?" His gaze turned soft. "I don't mean to pry into your finances, but I'd be happy to help you with this expense."

Her chest swelled with emotion. "Thanks, but I've got this," she replied.

Before she could say anything more, Mitchell Blackmore of Blackmore Windows and Glass and his assistant, a kid named Kurt, arrived. Mitchell and Jake removed the plywood from the window and then Mitchell measured the space.

"I drove by here earlier and eyeballed the window. I guessed at the size, which is fairly common in these homes in this neighborhood, and I have a window that will fit on my truck," Mitchell said.

"Great, then let's get it done," Monica replied.

She sat on the sofa next to Jake, and as Mitchell and Kurt worked to replace the window, the three men talked about sports. Monica fell into thoughts of everything that had happened since she met Jake.

His offer to help her pay for the damage had touched her heart. Heck, everything about him touched her heart. Making love with him had been her idea and she now realized it had been a big mistake. She'd thought she could have sex with him and not get emotionally involved.

She'd been wrong.

She was more than a little bit crazy about him and she hadn't seen that coming. She watched him now as he laughed at something Mitchell had said.

Why didn't he want a relationship? Was it just that he didn't want one with her, or was it that he didn't want to have one with anyone?

Didn't he want a family? Children? They hadn't really talked about these things and now she was curious. And then she told herself it didn't matter what his answers were to those questions. She just wanted her story.

Why couldn't you have your story and your man? a little voice whispered inside her head. She'd always thought that it had to be one or the other. Her career or love. So, why couldn't she have both? She dismissed the very idea. No matter what she felt for Jake, he'd made it clear there was no future with him.

The window was done. Monica paid them with a check and then Mitchell and Kurt left. "Is there anything you need to get from here before we leave?" Jake asked as he got up from the sofa.

She should tell him she was just going to stay here. It would be the smart thing to do. That way she could gain some much-needed distance from him before she fell for him so hard her heart would be scarred forever.

However, she had to admit she wasn't ready to be here all the time and all alone. In fact, she couldn't wait to get out of this place right now. Even with the brightness of late afternoon drifting in the new window, she still felt a darkness that lingered. Maybe in another day or two she'd be ready to return here.

"Yeah, I might grab a few more things." She could use a couple more T-shirts and maybe a few more blouses for her podcasts. It didn't matter what kind of pants she had on because her viewers saw her only from the waist up. But she always wore a professional businesslike blouse when she was being reporter Monica Wright.

"It will just take me a minute or two."

"Take your time," he replied, and sank back on the sofa to wait for her.

She went back in her bedroom and dug a duffel bag out of her closet and then packed it with the items she thought she might need.

When she was finished she realized she'd packed far more than she needed if she intended to move back here in the next day or two. Oh well, she could always carry it back here when it was time.

She returned to the living room and Jake stood.

"All set?" he asked. He reached a hand out to take the duffel bag from her.

"Thanks, but I've got it," she said.

"Okay, then, let's get out of here," he replied.

She locked the front door and they stepped out into the late-afternoon sunshine. She tossed the duffel in the backseat and then slid into the passenger side of his car. He was about to slide in behind the steering wheel when a gunshot sounded and the bullet slammed into Jake's car door.

"Jake!" she screamed.

Chapter Eight

"Get down," Jake yelled at Monica frantically. "Get down and stay down!"

He crouched low behind his car door and looked in the direction from which the bullet had come. Another shot and another bullet slammed into the door. At the same time Jake spied the shooter hiding behind a tree in the distance.

He grabbed his gun and returned fire. Adrenaline spiked through him and his heart beat so fast it felt as if it might explode right out of his chest.

He was vaguely aware of Monica crying, but he had no time to comfort her. His focus was solely on the shooter, who, to Jake's surprise, left the cover of the large tree and began to run away.

There was no way Jake was going to let him get away. This was his best chance to catch and identify the man once and for all.

He stepped away from the cover of the car door. "Jake, no!" Monica screamed.

He didn't listen to her; instead, he took off running after the man. He had a big lead on Jake, but Jake was determined to catch him.

Not only was Jake running all out, but he was also trying to stay close to trees or anything else that might provide cover if the shooter stopped, turned and fired on him.

Yet he half hoped the man would turn around so Jake could get a good look at him. Was he chasing Adam or was it Matt? Both men were built about the same, so he couldn't identify him just from body size alone.

His breaths became pants as sweat rolled down the sides of his face. He fought past the hitch in his side as he raced after the man.

He knew it was the killer. Nothing else made sense and if he could just take him down, then this would all be over. And God, but he wanted it over.

With this thought in mind he pushed himself harder, but the man was apparently running just as fast because Jake wasn't gaining ground on him.

Look back, he willed the person. *Just look back for one minute so I can see your face. Dammit, look back so I can identify you.*

He thought about shooting him and then quickly dismissed the idea. If he shot the man in the back, then he'd probably be the one who wound up behind bars.

The man cut through a yard and quickly climbed over a chain link fence. A dog began barking frantically. Jake followed right behind him, stumbling a bit as he got over the fence.

Another fence rose up before him and he got over it, too. The man disappeared around a corner and when Jake went around the corner as well, the man's gun fired again.

Jake hit the ground. What little breath he had left whooshed out of him. Thank God the man didn't have a perfect aim. Dammit, he hadn't even had a chance to see his face and now he was running once again.

Jake made it to his feet and continued his pursuit.

Once again he pushed himself harder and faster and just when he was beginning to gain some ground, the man jumped into a car parked at the curb and roared off.

"No!" Jake yelled. He instantly bent over at the waist and drew in deep lungfuls of air in an effort to catch his breath. "Dammit." He released a mouthful of curses. He couldn't believe the man had gotten away. He couldn't believe he hadn't been able to identify him.

He turned to head back in the direction of Monica's house. He hadn't even managed to get a license plate number and the dark sedan the man had left in had been completely unfamiliar to him. Neither of the men he suspected of being the killer drove that color car.

He heard a siren coming closer. Monica must have called the cops or perhaps it was one of the people in the neighborhood.

Monica was probably scared out of her mind for him. Or maybe she was terrified for herself, fearing that Jake would be shot and then the man would come after her.

As his car came into view, he saw Monica leap out of the passenger seat and run down the sidewalk toward him. She was crying and when she reached him she threw her arms around his neck. "Jake, thank God you're okay. I was so afraid for you."

"Hey…stop those tears." He swiped her cheeks with his thumbs and then framed her face with his hands. "I'm okay, Monica. We're both okay." He dropped his hands and led her back to his car.

They had just reached it when a police car turned up her street and cut the siren. "I called them," she said. "I… I was so afraid I didn't know what else to do."

"It's all right," he assured her as an officer with a familiar face got out of the patrol car.

"Can't you two stay out of trouble?" Officer Brian McDonald asked as he approached where they stood.

"Apparently not," Jake replied ruefully.

"So, tell me what happened," he said. "I was called out here because of shots fired."

Monica explained about meeting the glass guy to put in the new window and then Jake took over the story when it got to the bullets flying.

"And you didn't see the man's face?" McDonald asked.

"No," Jake replied in frustration.

"He got into a black sedan?"

"It was either black or dark blue." Jake released a deep sigh. "None of this is going to help you, is it?"

"Not really," McDonald replied. "Is there anyone you can think of who might want you dead?"

"Nobody I can think of," Jake lied. How could he possibly tell the truth about things right now?

"What about you, Ms. Wright? Are you still running those stories about gangs on your podcast?"

"The final one aired last night," she replied.

"Then my advice to the two of you is the same as it was last time I spoke with you. Stay away from here until things have had time to cool off." He looked at Monica. "While I appreciate what you were trying to do with your gang-related reporting, that can be a dangerous world to deal with. It's obvious this guy was sitting on your house and just waiting for you two to return here."

They spoke for a few more minutes and then McDonald waited until they were in Jake's car and pulling out of the driveway before he got into his patrol car and left.

"We both know this had nothing to do with gangs," she said after they had driven a couple of blocks.

"I just wish I'd seen his face." He tightened his grip on the steering wheel as a deep frustration once again swept through him. "Then I would have been sure who the killer is."

"We'll just have to keep sitting on Adam's place until something breaks," she replied. "I was actually thinking about telling you that I was ready to move back to my place before this happened."

"You can move back home when this killer is behind bars," he said, and then realized his voice had been harsher than he'd intended. But the idea of her being in that house all alone right now was untenable. "Sorry, I didn't mean to growl at you, but there's no way I want you alone through this. If I had my way I'd buy you a plane ticket and send you off someplace for a nice vacation."

"And where would you send me?"

"I don't know. Maybe Aspen. You could ski during the days and then sit in front of a fireplace and enjoy hot rum drinks during the evenings."

"I really don't see myself as a snow bunny," she replied lightly. "And besides, there's no snow in Aspen in August."

"Then I'll send you to a Caribbean island."

"Hmm, I'm not much of a sun worshipper, either. You know, the whole skin cancer thing. I guess this nails it, you're just stuck with me until the very end."

He knew she was trying to lighten the mood, but he didn't want her with him until the end. The gunshot coming out of nowhere had scared him in a way nothing else had. Despite her window being shot out, he hadn't expected a gun. He definitely hadn't expected anything in the middle of the afternoon.

The bullets today were meant for him, but that didn't mean tomorrow there wouldn't be bullets aimed at her. The bad news was the killer probably knew she was a reporter and so she would be seen as a threat.

Nothing was going to change that. Even if Jake was killed, she'd still be a target. The killer didn't want her to talk and tell whatever she might know, just as he didn't want Jake to talk. They both would continue to be in danger until the killer was behind bars. This had gotten far more dangerous than he'd ever thought it would be.

When they reached his house he pulled into the garage and closed the automatic door behind them. Only then did they both get out of the car.

"How does a frozen pizza sound for dinner?" he asked when they were in the kitchen. "I don't really feel like cooking tonight. I've got a meat-lover's in the freezer."

"I don't feel like cooking, either, so that sounds good to me. Can I do anything?"

"No, I've got it." As he turned on the oven to pre-heat, she sank down at the table. "Beer?" he asked.

"Absolutely," she agreed.

He pulled two beers from the refrigerator and then joined her at the table. It didn't escape him how normal it felt for the two of them to sit together in his kitchen.

It also felt normal for them to sit on the sofa together and laugh about a sitcom or fall into a deep discussion after watching a crime drama. It worried him that he liked her in his house and sharing his life.

He hadn't allowed anyone to get emotionally close to him since Suzanna's murder, but somehow Monica had gotten in. He not only liked her but he believed he was falling in love with her. And no matter how much he loved her, he couldn't have her.

He had to distance himself from her, but not right

now. Despite her chatter, he could feel her fear wafting from her. They had just been through a traumatic experience and now was not the time to pull away from her.

He definitely felt the end coming. He just hoped when all was said and done Monica was safe and sound and could go back to her life with a big story and a few good memories of him.

AS THEY ATE their pizza Monica kept up a stream of inane talk. She told him about being a pest to her older sisters when she'd been little and her few memories of her mother when she'd been alive.

"All I remember of my mother is her soft hands brushing my hair away from my face right before she kissed me good-night and the way she smelled of roses and vanilla. Do you have any good memories of your mother?"

"Not really. She was pretty much an absent mother once she started doing the dope. Suzanna and I used to joke that we could be on fire and my mother would use us to cook her stuff."

"That's so not funny," she replied.

"I know. So tell me more about you and your sisters."

"I remember one night my oldest sister and her boyfriend were sitting on our porch swing. I hid in the bushes and watched them because I was sure they would do something scandalous that I could then report back to my father and get her in trouble."

"And?" His eyes held laughter waiting to be released. She loved that look on his face.

"And nothing. They were so boring I fell asleep. I got in trouble for scaring my dad when he couldn't find me anywhere in the house."

The wonderfully deep and warm laugh she'd waited to hear was released from him. She needed the laughter and the talk to keep her fear at bay.

Those long minutes when she'd been sitting in the car all alone and Jake had gone running after the bad guy had been the most torturous she'd ever experienced.

She hadn't been afraid for herself; rather, all of her fear had been for Jake. She was terrified that he'd be hurt and she couldn't imagine the world without Jake in it.

And in that intense fear for him, the depth of her love for Jake had been realized. It didn't matter that they'd known each other only a short amount of time. It didn't matter that the timing wasn't right for her to be in love. The truth of the matter was she was in love with him and timing be damned.

Now she had to figure out what she intended to do about it. Right now she wanted to deal with none of it. She just wanted to laugh and eat and relax after the harrowing afternoon they'd had.

"Then there was the time I put a frog in my sister's bed," she continued, wanting to make him laugh again.

"I'm sure that didn't go over well," he replied.

She gave him a slightly wicked grin. "I can still

hear her screams in my head. Sadly I was grounded for a week. When my dad asked me why I would do such a thing, I told him she acted like she was a princess, so I thought if she slept with the frog he'd turn into a prince who would take my sister to his castle."

He laughed again. "You must have been something else. I almost feel sorry for your sisters."

"Oh, trust me, they deserved everything I did to them. They were both mean to me when we were all young. When I was nine they had me convinced that I was adopted and Mom and Dad had taken me in because nobody else in the whole world wanted me."

"So, you never got close to them when you got older?" he asked.

"No. I think a lot of the problem was they were so much older than me. They had different interests than me and we just never really connected. I love them both and we get along fine when we get together for holidays. We just never really became friends."

"Maybe it isn't too late to change things with them," he replied. "I'd love to have more siblings. Wouldn't your sisters be the keepers of your mother's memory?"

She looked at him in surprise. "I never really thought about it that way before." There had been several times in her recent memory that her sisters had invited her to lunch, or to coffee, and she'd always come up with an excuse not to meet them. When this was all over maybe it was time for her to do things differently when it came to her sisters.

She continued to chatter as they finished the pizza and cleaned up the kitchen. After dinner they moved into the living room and turned on the television. It was then that the fear she'd suffered while waiting, while wondering if Jake would return to the car, began to simmer once again inside her.

He sat close enough to her that she could smell the comforting scent of him; she could feel his body heat radiating toward her.

She'd thought he might not return to the car when he'd taken off after the gunman. She'd been so afraid he'd be shot and fall to the ground and die before anyone could get to him.

As these dark thoughts continued to fill her head, she moved closer to him. Emotion permeated her chest and tears pressed hot at her eyes.

"Monica, are you all right?" he asked.

She turned and looked at his beautiful face and the tears that had only burned at her eyes began to fall. "No…no, I'm not okay," she managed to say. "I… I think I'm having some kind of stupid delayed reaction."

"A delayed reaction about what?" His gaze was soft, but obviously bewildered.

"I was just so afraid for you when you took off running after the gunman." Her emotions were spiraling out of control and at the moment she couldn't do anything about it. The tears chased each other down her cheeks as a choking sob escaped her.

"Hey, hey," he said softly, and then he did what

she wanted him to do more than anything in the world…he drew her into his arms.

She clung to him as her tears continued to fall and she was grateful that he held her so tightly that she could feel the reassuring steady beat of his heart.

His arms warmed every cold place in her body and she welcomed the warmth. They also offered strength and the assurance that he really was okay.

At this moment her getting her story seemed unimportant. What was important was that Jake survive through this. It was important that he keep building beautiful structures that inspired people. He needed to continue to live and breathe and laugh until the natural end of his life. And she'd like to live that long, wonderful life with him.

Her tears slowed and finally stopped. Reluctantly she pulled back from him and gave an unsteady laugh. "Sorry about that. I don't want you to see me as a big crybaby."

"I don't, and I'm sorry you were so frightened," he replied.

"I really was. All I could think about was you being wounded and lying all alone in somebody's yard."

He smiled at her. "I feel like we're a couple of old cats who have nine lives."

"What scares me is I think we've already used up several of those lives," she replied.

He sobered and held her gaze. "Monica, there's no reason for you to use up any more of those cat lives."

She shook her head to stop anything else he was

about to say. "We've already had this discussion more than once and there's no point in having it again. I'm in this until the very end."

He frowned. "You're extremely stubborn."

She grinned. "Yes, I am, and you should remember that."

"So noted."

They returned to watching television. But she was still deep in her thoughts. Without her fear, there was nothing to stop her from thinking about her feelings for him. She began to nibble on her fingernail.

"I thought you were trying to stop that," he said.

She gave him a sheepish smile and dropped her hand back to her lap. "Thanks for reminding me. I'd like to have pretty nails, but I can't achieve that if I don't quit chewing on them. It's a nervous habit I need to stop."

"Are you nervous right now?"

"Not really," she replied.

As they continued to watch television, her thoughts were all over the place. When had her emotions toward him gone from liking him to loving him? Had it been when he'd released his last burst of laughter? Or when he looked at her with that soft, warm gaze that made her feel like the most important woman in the world?

Had she fallen from like to love the first time he'd kissed her? Or had it been when he'd told her about his sister and she had shared his pain?

She didn't know the answer. All she knew was that despite her desires to the contrary, she was in love with Jake Lamont. And she believed he had feelings for her, too.

When the show they had been watching ended, she turned to look at him. "Jake, why don't you want a long-term relationship in your life?"

The question obviously took him by surprise. "I just don't."

"Do you mean right now you don't want one or you never want one for the rest of your life?"

"I intend to be alone for the rest of my life," he replied. Tension had straightened his shoulders and his eyes became dark and hooded.

"Don't you eventually want a family? Maybe children?"

He leaned forward and raked a hand through his hair. "I thought about it at one time," he answered after a long pause. "But then I changed my mind."

He looked achingly sad. She placed her hand over his. "Was your change of mind because of Suzanna's murder?"

He hesitated once again and then gave a curt nod of his head.

"Oh, Jake. Do you really think that's what Suzanna would want for you? To be alone for the rest of your life?"

"It doesn't matter what she'd want. She isn't here and this is a choice I've made for myself," he replied. He pulled his hand from beneath hers.

"Then it's a choice that makes me very, very sad for you," she replied softly.

"Don't be sad for me. I'll be fine. I have my work and that's all I need."

"Work doesn't keep you warm on a cold night."

"When my bedroom gets cold, I just turn up the heater," he replied.

"Work doesn't make a good conversationalist," she countered.

"I like talking to myself just fine," he answered flippantly. "Besides, you've said the same thing, that you don't want a long-term relationship."

"That's just for right now. Eventually I do want a family. I want to be married and have two children. I want to wake up in the morning and see a man who loves and adores me every morning across the kitchen table. I want to sleep in the same man's arms every night until I die. I can't imagine that you wouldn't want that same thing for yourself."

"Well, I don't."

She released a deep sigh. The conversation was going nowhere and she knew for sure now wasn't the time for her to confess that she was in love with him. That definitely wouldn't make the remainder of their time together comfortable.

It was funny…a couple of weeks before she would have been arguing that her work was enough, that she didn't need or want any relationship to take her mind off her ultimate goal of success.

But what really defined success? Was it a thousand more blog followers or looking at the same man across a dinner table for the rest of your life? Was it getting the big story or was it having somebody

who wanted to share the little moments of your life
with you?

All she hoped for right now was that somehow
before this all came to an end, Jake would decide he
wanted love and a long-term relationship in his life
and she desperately hoped he'd realize he wanted
that with her.

Chapter Nine

It had been an awkward conversation the night before and the next afternoon Jake found it playing and re-playing through his mind. He sat at the kitchen table with a sketch pad before him, but the last thing on his mind at the moment was building designs.

All he could think about at the moment was the warmth of Monica's body in his arms while she'd cried with her fear for him. When he'd told her he intended to live his life alone, her beautiful blue eyes had radiated sadness...and something else...something that had made his breath catch in the back of his throat.

For a moment he'd thought he'd seen love shining true and strong from her eyes. He didn't want her to love him. Dammit, she was supposed to just want her big story and nothing more from him. Her loving him would only make telling her goodbye that much more difficult. And he had every intention of telling her goodbye when this was over.

Once again they had spent a couple of uneventful hours of the night staking out Adam's house. They had both been quiet during those hours and he'd been grateful to get home and go to bed.

Unfortunately his sleep had been filled with visions of her. In his dreams they had been sitting on a metal beam, staring up at the stars overhead, and then they had been in his bed and making love. He'd finally awakened with a bittersweet longing for what he couldn't have.

She was now in his office, doing research for the podcast she did every night at eight. He never told her but when she was doing her podcast from his office, he was usually in the kitchen watching it on his laptop.

She always looked professional clad in dress blouses, although beneath his desk where the viewers couldn't see she was in shorts and sandals.

Her takes on the news stories of the day were different and thought-provoking. She offered the viewers human-interest stories that were sometimes funny and sometimes sad.

Once she left his house and they returned to their own private lives, he would never watch her again. It would be too painful to see her on the air every night and remember her time here with him.

She'd told him that she hoped they would be friends at the end of all this and he'd agreed that would be nice. But he realized now he couldn't be her friend. When this was all over he had to completely cut her from every aspect of his life.

He'd pray for amnesia where she was concerned. He'd open up all his doors and windows to rid the house of her exotic scent and make sure not an article of clothing of hers remained behind when she left here.

There was no way he'd want to meet her for a friendly lunch or for coffee. When they said their final goodbyes, he needed to somehow never think about her again.

He looked up as the object of his thoughts bounced into the kitchen. "Guess what?" She sat at the table facing him, her eyes sparkling brightly.

"What?"

"My snitch just called me. He said earlier this morning some man walked into the North Patrol station and confessed to being the Vigilante Killer and they're taking his claim very seriously."

"Did he tell you who it was?" Jake sat up straighter in his chair as a burst of adrenaline filled him. Was it possible? Would the killer really turn himself in?

"No, he said he'd call me with more details as soon as he could." She leaned forward, a simmering energy wafting from her. "Do you think this could really be the end?"

"I don't know. The guy taking shots at me yesterday didn't seem to me to be the kind of man who would suddenly develop a conscience and feel remorseful enough to turn himself in," he replied dubiously. "But I suppose anything is possible," he added. "Did he give you any indication when he might get back to you?"

"I got the impression it wouldn't be that long. He said things were popping very fast on the case."

"Who is this source of yours?" he asked curiously.

"He's a lieutenant at the North Patrol."

"And how did you get hooked up with him?" he asked. "Did you show up on his front porch, too?"

She laughed. "No, we dated for a while in high school and remained good friends after we broke up."

"Is this somebody who still might have a thing for you?" He wasn't sure why he held his breath waiting for her to reply.

"Heavens, no," she said with another laugh. "In fact, he married one of my best friends and they have a four-year-old and a new baby."

He didn't want to examine the wave of relief that shot through him. She obviously had him twisted up in his brain. "So I guess we just have to wait until we have more information," he said.

"Even though this wouldn't exactly be a big and dramatic end to a story, him turning himself in would be the best way for this to end for everyone," she said.

"As long as he can't kill another person, that's all I've ever cared about," he replied. Right now he had too many questions to feel confident that this was really the end. It just seemed strange that the perp would decide to give up and turn himself in.

"But I'm sorry that it sounds like you won't get your big story...unless you decide to go public with everything I told you about the murder pact. Now that would probably be the kind of sensational story you want."

She stared at him with eyes that suddenly held a touch of frost. "I would hope you knew me better than that. You told me that information in confidence and I would never run with that story. It offends me that you even entertain the idea that I might."

She continued to stare at him, apparently waiting for him to offer her some sort of an apology. But he remained silent. Maybe it was a good thing she was irritated with him. If this really was the end of things, then maybe making her a little angry with him wasn't all bad.

"I'm going to go check and see if any other newscasts have this as breaking news," she said, and jumped up from the table. "I'll let you know if I get more information." Her tone of voice held the frost in her eyes.

He watched her leave the kitchen and then he stood and walked into the family room. He was now too restless just to sit. Instead he paced back and forth in front of his sofa as thoughts whirled around in his head.

He was sorry if he'd hurt Monica's feelings, but maybe that's what he needed to do. Maybe he needed to show her that he was a miserable man who deserved to be alone.

Thoughts of Monica were overtaken by thoughts of the latest development. Once again he wondered if it was possible this really was the end. That the killer had turned himself in. Even though he found it hard to believe, he hoped like hell it was true.

He and Monica would no longer be in any danger. There would be no more heinous deaths of people with Vs carved into their foreheads and Jake would be able to finally put this all behind him.

And it would be time to tell Monica goodbye for good. He was surprised at the wave of depression that swept through him at this thought.

He needed to tell her goodbye, but that didn't mean he wouldn't miss her smiles and the sound of her laughter. He'd miss her chatter and even her grumpy face in the mornings. He was just going to miss her like hell.

Fifteen minutes later she joined him in the living room where he'd finally sat in his recliner and turned on the television. "I checked every news source I could think of and nobody is reporting anything on the killer." She sank down on the sofa with her cell phone in hand. "I'm just hoping my snitch will let me know what's going on sooner rather than later."

She gazed at him for several long moments. "If this really is the end of things, there's one thing I want us to do before I go back to my house."

"What's that?" he asked tentatively.

"I want you to take me up in the beams and show me Suzanna's stars."

Myriad emotions rushed through him. Memories of his sister…his love for Monica…and the pain of a final goodbye to both. For a moment he couldn't speak as a huge lump rose up in the back of his throat.

"I'm sorry. Maybe it's not such a good idea after all," she said.

"No, I think it's a great idea," he finally said. He'd take her up to the stars and then he'd send her back to her house, back to her life, and he would return to his life of isolation.

As they waited for her to get another call from her snitch, he channel surfed to see if they could find any breaking news about the killer. But there was nothing.

He glanced over at her and noticed she was chewing on her fingernail once again. "Nails," he said.

She dropped her hand to her lap. "Thanks."

"Have you always been a nail-chewer or is it something you picked up when you met me?" he asked half-teasingly.

"Unfortunately, I've always been a nail-biter, but there's no question that the more stress I'm under the more I chew. What bad habits do you have that I haven't seen yet?"

It was a silly conversation considering they were waiting to get more information about a serial killer, but during their time together he realized she not only chewed her nails when she was stressed, but she also chattered.

"Socks," he replied.

"Socks?"

He nodded. "I have a bad habit of taking them off at night and leaving them at the foot of the bed instead of throwing them in the dirty clothes basket. Sometimes I have three or four pairs at the end of the bed before I pick them up."

"Thank goodness," she replied.

He quirked an eyebrow. "Thank goodness?"

"Yes, thank goodness you aren't as perfect as I thought you were. You do have some flaws."

"Trust me, I'm far from perfect," he replied. If she only knew how imperfect he was, she'd probably run for the hills.

"There's got to be more than socks," she said, her eyes holding a teasing light. "Do you leave the top off the toothpaste? Or maybe when you refill a toilet paper roll you do an under instead of an over?"

He laughed. "Is that really a flaw?"

"Definitely," she replied, and then laughed. "I can't believe we're talking about a serial killer and toilet paper."

"You started it."

Her laughter faded as she stared down at her cell phone. "I just hope he calls soon. I feel like my nerves are jumping out of my skin waiting to find out if this guy who turned himself in is for real."

"I feel the same way. I'm just hoping he's really the killer.

"If he is, then I don't have to worry about you doing something stupid." She held his gaze.

"What do you mean? I try never to do stupid things."

"Your plan to take this guy down while he was in the act of committing murder was a stupid and reckless idea."

He frowned. "It was a plan to get him under arrest once and for all."

"It was a plan that put you at deadly risk," she replied.

"I'd still do it if it meant getting this guy off the streets once and for all."

"You're very stubborn," she observed.

"Yes, I am, and you'd do well to remember that," he said teasingly.

"Duly noted," she replied, parroting his response about her stubbornness.

Fifteen minutes later she got a call from her friend, who told her there would be a news conference at four o'clock that afternoon, and that's all the information he had for her.

Would they learn the identity of the man who had confessed during the press conference? Had Matt or Adam walked into the police station and turned himself in?

Waiting was a study in torture. Monica went back to Jake's office to work on her podcast for that evening and he once again found himself pacing restlessly as he waited for the news conference. He hoped this was the end. This had been a burden on his soul since the very first murder. He couldn't even imagine how he would feel if that particular weight was finally lifted.

It didn't escape him that a new burden had been carved into his heart, and that was his feelings for Monica. When she left, there was no question she'd leave a huge hole and memories of what life might have been like if he'd made a different decision on the night of Suzanna's murder.

At four o'clock they were both back in the living room and seated on the sofa with the television tuned to a local channel that would broadcast the news conference.

A red banner appeared at the bottom of the picture, announcing breaking news. On the screen a lectern appeared and police officers began to fill the space. Chief of Police James Donahue stepped up to a lectern.

James Donahue was a popular man in Kansas City. He was a big man with a burly chest and a head full of snow-white hair. He was beloved not only by the officers who worked beneath him, but also the people of the city. He was known as a straight shooter who didn't give a damn about politics.

"I'd like to begin by introducing the officers who have been working around the clock on the Vigilante Killer case. When I call your name please step forward. Detective Chuck Baker…"

As the officers were called forward, Jake glanced over at Monica, who was chewing on her index fingernail as she leaned forward and watched the television. "Nail," he said softly.

"Right," she replied, and dropped her hand to her lap.

"This morning a man walked into the North Patrol and turned himself in, claiming he was the Vigilante Killer," Donahue said. "After questioning this individual at length, we believe he is who he claims to be."

Reporters began shouting questions. Donahue held up in his hands in an effort to quiet everyone and then he continued, "The man is forty-year-old Grant Timmons and we are still determining motive. That's it, folks. I am not taking questions at this time."

He left the lectern with reporters shouting questions. The channel went back to regular programming and then a local reporter came back on screen with an interview with one of Timmons's coworkers.

"Of course we were all stunned to find out about Grant, but we also knew he seemed to be struggling a bit in his personal life. He lost his parents in a car accident about three months ago and he wasn't the same after that." The reporter spoke to the man for another few minutes and then regular programming returned. Jake lowered the volume on the TV.

It wasn't Adam and it wasn't Matt. Jake was positively stunned.

"Grant Timmons. Do you know him?" Monica asked.

Jake frowned. "The name doesn't ring a bell."

"Let me see what I can pull up about him on the computer," she said, and jumped up off the sofa.

"My laptop is in the kitchen. Why don't you bring it in here?"

As she went to retrieve the computer, he racked his brain for any memory of a Grant Timmons. If he really was the killer, then why had he killed the perps of the men who had been in their murder pact? Why had he come after him and Monica? It didn't make sense.

Monica returned with the laptop and placed it on the coffee table before them. Her fingers danced over the keys and within moments she had a picture of Grant Timmons pulled up.

The photo was on a law firm site where Grant was listed as a paralegal. Jake leaned forward and studied the picture of the dark-haired man.

"He looks vaguely familiar," he said slowly.

"Is it possible he went to the Northland Survivor Group, too?" Monica asked.

"Maybe. I'm thinking maybe he sat in the meetings and never interacted with anyone. We had several men who never introduced themselves or spoke at the meetings. But I can't be sure that the guy I'm thinking about and this Grant are the same person."

"Surely the police wouldn't come out publicly and name the subject without vetting the story," she said.

She was right. The authorities had to have found some kind of corroborating evidence that proved Grant Timmons was, indeed, the Vigilante Killer. Otherwise they wouldn't have held that press conference.

Thank God he hadn't said anything to the police about Matt or Adam. If he had he could have potentially ruined the life of an innocent man.

"So I guess it's really over," he said. "I'm sorry you weren't the one to break the big story."

She shrugged. "There will always be another

story at another time. I'm just glad the killer is behind bars and you and I don't have any bullet holes in our body."

"That is definitely a good thing. So, I guess since we don't have to do our middle-of-the-night surveillance we can go star-watching tonight to celebrate."

"I can't wait. And then tomorrow morning I guess I'll pack up my things and move back home." She looked at him as if waiting for him to say something, anything, that would change things.

But he couldn't choose to change his future. It had been decided for him on the night he'd made a selfish choice that had resulted in the brutal death of his sister.

IT WAS A BEAUTIFUL, clear night and at midnight Jake came out of his bedroom wearing jeans, a T-shirt and one of his black blazers.

"Are you wearing your gun?" she asked in surprise.

"I am."

"But with the killer behind bars surely we don't have anything to worry about."

"It's just a precaution. I'm not thinking about the Vigilante Killer, but I am thinking maybe I should have it with me just in case the drive-by shooting at your house was either the work of gang members or even Larry Albright."

"I don't think it was either of those. I can't help but believe it was the work of the killer."

"But why? Why would he go after the two of us?

We weren't anywhere close to outing him. Neither of us knew him."

She held his gaze and frowned. "I don't know. I don't think we'll ever know the answer to that question, but I guess the gun is a good thing. It doesn't hurt to be prepared," she replied.

"My thought exactly. Besides, when I go downtown at this time of night I always carry."

Minutes later they left his house for his job site.

Although she was looking forward to the night activity of stargazing, overall she was depressed. It wasn't the loss of a big story that had her disheartened; rather, it was the loss of something she'd thought would be wonderful, something she'd somehow thought would happen with Jake.

She'd believed he might be in love with her. She'd thought she'd seen it in his gaze and felt it in his touches. She'd tasted it in his kisses and yet he hadn't said anything to stop the plan of her going home in the morning. And she'd given him a perfect opportunity to do just that.

That upset her far more than not getting the story. She couldn't believe how much she'd changed, how her priorities had shifted since Jake had come into her life.

When they had first met, they had been just alike in their assertions that work was enough, that they didn't want or need anything else in their lives. She was still passionate about her work, but she also had a passion to have Jake in her life forever.

"You're very quiet," he now said, pulling her from her thoughts.

"I've just been thinking about everything that has happened since I so rudely shoved my way into your life," she replied.

He flashed her a quick grin. "It's definitely been a wild ride."

"Definitely," she replied. She'd been kissed and shot at, she'd feared for Jake's life and her own, and through it all she'd fallen in love.

"How often did you and Suzanna go stargazing?" she asked. She needed talk to keep her brain off the emotions that were far too close to the surface.

"Not that often. Maybe once every six weeks or so. It always depended on the weather and the cloud cover and how busy we were with our personal lives and what building was in a state to allow us to go up in the beams," he replied.

"Tonight looks like a perfect night. There isn't a cloud in the sky."

"That's supposed to change. Storms are supposed to move in sometime before morning."

"Then thank goodness we didn't wait any later to come out, and hopefully we'll have time before anything moves in." She looked out the passenger window. The houses they passed were dark and there were few cars on the road.

It was nice to know they were on their way to see nature's beauty and not going to spy on a man they thought was a killer.

She turned to look at Jake, loving the way the dash

light illuminated his handsome features. There was a faint five o'clock shadow on his jaw and it only added to his attractiveness.

"Will this be painful for you?" she asked softly.

"What would be painful?"

"You're taking me to a place where you always took your twin sister." She watched his features closely and relaxed when a soft smile curved his lips.

"When we get up there, will I remember times spent with Suzanna? Absolutely. But they will be good memories about her life."

"And when we get up there, I want you to share more of Suzanna with me." For a moment she wondered if she'd pushed him too far, but he smiled once again.

"I'd like that."

They rode the rest of the way in silence. She released a soft sigh. Her heart was going to be completely crushed when she packed up her things and left his house in the morning.

It wouldn't be because she didn't want to go home; rather, it was because his house had become her home. She didn't want her time with him to end. But he'd never wavered from his declaration that his desire was to spend his life alone.

She'd been such a fool to allow her emotions to get so tangled up with him. Still, there was a tiny nugget of hope in her heart that when tomorrow morning came, he'd confess that he was in love with her and ask her to stay with him forever.

Dammit, she hadn't imagined him falling in love

with her. She hadn't misread his soft glances, the caring touch of his embraces and the desire that still simmered between them like unfinished business. She knew in her heart he was in love with her. What she didn't know was why he would deny himself her love.

When they reached the job site, Jake parked and they both got out of the car. She looked up at the huge skeletal structure silhouetted against the night sky and lit slightly by the streetlights in the area.

"Seeing it in the daytime and at night are two very different things," she said.

"I guess it could be seen as being a bit scary at night," he agreed.

She wasn't about to admit to him how nervous heights made her. She didn't ride the Ferris wheels at carnivals and she'd never chosen to go to a look-out point that was a cliff hanging in the air. But she believed she'd be fine as long as he was by her side.

"We'll go up to the sixteenth floor. The beams on that floor are about two feet wide," he said.

Two feet wide? Twenty-four inches wide? That didn't sound so reassuring. "Isn't there a floor where the beams are at least six feet wide?" she asked.

He laughed. "Afraid not." In the moonlight that spilled down, his features were visible. His smile fell away, and he reached out to shove a strand of her hair away from the side of her face.

There it was… She could swear it was love pouring from his eyes, in his gentle touch. She leaned toward him but he dropped his hand to his side and stepped back.

"You know, we don't have to do this. We can just go back home and call it a night," he said, as if he'd accurately identified the faint fear that whispered through her as she thought of going up on the beams.

"No, I want to do this, but I will admit I have this little thing about heights. As long as you promise me I won't fall, then I'll be fine."

"I promise you'll be fine," he assured her. He took her hand in his and led her to the cage that would take them up. Before they started the ascent, he helped her with putting on a safety harness and then he put one on himself. "I also promise this will be a wonderful experience for you."

As the cage began to take them up, he pulled her close to him. "Can you hear my heartbeat?" she asked.

He smiled at her. "No, I can't hear it. Is it racing?"

"Like a horse at the Kentucky Derby."

"You just tell me if and when you want to go back down and we will."

"I'm sure I'll be fine once I get up there," she replied. As they continued upward she kept her gaze on him, refusing to look down to the ground below.

Just looking at him and feeling his arm around her eased most of her fear. This was a man who had saved her life when bullets had flown through her front window. He'd tried to talk her out of partnering with him a dozen times because he was trying to keep her safe.

If he thought this was dangerous then they wouldn't

be doing it. He would have never put his sister in danger, either. Monica knew without doubt that he would never willingly put her at risk. Knowing this took away any lingering fear she might have entertained.

When they reached the sixteenth floor they stopped, and before she stepped out of the cage, he hooked her harness onto a safety line that ran waist-high across the beam. He then did the same for himself.

"Ready?" he asked. He pulled a flashlight out of his coat pocket, hooked it onto his belt loop and clicked it on.

"I think so."

"I'll go first and if you want to hang on to my shirt or whatever, then you can. We'll take it slow and easy and then stop when we get about midway across."

Midway looked like a long ways away as she stared across the narrow steel beam. "And you swear this safety line will hold me if the worst thing happens and I misstep and fall? You know I've put on a few pounds since I've been staying with you."

A low rumble of laughter escaped him. "Honey, these safety lines work for men three times your size, even if you have put on a few pounds. You ready?"

"Yes, I'm ready." She drew in a deep, steadying breath.

As he began to walk across the beam, she followed right behind him, her hand holding on to the back of his shirt. Thankfully he took small steps.

When they reached about the halfway mark, he turned toward her. "I'll help you sit."

He steadied her while she sat, her legs dangling into dark nothingness. When he sank down next to her, she immediately placed a hand on his thigh, needing to touch him in order to stay grounded.

There was a bit of a breeze that smelled clean and fresh, but held a faint scent of approaching rain. Up here the skies looked different than they did on the ground. The stars looked so much bigger and brighter without the effect of city lights dulling their brilliance.

"Whatever possessed you and Suzanna to do this in the first place?" she asked.

"It was actually Suzanna's idea. She wanted to be closer to the stars and so she talked me into going up in a building we were working on at the time."

Monica looked out and up. "I definitely feel closer to the stars up here. It's beautiful."

"Yeah, but I see a few clouds creeping in."

"Hopefully we'll have plenty of time for you to point out all of Suzanna's favorite stars to me before any storm moves in," she replied.

"I'm not sure she had a favorite." He pointed. "Can you see the Big Dipper there?"

She followed his finger and spied the constellation. "I see it."

"Suzanna used to say the Big Dipper held all the rainbows and occasionally those rainbows would spill over and fall to the earth."

"That's beautiful," Monica said. She couldn't help it, she felt so close to him at this moment she grabbed his hand in hers. "I think I would have liked your sister."

"I think she would have liked you, too," he replied. "You probably would have been good friends."

"I don't have many friends right now. I've been so focused on my work I've kind of neglected all the friends I once had."

"Maybe it's time you rectify that," he replied.

"Maybe. What about you? Do you have friends?" During the time she'd stayed with him, she didn't think he'd received any calls except business ones.

"No. All the friends I once had went away while I was going through my grief and rage period. I pushed them all away."

"Maybe it's time you rectify that." She echoed his words back to him.

"I really don't want to rectify it. I'm good alone."

Once again her heart broke for the wonderful man seated next to her. He was a man who laughed easily, a man who appeared to love life, and yet he intended to live only half a life.

For several moments they both gazed up. "Oh, did you see that?" she exclaimed. "A shooting star."

"I saw it." His voice was soft. "Suzanna used to say that shooting stars were the souls of people who have been released from purgatory and are now on their ascent to heaven."

She squeezed his hand as she heard the deep emotion in his voice. She had a feeling for some reason Jake was trapped in his own purgatory. She just wished if that was the case, that he'd find his way out before she was forced to walk out of his life in the morning.

Chapter Ten

For the next half an hour Jake continued to point out the various constellations in the sky. He was vaguely surprised by how many he remembered Suzanna teaching him about.

He was also surprised that thoughts of Suzanna didn't evoke the piercing, agonizing grief anymore, but instead just brought up a deep and profound sadness that he would never be able to spend time with her again.

Even though he was sharing Suzanna's stars, most of his thoughts up here belonged to the woman who sat next to him and held his hand.

If things were different he could have easily imagined a life with Monica. She enchanted him with her humor. She challenged him with her intellect and she humbled him with the love he felt radiating from her to him.

It was possible she might be brokenhearted when she left his house in the morning, but she'd get over him. Even though he'd jokingly told her he had no skeletons in his closet, he had lied.

Eventually she would find a good man who truly had no skeletons, a man who could love her with open arms and an open heart. But that man wasn't him.

"Was Suzanna always into the stars, or was it an interest she developed as an adult?" Monica asked.

"I think it all started when she was about ten and I bought her a poster that showed all the constellations. I tacked the poster on the ceiling above where she slept. Whenever we moved I made sure the poster always came with us."

He paused thoughtfully. "We never knew where we would live or when we'd get our next meal. Sometimes we were awakened in the middle of the night to sneak away from a landlord my parents owed money to. With all the chaos of our childhood, me and the stars were the only real constants in her life."

"You shame me," she replied.

"How so?"

"I complain that my father doesn't respect my work and I don't believe he loves me as much as I'd like, but I always had a beautiful bedroom and woke up in the same house every morning. I always had food and heat and water and I can't imagine what horror you and your sister went through as children."

"Unfortunately we don't get to pick our parents," he replied.

She squeezed his hand. "I would have picked far better parents for you and your sister."

"Thanks. But that all seems like a lifetime ago."

"So, are you already dreaming of the next building you'd like to see or have you been commissioned by somebody to build another one?"

"I've had a developer contact me about another project, but we're just in the talking stage. It's a smaller office building up north. I'm sure in the back of your brain you're always working on a story for your podcast."

"I thought I had my big story, but that's all fizzled away. I know there will always be another story."

"I still find it hard to believe this man turned himself in. It just doesn't seem to be characteristic of that particular killer."

"I can't imagine the police doing that press conference without having corroborating evidence," she replied. "But I don't want to talk about killers, I want more talk about stars and hopes and dreams."

And that's what they did. He talked to her about his ideas for buildings that would transform the modest skyline of Kansas City into something magical. "We're never going to be a New York or San Francisco, but there's no reason why we can't make the skyline here something people talk about," he said.

She then talked about wanting to be the reporter Kansas City looked to for local stories and news they could trust. "I like going beyond the stories and talking to the people who are affected by crimes. That's why initially I wanted you on my podcast."

He chuckled. "You were rather tenacious. I couldn't believe it when you turned up at my house."

"I'm not sure I would have done that if I hadn't gotten the information about you attending those meetings."

They fell silent for several minutes. The breeze had picked up a bit and cooled off. Thoughts of his sister flitted through his head. He was confident Suzanna would have approved of him bringing Monica up here to see the stars.

Yes, he was certain Monica and Suzanna would have been great friends. They both shared a zest for life and a great sense of humor.

"Have you ever thought about living someplace else?" she asked, pulling him out of his thoughts.

"Never," he replied easily. "This is my hometown and I love it here. What about you?"

"Same. I think this is a great city to live in and I've never wanted to live anyplace else. It's not only a great place to live but I think it's a great place to raise children."

There was part of him that never wanted this time…these moments with her to end. Unfortunately the clouds had begun to thicken, the cooler breeze had begun to blow, and he thought he heard a distant rumble of thunder.

"I think it's time for us to head down," he said reluctantly. "It looks like a storm is moving closer and this is the last place we want to be if it starts to lightning."

"Okay, but there's just one more thing I need to say to you," she replied.

A new tension wafted from her and he knew instinctively he didn't want to hear what she was about to say. What little moonlight was left shone on her face and bathed her features in a silvery glow as she gazed at him.

"I'm in love with you, Jake."

He stared at her in dismay, wanting her to take back the words that had just fallen out of her mouth. From the corner of his eye he caught a movement. He gazed past her and froze.

Matt Harrison stepped out of the cage, a gun in his hand. And there was only one reason he would be here. The police had gotten things wrong.

Adrenaline spiked through Jake's body. In an instant he made a decision… He shoved Monica off the beam. She screamed with terror as she went flying down below the beam and into the darkness.

Jake got to his feet and grabbed his gun. With the other hand he clicked off his flashlight, knowing that it would make him more of a visible target if it was on.

"Matt, what are you doing here?" he yelled above Monica's panicked screams. Jake was sorry about what he'd just done to her, but at least with her dangling in the air below the beam and not between the two men, she wasn't an immediate and easy target.

"You know why I'm here. You're weak, Jake," Matt yelled back.

Monica finally grew silent and he wondered if she'd passed out with fear. "What are you talking about?" Jake asked.

"You know what I'm talking about. You broke the rules by working with that reporter. Have you told her everything? Is she going to break a big story and out me? Have you told her about our murder pact?"

"What murder pact?" Monica screamed from out of the darkness. "Nobody told me anything about a murder pact." Jake drew a breath of relief, knowing she was okay. "Jake is my boyfriend and I don't have any idea who you are or why you're bothering us."

Jake's hand tightened on his gun as a flight-or-fight tension overtook him. Only there would be no flight. He couldn't run from this, especially knowing that Monica wouldn't be safe. But he wouldn't have run even if she wasn't here.

This was what he'd wanted. The ability to stop the killer. It pained him that it was Matt and that the man was now here to continue a reign of terror.

"Matt, what are you doing? I thought we were good friends. Why don't we all get down from here and go someplace where we can have a beer together and really talk?" He didn't want to have to kill Matt. What he'd like to do was talk Matt into turning himself in.

"We were friends, Jake, but that all changed when you hooked up with that reporter. I'm not letting you take me down."

"I don't want to take you down. I want you to turn yourself in and get some help." A flash of lightning split the sky, followed by a rumble of thunder. "Come on, Matt. Let's go have a few beers and then I'll go with you to a police station."

"You don't understand, Jake. I have a calling now. It's my moral duty and job to kill all the guilty people in this city."

"Did you shoot out Monica's front window?" Jake inched backward on the beam.

"Yeah, that was me. You two have been a bit of a problem when it comes to killing you." Matt didn't move from his position. Jake suddenly realized that apparently the man had been so eager to get to them he hadn't put on a safety harness and wasn't tied into the safety line.

Jake continued to inch backward, so that he was next to an upward beam. "Matt, this isn't a calling. It's a sickness. I think something broke inside of you when your mother was killed."

God, Jake didn't want to shoot Matt, especially knowing even if he only wounded him the man would probably fall to his death. He didn't want Matt dead; he wanted him arrested.

He didn't want to be killed by Matt, either. If Matt managed to kill him then he would surely kill Monica as well, and Jake couldn't let that happen.

"Damn straight something broke inside me," Matt screamed, his voice filled with rage. "She was a saint, Jake. My mother was such a good, loving mother. She was a God-fearing woman who volunteered at a homeless shelter and that piece of crap beat her to death. I have nightmares about the pain and suffering she endured in those horrific moments before her death. This is my job, to rid the world of creeps, and you know what the best part is? I like it. I like it a lot and nobody is going to stop me."

In another flash of lightning, Jake saw his intent. Jake jumped behind the beam as Matt fired his gun. Monica screamed once again.

Lightning once again split the sky as Jake leaned out and fired on Matt. He missed and Matt laughed. It was the hysterical laughter of a man who had lost touch with reality.

"God is speaking, Jake. Don't you hear him in the thunder? He's telling me that I'm his warrior on earth." Matt fired his gun once again.

Sirens whooped in the distance. Had somebody heard the gunfire and called the police? Jake would gladly tell them his role in this if it meant getting Matt off the streets.

Still, even if the police arrived they couldn't exactly get up here and place Matt in handcuffs. There could be a hundred cop cars parked below them and they would be no help in this situation.

Ultimately only one man was going to come down from here. It was either going to be Jake or Matt. If it was Matt who survived then he prayed Monica would be able to tell the police enough to get him arrested.

The sirens grew closer and the thunder and lightning added to the chaos of the standoff between Jake and Matt. "Matt, the police are coming. You need to turn yourself in," Jake yelled in a final attempt to end this without anyone getting hurt.

A bullet ricocheted off the steel column behind

which Jake was hiding. It was obvious to him that Matt had no intention of turning himself in.

Several more shots sounded and Monica screamed once again. Jake's heart stopped. Matt was now firing on Monica. She screamed and then moaned and then her screams stopped, and there was nothing but the thunder and the lightning and Jake's terrified rage. Had she been hit? Oh God, was she dead?

Not caring for his own safety, driven only by his fear for Monica, he stepped out from behind the column. Half-blinded by the rain that had begun to fall and his own tears, he fired his gun over and over again.

MONICA CAME TO SUDDENLY. Her upper arm hurt like hell and a steady rain had begun to fall. From somewhere Jake was calling her name over and over again.

She still dangled in the air, a breeze buffeting her hanging body. She realized that her fear of heights and the pain in her arm had apparently made her pass out. What had happened? Where was Matt?

"Monica," Jake cried. His voice was filled with desperation.

"Jake?" she finally answered.

"Oh, thank God. Are you okay?"

"No, I'm not," she replied, and a sob caught in her throat. "I want to get down. Please get me down from here, Jake. I just want to go home."

"I'm going to pull you up to me," he said. "And then I promise I'm going to take you home."

She looked down to the ground, surprised by

a half a dozen patrol cars that shone their bright searchlights up to where they were.

Where was Matt? Had he gotten away? Was this not the end but rather the beginning of a new cat-and-mouse game? She moaned as the pain in her upper arm intensified as Jake began to pull her up to the beam where he now stood.

It wasn't until they were both in the cage that she collapsed against him. "Where's Matt?" she asked.

"Dead." Jake pulled her closer into his arms and then gasped. "Oh my God, you're hurt."

She followed his gaze and was shocked to see blood running down her arm. "I… I think I was shot. It hurts, but I'm okay." She pressed closer to him. "Are you okay?"

"I am now. I… I thought you were dead. I thought he'd killed you." Emotion was thick in his voice. She looked up at him and she couldn't tell if his cheeks were wet because of the rain or because he'd been crying.

When they reached the ground the police were waiting. "She needs medical attention before we talk to anyone," Jake told the man who had identified himself as Sergeant Ben Wallace.

"I have a dead man on the ground and I need some answers," the sergeant replied.

"She's been shot. Right now that's more important to me than a dead man on the ground," Jake said gruffly.

He didn't leave her side as she was led to an awaiting ambulance. He stood by silently as the medical team cleaned the wound. Thankfully it was only a graze. She was bandaged up and then they were ready to speak to the officers, and Monica wasn't about to let Jake incriminate himself in any way.

"The dead man is Matt Harrison, the real Vigilante Killer," she said. "Jake met him in a grief group and had some suspicions about him. He came to me with those suspicions and we were trying to find out if those concerns were true. Tonight he tried to kill us to keep his secrets safe."

The two of them were taken to a nearby police station where they were questioned for hours. Jake said nothing about the murder pact, but he did say that there were six men who had become friends during their meetings at the Northland Survivor group.

They had been in the sergeant's office for about two hours when another officer walked in to tell them a search warrant had been executed and in Matt's house they had found evidence that supported the fact that Matt was the serial killer Monica and Jake claimed him to be.

It was nearly dawn when they were driven back to the job site and Jake's car. "It's finally for sure over," she said in exhaustion.

"And now you know it was all Matt…no gangs and no Larry Albright. Matt did it all."

"I'm just so tired I feel like I could sleep for a month," she replied. She stared out the passenger window, where lights had begun to appear in homes as people got out of bed and readied themselves to face another day.

Even though she was tired, there was still a streak of residual fear that had a grip on her. Although it was over, she had a feeling it was going to take her a while to put this night behind her.

She turned back to look at Jake. "I've never been as scared as I was when you shoved me off that beam. Swinging in the air sixteen stories high was terrifying."

He grimaced. "I'm sorry. It was the only way I knew to make you less of a target. Unfortunately, it didn't completely work. How does your arm feel?"

"It hurts, but not too bad. I'm sorry you had to kill a man you considered a friend."

"Yeah, me, too. But when he started shooting at you I saw red and I knew he had to be stopped immediately. He was so busy shooting at you he didn't see me shooting at him." He released a deep sigh. "It's been a hell of a night."

That was an understatement. They didn't speak again until they reached his house and walked in through the front door. "I think we could both use at least a couple hours of sleep," he said.

"I definitely second that," she replied. Her eyes itched with tiredness, and a slight headache had begun to pound across her forehead. Her arm hurt and it was going to take some time for her brain to unscramble and process everything that had happened.

"I'd say you have a pretty riveting story for your podcast tonight. You not only helped in identifying the killer, but you were shot by him and survived. You've got your big story, Monica."

"Maybe I'll be excited about the story later after I've slept. Right now I'm just too exhausted to care."

"Then I'll just say good-night for now," he said.

Together they went down the hallway where she went into her room and he walked on down to his. She peeled off her clothes and pulled a nightshirt over her head. She then went into the bathroom and washed her face and brushed her teeth.

Minutes later she was in bed, but the minute she closed her eyes she was flying in the air…in the dark…with nothing to hold on to. Gunshots echoed in her head and fear closed up the back of her throat and iced her body.

She gasped and opened her eyes. Fear still pounded through her veins and she knew she'd never get to sleep in this bed by herself.

She needed…she wanted… Jake. Without any other thought in her mind, she got out of bed and walked down the hallway to his bedroom.

He was in his bed, covered up by a sheet, and his eyes were closed. "Jake?" Her voice trembled.

His eyes opened drowsily and he looked at her. "What's wrong?"

"Nothing, but can I…can I sleep in here with you?"

He held her gaze for a long moment and then raised the sheet, a silent invitation for her to join him. She moved quickly across the room and slid into the bed.

He immediately pulled her back against his chest and his arm went around her waist. His warmth took away the ice inside her. The strength of his embrace comforted her.

Her last thought before she fell asleep was that neither of them had mentioned the fact that just before Matt had appeared on that beam, she'd told Jake she was in love with him.

Chapter Eleven

Jake woke slowly, and instantly all his senses came alive with Monica. Her soft curves were tight against his body and her scent surrounded him.

He'd been asleep for about two hours. Monica was still soundly sleeping in his arms. He knew he wasn't going to go back to sleep, but he remained in the bed anyway.

He'd love to wake up like this every morning for the rest of his life. She fit so perfectly against him, as if she had specifically been made for him. He'd definitely love to have her in his arms all night long for every night he had left on this earth and then wake up each morning and see her across the breakfast table from him.

But that wasn't going to happen. What was going to happen was that this was probably going to be one of the worst days of his life. It was the day he had to tell her goodbye.

He drew in the scent of her and remained perfectly still, wanting to savor these last moments with her in his arms. He wished things were different. He wished he were the kind of man who could welcome her love with open arms. He wished they could get a black schnauzer and have a couple of children and live happily ever after. But that just wasn't going to happen.

With this thought in mind, he eased away from her and out of bed, grateful that his movements didn't wake her up. He grabbed clean clothes and then padded down the hall to the guest bathroom. He didn't want to shower in his own bathroom where the sound of the water might disturb her.

When she'd appeared in his bedroom doorway and had asked to sleep with him, he knew it had been residual fear that had driven her into his arms for the last time. One thing he had learned about her was that she tended to process events long after they happened, and then she got emotional.

Standing beneath a hot spray of water, he felt as if he needed to scrub himself clean of the scent of her and wash away the feel of her body against his.

When he was dressed, he went into the kitchen and made a pot of coffee. It was a gray day. It was as if the dark clouds from the night before had decided to stick around and might at any moment spit down more rain. The gray day mirrored the condition of his heart.

He poured himself a cup of coffee and then moved into the family room, where he turned on the television and searched for any news stories concerning the events of the night before.

While everyone was reporting on the death of the serial killer, nobody had the story of the life-

and-death struggle that had taken place high on the beams of the building. Monica would be able to report that story.

However, the news reports did let him know Grant Timmons had been released from custody. He was not the killer, but he was a troubled man who had professed to be. There was no question that there had been a rush to justice where he was concerned.

He and Monica were both mentioned, him as a respected architect and her as a podcast reporter. She would be pleased by the publicity the news would generate for her. She was definitely going to gain new viewers.

Several reporters spoke about the issue with Grant Timmons, finding it inexcusable that the police had trotted him out at a news conference before fully investigating him. The reporters called for an investigation into the release of Grant's name.

Then there was Matt.

A picture of him appeared on the television with the reporter talking about the murder of his mother and the evidence police had found in his home. It not only included a hit list of sorts, but also pictures of his victims taken right after their murders and tacked to Matt's bedroom wall.

Pictures… Jake's mind couldn't comprehend that the man he had once considered a friend got up every morning and went to bed every night with pictures of the heinous murders he'd committed on his bedroom wall.

Jake turned off the television and went back into

the kitchen and sat at the table. He didn't need to see any more news. What he needed to do was prepare himself for telling Monica goodbye.

I'm in love with you, Jake. Her words whispered over and over again in his head. It was the last thing she'd said to him before he'd shoved her off the beam.

He hoped he didn't hear them again today. Dammit, he'd warned her from the very beginning that he wasn't interested in any meaningful or lasting relationship. Even after they had made love she'd indicated they were both on the same page and it hadn't meant anything emotional between them.

He released a deep sigh and swallowed hard against his own emotions as he thought about what the rest of the day would bring once she woke up.

Walking down the hallway toward his bedroom, his mind told him to go back to the kitchen, but his heart wanted just a moment to gaze at her while she was unaware.

She was curled up facing him as he stood in the doorway. Her hair was a silky spray of darkness against the white pillowcase. He'd never seen her animated features at rest. She looked peaceful and achingly beautiful. Her eyes were closed and her long dark lashes dusted her upper cheeks. Her mouth was slightly open, as if awaiting a lover's kiss.

He clenched his fists, stepped back from the doorway and then went down the hallway to the kitchen. He poured himself another cup of coffee and once again sat at the table to wait for her to wake up.

An hour later she walked into the kitchen. Clad in

her navy robe and with her hair tousled, she looked as beautiful as he'd ever seen her. His heart squeezed tight.

As usual she beelined to the coffee and poured herself a cup and then sat at the table across from him. A sleepy smile curved her lips. "It seems odd to say good morning at this time of the day, but good morning." She raised the cup to her lips and took a deep drink.

"Back at you," he replied. "Did you get enough sleep?"

"For now."

"We made the news."

"Tell me all."

While she drank her coffee, he told her everything he'd learned from listening to the various news reports on television. All the while he talked to her he was already starting the grieving of her absence.

There would be no more shared coffee in the mornings or cuddling on the sofa in the evenings. He would no longer hear the sound of her laughter or see the tiny frown line that occasionally danced between her eyes when she was thinking.

By the time he'd finished telling her everything he had heard on the various news reports, she had finished two cups of coffee. "I'm going to go take a quick shower and get dressed." She stood. "I'll be back in just a few minutes."

When she left the room he cleaned up the coffee cups and then went back into the living room. Rain had started to patter against the windows.

He stared out the window and a knot of tension twisted in his chest; it was tension based in grief. This would be the second time he'd had to tell a woman he loved goodbye. He would never, ever put himself in this position again.

He was still standing at the window when Monica came in the room. She was dressed in a pair of jeans and a deep blue T-shirt that made the color of her eyes pop.

"Let me know when you're ready to pack up your equipment and I'll help you," he said.

She didn't move. She stared at him with an intensity that threatened his breath. "Please, don't send me away, Jake."

"It's over, Monica. It's time for us each to go back to our own lives." The pain of his words reflected in the blue depths of her eyes.

"But it doesn't have to be over." She took several steps toward him. "Jake, did you not hear what I said to you last night? I'm in love with you."

He stiffened his shoulders and tried desperately to erect a mental defense against her. "I'm sorry, Monica, but that changes nothing."

She took another two steps forward, now standing so close to him if he leaned forward he'd be able to capture her lips with his.

And heaven help him, that's what he'd like to do at this very moment. He wanted to draw her against him and take her mouth with his. He needed to tell her that he never wanted her to leave, that he needed her to be here with him forever. But he did none of those things.

"I believe you're in love with me," she said softly.

He shook his head. "I'm sorry if I gave you that impression. I thought we were both on the same page and knew that when the killer was no longer a threat, we'd go our own separate ways."

"I believe we're still on the same page." She now stood so close to him he could smell not only her dizzying perfume, but also a minty scent from her toothpaste. "Jake Lamont, you look me in the eyes and tell me you aren't in love with me."

He couldn't do it. He couldn't lie to her. "It doesn't matter what I feel or what you feel." He desperately tried to hang on to his emotions, but he already felt them slowly spiraling out of control.

He stepped back from her and sought anger rather than the killing pain that caused hot tears to press behind his eyes. "Dammit, Monica. I warned you that I intended to live my life alone. I warned you that I didn't want love in my life."

"But why? Tell me why you don't want love. Don't you want to grow old with a partner? Do you really not want any children or a family...a safe place to fall in a world of chaos?"

"Monica, please don't make this any more difficult than it already is." He hadn't expected her to fight him...to fight for him.

"I'm not trying to make it difficult, I'm trying to understand. I love you and you love me so why does this have to be so complicated? Why does this have to be the end?" Her features were taut with both pain and confusion. "Surely after everything we've been through together I deserve an answer," she added softly.

"You know what the answer is?" The guilt that he'd carried around for two long years came crashing down on him. "I don't deserve any happiness or laughter or love in my life because I'm the reason why my sister was murdered."

MONICA STARED AT HIM. His entire body trembled and his shoulders slumped forward. His eyes misted with tears and he looked like he was on the verge of a complete breakdown. "What are you talking about?" she asked softly. "Max Clinton murdered your sister."

"She would have never been at her house that night if I hadn't been so damned selfish." Tears trekked down his face and he swiped at them angrily. "She was murdered because of me."

"I can't imagine you doing anything terrible, Jake."

A bark of laughter escaped him. "Really? Maybe you just don't know me well enough to realize what kind of man I am."

"What kind of selfish thing do you think you did on the night your sister was murdered?" She reached out to touch him, but he brushed her away and took several steps backward. "Tell me, Jake. Tell me what happened that night."

He collapsed on the sofa, as if his legs wouldn't hold him any longer. He dropped his head in his hands. When he looked back up at her, his eyes were nearly black with torment.

"Even though it had been two months since the last time Suzanna had spoken to or seen Max, she still believed he was stalking her. She'd go to work every day but when dinnertime rolled around she'd show up here and she stayed every evening here, more times than not falling asleep on my sofa."

He raised his head and looked beyond her shoulder. His voice was flat and weary as if he'd gone over this a million times in his mind. And in replaying it, someplace along the line he'd broken.

"That night I was tired of her company and I had a date. I wanted to bring my date back here and I didn't want a pesky sister hanging around."

Monica sank down next to him but knew instinctively now wasn't the time for her to touch him in any way. He was lost in the memories of that night "I made her leave. I knew she didn't really want to go, but I kicked her out of the house anyway." For a few moments he didn't speak as tears fell down his cheeks. His grief and guilt were painfully palpable in the air.

She finally broke the silence. "What else did you do?"

He looked at her in surprise. "That's it. Isn't it enough that I kicked her out of a place where she would have been safe and placed her right in the arms of the man who killed her?"

"Oh, Jake." She sighed and then did what she wanted to do. She placed her hand on his forearm.

"You're going to hold yourself responsible for the rest of your life because of this? Because you were human and wanted a night to yourself?"

He started to pull his arm away from her, but she held on tight. "I made it possible for Max to kill her."

"Max wanted her dead and if not then, he would have found another time and another place. He was the monster, Jake...not you."

Her heart ached for him. He'd carried around this guilt, this sense of responsibility for his sister's murder, for two long years. And apparently he intended to carry it with him and punish himself for the rest of his life unless she could change his mind. And she desperately needed to make him realize he was in no way responsible for his sister's murder.

"Jake, let yourself out of the prison you've put yourself in," she said fervently. "You did nothing wrong." Tears of frustration burned at her eyes as she felt his resistance in the tense muscles of his arm.

"This isn't what Suzanna would want for you. She wouldn't want you to turn your back on love and happiness. She wouldn't want you to live your whole life alone. Please, Jake. Tell me I can stay. Tell me you want to build a real life with me."

He looked at her and in his eyes she saw a sadness that made the tears chase faster and faster down his cheeks. "Monica, I'm sorry."

He pulled his arm from her grip and stood. "Let me know when you're ready to pack the car and I'll drive you home." He turned and walked out of the room.

She remained on the sofa as sobs of heartache ripped through her. She couldn't believe this was how it was going to end. For several long minutes she remained seated, hoping and praying that he would come back into the room and tell her he'd changed his mind.

When that didn't happen she drew several deep breaths to stop her tears and rose from the sofa. Now all she wanted to do was get to her own house, where she could truly cry for what might have been.

It took her almost half an hour to pack up all her clothes and toiletries, and as she worked a curious numbness swept through her. She then went into his office and packed up all her equipment. She carried or dragged all the suitcases and duffel bags to the front door.

During all this Jake remained in his bedroom with the door closed. The coward. He'd destroyed her and then had run to his bedroom to hide from the emotional fallout.

She strode down the hallway and knocked on his door, a tiny flame of anger igniting in her chest. "I'm ready," she said when he opened the door.

He gave a curt nod and followed her to the front door. Neither of them spoke as they loaded her things into his car. They also didn't speak on the drive to her house.

She played and replayed what he'd told her and the flame of anger burned just a little bit brighter. He'd taken on the responsibility for Matt Harrison's actions and intended to carry the burden for Suzanna's murder for the rest of his life.

When they reached her house they silently unloaded everything into her living room and then he stood by the front door apparently to say a final goodbye.

"You're something else, Jake," she said as she allowed her anger to rise to the surface. "You must think you're some important person in the grand scheme of life. You alone unleashed a killer and you somehow believe you're responsible for your sister's murder. You know what I think?"

His eyes had become dark and hooded as he met her gaze and his features were stoic, as if he was going to allow her to vent and then he'd just leave.

"I think you're a big coward. I think you're hiding behind tragedies so you don't have to face real life and real love. You're a big coward, Jake Lamont."

"Monica," he said softly.

She raised a hand to silence anything he might want to say. Tears began to blur her vision. "I don't want to hear anything you have to say unless you're going to tell me you love me and want a life with me."

"I never meant to hurt you," he replied.

"You're hurting yourself way more than you're hurting me. In the last couple of weeks I've realized that I want love in my life. I love my work, but I want more. I wanted that with you, Jake."

A sob caught in her throat. "I know you love me, Jake. I didn't imagine your love. I know it's real and true and I think what we had…what we could have would be beyond wonderful. But you're too big a coward to handle it. You've made it clear to me that you're too scared to take a chance on love. You're going to wear a damned safety line through the rest of your life and that will keep you safe from any emotional ties you might build."

Another sob escaped her and suddenly her anger was gone, replaced by a wild grief. "Please Jake, don't make me beg for you. Look deep in your heart and tell me you want me as much as I want you." She stopped and bit her lower lip as she saw his answer in the darkness of his eyes.

Without another word she turned and headed down the hallway. When she reached her bedroom she heard the sound of the front door closing.

He was gone.

Chapter Twelve

Monica sat at her table drinking her morning coffee. It was a few minutes after ten and even though she had just gotten out of bed, she was exhausted. Her arm hurt but that pain didn't begin to compete with her wild heartache.

She'd cried for hours yesterday after Jake had brought her home. She'd half hoped he would magically reappear and tell her he was ready for her love, but that hadn't happened. She had only managed to pull herself together about an hour before her podcast. For the first time the podcast was difficult for her.

As she'd told her viewers about the terror of being up on the beams when confronted by a serial killer, all she could think about was Jake. When she'd reported about them being shot, her heart had cried for her man.

Somehow she had managed to get through the podcast and then had collapsed in bed. She'd cried herself to sleep, but thankfully she'd slept without dreams. However, the minute her eyes had opened, thoughts of Jake assailed her once again.

He was right. He had warned her, but the heart knew what the heart wanted. And despite her intentions to the contrary, her heart wanted him. And what really broke her was that she knew with every fiber of her being that Jake loved her.

He was the fool. A misguided fool who planned on keeping himself isolated from others because of a guilt he shouldn't own.

She'd hoped her love might heal him. She'd definitely hoped he would pick love over his guilt, love over fear, but that hadn't happened.

With a sigh she got up and poured herself another cup of coffee. Later today she intended to contact somebody to fix the Sheetrock in the living room. She needed to reclaim her house as a safe haven and she couldn't do that until the bullet damage was gone.

Maybe she should just let the damage remain. When she looked at it, her thoughts would always take her back to the night she and Jake had shared their first kiss, the first night he had saved her life.

No, she was going to get the wall repaired or replaced and then maybe she'd paint the entire room a new color to go with a fresh start.

Her doorbell rang. Every muscle in her body froze. Jake? Was it possible he'd changed his mind about things? She jumped up from the table, her heart beating wildly in triple time.

She ran to the door. She unlocked it and flung

it open. All the joy that had momentarily filled her whooshed out of her. "Dad, what are you doing here?"

"Aren't I allowed to visit my daughter? Hmm, I smell coffee."

"Come in and I'll make you a cup." She opened the door wider to allow him in and wondered what had really brought him here.

Neil Wright was a big man, with big arms from working construction all his life. He'd retired a year ago and Monica was glad he now had a life of fishing and golfing.

He went into the kitchen and sat at the table. "I watched your podcast last night."

She popped a coffee pod into the machine and then turned and looked at him in surprise. "You did?"

"Yeah, to tell the truth I've watched you several times, but I don't want you ever to put yourself in danger like you did with this Vigilante stuff. You're good at this reporting stuff, but you don't have to put yourself in dangerous situations to get a story."

She stared at him. He'd just told her she was good, words she'd been waiting to hear from him, but she hadn't been good enough for Jake. She suddenly burst into tears.

"Hey, hey." Neil got up from the table. "What's going here? For God's sake, why are you crying?"

She shook her head, unable to answer him with the raw emotions that had a grip on her.

To her surprise he pulled her into his arms as she wept uncontrollably. He patted her back awkwardly as she cried into his broad chest with his big arms encircling her.

She couldn't remember the last time her father had held her in his arms. She cried for a few minutes and then raised her head and looked at the man who had raised her. "He broke my heart, Daddy. Jake broke my heart."

"Give me his address and I'll go beat the hell out of him."

His mock bluster made her laugh. She swiped at her tears as he released her. "Sit back down and I'll get the coffee."

Moments later the two sat across from each other. "You have no idea how much I've wanted to hear you say something positive about me," she confessed.

He looked at her in surprise and then leaned forward in his chair and gazed at her thoughtfully. "Maybe I haven't been good at letting you know how proud I am of you. Your sisters were so easy to raise. They're both just like your mother. They're natural pleasers. But you, you scared the hell out of me. You were so much like me. You were a rebel and you questioned everything. You were a real challenge to raise, but honey, I've always loved you and I'm always proud of you. You just never seemed to need me as much as your sisters."

"I really, really needed to hear everything you just said to me," she replied. "I really needed to know that you love me."

Neil frowned. "I'm sorry. I didn't know. When your mother passed, I was terrified. I was suddenly the single parent to three little girls. You know, there wasn't a manual to tell me how to do it."

"You've been a great father. Maybe I should have asked for what I needed from you."

He smiled at her. "Once and for all, I love you, Monica. I love you with all my heart."

He leaned back in his chair. "Now, enough of this emotional stuff. I see you have a bandage on your arm. How is that doing?"

Monica's heart swelled with the words her father had spoken to her. They were what she'd wanted… what she'd needed to hear from him for years. And she had a feeling she would never hear them again.

"Dad, you have to respect that doing the podcast is my career. It's what I want to do."

He frowned. "I understand that, but you can't blame me for wanting the best for you. Last night when I heard what happened to you, it scared the hell out of me. I can respect what you do and still want you to be safe and financially secure."

"I seriously doubt I'll ever be in a position again to face a serial killer."

"I hope not. I know you and your sisters aren't close, but before I die I'd like to see that change. They are your family, you know."

"They don't seem to want a relationship with me," she replied. "They just ask me out for coffee and stuff because they feel obligated."

"I think you're wrong. They care about you, Monica."

They talked for about a half an hour and then he

left. If nothing else came from this, at least she felt a new closeness to her father.

But with him gone there was nothing left except her heartbreak. Half a dozen times throughout the day she thought about calling Jake.

But what for? To ask him if he'd changed his mind about them? If that had happened, then he would be here with her right now. She wasn't going to beg for his love.

Around two she decided to take a nap. She'd gotten little sleep the night before because she hadn't been able to stop crying.

She immediately fell asleep and into dreams of Jake. And in those dreams she was in his arms and he was making sweet love with her. Then they were sitting at his kitchen table and laughing together. Finally they were walking down the sidewalk with a double stroller in front of them. In the stroller was a little dark-haired girl and a little dark-haired boy. Twins.

She awakened crying for all she would never have with the man she loved. She had to get back her excitement, her wild passion for her work, and stop thinking…somehow stop loving Jake Lamont.

Over the next five days the news cycle changed and stories about the serial killer were few and far between. Her podcast subscribers grew in number and she told herself she was fine. She saw her family doctor, who rebandaged her arm and prescribed some antibiotics.

A cool front had moved in and suddenly it felt

more like fall than summer. She packed away some of her lightweight things and pulled out sweaters and blankets. She gathered two bags of clothes and shoes to donate. Two men spent two days fixing the Sheetrock in her living room and then she spent an afternoon painting. She went shopping for new pictures to hang on the wall and kept up a frenetic pace that gave her little chance to think.

She managed to convince herself she was fine until the long, dark hours of the night. She sometimes felt as if he were haunting her. She imagined she could smell him in her sheets and feel the heat of his body warming hers.

She kept telling herself it was just going to take more time for her to forget Jake. But each day she awakened with the same heartache of what might have been.

This morning she had decided to scrub the kitchen from top to bottom. She needed to clean out her pantry and wash down tiles. She threw on a pair of jean shorts and an old navy T-shirt and then drew her hair up in a messy ponytail.

The only way she had gotten through each day was to stay busy. She didn't want to give herself time to think because her thoughts always ended up on Jake. And those thoughts always brought on another bout of tears.

Another good outcome of the big story of the killer was that both her sisters had called her, offering their love and support. She'd made plans to meet them for lunch the following week. She might have lost at love, but she'd gained a new relationship with her family.

She started scrubbing the tiled area behind her sink with a lemon-scented cleaner. As she worked she tried to stay focused on her podcast and what she intended to report that night. There weren't a lot of stories that had really captured her and begged her to dig deeper.

With school starting in the next couple of days, tonight she had a taped interview from a security expert talking about school safety.

A knock on her door pulled her from her work. It was probably her father stopping in for coffee. He'd mentioned on the phone the day before that he might come by again.

She yanked open her door and a small gasp escaped her. Jake. "Can I come in?" He looked like he hadn't slept in weeks. Lines of exhaustion ran down the sides of his face and there was a hollow darkness in his eyes.

She opened the door to allow him in. Why was he here? She steeled her heart against him. He didn't look like a man who had come here to profess his love for her; rather, he looked like a tormented man.

"The wall looks nice," he said when he entered the living room. "I like the new color."

"I know you didn't come here to check on my home repair. Why are you here?" Her heart beat a faster rhythm as she gazed at him.

He sank down on the sofa and released a deep sigh. "From the moment Suzanna was murdered I decided that I would be alone for the rest of my life. It had always been her and me against the world, and without her I was utterly lost."

Monica sat on the chair facing the sofa. Was he here to clear his soul? Did he feel the need to once again go over all the reasons why he couldn't return her love? Was he here to once again reject her? She said nothing but continued to gaze at him.

"You were just supposed to stay a partner in finding the killer. You were never supposed to be anything else."

"Why are you here, Jake?" she asked again. Seeing him again was killing her. This might be something he felt like he needed to do, but she couldn't just sit here while he told her all the reasons he couldn't be with her.

"I'm here because you were right. I've been a coward. I was afraid to face life. My grief over Suzanna made me afraid to care about anyone else again. Intellectually I know that I'm not responsible for her murder, but it was easy to grasp on to that to keep people away."

He stood and walked over to her. He took her hand in his and pulled her up out of the chair. Her heart quickened its pace as she gazed into his eyes…eyes that now held warmth.

"I thought I'd get over you. I thought I could push you out of my house and out of my heart. Monica, these past five days have been the longest in my life. All I could think about was what a fool I was. I watched your podcast each night and longed for you."

"You longed for me? Tell me more." She knew now why he was here and joy filled her heart. But as much as she loved him, as much as she wanted him, she also wanted him to grovel a bit. He owed her a little groveling after the five long days of grief he'd put her through.

He reached up and stroked her cheek with his thumb. "I missed seeing your cranky face across the kitchen table each morning. I missed hearing your voice and smelling the scent of you. You're right— Suzanna wouldn't have wanted me to live my life alone. I want you, Monica. I need you. Please tell me I'm not too late, that you're still in love with me." He dropped his hand to his side and his eyes burned with a fierce intensity as he gazed at her. "I love you, Monica. For heaven's sake, tell me you'll come home with me and be my wife…my partner through life."

For a moment she couldn't answer. Her joy, her happiness, was too big for words. She nodded and then a laugh escaped her. "Yes," she finally said.

He pulled her into his arms and kissed her long and deep. She tasted his love for her. She felt it in his strong arms that surrounded her.

When the kiss ended he stepped back from her. "Wait right here," he said, and then he went back out the front door.

What now? She stood staring at the door, waiting to see what was going on. Jake came back in, and in his arms was a small bundle of black fur. Two black eyes gazed at her curiously.

"Her name is Cookie. She's eight weeks old and

as you see she's a black schnauzer. I figured taking care of her would be good practice for when we have kids."

"Oh, what a sweet baby," she said as she took the puppy into her arms.

"I want kids, Monica. I want a family and a dog and I want it all with you," Jake said.

"We'll have it all, Jake." The puppy barked as if in agreement. Monica laughed. As Jake took her lips once again in a tender kiss that spoke of their future, she knew this was the best story of all, a story that ended with love and laughter and puppy kisses.

* * * * *

COMING SOON!

We really hope you enjoyed reading this book. If you're looking for more romance, be sure to head to the shops when new books are available on

Thursday 13th June

To see which titles are coming soon, please visit

millsandboon.co.uk/nextmonth